BOOKS BY MAX CRAWFORD

Lords of the Plain
The Bad Communist
The Backslider
Waltz Across Texas

LORDS
OF
THE
PLAIN

LORDS OF THE PLAIN

Max Crawford

ATHENEUM

New York

1985

Library of Congress Cataloging in Publication Data
Crawford, Max, ———
Lords of the plain.
1. Comanche Indians—Wars—Fiction.   2. Texas—
History—Fiction.   I. Title.
PS3553.R293L6   1985   813'.54   84-45054
ISBN 0-689-11475-3

Published simultaneously in Canada by McClelland and Stewart Ltd.
Composition by Yankee Typesetters, Inc., Concord, New Hampshire
Manufactured by Fairfield Graphics, Fairfield, Pennsylvania
Designed by Kathleen Carey
First Edition

For
those who were there first and
those who are there now

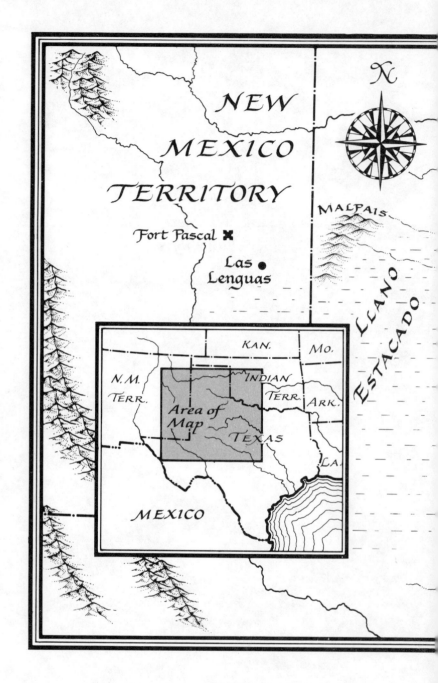

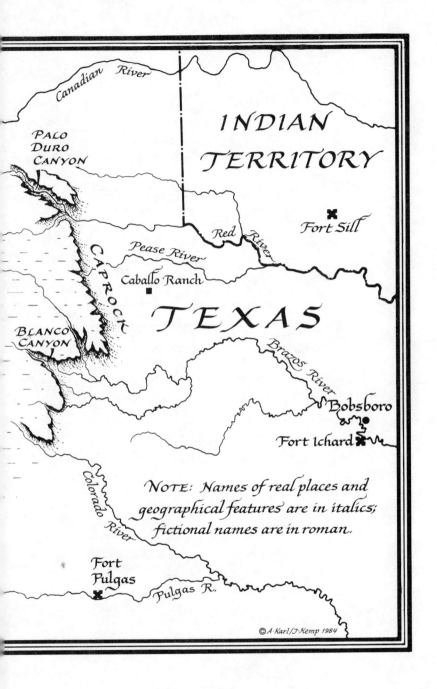

In nine days' march I reached some plains, so vast that I did not find their end anywhere I went . . . plains with no more landmarks than as if we had been swallowed up in the sea, where our guides strayed about, because there was not a stone, nor a bit of rising ground, nor a tree, nor a shrub, nor anything to go by. . . .

Francisco Vasquez Coronado
20 October 1541

LORDS
OF
THE
PLAIN

ONE

No one knew when we would commence our second campaign. Our horses were fat, the men restless, all equipment and tack and supplies stood ready, and still we did not march out. We had received our orders from Leavenworth, but Colonel Mac-Swain confided in no one, not even this writer, his Adjutant for a year now. We would be on the trail of the Indians once again, come spring, but none knew when or where. There had been no rain since the previous fall, and the winter's snow had fallen light and dry and had blown off the ground and left no moisture. I would tell the company officers that MacSwain was waiting for rain, but few of them believed me. I feared MacSwain's failure of nerve worse than they, for I knew the longer he delayed the more violent and irrational would be his action when he moved. The days were spent in endless drill and maneuver, most of which little served our purpose. Only the trail would make the men and horses hard, and the tactics we practiced, the skirmish lines and frontal assaults of the Civil War, would be useless against the Indians, who fought by no rules that we taught. The men debauched in Hidetown and the horses grew heavy and slow on corn. Our officers hunted in secret, for that pastime was proscribed, and gossiped and gambled and dreamed of glory. Our equipment and tack were in superb condition, but our will to fight withered as we delayed. There were only three Regular Army officers among us—MacSwain, myself, and Major Hoeme—who were veterans of the Indian wars, and their comradeship brought me scant solace. There was Devereaux, head of the Indian scouts, but though he was a good soldier, he had been a Rebel and as well would be away from the column with the scouts for great periods of time and could not be counted on during these absences. With Jeremy Jones's death there were no officers of my generation in the Second Cavalry, all of the troop commanders having come of age after the Civil War, and none that I trusted.

It had been three years since the four of us came to this desolate outpost on the Texas border. Two husbands and two brides, we called ourselves, though Ann and I had been married more than two years then, she carrying our daughter in her womb. In those days it had taken six days to travel from Boston to New Orleans by rail, and in that city we were further delayed by a quarantine against an epidemic of yellow fever. We made few precautions against the fever, though we did not go about the city at night and took care with our diet, and our hotelier plied Jeremy and me with the city's good whiskey, which he assured us would be serum to ward off any plague. After such idleness we were anxious to sail and on September 20, 1872, we eagerly boarded the *Mirador*, a steamer of the Morgan Line bound for Galveston. None of us had ever been so far south, and we observed the low, steaming land that fell off our starboard bow as if it were a foreign country. We sailed across the Gulf of Mexico by night and crossed the shifting bar of Galveston Bay at dawn. Church spires reached out for us like arms from the sea, the low island of Galveston rising from a bank of blue fog to

4

hang suspended by mirage in midair. From Galveston we entrained to Columbus, on the Colorado River, where we boarded a stage for San Antonio. None of us had dreamed of the vastness of this land. We entered onto an endless, climbing prairie, passing through herds of cattle that spread to the horizon, till it seemed that every beast that had lived since creation had been brought to these limitless plains. As we went west, the men we saw grew rougher and, to our eye, more picturesque—cowboys in great wide-brimmed sombreros, jingling Mexican spurs hanging from their boots, Irish and Negro railroad workers, German farmers, many dressed in the costumes of their native land—and much of our time was passed in describing in postal cards and letters home these men and the countryside, as we all thought this was the Texas we were destined for. The old Spanish capital of San Antonio de Bexar appeared to us like a city from *The Arabian Nights*. No railroads served San Antonio then, and its isolation, its ancient missions and narrow twisted streets, its aristocratic grandees one might have thought imported from Spain solely for our entertainment, touched the city with timelessness. Daily I rode down the winding, shaded banks of the river to the Missions San Juan La Espada, San José, La Purissima and there studied the architecture, the religious wall carvings and statuary crumbling and defaced by vandals. I found a melancholy there, a sense of lost hope that I had not felt among the ruins of Rome and Greece. To the interest of some and the amusement of others, I practiced my Spanish among the priests and the antiquaries of these missions and learned of the Spanish adventurers who had crossed this netherland three and a half centuries before my arrival.

Given our choice in San Antonio, Jeremy and I had asked to report for duty at Fort Pulgas. We proceeded there in an ambulance wagon drawn by four mules, under a cavalry escort commanded by Captain Lawrence Billings. Billings was a teasing, good-humored officer, and though this area had been cleared of hostile Indians, he entertained the women with tales of the massacres that had occurred here and there along the trail, tales that aroused more than a general curiosity in the men. Our road was a dim stage trail, and as we went west we left behind the rolling prairies and their waist-deep fields of grass and forests of wild flowers and entered a stark, inhospitable terrain. With this sudden change in landscape came our first taste of the capricious violence of Texas weather. Our column was struck by a wet norther, and the gentle limestone-bedded creeks became booming rivers and our progress was slowed by perilous fordings and grueling pulls through the grasping desert mud. We did not make Fort Pulgas till mid-November and found nothing there to our liking. Lumber had been scarce that year, and the post was little more than a canvas stockade. A few stone buildings had been erected; except for these only cloth walls protected us from the hostiles and the savage cold and rain and wind. Ann gave birth to our daughter, Katherine, in early spring, during a late norther, when the earth was covered with ice. Men held the guy ropes against the tearing wind, and the difficult delivery was accomplished, and this bleak region knew its first native white citizen. It was not long afterwards that Jeremy and Eliza Jones lost their child, two months into pregnancy, and their melancholy began.

Pulgas was commanded then by Colonel Rufus L. Dougherty, an able officer at his desk, but a tired man, old, with little taste to fight the Indian or learn a new way of war. His age, dimming vision, his drinking and cowardice were what our junior officers spoke of when they spoke of our command's inaction. I fell prey to these easy conclusions. I listened but did not understand when Dougherty would talk far into the night about our true purpose in the wilderness. He spoke not of protection of our settlers but of annihilation of the natives. I had heard these theories since childhood, from my father and later from his friends, whom the Army had taught me to call the Indian Ring. The only difference between Dougherty and my father, I thought, was that my father would have been sober.

Dougherty talked of Darwin, whom I had not heard of then, and his clear, brutal theories. Our wilderness nation had been like an island in Darwin's archipelago. The natives had lived among themselves, not always at peace, but fruitfully. Then like some windblown spore we had come to the island. Our ways were not better or worse than theirs, Dougherty said, merely stronger—like disease. Not only were our methods of war more destructive, even more devastating to the Indians were our ways of peace. "Hunting and forage can never produce the energy of grazing and planting," Dougherty said, parting his clean-shaven lips over teeth that were yellowed and decayed by drink. "They would have become extinct anyway, Captain, without our slaughter. Please do not lose sleep over that." A fit of coughing took him and he doubled over, racked by it for minutes. Recovered, he drank my health and spread his mouth again. "Don't be a fool, Chapman, like me. Don't think you can turn it back, ever. Don't think you can halt it. Don't try to slow it, soften it, nothing. Be swift. That is the only mercy you can show these doomed brutes."

I tried to make these words out as drunken raving. I could not stand the touch of the old man's common embrace. How did he know of my doubt when I had yet to recognize it in my own mind? When doubt did come, I chose to think Dougherty knew it by knowing of my father and his writing and his friends. Or I chose to think he had taken down my record from the Civil War and somewhere in its dry recital of battles and promotions and citations had seen my weakness. For a while then I took great care to disguise my misgivings. I became rigid and zealous, not only in my duties, but in my philosophy. I propounded the official War Department line on our Indian wars, I was the model of blue-coated reason among officers and men. It took little dissembling to repudiate my father and his ideals. Surrounded by soldiers and settlers who had fought and suffered the cruelty of these cornered savages, contempt for Eastern preachers and papers, Washington politicians and pacifists,

7

came easy. Only Ann knew of the hatred of war that was gathering in me, but she said nothing of the new persona that hid it.

I greeted MacSwain, then, with more enthusiasm than the others. Under Dougherty our command had become little more than a hunting outpost. Dougherty had taken some care that we move about like soldiers, but there was scant result from our scouts. Twice monthly we sent columns to the nearest links in the chain of forts that stretched along the frontier from Sill to Bliss. If a ranch had been raided or a stage robbed or a corn train attacked, we dispatched a troop to the scene, but our arrival came too late for action. We buried the dead and took the survivors into custody. We made no offensive moves against the Indians, and in truth none seemed called for. The Indians were moving north, away from the encroaching settlers, onto the great reservation at Sill or into the badlands bordering the *llano estacado* or onto the *llano* itself. As my second year at Pulgas began, contact with the Indians ceased. Our scouts became hunting parties. The depredations we observed among the settlers and the wagon trains and the stages moving through our lines were more often committed by *comancheros* or drunken buffalo hunters or by common outlaws. We came to believe, as Dougherty preached, that our mission had been a success. From Davis to Stockton, the nearest forts in our chain, the land had become safe for settling. When MacSwain came, with his zeal and a new policy from Washington, I stood alone in welcoming him.

By his second year, the year of this account, MacSwain had become what Dougherty had been, though without the old man's protective cynicism. I would not have dreamed of it then, that two years hence it would be I urging the sluggish MacSwain into the field. Rather MacSwain came to Fort Pulgas breathing fire, as ambitious an officer as I had ever known. He had brought a select troop with him from the wars in Kansas, and those veterans of Pulgas who did not stand to their measure, who did not accept the drill and discipline and danger,

8

were transferred to San Antonio and the rear. Over the first half year the six troops of cavalry and two companies of infantry under MacSwain's command were hardened for battle. Our orders were to march north with spring and engage the enemy. "To force the Indian onto the reservation," MacSwain said, "or punish him. Those were the words of General Sherman. Contain and punish, Captain Chapman. No more sitting by our stoves like women or hunting rabbits like boys. By God, if they want to hunt, we shall hunt Indians! Do you agree, Captain Chapman?"

So in March of that first year, in ideal spring weather, so unlike this year, we rode north toward disaster—the disappearance of Jeremy Jones and his scout, the collapsed command of Colonel MacSwain, and the defeat of our mission on the *llano estacado,* an empty plain that had not been crossed by white invaders for more than three hundred years.

The second winter of our tour at Fort Pulgas was MacSwain's first and, though none could have foreseen it, proved to be his acme. We received word in September that Dougherty was to be replaced. None were surprised by this, least of all Dougherty. The old man had predicted a shift in the War Department, that the Indian policy in the borderlands would be turning aggressive, that there would be younger men sent out to command the new war that was to be waged against the savages. Dougherty knew the identity of his replacement long before he made it known. "I have had a good reason to keep his name from you, Phil—that I have been trying to reverse his appointment. Without success, of course, but I have registered my complaint. MacSwain has far more important friends in Washington than I." Dougherty rose and shambled to the wall map. He spread his hand over Kansas and dragged his clawed fingers west and north. "He will be the youngest general officer in the United States Army when he receives his promotion, this year or the next. Still, he feels himself in the shadow of Custer and Miles. He has chosen to remove himself from the central battlefields in Kansas and Nebraska and has come to make his name here in Texas. He is far too ambitious a man for Fort Pulgas. What he has in mind for the Second Cavalry and Pulgas and you, I, of course, can't say." Dougherty returned to his desk and placed objects here and there to illustrate his words. "He is known for long, forced marches—hell, he is famous for them. From Kelly Ford to the Battle of Five Forks, I'm sure you've heard it all. There is another aspect of this commander, Chapman, that is little known to any but his closest colleagues. His theory of war. He believes that wars should be fought—unconditionally. It is no accident that his idol is Sherman. They loved what happened in Georgia, Phil, they adored it." The old man drank from his cup. "He will want to wipe out the Indians, Captain Chapman, to sweep them from the face of this earth."

The first we saw of their column was a lone rider on the horizon, the touch of drama that I was to come to associate with MacSwain as I would the nervous snapping of his stubbed fingers. The rider was Hoeme, his uniform darkened by exertion, moving his great black horse in an even, relentless fox-gait, as if he were some angel of affliction bearing the greetings of plague. As the man rode down toward us, before I could distinguish his insignia, I took the threatening figure to be Mac-Swain. "No, his German mercenary," said Dougherty, ordering the bugler out and the fort gate swung open. "MacSwain will be giving us a better show. And we are expected to respond." Dougherty's contempt swept over Hoeme, who had entered the fort and was reporting mounted to the Officer of the Day.

Jeremy Jones was ordered to mount fifteen men from the regiment and ride out to MacSwain's column and as a guard of honor escort them to the post. As mockery that I did not understand, Dougherty had Jeremy take four black mules from the post water wagon and tender them for use on the spring ambulance that accompanied MacSwain wherever he went. I was then ordered to form up two gun detachments and wheel into positions of honor the pair of three-inch rifled guns which we had never fired. My First Sergeant and I experienced a moment of concern and comedy when it seemed there were no men in the post who had ever drilled a gun squad, but two old soldiers who had served an enlistment in the artillery were located and in no time they were sharply drilling green infantrymen around the ceremonial cannons. At four in the afternoon the head of a column of twos appeared on the horizon, riding at a gallop. Jeremy's escort and the four fresh mules had been spurned by MacSwain, and he rode at the head of his detachment of seventy well-mounted men. MacSwain's troop swept down along the river, circling past Hidetown, to the astonishment of its citizens, and wound up toward the fort in the sinewy movement of a snake. The column passed through the gate in a graceful canter, then traversed the length of the parade ground, where the column turned sharp left as if to ride about the inner walls of the fort. But then, strung out along the south wall, the column made an abrupt left face and at a walk returned in a single unwavering rank the length of the parade ground, the seventy horses so arranged that their colors faded from black to brown and bay and sorrel, from buckskin to dun and gray to MacSwain's white pacer. The cannon fired, the men cheered and tossed their hats, and Colonel MacSwain was presented the sword of command and received our allegiance.

I was not used to the ways of a man as subtle as James John MacSwain. The officers I had been drawn toward and generally assigned to had been fighters, such as my mentor Cushing, whom I had seen killed at the Bloody Angle, or philosophers, a variety of men I had known in my service at the War College and at such outposts as Pulgas, so isolated from war they took on some aspects of a monastery. I had yet made no contact with the politician in blue and so readily succumbed to MacSwain's blandishments. I was ordered to report to MacSwain the day following his arrival. Colonel Dougherty and those men who would accompany him to San Antonio had not yet cleared themselves and their belongings from the post, and MacSwain and his detachment had erected tents outside the fortress walls, a gesture that could have been taken for courtesy or contempt. I expected that word had reached MacSwain of my friendship with Dougherty and so did not reckon for the new commander's reception. I was greeted as a long-lost comrade by MacSwain, though some of his staff remained cool, and was put thoroughly at ease by his knowledge and, it would seem, approval of my military record. Nor did he decry my father's politics, or if he did so it was with humor and charm. "I know you hail from a race of warriors, albeit your mother's men. I, too, have received much of my blood from the distaff of my family. The Hows or Howes or Houghs," he said with a smile, "stand with the hallowed names of Knox, Wayne, Greene, Lafayette, Pulaski, and Sherzer"—he spoke the last, the name of my mother's family, as if it quite naturally belonged to that list to which any fighting man would aspire. "I have the records of thirty-four ancestors who fought in every war this country ever engaged in, from the Siege of Oswego to Chancellorsville. I have reason to believe that our ancestors, Colonel Josiah Sherzer and a certain Captain Thomas How or Howe or Hough, served side by side during Lord Amherst's expedition to Crown Point. Though our patrimony may be from Chapman and MacSwain, I trust that Sherzer and Howe are still in our blood and that our association will bring them honor. And as well, Philip, if I may so address you informally, I do not disapprove of the years you spent as an enlisted man. I know from good sources that you postponed your appointment to West Point so that you might fight immediately in the War of Rebellion and further that you declined political commission, which you might easily have secured through Governor Andrews, because of your extreme youth and inexperience. Also," concluded MacSwain with an ironic smile, "I believe that you are not thirty-one years of age, as your records indicate, but twenty-nine. I do well understand how a boy of fourteen might long for the passage of those two interminable years that will place him in the ranks of fighting men. I will make no mention of this inaccuracy to the War Office or your very attractive wife."

I was thus captivated by flattery, humor, friendship, and charm. MacSwain wooed me further by asking that I retain my position as Post Adjutant, though I had expected to relinquish those duties to a senior officer, such as Major Hoeme. Far more ingratiating than winning this informal promotion (I had for months desired to return to my field command of I Troop) was the role I was to assume as MacSwain's confidant, again a function I thought would have fallen to a longtime associate such as Major Hoeme. But then I did not know how the two of them worked. Hoeme was everything that MacSwain was not. A huge, glowering, sullen-visaged man, Hoeme made no friends among officers or their wives, established no contact or rapport with the men, took no part in the social life that swirled through the post the first winter of MacSwain's command. Hoeme passed his time drilling the elite troop of cavalry that acted as MacSwain's bodyguard. The German spoke little English and that with a heavy accent. Nothing was known of his military record, though rumors circulated that Hoeme had been a soldier of fortune in South America, that he had acted as a spy during the Civil War. Little could be discerned of his character, for everything about the man was distorted by his universal contempt of life: Indians, horses, the women of the post, the scum of Hidetown, he hated them all, as well as the officers and men of the Second. He showed, in particular, a bright loathing for me. Though the German spent practically no time with MacSwain, I saw they once had been quite close. There was a way about them together—whether during drill, on scout, or in conference—of communicating positions and thoughts without words. While as MacSwain and I talked and talked, the more clearly did I understand we were strangers.

The first winter of MacSwain's command was a period of excitement and activity, of social intercourse and military preparation. Though MacSwain was a bachelor, like Dougherty, he had a way with the ladies that charmed them all. During that winter, as he vigorously drilled the men, expunging every trace of Dougherty's hunting club, he took pains to see that the lives of the women and their children were made to run as close as possible to what they had known at home. Regulated schools were established, a decent laundry constructed, our living quarters refurbished with rugs and curtains and furniture and other homely objects, all brought from San Antonio at the post's expense. The enlisted men's barracks were separated from the officers' quarters by an interior wall, and the women knew a privacy nonexistent during Dougherty's relaxed command. Even more winning than attention to such niceties were the weekly balls MacSwain gave in the officers' mess, with feasts, dancing, and games. MacSwain moved among the couples with genial charm, exuding a chivalrous manner that transformed our rude fortress. During Dougherty's command men and women had gathered as if in cafés, and arguments, brawls, and liaisons were not uncommon. If, as my wife argued, MacSwain's formal society did nothing to discourage fighting and adultery, the illusion that we were idling in a great house's ballroom made these transgressions bearable. At length Ann refused to attend these galas, and our estrangement sharpened. Ann had been a favorite of Dougherty and in turn quite fond of the old man, who had something of her father about him. Of all the officers and the wives of the post, she was the only one to express regret at the departure of our former commander, or so it was during that first winter of MacSwain's command.

That first spring we struck out on the trail of the Indians far too early and nearly perished of it. The winter had been mild and brief, and we were in the saddle by early March. The air was soft and fragrant, like balm, the rolling prairies around

Pulgas blanketed with wildflowers and rich grass. None of us respected the warnings of the old-timers when they spoke of the freak ice storms that might strike this region as late as May. We took down our atlases and our globes and saw the thirty-second parallel running to the east through Savannah, Georgia, and scoffed at such reports. The weather held fine till we had ridden out our horses and outdistanced our supply train by three days on a dry road, by a week or more when the earth became a mire or was covered with a sheet of ice. The norther struck first dry and bitterly cold, and we huddled in our icy tents, praying for warmth that we would curse when it came. With the thaw, our horses mired in the mud, even more helpless than they had been on the ice. The weight of the ice had cracked and rent our canvas tents, and we found no escape from the rain anywhere. The horses suffered terribly. The weaker animals froze to death, the stronger survived the cold to rip muscles and shatter bones fighting against the clay mud. When the weather cleared and we could ride again, we doubled back on our trail to find that the supply train had been set upon by Indians, who had allowed our main force to pass their ambuscade before attacking. We regrouped the supply train and now riding together, fearful of any darkening in the sky or the slightest movement on the horizon, turned north again toward the *llano estacado*.

I do not clearly remember what I had expected of the *llano* that first spring, before I had been on it. Another prairie, perhaps. I did not understand the words of our cartographer one night as we were studying the maps. These early maps of the Texas frontier were crude affairs, rough sketches compiled from the scrawlings and hearsay of *comancheros* and buffalo hunters and captured Indians. Rivers were shown with little accuracy, and their tributaries drawn in by hand with none. Hills and valleys, gorges and buttes were sketched in, and some lines corresponding to elevation had been made. There was a vast area on the map that was unmarked except for what it was called, *llano estacado*. I commented on this unfinished part of the map, and the cartographer studied me with a slow smile. "I think, Captain, there may not be much more drawing to be done than this, even once we have finished our work. Those who have been there say a mere outline to discern its border is the only way of describing the place. The Indians think the gods have removed all things that were once there, and have left the earth there as it was before man and beast came onto it. Part of some curse that I don't know of."

I was amused by the legend, but the mapmaker seemed to think there was some reason in it. "I spoke of it once with Marcy's cartographer, an old man who had ridden on the *llano* twenty years before, and he could not forget the place. He said that they learned that the earth itself could drive a man mad, as if all along the truth has been that man has no right here on earth and will be swept off it someday and that the likes of you and me and those of us poor souls who will go up on that plain will know how doomsday will be."

When these distortions of reason became mine, during our first trek across the staked plains, as we searched for Jeremy Jones and his scout, I denied them. Being a rational man still, I looked to my body to explain my mind's malfunction. And there was good cause to understand our despair as hallucinations of exhaustion. After reforming the supply train, we had ridden north into a second norther—ice and rain and ice again. A warm wind blew from the southwest and the sky cleared, treacherously promising spring, and again we galloped ahead of our supply train, two days, three, a week beyond our provisions and forage. Winter struck anew, and we remained frozen in camp for three days, and when ice turned to rain we retreated south, walking our broken horses through mud that often reached above their knees. We found the supply train a mass of shattered wheels and axles and frames and our goods and grain rotted and fouled by the deluge. We camped around the supply train and waited three weeks for the weather to clear, a hiatus that none disputed then, but pointed to Mac-Swain's fits to impulsive adventure amidst long, tedious periods of inaction. By this time we were well into April, and though the ice was gone we were struck by another wet storm—sleet, hail, and near-freezing rain—and might have welcomed winter's return. We mounted our column and rode pitifully slowly north, preceding our supply train by only a day or two at most. Our horses were ruined, the men's morale in tatters, their mood mutinous, but then our cautious advance brought pleasure, it would seem, to the gods. The weather turned, and for days the skies cleared and the sun shone and the earth dried, though by now no man among us could ever celebrate spring again, as if the seasons had lost all order and ice and sun and wind were flung at us helter-skelter, with no natural reasoning. With the good weather came fresh signs of Indians: abandoned campgrounds, the Tonk scouts reporting war parties riding our flank beyond the horizon, a lone Comanche scout observing our progress from a canyon wall. But we saw no massed Indians and heard only of their retreat before our advance. As we warmed and dried, the horses mended and the men's spirits lifted. We rode more quickly, with greater purpose: it seemed that we would win this Indian war without fighting a battle, the savages fleeing before us toward the reservation. Daily we grew more arrogant, spoiling for a fight. Men who two weeks before had stood ready to desert now boasted of their martial prowess and taunted the retreating Indian to battle. MacSwain had recovered his ambition and sent large scouting parties out great distances from the column to engage the enemy. At night in his tent he spoke for hours, not only of the need to win the Texas Indian wars, but to do so with a great battle, with a military flourish that would make him known in the minds of men as the greatest Indian fighter in the history of our nation.

In late April, we came to the southern border of the *llano estacado,* its escarpment rising two hundred feet above the broken countryside we had passed through. MacSwain turned our column, and for two days we rode beneath the walls of the *llano,* following its ragged border in a northeasterly direction. On the third day the Tonk scouts reported they had found a way up onto the plain, and MacSwain detached a scout of twenty troopers and ten Tonks under the command of Lieutenant Jeremy Jones. On May 2, we stood in camp and watched the column of thirty men disappear into an arroyo twisting up through the sheer cliffs that capped the plains. These men were never to return. No trace of them, their horses, or their scouts was ever found. We waited two days for word from the column, then a third, then a fourth. On the fifth day we rode up onto the plain to search for the lost column, but we found nothing. Even now I must refer to my diaries to recall in any detail how we passed the next weeks searching for them. The jagged words strewn across the ledger page reflect our growing despair as we wandered over that endless terrestrial sea as helpless and lost as Coronado three centuries before, finding nothing.

We returned to Fort Pulgas in the fall. There we mended tack and cleaned equipment and rested our horses and healed our bodies' wounds. The business of the post was bitter those first weeks of our return. Recrimination for our failure swept through the headquarters, and MacSwain caused all those near to him to suffer. I was neither singled out nor spared. Round after round of hearings were held among the officers. Mac-Swain abused all others, then would turn and blame only himself. During our absence the post had lost all discipline, falling beneath Dougherty's lax standards. The men drank and gambled and fornicated in Hidetown, and the pimps and whores and gamblers of Hidetown came to the fort at their pleasure. Returned to my duties as Post Adjutant, I saw the worst of these abuses stopped, but it was only the onset of winter that brought the men into line. Much of my time was occupied with domestic trials. For the first time in our marriage, Ann spoke directly of my resignation from the Army. I discovered letters written to her from my father urging her to join in his campaign against our Indian wars. Ann and I quarreled, the first cross words we had ever exchanged. Ann sorrowed over Jeremy's death, sorrowing not only for our friend, but for the death she imagined might one day be mine. But my mind was still spent from our campaign and diseased from our separation, and I grew angry at her mourning. My jealousy, or envy, soon fell away, but it left wounds we were not to have time to heal. The sufferings of Eliza Jones obsessed my wife. Her concern for her friend wasted her own frame and, I thought, gave to our small daughter the melancholy that aged so many women who came to this desolate place. I arranged for Eliza Jones to be transferred to San Antonio, from there to be returned home, but she grew ill and could not be moved. We feared for a time she was pregnant again, for there were rumors she had taken a lover during her husband's absence, but the surgeon's examination revealed nothing. "The men she claims to have had, they are imaginary, Chapman. It is part of her dementia. She has had no one, she is carrying no child. She pines for the dead, and I don't have to tell you, sir, what good that does any of us." It was not long afterward, a few weeks before Christmastime, that Eliza Jones died, joining her husband and her deadborn baby as those sacrificed to this region.

MacSwain soon regained his balance, perfectly, as if he had never wavered. The men were brought under discipline, the post was cleaned and made straight, and fresh plans for the following summer's campaign were laid. The War Department had been made to see our futile wanderings as a successful war, and MacSwain's reports on the *llano estacado* were received warmly by Sherman. That alone became our mark of valor, that we had gone onto this plain and returned, but it was sufficient to raise MacSwain in the eyes of the generals at Leavenworth. MacSwain gloated over his success. The officers cheered when he sent off his request to Leavenworth to conduct a second campaign on the *llano estacado*. We waited and drilled and fattened our horses. A reply came in February, not quite a year since we had last ridden out. In a fury, Mac-Swain called in his senior officers. His plan, he raged, had been rejected. "The Red River, the Red River," he hissed as he clawed the map. "They are *concerned* with settlers there. They want us to *contain* reservation Indians. Not Comanches, but Kiowas. There, there!" He tore at the wrinkled blue line between Texas and the Indian reservation at Fort Sill. Later that night he confided in me, alone, as he was to take aside each of his senior officers, singly. "They are not rejecting my plan, Phil, that is the worst of it. Don't you see, they will only postpone my plan for the *llano* till next year. But I know what that means. It means that by next year Custer will be free from Kansas and the Dakotas, that they will want Custer to lead the extermination of the Comanche in Texas. James John Mac-Swain is no fool. He knows what this means. It means that if I do not have my victory this year, I will have none at all." He offered these last words wearily, his passion declined. He pushed about the loose skin along the line of his jaw with the stubbed fingers of his right hand. "We will wait. We will wait. Perhaps things will change." He cast a quick indefinable look toward me and shifted his eyes to the map. "You do want to go back up onto the *llano* with me, don't you, Philip? Tell me you want to be a lord of that plain!"

TWO

ON May 9, 1875, the Second U.S. Cavalry under the command of James John MacSwain rode out from Fort Pulgas, Texas, to protect settlers from Indians and Indians from their foes on the Texas frontier area that stretched from Indian Territory on the north to the Cross Timbers settlements in the south. These words were the first entry in the diary I intended to keep during the second campaign on the *llano*. I have the unused ledger before me, having never written further in it, abandoning the notations of how far we rode each day, where we camped, the direction of our march, was there wood, grass, water, the times of day we rose, ate, and slept. The unprompted memory has lost some of these things, but it sees others more clearly for it. It was May, it had not rained, the air crackled as if it were the dead of summer the day we rode out of Fort Pulgas. It was as if a mirror had been held to last year's leave-taking, but that mirror had darkened and been cracked by drought and the failure of our first campaign. The band played

21

an air, the wives and women of the post stood on the review stand, their dresses flashing in the breeze like flags of a multitude of nations. We rode past their review in a single rank, the line of horses colored from black through every brown to gray and white. The parade had been watered, but as we swung from our single rank into a column of twos and passed through the main gate we were shrouded in dust. The denizens of Hidetown had gathered at the far bank of the river to see us go, but instead of crying out in celebration they drew back, for our uniforms were coated gray with dust and the thick dust that lay on the ground muffled our horses' hooves, and so we passed by them like specters, in silence.

Our orders had not changed since February. The Second Cavalry was to ride northeast to the Red River, three hundred and thirty miles distant, to relieve the Sixth Cavalry, which was under marching orders to Kansas. We were not to pursue the Comanches, the last free Indians in Texas, led by their legendary chieftains Bad Hand and the half-white Tehana Storm. Instead, we were to protect and discipline the Kiowas, Indians who had come in to the reservation, to fatten on government rations, while using the enclave of Sill as a base from which to raid into Texas. We were not to go out onto the *llano estacado* as an army but were to patrol its border as a police force. There would be no glory for us, only duty; we were not to make war but to keep a false peace. As the sharpest humiliation, the Second Cavalry had been placed under the command of the Eleventh Cavalry. MacSwain was to be subordinated to Greer, the Commandant of Sill, a prominent advocate of the current Peace Policy.

By climate and topography Texas was divided in two by the hundredth meridian. The eastern half belonged to the South in all its aspects—deeply wooded land, rich in farming in the black soil where timber had been cleared, a gentle rolling countryside throughout that directed its compliant rivers toward the Mississippi and the Gulf of Mexico. The weather there was temperate and rainfall normal to the Eastern regions of the nation. Cities were being spread inland along the river network, and railroads were linking the valleys: it seemed only a matter of time before that half of the state would be home to us. In contrast, to the west of the hundredth meridian was a place alien to civilization. The land became desert—rugged, unpredictable. The plains could be barren for eleven months, then cloaked in green wispy native grass—soft as velvet to the eye—for one. Stands of trees were sparse or occasional: shin oaks, scrub cedar, gnarled mesquite; near water one found majestic willows, cottonwoods, live oaks. The earth was raw, of rock and sand, incapable of supporting much vegetation but cacti and the native grass. In the west, the weather was violent and capricious, cold as the Arctic in the winter, scorching in the summer, while the temperate seasons of fall and spring could know ice or fierce heat at almost any time. The rivers that crossed the barren stretches of western Texas were desert rivers, filled only during sporadic storms when they would attack the countryside like something gone mad, slashing through the earth's crust, leaving ragged empty scars as the storms passed and their beds dried. Of all of the desert that was alien to the Easterner, the most difficult to understand by us and the most dangerous was that: that there was no water other than what fell from the sky. All but the veterans among us rode out that late spring from Fort Pulgas like spoiled children leaving home, little understanding that nature was not a gift set down by a kind parent to sustain us, but rather an implacable foe bent on our destruction.

We set out from Fort Pulgas with two water wagons attached to our trailing supply train; these lasted men and horses four days, and still we had not found water. We had ridden well over thirty miles a day, a punishing pace on man and animal and ruinous to our supply train. Lawton, our Quartermaster, kept the wagons rolling by means that seemed magic to us, by soaking strips of rawhide in water and then binding them around

shattered spokes and axles and frames, the strips of hide dry-
ing to fit these broken pieces together like bands of steel. But
even Lawton's genius could not keep up with our pace, and
MacSwain called a halt short of the West Fork of the Brazos,
allowing our battered supply train to overtake us. Here a temporary supply camp was established, eighty miles from the permanent camp MacSwain had planned. The wagons that were
unloaded, the most damaged of the train, were returned to Pulgas for repairs and water and parts for the wagons that remained with us. The country around the West Fork, where we
made our next camp after a two-day ride, stood black and
burnt-over by the drought. The ground had dried and cracked,
the withered grass had fallen from its roots and was swept
away by the wind, leaving the earth bald and scorched. Great
fissures broke open the road, and our wagons were shattered
crossing them. MacSwain had taken on a guide, an old man
who had once ranched in this region, and he had promised water at the West Fork. There was none, the riverbed filled with
dust, the deep holes we dug dense putrid mud.

"Buffalo Springs will have water for certain," the old man
brayed the night before we decamped. "I ain't never seen it
dry, not during the worst of days."

"Then, Clinton," said MacSwain, "you do not think we
should turn back, upon your word?"

The old man shifted his eyes from side to side. " 'Pon my
word I do not think Buffalo Spring wells have been dry of water the many years I have been here, near twenty, in all."

We rode the next day, thirty miles, our horses heaving and
staggering from thirst, to Buffalo Springs. A rotted odor reached
us on the trail, and several of us and the scouts went ahead to
find the water hole buried under the carcasses of hundreds of
dead cattle. The air was suffocating with the stench. Devereaux
and two Tonks wrapped their faces in bandannas and went
down to the water hole and attempted to clear it by lashing
ropes around the dead cattle, to drag them free of the water,

but the animals' legs split from their bloated bodies, blowing a decayed matter on the men that made them violently ill from its filth. We rode back to where the column had dismounted. The men had dispersed over several hundred yards, seeking shelter from the brutal sun beneath the shade of the mesquite or under lean-tos made by hanging ponchos or blankets from ropes strung between trees. The sweat on the men's faces had collected trail dust, the grime darkening them, so that as they lay in the shade they appeared to be Mexicans or Negroes or the Indians we pursued. The men half rose, slowly coming to their knees to watch our return, and, reading failure in our slow pace, lay down to sip fitfully at the quarter-canteen ration each had been allowed. Some of the older men cupped water in their hands for their horses, though they knew this taste could not possibly slake the animal's thirst, for water, far more than for man, was fuel for these beasts of burden. We found MacSwain crouched beneath a lean-to, his small frame twisted in repose. That his old wounds gave him great pain on horseback could be seen by all, by the manner he sat in the saddle, hunched, tight as wire, racked by the easiest gait, but few men knew the pain he suffered when he became too tired to stand or sit and was forced to lie. He was lifted by an aide-de-camp and received our report without comment but to call for the old guide, Clinton, squatting nearby.

"So, Clinton, what do you think now? Is there water farther on, or shall we turn back?"

We had spread out our maps, those which the cartographer had drawn from Marcy's expedition of 1851 and from our own knowledge gathered last year, on a camp table, and we watched the old man fumble with pen and rule and prismatic compass. He did not know maps and had gone beyond the scope of his knowledge of the land. He was dismissed and sent back to Fort Pulgas. Devereaux then brought forward Poor Man, the chief of his Tonk scouts.

"The Tonks say there is water here, Cap," said the Rebel

scout. "But it's badland and bad water, but beyond it, here, the Red and the Deep Fork that flows into it, the Red for sure, during the worst of droughts, has running sweet water."

"How far is it across?" said MacSwain, rubbing his stubbed fingers over the territory Devereaux had washed with ink, the badlands.

Devereaux spoke to the Tonk scout and related his words to us. "It would be, I reckon, a hundred and twenty miles to the Red. Twenty to thirty less to the Deep Fork, but that may be dry, Cap. Poor Man says it's a two-day walk across gypsum country, gyp water tonight."

MacSwain gave orders to the Sergeant Major to mount the men. He then had a young private named Dixon brought forward. The man, or boy, for he could not have been eighteen, had been caught by the sentry trying to tap into the water wagon. The boy had to be held erect by the guards, he had grown so weak from his fever. Captain Sanders of F Troop, to which the boy was assigned, spoke for him.

"He is a good man, Colonel. He has been given an old horse, sick and lame, and he was taking the water for the beast."

"Is that what the lying dog says? Does he love his horse so that he would walk to save it, Captain?"

And MacSwain saw that a shattered caisson wheel was strapped to the youth's back and that he walked in the column's dust till he choked and fell. The Colonel bade the column ride on for several miles till he allowed men to return for him. He then had the youth stripped of his shirt and spread-eagled across an open wagon frame, and the searing sun did to his back worse than what a bullwhip might have done.

MacSwain deemed our halt there two miles above Buffalo Springs another temporary supply camp, though we merely dumped excess baggage there, the large walled command tent among it, and cut free all ailing animals, mules and horses alike, and shot them rather than leave them to die in the sun.

We marched, now all but the officers dismounted, toward gypsum country. The sun heated the air till it cooked, the light so distorted that all we saw danced before our eyes. One could not touch the barrel of a pistol or carbine without blistering one's hands. Several men fell to heat prostration, and one officer, a lieutenant in infantry, dropped in his tracks. Of these stricken men, one grew seriously ill and succumbed before nightfall. We marched across the low, rolling plain till late that afternoon, believing to a man that the heat and the dust-choked air and the monotony of the burnt landscape would never end, when we came upon a deep canyon, approaching its precipice so suddenly that our forward riders almost tumbled their horses down its walls. We found a road down into the canyon and were soon surrounded by high gypsum bluffs that rose with a majesty I had previously thought reserved for the architecture of man. The valley walls were littered with nature's art: detached mounds, buttes, domes, and a great variety of other forms that in the shimmering heat resembled monuments, vases, urns, spires, colonnades, arches, all striated like the canyon walls by rockbeds bearing a spectrum of colors—pale dry pink sandstone layered between green rock porous as sponge, thin lines of dark burnt red, thick cakes of decaying yellow chalk as soft as powder, pitted caps of hard white stone, coral-like formations of purple and washed blues that recalled to us that the plain we descended through had once been an ocean floor. The road soon gave way to a narrow, crumbling path, and we dismounted and leaving the supply wagons behind walked the horses into the valley. There we came upon gypsum rock of every hue and form: clear white bricks of selenite, delicate needles of pink and rose and oxblood, coinlike stones pale green and blue and purple worn smooth as polished jewelry. By the time we had made our way down, the sun had set on the canyon floor and the light we came into was blue, cool and liquid, as if we were riding underwater. The cliffs above still caught the late sun, the canyon walls bathed blood-red, the gypsum crystals sparkling as if the rock were encrusted with diamonds. When the sun dropped beneath the horizon of the plain, the colors darkened and the brilliance faded and we on the canyon floor were cast into night.

We came upon water immediately, but it was bad—low limestone pots bubbling with sulfurous waste—and we pressed on through the dark and came onto a riverbed whose coarse sand was damp a few inches beneath its surface. As we went upriver, the moisture grew nearer the surface, till it was broken by the horses' weight and a scum of water stood in our tracks. Some men threw themselves onto the sand and sucked at the water, but it was foul, the taste of it throwing them into fits of retching. The scouts promised good water farther on, and as we made our way upriver, the banks became lined with thick stands of reed and willows and a rank sedge grass so tall it could not be seen over on horseback. Toward midnight the scouts came back with word they had found a stream a mile ahead, and we mounted and rode toward it. The men were not disciplined, and many of them broke ranks and ran into the pools that spread out around an artesian spring. This water was thick with gypsum, nauseating to smell and taste, and the men who drank more than a few spoonfuls became ill, vomiting till their stomachs were dry, and still they were convulsed by the gypsum salt. The men who had thrown themselves into the water suffered worse, the gypsum becoming encrusted on their bodies and uniforms, lacerating the skin, raising raw bleeding sores where there was the slightest friction of cloth and skin or skin against skin. The wisest among us thought to add some corrective fluid to the ruined water, but neither citric acid nor lime juice nor brandy made it potable. Boiling the water only distilled its fragrance. That night the entire command was ill, the horses and mules suffering the worst. The following morning we left ten horses and three mules behind, shooting the dying.

We decamped before dawn, sleep being useless to us. The

morning was spent finding a way down the canyon wall for the supply train. That was accomplished by noon, and we set out over a low divide and saw as we ascended that the canyon opened to the east into a broad valley. We tried to find this topography on our maps without success. Much of my time was spent noting formations and dry streambeds and other points for the cartographer. We saw our first herd of buffalo that afternoon, a great black blanket flowing across the prairie ahead of us, and the first signs of Indians since we had departed from Pulgas. MacSwain and I rode out to one of the abandoned villages that the Tonk scouts had discovered. "Comanches," said Devereaux, showing us the outlines of the council lodge, where the individual tipis and wickiups had stood. "It's been long deserted, Cap, maybe a year, but look here. A fire was built in one of their old pits not long ago. Maybe three days. The boys found these." He held out three cartridge shells, and we examined them: Winchester .30s, of Army issue. Then he showed us a red clay pipe and an arrow with a mulberry shaft tipped with wild turkey feathers bound to the shaft with buffalo sinew. The arrow spike was made of hoop iron that had been tempered and hardened. "Only a smithy could've done this job, Cap. The Tonks say Kiowas, and they are a raiding party from Sill. They camp in old Comanche villages to cover their trail." He pointed the arrow toward a track running northeast. "Maybe fifty, sixty head of shod horses, going back to Sill."

"Can we catch them, Dev?" said MacSwain.

"No, Cap," said the Southerner with a grin. "But do we want to?"

MacSwain came up at the scout but gave away with a side-long look of resignation. He ordered me back to the column. As I rode away, MacSwain and Devereaux were conferring between themselves, the scout's grin flashing beneath the white felt sombrero that he alone among the Regulars was allowed to wear.

29

We came upon water in midafternoon and camped there. This water proved bitterer than before, gypsum held in solution, sickeningly fouled with buffalo excrement and urine. Brown scum covered the ponds, and even after this had been scraped away, the water had to be cleaned not only of fecal matter but buffalo hair, which those men who had some humor left claimed was best strained by drinking with teeth set on edge. The men became ill, but minutes after vomiting they would be back sucking at the warm stinking liquid, such was our thirst. Coffee best covered the nauseating odor and taste of this cocktail of gypsum and buffalo waste, but even if the water could be made palatable, our bowels were stricken by the salt and the troop suffered debilitating diarrhea. Of the men, the oldest suffered worst. The surgeon could barely sit his horse, and many others were carried along on litters. Our lips and mouths and tongues and throats had been scraped raw by the alkali, and there were few who were not spitting or vomiting blood. We smeared our lips and faces with camphor ice and wore goggles to protect us from the searing sun. We marched till late morning, when the heat overcame our horses, and we camped at midday, pitching lean-tos strung from our stacked rifles, seeking shade. We remounted at three and continued across this high divide, a humped plain that seemed to slope downward in every direction but that in which we rode. A peak became visible to the east as we struck the divide's crest, towering above the plain, but our eyes were so inflamed from the sun and wind and gypsum salt that we had no sense of its true size: most could barely see beyond the rider ahead. We camped at dark, without water or wood and with poor grass. But MacSwain allowed a hunting party to go to the buffalo herd that had been trailing on our flank throughout the day, and that night we feasted on bison steak and roast, whose blood we drank as though it were wine. During the night I was waked by a fresh breeze and rose and saw the wind had shifted to the north. I walked away from the camp, to a low promontory overlooking the folds of ridges and deep-cut arroyos that lay before tomorrow's march. Lightning flashed beyond, on the distant northern horizon, like cannons in a war being fought in the sky. The storms—there must have been a half-dozen of them—were too distant for their thunder to reach us, but the air was perfumed with rain. As I made my way back to the camp, I could hear the horses shuddering at its promise.

It was natural to this region that the rain we prayed for to-day would be cursed on the morrow. We broke camp late the next day, MacSwain allowing the men to rest not for what they had gone through but for what they would, and did not ride out till Devereaux and the Tonks had returned from their scout. They reported the country ahead wild and broken, but so for no more than thirty miles, after which we would come upon an easy plain, the scout said, that would lead us into the Red River drainage. The arroyos were steep and cuts would have to be made in the creek banks, but there did not seem to be one that could not be headed, if the supply train could not pull the ridge. "Better news than that, Cap," said Devereaux, ordering the Tonks to bring up a packhorse. "Fresh water in the arroyo springs, sweet as milk." And like a children's Christmas, the canteens with good water were broken out and passed throughout the command, each man rationed no more than a mouthful, but by three that afternoon we had ridden off the divide out of the badlands and were feasting on sweet fresh water from a spring-fed pond. To bring further relief, the wind continued to blow from the north, the air growing soft with rain. Clouds gathered till by late afternoon the sky was overcast and night came early. There was good grass, and the Quartermaster located a grove of cottonwood that yielded abundant firewood, and for the first time during our march, there was a camp made in which neither man nor animal suffered. We rested that evening, dozing and smoking before the campfire embers, spitting out cuds of gypsum and washing the salt from our throats with brandy.

31

That night wind crackling in the cottonwoods woke me. I heard through the pitch black two horses rearing at their lariats, as if in play. I was able to secure my own horse, but before I had gone beyond the camp perimeter toward the herds, lightning struck in our midst—probably in the cottonwood grove farther upstream, but its fire flew all around us—and the thunder from the bolt shook the ground. The horse herds had been staked and secured with sidelines, but these precautions had been made against Indian attack and, with no sign of hostiles, poorly executed. Most herd riders and sentries were asleep in the saddle if they remained mounted at all. The herds broke free from their ropes and picket pins, and with lightning blasting the sky and thunder blasting the earth the crazed animals stampeded down the arroyo. Cries to hold the horses could be heard along the line, and those of us who had managed to secure our lariats and tie down our mounts were sent off into the night after the scattered herd. Devereaux and the Tonk scouts had leapt to their ponies bareback and had galloped out after the herd so close behind as to be part of it. By the time my men had saddled and mounted, the scouts had circled and turned most of the horses and had corralled them not a mile from camp, to wait out the storm there. Devereaux and I and several men rode out to locate the horses that had broken away from the herd. The lightning flashed all around us, painting ourselves and the land in a lurid light that for the time of its flash was bright as day but unnatural, for it reflected no colors, only stark white and black. The thunder was a continuous roar, as if thousands of crazed beasts were stampeding around us. The storm had been dry in coming, but now well-spaced drops of rain began to fall, so heavy they struck at us like hammer blows, spooking the horses already made frantic by the thunder and lightning. In a prolonged flash of lightning we saw four strays making up the slope of a prow of land that rose between two arroyos. We whipped our horses and crossed the arroyo, now only Devereaux and I in pursuit, galloping up the ridge, quickly gaining on the horses, who were dashing left and right, maddened by the storm. We ran up alongside the four strays—then Devereaux fell back to turn them and bring them back to the arroyo. The four horses made a sudden dash to the left that jerked my horse up and nearly sent him to his knees. Devereaux's horse collided with mine, and as we were untangling our animals, who were rearing and lashing their hooves in terror, a webbed tree of lightning illuminated the country for miles around. We saw in that instant that the four horses had turned at the brink of a precipice and only the instinct of my mount had saved us.

"My word, Cap," said Devereaux as we stood only feet away from the cliff, and then as the dazzling lightning struck again, "I do owe you one, I do believe I do. Oh my." He whistled as the lightning crackled over the valley below.

We did not find the four strays, or make much attempt to, and went back to what we had corralled of the herd and saw that the Tonks had them well in hand before returning to camp. The first line of the storm, the wind, lightning, and thunder, had moved across us, and now it had begun to rain. Our horses were taken by an orderly, and we were told to report to Mac-Swain's tent. There were collected the officers of the command but for two troop leaders who could not be found. Poor Man, the Tonk scout, was there, and Isle, the regiment's surgeon, still clad in his long white nightshirt. MacSwain was enraged, suspicious of everyone in his presence, as he had been so often during our first campaign. I reported on the horses gathered, which MacSwain received with a curt gesture. With a few muttered comments we were all dismissed but for Lieutenant Beaumont, the Officer of the Guard, whom we expected to see broken by dawn.

The next morning the camp was waked by a roar as ominous as stampede or thunder. During the night the dry creek-bed had been taken by a torrent of frothing red water that hurled down the arroyo with a ferocity that made it seem mad

to destroy everything in its path. No word came from Mac-
Swain till noon, when the rain had slacked and the sky light-
ened. Hoeme emerged from the commander's tent to report
MacSwain was suffering from his wounds and the alkali he
had ingested. We had been ordered, the German said, to
bridge the river by nightfall. To crown this comedy, Hoeme appointed me Engineering Officer in lieu of one and pressed upon
me Mahan's text on civil engineering, which would have served
us well had we a dozen trained engineers and a car of steel
beams and weeks to work in. I approached the Quartermaster,
Lawton, who began our task by adding Mahan to the flotsam
being swept down the arroyo by the flood. Ropes were shot across
the river till one snagged a fallen tree, and a brave lad made it
across, soaked but well, and more ropes were flung over, which
he tied off. A dozen men crossed the river, with axes and saws,
and parties on both sides began to construct cribs made of
green logs, notched and well fitted, and then to fill these cribs
with the largest stones we could carry. Meanwhile a larger party
of men began to cut down the steep bank the flood had gouged
into the ravine. This work went more slowly on the far bank,
for still only a dozen of the ablest men were able to cross the
ropes without being swept away. On the near side a crew began
to lay down an approach of corduroy, small tree trunks lashed
together and pinned to the earth by heavy stones. Two long
stringers were made by splicing saplings with rawhide; these
were floated into position and fastened to trees on the near and
far banks. The first wagon was sent across the torrent too soon,
before the corduroy approach on the far side was complete: it
slid into the current and was lost. The Mexican teamster was
saved but four mules were drowned, nothing of them seen
above water but their ears floating downstream like aquatic
plants, a sight that caused some to laugh till they stepped into
the grasping water.

The fording of the river was halted at dusk and completed
the following morning when the water had dropped by several

feet and the current did not flow half so swift as before. The Mexican teamster left during the night, our first deserter. Many more men would have gone before him had we been near a California trail or any civilization, but the men loathed the Army less than they feared Texas, and we were near full strength entering the Red River drainage. We encountered no more booming rivers, but the rain continued and the earth was turned to mud; the riverbanks and bluff trails became slippery and unstable, often caving in under the weight of a single horse. The bottoms had turned to gumbo, a thick sucking clay that tore wagon wheels from their axles and snapped horses' legs as they fought to break free of the mire. Wagons had to be double-teamed for any grade over three degrees. On steeper slopes every wheel had to be winched not only up but down, for the mules could not keep their footing on the downslope and they foundered and fell, pulling the wagons down on them, destroying the animals as well as the wagons and their cargo. We passed three days at this hideous labor, a steady drizzle of rain tormenting our efforts. There was nothing that was not wet—tents, tack, uniforms, provisions, the animals' grain and forage, papers, maps, weapons, boots, everything ran with water. The fires that we could ignite smoked and steamed. Nothing could be dried or cooked. We existed on jerked beef and canned rations. At night we rolled ourselves in ponchos and rubber-coated blankets, but the slightest movement opened a fissure and water poured in, everywhere. The sun and heat and gypsum had broken the skin around the men's mouths and noses and eyes and anuses, and these lesions and ruptures became infected and turned to sores that could not be healed in the damp. The horses did not suffer as did the men at first, but then they were struck by flu and many were lost to fever and chills. By the time we came out of the badlands we had lost thirty mounts and dray animals to disease or accident, and another twenty had not been recovered from the stampede.

MacSwain goaded every officer, man, and beast in pursuit of

Indians that none but he believed we could find. When we stumbled across the trail of the Kiowa raiding party whose signs we had first seen in gypsum country, MacSwain gloated at our defeatism, bragging before the regiment in formation of his nose for the enemy, so that morale worsened as we closed with the Indians. We had come to the end of the broken country but for a last formidable gorge. The rain had stopped, the rivers dropped to streams, the roads and trails had firmed, so that we climbed and descended the network of arroyos with a swift technique and felt little threatened by the last chasm. We arrived at the gorge in midafternoon, and after some argument from the staff, MacSwain relented and ordered that we pitch camp on the high ground and cross the gorge the following morning. Toward sunset we looked over the gorge and saw Devereaux and his party returning from their scout. Devereaux whooped and waved his floppy white hat above his head, and we saw that one of the Indians with them was a captive. The trumpeter sounded assembly as the scout and his party came at breakneck speed down the gorge walls. The weather had turned mild, the sky was smudged with pastel blues and pinks; innocent clouds trundled by in unison; the walls of the gorge were bathed in faded reds and yellows of sunset as the scout and his party flew down the slope, whooping and waving their hats and weapons as they rode. Such were the canvases we had seen as young men, before coming west, the pastorals that had induced so many dreamers to take up lives that came to nothing but hardship and defeat, often ending in deaths that no artist had ever drawn.

Nature continued to mock us with her beauty that evening, as the staff officers and Devereaux and the Tonk scouts and the captured Indian gathered around the campfire, lying or sitting at ease, smoking hand-rolled cigarettes, our faces ruddy in the fire's glow, the canopy of stars shivering in the black sky as bright as paint. The captured Indian proved to be a Lipan. According to Devereaux, early that day they had seen a column

36

of smoke to the northeast, toward the Red River. Poor Man, the chief Tonk scout, had said the signals were from a large Kiowa party warning of our approach. They had ridden toward the smoke and had jumped a Kiowa scouting party. A few shots were exchanged, and the Kiowas had turned their ponies and made back toward their camp, easily outdistancing Devereaux and the Tonks' weary mounts. But the Lipan's pony had taken a fall, and after a chase they had captured him. The Lipan was questioned by our scouts, then led away. Devereaux scratched a design in the earth and tossed the stick in the fire. "Well, Cap," he said to MacSwain, who had been restlessly prowling beyond the campfire, "you ain't going to like it, but the Lipan says the Kiowa ain't a war party but a large hunting party. He says they got permission, Cap, to hunt off the reservation and that from the Big Chief from Sill. Greer."

MacSwain flung out: "By God damn, sir! If we are not to capture and punish these hostiles, then why are we ordered to ride after them to the Red River!"

The scout narrowed his eyes and cocked his head. "The Lipan says the Big Chief's camp is one day's ride, direct on the Kiowa trail. Then, mebbe, we shall see."

MacSwain cursed. "Then we *shall* see! And we shall have a night march too!" And in a rage the Colonel went back to his tent. MacSwain was at length dissuaded from punishing the men and the animals to vent his frustration, but it cost those of us who spoke out in doing so.

The following morning it was decided that the Quartermaster and L Troop, whose inferior horses were hurting, and the infantry companies would escort the supply train and head the gorge, a ride of thirty or forty miles to the northwest, we figured from our maps. The remainder of the regiment, five cavalry troops, crossed the gorge with ease and, picking up the Kiowa trail from their last encampment, rode at a trot or quicker gait after the Indians, our horses laboring at the pace. We had gained to within a day of the Kiowas, perhaps less, when we

37

came upon a rocky stretch and lost the trail. When we took it up again the Indians had gained a day, and at that night's camp we stood less than fifty miles from the Red River and the reservation border. We broke camp that night at eleven and made a good night march across easy country, but at dawn, when it seemed possible that we might overtake the Kiowas, we were encountered by a scouting party from Greer's command, the Eleventh Cavalry, which we were told was camped five miles distant. The Captain commanding the scout relayed orders from Greer, which he presented as informal invitation, to camp our regiment near theirs on the banks of the Red River. MacSwain replied that we were in hot pursuit of Kiowa raiders and, continuing the charade of diplomacy, said that the Second Cavalry would accept the general's hospitality when these hostiles had been detained. The Captain deferentially drew MacSwain away from the column, and they conversed beyond earshot, though we did not need to hear to understand that Greer's orders were not to be breached. As the two rejoined our column we heard MacSwain's shrill voice: "My God, man, we will not be escorted there!" And the Captain, his manner cool and civil, his uniform pressed and spotless, saluted and turned his men and rode away at a gallop. MacSwain waited till their column had cleared the horizon, then in a voice cracked with anger and humiliation said, "By God, Phil, I have been relieved of my command!"

Greer's camp was set by an open grove of cottonwood in a graceful bend in the Red River. So picturesque was the site that MacSwain commented it could have been chosen by an Indian. The others did not share the commander's bitterness, and we rode down to this oasis as full of wonder as savages come upon civilization. The camp was laid out in streets that bent with the riverbank, four lines of dog tents in a sweeping arc that ended in a cluster of wall tents connected by a system of strung flies and board walkways. Our weary column was led to an area not distant and, though away from the whispering shelter of the cottonwoods, far from unpleasant, the loose, sandy soil pillowy as goose down beneath blanket and canvas. We set out our ragged, discolored tents in no great order and dismissed all men from duty, as guard and picket were mounted by the Eleventh, and allowed our soldiers to bathe in the river. Their shouts and calls came to us like the sounds of children at play. Word was brought that that evening's mess would be provided by Greer's polished kitchen, and our cooks and orderlies were given leave to join the others. With this came an invitation to our officers to join Greer's command for dinner that evening. Petulantly MacSwain refused this hospitality for all, then relented and ordered every officer to attend but himself, saying a fever had struck him and that he would be indisposed. Several officers who were in fact ill attempted to stay back, but they were not allowed to rest. We cleaned and mended our soiled and tattered uniforms as best we could and at dusk ambled through the Eleventh's tent city like gentlemen on promenade.

A banquet hall had been fashioned by placing two fresh white wall tents end to end, with flies stretched between the two tents and a floor laid. Tables had been set up and laid in one tent, while the other acted as a lounge, with Greer and his men sitting and standing about, sipping whiskey and exchanging gossip. These officers of the Eleventh were spit-and-polish, sleek, tanned and fit, while we felt raw, disheveled, and uncouth in their company. There was a moment of discomfort when we entered and it was noted that MacSwain was not with us. Greer's Adjutant sensed the insult and attempted to greet us formally, but Greer eased him aside and laughing off our salutes shook hands around and saw that we had drinks and were made comfortable. Greer was an affable, plump man, with silver hair and heavy waxed mustaches. He was a Philadelphian, friend and confidant, it was said, of General Grant. His manner was civil and candid. He laughed openly but without

39

malice at MacSwain and those officers in the Texas Department who chose to make war against the Indians. "Play at war" were the words he employed in repeating his jest to his own men. He was solicitous to a fault about MacSwain's illness. "Has he been wounded, Chapman, and again not reported it or had it treated properly? Shall we send our surgeon to his tent? Such an iron man he is or was," Greer said to those who had gathered around us, principally officers of his command, for ours had been given camp chairs and were being served drinks and canapés by brunette soldiers. "Whiskey and good cooking will do him no harm," said Greer and sent his Adjutant to MacSwain's tent to reiterate his invitation. "If our hospitality has to be offered a third time, then I shall deliver its invitation myself. I am sure that then," said Greer, turning to us, "he would not be able to refuse my charm."

Greer ordered a map of the region, one superior to any our command possessed, hung on the wall, and I was asked to point out this badland we had passed through. I traced the route of our march, and one of Greer's officers, an insolent office fighter, pointed to another line. "True, you came on a straight path, very nearly, from Pulgas to here, but sometimes these straight paths can be deceiving in the field, being far from the shortest distance between two points. Wouldn't it have been a quicker, and less eventful, march to have come here, swinging to the north and skirting these badlands and the trials that have laid your commander low?"

Before I could reply, another officer spoke: "Ah, but that would have taken MacSwain dangerously near the *llano estacado,* and we hear he has no desire to go there again."

I found myself defending what I might otherwise have attacked, irate at MacSwain's absence, that I would have to speak for him. "To the contrary, Major. Colonel MacSwain did choose the direct route to avoid the *llano estacado,* that is true, but only because he has a great desire to go there again and fight the Comanche and has been ordered to avoid them."

"Does he indeed have this grand desire?" said Greer. "Does he indeed?" And Greer's acolytes laughed.

There followed an uncomfortable silence that was broken shortly by the entry into the tent by four men in civilian dress. Like homely maidens at a ball, myself and our sunburnt, exhausted officers of the Second were abandoned by Greer's sleek subordinates as they flocked to these civilians. The first of these men all recognized, for, other than Custer perhaps, none was better known in the plains region than Johanes Kidder, the Indian Agent at Sill. A Quaker by religion, Kidder in dress and manner resembled the two interpreters and guides who accompanied him, weather-worn men, garbed in soft leather jackets and britches, one affecting a high-topped moccasin boot usually worn by squaws. The fourth man, in a cheap gabardine suit and low-cut shoes, was named Chivington, according to Lieutenant Bass, the latter a young officer from I Troop who had passed through Leavenworth before being transferred to the Second at Fort Pulgas. Bass remarked that Chivington was the principal civilian contractor for provisions and supplies to the reservation at Sill. "It is understood that Chivington has made millions," Bass said without particular regard for who might overhear, "in overcharging Friend Kidder's noble red men, packing the grain with chaff, loading wagons of flour with rocks, and at that the grain and the flour are often mangy stuff, some dating from the Civil War. Such is the case too with the tinned meats and tea and molasses—war surplus. Some say that is the point of collecting these noble red men on the reservation—that the Quartermaster may rid itself of the glut of maggoted and rat-ruined provisions left from the Civil War. Should a true history of these Indian wars be written, sir," said Bass, "it would be seen that greed has shown the way for enmity."

I asked Bass to hold his opinions, for the Sill party had been apprised of our presence and we were being approached by Kidder and Chivington, flanked by the Indian interpreters and General Greer and the sleek members of his staff. By the formation of their approach, a phalanx that showed a comic aspect of having been practiced, it became apparent that the Indian Agent was chief at Sill. Johanes Kidder appeared a man far less interested in keeping the peace or protecting the noble savage than in making it clear to all, and in particular the officers of our unit, that the Indian Department, and not the Army or Department of War, retained control over these Indian wars, the last phrase so outspoken by Lieutenant Bass that it had drawn the Indian Agent's attention to our party. For reasons of rank, perhaps, Kidder chose to address his rebuke to me:

"Do you think these be wars, Captain? Do you think driving these poor savages like beasts from their homelands, to herd them, to corral them, to manage them, to punish them, to deprive them of their ancient customs, to take their manhood, their gods, their lives and way of life from them, be *war,* Captain?" Aware that these words might not rest well with many of the officers of the Eleventh lined at his side, Kidder shifted: "These men from Sill, brave one and all, have seen real war, Captain. They have no need to strut across the plains like blue-shirted bullies, swatting down these natives, be they warrior, squaw, or papoose, like flies and call that war. No, these are men, Captain. They have had their fill of war, real war, when brother slew brother and the land from Vicksburg to Atlanta ran red, they have seen the monstrous face of it and do not go swaggering through the lands of those who are native to it calling their peacekeeping war."

"Nor would I, sir, before I came to these regions, have called this war. But now I have been two and a half years here, and it is war, sir. It is a different sort of war, to be sure, but it is still war. That it is not a conflict where soldier fights soldier over some gain in ground or to prove the power of some witless philosophy or to extend the reign of an even less witted ruler, that does not mean that we are not fighting, and when men fight that is war."

Kidder smiled and made his reply. "Tell me, Captain, when

you ride out from your forts, as your command has just ridden out from Pulgas, do you go out to make war? By whose orders do you go out and make war? Tell me, General Greer," he said without turning, "by what orders has the Second Cavalry of James John MacSwain ridden out from Fort Pulgas to make war on these peace-loving Kiowas?"

"There are no orders for the Second Cavalry to make war against the Kiowas," said the supple Greer, "other than orders that Colonel MacSwain seems to have issued on his own."

"If you will give me leave to speak, sir," said Lieutenant Bass, and being in so foul a mood as to toss this opinion-monger to these wolves, I allowed him to do so, "if I may speak on behalf of these younger officers, such as myself, who have not served in a real war, as has Captain Chapman, if there is no war on the plains, sir, what is the point of placing an army here?"

"To keep the peace," said the Indian Agent. "Not to disrupt it."

"Then are we policemen, rather than soldiers, sir?"

"The role of the soldier may be to keep peace as well as make war, Lieutenant."

"Indeed, sir," replied Bass, who had now won many of the officers of the Eleventh to his side, despite their commander's displeasure. "But then, wouldn't you say, sir, that our presence is disruptive of peace, that if true peace were desired by the civilians in Washington, then civilians, policemen, if you will, would be sent to the plains and the plains would be regulated by these police as are the streets of Boston or New York? But that is folly, as even the most pacifistic Friend must know. These aren't city streets, not even country lanes, we ride over. Nor are these noble red men you speak of common lawbreakers who may be imprisoned and punished for their crimes. It is true that the Indians are often lawbreakers by our definition, but isn't it also true that they are often criminals *only* by our definition? As an example—when an Indian party raids a frontiersman's ranch and steals his cattle, isn't it usually because these frontiersmen have driven off the buffalo and have replaced it with cattle? How is the Indian to know that the buffalo is free and of little value while the cattle is owned and highly prized? Particularly since the latter seems such an inferior meal when compared to the former."

There was muffled laughter from the officers. The Indian Agent seemed unsettled by their amusement. General Greer spoke out: "Your point, sir?"

"This, General," replied Bass with aplomb. "We, as soldiers, are sent here to do our duty. We are told in Washington that this duty is peacekeeping. However, to the Indian, our very presence here is an act of war. Now, sir, my point is this: if our leaders say we are at peace and our enemies say we are at war, whom is a poor soldier to believe?"

The laughter swept us all, but our amusement was cut short by the appearance of the ladies of the Eleventh, the wives of General Greer and his favored officers, and we were called into the adjoining tent, where a feast had been prepared. The officers of the Second, starved for such a table because of Mac-Swain's ban on hunting and his allowing no officer to eat other than those rations given the men, soon forgot the insults they and their bodies had suffered the previous weeks. To us, wine fermented from local wild grapes had the bouquet of burgundy, thick cotton tablecloths spread like linen under our hands, the rude camp chairs sat plump as chesterfields. Negro servants brought course after course—fried catfish and perch from the river, wild turkey, quail, antelope, and buffalo roasts and sweetbreads—till the dinner concluded with brandy and cigars. Conversation turned away from our earlier debate, away from all talk of war, and, as the women placed among us laughed and chatted gaily, we offered more of ourselves, of our youths and our dreams, than might have been wise, had wisdom been sat at our table. We found a sustenance in the women, were they beautiful or not, greater than from food or drink.

I retired early to my tent and wrote Ann for the first time since our departure. I set the letter aside and went out of the tent, intending to walk to the river or to the horse corral. It was near midnight; from what I could hear the banquet was continuing in full swing, the sound of fiddle music and dancing and women's laughter carrying across the darkened camp. As I turned away from the ball, I saw a light in MacSwain's tent and made for it. I could hear no voices within and, thinking the Colonel was reading or studying maps, asked permission to enter. There was a sound within, and I entered the tent to find MacSwain asleep, half-sitting, crouched on the cot, leaning against the tent wall, the only position in which he could find rest. He was scarcely sleeping at all, muttering to himself, grinding his teeth, breathing in shallow gasps. Thinking the light caused him discomfort, I turned down the lantern and extinguished it. He woke in the darkness, crying out,

"My God, light it! Light the dark!"

During the following days of rest and recuperation and repair, the course of the Second Cavalry became clear. For the moment, the Interior Department in Washington reigned over the Army, and all units on the Western frontier were placed in defensive positions with orders not to ride out against hostile Indians till a period of negotiations and diplomacy had turned, or failed to turn, these free Indians to the reservation. As well, the Army units strung along the Texas frontier, particularly those near the border of the Sill reservation, were to act as buffer between the reservation Indians and settlers, to keep the adventurers among both from encroaching on the other's territory or rights. These restrictions satisfied older men—were they Indian, settler, or soldier—but the young worried at the halter and made plans to break the peace before its purpose was served and make war for the sake of warring. None was more excited by this inactivity than James John MacSwain, who, during our ten-day encampment at the Red River, bombarded his friends in Leavenworth and Washington with reports on the growing savagery of the unfettered Indians, the grief being suffered by the heroic settlers, and, no doubt his most telling argument, the deterioration caused a fielded army when it must bow to civilian dictate. Nor did he reserve his argument to paper. During our time at Red River he lobbied ceaselessly among the young officers of both the Second and Eleventh and made many converts among them to his policy of war.

There was a celebration that rivaled Greer's ball when the Second Cavalry received its assignment. The weather had continued mild and dry, and the operations map was taken from the headquarters tent and hung from the fly outside and the officers of the Second were sat around in camp chairs with many of the men gathered behind them, as if attending an entertainment. MacSwain conducted the briefing himself, in good humor, physically as well as mentally rejuvenated. His eyes shone with health, and his gestures and stance showed no sign of fatigue or pain. "Gentlemen, we have been sent our marching orders!" he began, and the officers and the men who a fortnight earlier had been near marched to death cheered. "Your commanding officer has been thoughtfully returned to command," which was followed by a second ovation that surely reached into General Greer's tent. "And finally, the Second has been given a command post of its own, not one here on the fringe of some reservation, but in the very heart of Comanche country, from which, when the orders come to reengage the enemy, the Second Cavalry will be the first to war!" A third ovation carried through our ranks. MacSwain pointed on the map to a place one hundred and forty miles a few degrees south of west of our present position: "We shall establish a base supply camp here—at Fort Phantom Hill—to make ready to march out onto the *llano estacado* when the Indian Ring and its friends in Washington have been routed!"

The men cheered and cheered, ready for war.

46

The legs and wind of our horses, however, did not repair like the wills of men. We fed and rested the exhausted and damaged animals that we had ridden from Fort Pulgas, trusting they would last till replacements could be found. Within a week, Major Frank Clous and two troops of cavalry arrived from Fort Richardson and were attached to the Second Cavalry. Many of our more damaged mounts were replaced, and Major Clous, an officer respected throughout the Department of Texas, was appointed MacSwain's second-in-command. On June 14, the Second Cavalry marched out of the Red River encampment at full strength and in high spirits.

We rode as quickly as we could without ruining the horses and covered nearly one hundred miles the first four days. Thereafter we entered Comanche territory, or what had recently been, and proceeded more cautiously, though we saw no sign of Indians. Our progress would have been slowed in any case by the terrain, a stretch of low broken hills that we did not ride out of till late our fifth day in the saddle. The guide who had come from Sill thought that our destination, Phantom Hill, a ruined fort that dated from before the Civil War, lay forty miles distant, though the exact position of it was not given on any of our maps. The scout knew only that the fort stood on the old Fort Richardson wagon road and opined that if we turned south and joined that road we would at least know the line of our march if not its exact distance. We camped that afternoon and rose at two in the morning and were in the saddle by three and had ridden seven miles before dawn. At noon we came upon the Fort Richardson trail and turned west. We had not reached Phantom Hill by sundown, and, after a brief rest, we pressed on. The night was moonlit, the countryside flat or nearly so and open, the wagon road well-worn, and we made good time and shortly before one in the morning were greeted by our scouts riding back to us. They reported that Fort Phantom Hill had been sighted, and we went at a quick pace toward it. The old guide from Sill, his job now accomplished, at-

47

tached himself to Lieutenant Bass and me and spoke of the legend of Phantom Hill, which was one of a chain of forts built after the Mexican War and closed when, during the Civil War, the Texas frontier was abandoned. The fort had been founded and named by a Major Theder, who had, according to our yarn-spinner, later gone mad and committed suicide.

"The story goes," said the guide, "that Theder and his men came upon this place one evening when the mists was rising from the Clear Fork and the moon bright as your face, as it is tonight. On approaching the river valley from the north they seen a great hill rising from the mists, shining like bone in the moonlight. About the hill stood groves of trees, some sixty feet high, their branches waving, beckoning them. On the plain lay a mist that rolled like the sea so that the men and horses was feared of riding into it for drowning. Theder laughed at his men and ordered them down into the river bottom and crossed over and come up to the hill, but they found it gone." Lieutenant Bass was amused by this disappearance, and the old guide shot back: "Beware, young feller, of taking this tale for a tease, for that was in the mind of Major Theder—he scoffed and laughed at the Phantom Hill as he rode down into the valley that night, and he ended his days driving a nail into his ear and into his brain."

"Sorry, old-timer," said Bass. "Please go on. Now where did this hill go?"

"It had gone, sir, it had gone. Some said it had never been, some said it had been only in the mists and fogs from the river and was mirage in the twists of the moonlight. Whatever you want to think, it was gone, and Theder laughed at them that hung back in fear and showed them how the hill had been mirage and fogs and the scrub mesquite had been magnified to look like great trees and the cries of the owl and the bobwhite had been the ghosts that had spooked the horses. Theder found plentiful wood and water and good grass near at hand and not far away good logs and hard stone for building, and they erected a fort there where Elm Creek feeds into the Clear Fork. When asked what he would call it, Theder laughed, 'By damn, we'll call it Fort Phantom Hill.' But it should not have been done, sir. Them grounds was swampy and full of sickness. Both man and horse got ill there, and some died and some saw visions, specters and forms rising from the river and walking in the moonlight, such as there is tonight.

"And then there is the end of Phantom Hill," said the old guide, as the column stretched out silent behind us, the men dozing in their saddles. "It was the first year of the Rebel War, and the garrison was but a handful of Union boys. A troop of Texas Rangers led by Barry marched up to the fort, but the six Union boys inside would not surrender. Barry and his com- mand surrounded the fort and besieged it. One of their shots, they figger, set a fire that swept through the fort and burned it all but the stone to the ground. When the wreckage cooled, Barry went in—but there was nothing to be found of the Union boys! There was not the remains of a single man found in it. No trace of them six boys living or dead was ever seen again! Now you tell me the ruins of this old fort ain't haunted by the ghosts of them six bluebellies!"

Shortly thereafter we topped a low bench and the ruins of Fort Phantom Hill rose up in the distance. As the old man had foretold, all that remained of the old fort were the stone end walls and chimneys, tall white columns rising like monuments in the moonlight, giant shrouded figures standing in loose ranks, waiting our arrival. We rode on past the ruins and made camp and passed a restless night beside the Clear Fork of the Brazos. A soldier had grown ill during the march, and I was waked by his coughing and rose and walked out of the encampment. Bass was Officer of the Guard, and I came upon him and together we went back to the ruin, less than a mile distant. Bass applied reason to the old guide's tale of the six disappeared Union soldiers.

"I should guess that the Union soldiers knew of some secret

escape from the jail and burned the fort themselves, to cover their escape, and then deserted, though for what reason I can't really imagine. Or it is possible the Rangers killed the Union soldiers themselves, murdered them perhaps and destroyed the bodies and created this legend to hide their guilt. These are two rational explanations of why the Union boys were never heard of again. It is an easy matter to explain legends and myths if one thinks about them in a careful, rational way."

We had come upon the ruins. The monoliths stood on the plain like headstones, and there were, as Bass noted, six of them, one for each of the vanished Union soldiers. "Do you believe in any of these things, sir—ghosts, specters, of any sort?"

"Not ghosts, as such, but I do believe that a man's thoughts exist as solidly as his flesh and that his beliefs may be real as wounds—whether these imaginings be political principles or the love of a woman or visions of ghosts."

Bass said, "Ghosts—of course not. Not figures in sheets or headless horsemen or the like. But, yes, you're right, I do believe that men's minds can be taken, haunted, if you will, by things we don't understand. I sometimes see myself as alone in this world—everything is gone. My family, my sweetheart, my people, everything is gone. I am on a plain and it is empty but for me. My father, who is a physician, says these states of mind are only the reasonable fear of the unreasonable."

"And what does your father consider unreasonable?"

"Battle would be one."

"Ah."

We had walked around the old fort and had stopped before returning to camp. Soon Bass would be called to mount the changing of the guard. We could see that the interior of the stone walls was blackened, not by shadows but charred by the fire that had destroyed the fort. Bass said, "Shall we be riding up onto the *llano estacado* this summer, sir?"

"Our orders are to stay off it," I said and left it at that, to allay whatever unease the officer had before his first combat.

The young man pondered some marks he inscribed on the earth with his boot. "Are you married, sir?" He continued without waiting for an answer: "I wish that I were married, before we ride out on the plains."

"There will be time to marry when you return."

"I sometimes fear that I shall not."

"You will return. We all will."

"Yes, of course. We shall all live, I suppose," said the young officer, whose fear of death would be fearfully met.

A few other words were exchanged, then Lieutenant Bass strode off toward the guard, who were assembling for his inspection.

Shortly before reveille I was visited by the Colonel's aide-de-camp. The regiment was striking all tents and mounting. Mac-Swain had decided during the night to abandon Fort Phantom Hill and establish our summer camp farther on, nearer the *llano estacado*. The command mounted without fire or food and followed the old wagon road ten miles to the west; there we left the road and turned northwest, toward the staked plain and Comanche territory. The men were given breakfast at ten and the horses were cared for, and we were in the saddle by midday. The regiment made good speed throughout the day, and the following morning we began to see Indian signs, campgrounds and trails, that had been left no more than two days ago. We rode steadily that day and made an uneasy camp that night. We ate cold rations, and the men slept in their boots. When light came we read signs that Indians had been in the horse herd during the night; the wranglers reported five mounts missing. Chilled that the Comanches could come so close undetected, we saddled and mounted and rode ten miles before halting for breakfast at midmorning. MacSwain ordered that camp be pitched here and attached the troop under my command to the scout. Accompanied by Devereaux and his Tonks, the troop rode hard on the Indian trail and had gained a day on them by nightfall. Devereaux sent a party of Tonks out on our flank, and they returned in an hour's time to report a trail of ten Comanches and a like number of unmounted horses riding parallel on our flank. "The raiding party that stole the horses last night," said Devereaux. "Keeping track of us, I figger. They're little danger to us or the regiment. They need ponies, not scalps."

Even so, Devereaux counseled against making a camp that night, and we remounted our exhausted horses and rode throughout the night back toward the safety of the main column. An hour after daybreak we saw a black line draped across the horizon, about four miles distant, the previous night's rain depriving us of a warning plume of dust. We took refuge in a wooded ravine and surveyed the column, which to our relief moved in good order. When we saw the white sails of the wagons we remounted and rode forward to meet our comrades. The forward guard of the main column were as frightened of our troop as we had been of them and they dismounted and fired several shots before we made ourselves known to them. The united command made a midday camp. A hunting party went out and returned with antelope and pheasant, abundant in these parts. After the roast, officers' call was blown and every officer of the regiment, line and staff, gathered in the command tent. Mac-Swain half lay, half sat on a cot at the rear of the tent. Mac-Swain was a frail man in the best of health, and only rarely did he shed his tunic, even before his closest aides, but now no uniform could mask the wasting of his frame. His head and eyes had grown large and luminous, his face ravaged from lack of sleep and food. At best his leadership had come from an energetic movement of body and mind that had left his most active subordinates feeling sluggish and slow-witted. But now, as he reclined, served by his aides and orderlies like an Arabian potentate, his swollen eyes pleading for our obedience, one could only sorrow at the sight of him. We had been in the saddle little more than a week, and he was a near cripple for it.

I gave my report of the previous day's scout, that we were a two-day ride behind the main body of Comanches, perhaps less.

"Two days?" said MacSwain. "Then we are within striking distance of the Comanche, sir! Clous!" he snapped, and the new second-in-command unrolled the maps and MacSwain was aided to his feet. We gathered about the camp table. I traced the Indian trail we had followed. "Comanches? Are these savages challenging me?" Devereaux was called in to attest my report. That done, all but the senior officers were dismissed and the fly dropped. "Then we shall have a night march—*two* night marches! We shall overtake them and punish them—as if they were children—is that clear? Clous, form up an attack column. You shall command it," MacSwain concluded, and we were dismissed, like children.

Major Clous accosted me outside the command tent, and we walked a distance away from the others. I had not known Clous previously, and he spoke to me as an adversary: "I don't know whether you are one of MacSwain's clique or not, Chapman, but as second-in-command I am speaking to every officer in the Second that they may know we are pursuing these Indians under verbal orders from the Colonel. Is that understood? These verbal orders contravene our written orders that the command was to establish a summer camp at Fort Phantom Hill and that we were to avoid direct contact if at all possible with the Comanches till they were allowed to go peacefully onto the reservation at Sill. Is that understood?" When I said that I did understand, with perfect clarity, Clous spoke with weary disgust: "This so-called war we are fighting is destroying the discipline, the very nature of our army. Ah! Maybe it will be tonic for the officers and men to ride into action, though I can't believe we will see much of a battle. At least I will be in command. He won't be given the chance to emulate Custer's so-called victory on the False Washita. There will be no massacre under my command, is that understood, Chapman?" Clous looked back to the command tent. MacSwain had just emerged, holding himself stiff from pain. "I suppose I shouldn't be so hard on the man. The surgeon has only now told me how he is suffering. Sitting a horse is a torture, making him more woman than man. The man should resign from the horse cavalry," he said and turned back to me. "But I suppose that is impossible. Perhaps he will regain his strength and his sense while we are away. How are your horses, Chapman?"

"Not good."

"See if you can find some beasts that can run. I want your troop attached to this column."

I went to my exhausted troop and informed them we would be riding with the attack column. Lieutenant Bass and I then went about finding what fresh horses there were. I took a good horse that I had ridden before and saw it saddled, but did not notice that Bass retained his weakened mount. As Bass and I were preparing the troop to ride out, Clous approached with a dark foul look. "He has changed his mind, God damn him. He will be riding with us. With his German."

The attack command was composed of Cavalry Troops A, D, and F, and Company I of the Twenty-second Infantry, with two surgeons in attendance and four wagons that would carry the infantry, ammunition, and two days' forage and rations for horse and men—in all twelve officers and one hundred and seventy-two men, with fifteen Tonk scouts under the command of Captain Devereaux. Left behind at the base camp were L Troop along with two infantry companies and a body of support troops. This force was to remain in place until the supply train arrived from Red River.

The attack command made a night march, and early the following morning we picked up the trail of the main body of the Comanches. There were many lodgepole marks, and the Tonk scouts read from this that we were following a large village on the move north toward the staked plains. "I'd say eight hundred ponies," reported Devereaux, "and a good number of squaws and camp followers. The Tonks feel there ain't many warriors with 'em, Cap, that they're off ahead of the village following a buffalo herd. The ponies and the squaws will be easy picking, but that is very likely to turn the warriors' minds from the hunt to war." We pushed forward at a rapid gait and at about one in the afternoon found a creekbed where wild grape vines had been stripped of their fruit, the broken grapes still damp and fresh on the ground. We followed the trail of grapes and after a rapid march of three or four miles came upon the village pitched in a cottonwood grove along a stream that we took to be the Rio Blanco. The column was closed up, and after a brief rest we formed into tight ranks and charged into the unsuspecting village, MacSwain and his handpicked F Troop leading the assault.

The fighting lasted scarcely half an hour, and the village was captured. But our charge had been hastily conceived, and though we rode through the village at will, no plan had been laid to seal off its lower end, and the fifty or so braves camped there escaped with only a few killed and captured. That these warriors would so readily abandon their ponies and their women should have acted as warning, but basking like hounds in victory, the Second's first real battle with the Indian, we chose to imagine our enemy cowering and retreating before our power. About a hundred squaws and children were captured, along with four hundred ponies that had not been driven off by our wild charge. We counted twenty Indians killed, all but a few women and children. Except for a store of meat and a number of choice buffalo robes, the entire village of one hundred and fifty lodges was destroyed by fire. MacSwain showed keen disappointment when he learned the village was not that of a major band of Comanches, but the Wasps, a tribe of little stature. Our command suffered four casualties—three were wounded, and one man who was struck in the throat with an arrow perished from the wound while the arrow was being removed.

MacSwain made a great opera of this trooper's death, swearing before the assembled command to avenge his murder, and instead of turning back to our base camp with the captured squaws and ponies, placed both women and horses in corrals and turned the column north on the trail of the escaped warriors. Clous attempted to sway MacSwain from this advance, warning that the Comanches would never allow us to retain their women and horses without a fight, but our command and many of our officers and men were full of pride, and we rode like cattle into their trap.

We followed the Rio Blanco as it wound northwest through increasingly difficult terrain, the river canyon narrowing as it rose toward the *llano estacado*. We marched well ahead of the herd of Indian women and ponies and made an early bivouac to rest the men and horses. This allowed the captured Indian women and horses to close with us, while we sent a Tonk scout forward to reconnoiter the head of Blanco Canyon. At the point of our halt the Rio Blanco valley was a mile wide, the river running close to the west bluff. We pitched our tents there, on the high narrow bank between the river and the bluff. This provided us a natural defense against a massed attack from the valley floor, but with our forces strung out a half mile down the riverbank and with little room to maneuver in any direction but across the river, the position was vulnerable to attacks from up or down the river. The creek water was clear and fresh, and we set our tents beneath a rustling canopy of cottonwoods, and the men fished and harvested the wild grapes that grew along the banks. Fires were allowed during the day, and the men feasted and discipline was eased. The mood among the troops was lighthearted as the men held mock auctions among the captured horses and squaws and played at other games. There was good grass and plentiful wood nearby, and, to further dull our readiness, a pocket valley was found that provided a natural corral for the captured ponies. A meager guard was mounted, as if Indian country were thousands of miles away.

The Tonk scouts returned that evening, weary and covered with blood and dust. They had run upon four Comanche warriors and had pursued them out onto the staked plain, less than ten miles from our camp, they reported. One Comanche's pony had broken down, and they showed around the fresh scalp, which excited many of the younger men who had never fought Indians before. The Tonks were exhausted from their ride and ravenous at the smell of cooked meat, and they ate and rolled into their blankets and slept, depriving us of their keen senses. Devereaux felt the Comanches would surely try to rescue their women and horses, but he saw no force nearby or trails of any that could accomplish it. He, too, was fagged out and was seen asleep in his boots before sundown. Lieutenant Bass was still acting Officer of the Day, and I performed a brief ceremony of mounting the guard, without bugle call. I rode with Bass while he placed the guard posts, scouting the bluff wall, which seemed impassable but by rope, and the river, which, though shallow, was strewn with quicksand. I rode back to camp and, though some of my fears were allayed, slept without removing pistol, belt, or boots.

When I woke all the fires had burned out and the camp was sunk in black. I then felt what had wakened me: the earth trembled beneath my ear. The rumbling from the earth increased, as if its bowels were on fire, and then there was a single cry and a gunshot from somewhere down the line, and the earth began to shake and a deep roar came from down the valley, as if flood water were roaring up toward us. By now men were rushing all about, colliding and falling and cursing in the dark. Rapid gunfire came from downstream, toward the horse herds—only then did we understand that the horses were being stampeded directly through our camp. Despite the chaos I was able to mount my horse unsaddled, and saw flashes of pistol and carbine fire coming from the bluffs above. I heard the first warning cry of *Indians!* only seconds before they were upon us, driving the horses, both their ponies and our mounts, through the camp, shaking robes and ringing bells and screaming like demons to drive the terrified beasts over us. Our men sought to return the Indians' fire from the bluffs, but most men had lost their horses, and as the stampeding herds bore down on the camp many of them left their weapons to secure the animals that would save them. There was no light but muzzle flash, and so we saw still-frozen pictures of horses and mules and ponies, rearing, jumping, plunging, whinnying in terror, crashing against one another, smashing themselves against trees, boulders, crushing men and themselves in their frenzy. Trembling and groaning with fright, the tethered horses fought against their lariats, plunging and flinging their heads against their halters, tangling their ropes, which snapped and cracked like bullwhips, the iron picket pins being yanked free from the earth and flung about at the end of the ropes, whistling through the air like knives, tearing and ripping the flesh of horse and man. The dismounted men desperately caught at any rope, only to be pulled down in the tangle of ropes and slashing hooves, to be cut and dragged, lacerated and hanged, mangled and fearfully burned by the ropes, in the melee of terrified beasts.

The stampeding herd crashed on up the valley. The men regrouped, and those few horses that had not been driven off were secured, it taking three, often four men to bridle and saddle one of the frightened beasts in the dark. My mount was saddled, and with little thought to anything but pursuit a dozen or so of us galloped off, leaving the camp a tangle of injured horses and men. As we rode through the camp we fired at the bluffs above, like boys playing at war, for the Indians had gone from the heights and our wild shots would only have made us targets for their sharpshooters had they not. The east was showing faint light as we passed the last picket post, a corporal firing his carbine in the general direction the Indians had gone. We crossed the Rio Blanco at a ford with water to the saddle girth but with good footing, and picked up the blasted trail of the stampeded horses and made hard after them. The river meandered across the valley, and soon we came to another crossing. We pulled up, and in the gray light I was able to identify our number: Bass and several of his guard whose horses had not been unsaddled during the night, Devereaux and two Tonks who rode bareback, a collection of officers and men who had managed to saddle their horses before the stampede struck the camp, among them MacSwain's favorite, Major Hoeme, who assumed command. We dismounted and tightened our cinches and in our excitement fell to arguing whether to make directly up the canyon toward its head—to ford the river here, and later, if need be—or to follow the winding river course, the path the Indians had driven the main herd of horses. We read from the trail that a smaller group had broken away from the main and had crossed the stream, and our group was so divided—the larger body following the river course, while Hoeme, Bass, myself, and three men crossed the river and, picking up the trail, rode directly up the valley to intercept the main herd at the next river bend. We made the next river crossing quickly, and though we did not come upon the main herd, we jumped a dozen or so Indians driving as many horses. Coming out of the sun, we surprised this group and still riding like fools began firing beyond pistol range. By the time we had crossed the river, the Indians had abandoned the horses and were riding up the valley toward a capped butte that stood in the center of the valley floor. The horses the Indians had been driving scattered, and we sent two men after them, our number diminishing to four: myself, Bass, Hoeme, and a boyish trooper who was Dutch and spoke little English, so that he and Hoeme shouted at one another in Dutch or German, further lending to this ride's bizarre spell, for much of it seemed like a dream.

At this moment, as we paused to reload our pistols and peer up the valley where the Indians had gone, I was aware of the details, both sublime and absurd, of our surroundings, collecting them as if I were a gallery-goer leisurely studying a framed canvas. The rising sun had broken the horizon and hung red

59

and fat beneath gauzy bands of purples and blues that darkened to a night sky in the west. During the last few minutes the dawn gray had exploded in color: the soft greens of the rolling plain and the stark ochers and browns and yellows of the cliffs and hills, all were slashed by the black ragged shadows cast by ourselves and the trees that lined the curving riverbed. Looking for our comrades, we saw their grotesque shadows crawling across the valley floor long before we located the horsemen who cast them. They were two miles distant and seemed to be on their own trail, moving away from the river course that would have led them to us. We turned our horses to our own chase, with no fear that we were four riding after twelve, nor giving any thought to why there had been so many Indians herding so few horses. We rode for the butte that divided the valley and made our way around its southern base, cutting ourselves off from our comrades who had ridden north. As we circled the butte, any notion of the danger we were riding into was dispelled by the panorama spread before us. There, only two miles distant, stood the great wall of the *llano estacado*. We rode before it, mesmerized by its grandeur. Even those of us who had come upon it before gazed in wonder as this fortress loomed above us, like a bank of stone clouds. The colors were those I had never seen in nature or art: the sloping canyon walls were a fiery brick red dotted with dark green clumps of brush, the caprock escarpment mottled yellow and white, the sky behind the escarpment a curtain of black blue pierced by a bright solitary star mockingly luring us forward. We pitched down a steep embankment and crossed the river a final time and labored up an even steeper slope, and another formation came into view, a pure white mountain, a great cone of caliche or some alkaloid rock that rose two hundred feet or more from the valley floor, its summit equal to or greater than the high plains. Like all else, the mountain was bathed in the pink glow from the sunrise, its dark side cast in icy blue shadow. We could see that the Indians had found a trail along the mountainside and were scampering their ponies up onto the *llano*. We galloped hard after them, so that our horses were close to ridden out when we came to the foot of the plain wall.

We went up the mountainside but were forced to dismount and walk our horses the last few yards, so steep was the pitch of the trail that bridged from the mountain to the caprock. Hoeme led our group and was the first to gain the plains. Clambering a few feet behind him, I was struck by his transfixed state, as he stood paralyzed, still dismounted, gazing westward, his great black stallion fighting the reins. As I crossed the caprock I saw it was not the plain's relentless horizon that had transfixed Hoeme, rather that a fog lay on the ground so thick that there was nothing before us but a netherworld of shifting mists, as if the very earth had vanished.

"Fog. Fog," Hoeme said as Bass and the Dutch trooper joined us. "We have lost them in the fog."

Bass rode his horse out into the fog and disappeared under its gray mists and then came back, his horse making no sound as it came. "No tracking them in this, though it will burn away in an hour's time, I'd say, maybe less."

"Burn?" said the Dutch trooper, gazing at Bass as if he were just returned from the underworld.

"Der Nebel!" Hoeme spat at the Dutchman. *"Idiot!"*

We rode north along the plain's edge a way, and observing that the fog was thinning as Bass had foretold, we left the caprock border and went out onto the plain, searching for the Indians' trail. But the fog still lay thick on the ground here, and we could find no sign of the Comanches. We had grown discouraged and had turned our horses toward the way we had come when we saw figures emerging from the mist. At first they seemed to be trees or strange rock formations, for they were motionless; then we saw they were human figures, men on horseback, to which our reactions were various. The Dutch corporal's eyes grew large, and he began wheeling his horse and shouting in German, while Hoeme and I took the figures to be soldiers, the members of our detachment who had ridden off after the main herd. Only Bass saw we were among neither friends nor specters.

"Heavens now, but we are in a nest," he said. "Would you look at the Indians, Captain."

"Indians?" said Hoeme. "Bah!" He galloped his black stallion toward the figures. After a few yards, Hoeme reined in the horse and charged back. *"Indians!"* he shouted as he caromed through us. "Ride like the hell!" The Dutch corporal complied without a translation, and Bass and I followed close behind.

We had gone far enough onto the plain to have lost sight of the canyon and had only the sun to lead us back to the white peak and its bridge over the caprock. We missed that mark by a quarter mile, and as we turned to ride along the plain's edge toward it we saw that the Indians had blocked our escape. The valley and safety lay tantalizingly near—we could see riding toward us a blue line of troopers skirting the table butte—but here the caprock escarpment fell thirty feet sheer drop, and if the leap did not kill both man and horse it certainly would leave the horses injured and ourselves dismounted and easy prey for the Indians. Our only hope seemed to be to dismount here and, with our backs to the precipice, to deploy our horses as shields and fire on the Comanche, hoping that we could repel their initial charge and that our gunfire would then attract the rescuing column to us. We turned our horses and saw a hundred war-painted Indians, at least, fanned across the horizon, walking their ponies toward us with an insolent, idle pace. This gave us time to dismount and, incredibly, to argue. Hoeme demanded that we remount and make a dash through the Indian line toward the white peak, but I knew that this would sacrifice the riders on weaker horses, while those like Hoeme on his powerful black stallion might survive the gantlet. "By God I shall go alone!" shouted Hoeme and vaulted into the saddle. Spitting German at the terrified Dutch trooper, who needed no encouragement to run, he galloped off firing and shouting in his native tongue with a ferocity that caused the Indians to recoil from his path. Unfortunately the Comanches recovered in time to close in on the Dutchman; the last we saw of the youth, before we turned to our attackers, was his blond scalp being torn from his skull, one boot still kicking in the stirrup.

Working our carbines till they smoked, Bass and I repulsed the Indians' first charge, though still they did not send their mass at us, but attacked in gangs of five or six, the rest circling their ponies in an ever expanding and contracting line, whooping and brandishing their arms and spears, but making scant progress toward us. Rather than the deadly enemy that they in fact were, the Indians paraded before us like players in some costume piece, their faces and naked torsos painted like plumage, the bells tied to their wrists and ankles jingling with a childlike merriment, even their war whoops carrying a comic exaggeration. Their ponies were painted like themselves, and their manes and tails were tied with strings of red flannel and calico. Now we began to see and hear the Comanche squaws gathering behind the circling warriors, their high-pitched screams underlying the braves' manic whooping and yelling.

In the midst of this choreography of circling ponies we spied two standard-bearers, medicine men likely, who seemed to be directing the warriors' movements by changing the attitudes of two scalp poles decorated with feathers and tags of brightly colored cloth and pieces of mirrors that flashed in the sun and long scalp locks taken from women. Riding between the two standard-bearers was the tribe's chieftain, a man larger and more erect than the rest, who rode a white horse and was himself, his face and arms and torso, painted black. Placed along the milling line of warriors were subchiefs of some sort who relayed the scalp bearers' instructions by hand signals and flashing mirrors. There seemed to be no organized groupings among them, such as our squads and platoons, for when an order to attack was made, the warriors who rode at us would come from any point along the shifting line, advancing and retreating as individuals. This lack of organization alone saved us, for we were two against a hundred or more and the Comanches could have swept us into the canyon below at any time.

We repelled several attacks and reloaded our carbines and continued to fire without thinking that we might deplete our ammunition before the relief column arrived. Between attacks, as I continued to fire, Bass crouched behind me, reloading his carbine. Looking down into the valley, he cursed, "Damn, they are not coming for us!" I took Bass's position as he fired and saw that the column of troopers had made little progress toward us, that their line did not seem to be moving at all. It seemed inconceivable that they could not hear our firing and the Indians' cacophony, nor see us on the caprock horizon as we saw them on the valley floor. Before I could speak, Bass had remounted and, firing his carbine like a pistol as he reined back his horse, shouted, "We will have to ride for it, Phil, or we are done for!"

I leapt on my horse, and we turned north and rode along the canyon precipice with no thought but to take some action against our slaughter even if that action might hasten it. We shouted to one another, as our horses collided in their race, that we might find a way off the plain and that if we couldn't I, at least, planned to jump my mount off the caprock and die of a broken neck on the canyon wall below. We drew away from the Indians for a while, for, though they had sent their swiftest ponies after us, they paced them, believing that nothing but one's own life was worth the risk of a ridden-out horse. With luck I had drawn a good horse, a large awkward gelding who had been buckshot in the face at one time and was disfigured by pocked scars and had a bad glaring eye that caused many riders to look to a prettier mount, to their misfortune, for the scarred gelding was a courageous animal, with good speed and endurance and an intelligence rare in these cold-blooded beasts. Bass had been less fortunate. His regular horse had been stampeded, and he had grabbed at any rope and been able to hold on to a weaker animal, one of the scout horses that had been ridden out. We had not run far before Bass's horse began to heave and sway and fall off the pace. We pulled our horses up and saw that a wing of the Indian force was riding wide on our flank to encircle us at some place ahead where the plain was eaten back by an arroyo. The mass of the Indians came from the rear at a slower pace, their purpose being to prevent our retreat toward MacSwain's column. The Indians were still fearful of our carbines, but the range of this fast-working rifle was not great, and the sharpshooters among the Indians had dismounted and were firing their muzzle-loading rifles at us with fair accuracy. Only now that we had pulled up did I see that Bass had been struck in the hand, blood gushing from where two fingers had been. He continued to work the lever of the carbine, covering his tunic and face with blood, unaware he had been wounded till a shell jammed in the receiver and he saw that the fingers which would have withdrawn the shell were missing. As the Indians continued to deploy across the horizon, Bass turned to me and cried, "My horse is given out, Phil! Your only chance is to go on!"

"To hell with that! We'll jump our horses first!"

We rode to the canyon wall and saw that no horse could survive the thirty-foot drop and were ready to dismount and climb down the rock, equally suicidal, when Bass spied a quarter mile to the north a geological formation, a spiny ridge of rock that reached up from the valley floor like a prehistoric beast to feed on the brow of the caprock. This formation made a natural bridge and might hold the weight of our horses and lead us down to safety. We unlocked our carbine magazines and fired every round we had to drive back the Indians, then rode to the precipice with the few seconds we had gained. We saw that the rock bridge was no larger around than a man's trunk, the rock rotted and crumbling, so that we would have to leap our horses over it to safety. We rode back fifty feet to have a run at it, the Indians allowing us this game, anticipating as much pleasure in

65

the spectacle of our leaping our horses into the abyss as they would derive from crushing our skulls with their war clubs. As we turned for our run, Bass quirted my horse and the animal dashed for the bridge and made the leap with ease, as if it had trained for such acrobatics all its life. But as I rode down the spiny rock back I saw that the force of my mount's landing had crumbled the natural bridge and that Bass was faced with a leap that his horse had neither leg nor wind nor spirit to make. Still, Bass spurred his horse forward and made his run, but the frightened animal pulled up at the precipice, throwing Bass to the ground, itself falling on its forelegs like a condemned man pleading mercy from an executioner. Seeing that I had jumped my horse to safety, the Comanches unleashed a furious charge. Bass fired at his attackers with his revolver and dropped two warriors, at least, and as many ponies, but he was overrun. He had saved a cartridge for himself, and as he was being skewered by a warrior's lance and lifted from the ground, he took his own life by blowing off the side of his head, mangling his scalp as well as denying a kill to any of his attackers, his final act of defiance.

THREE

THERE was still such chaos at the camp—every tent had been downed by the stampede and equipment and supplies lay scattered a quarter mile along the riverbank—that I led my horse to the river and let him drink and sat, taking no action of my own. After some time I rose and gave my horse to an orderly and set myself toward duty. As I went through the camp, I saw that order was returning there. Tents had been righted, the men had been organized into details and were salvaging supplies and mending equipment and burning or burying that which could not be saved. Few of the stampeded horses had been retrieved. Those men not at defensive posts or assigned to cleanup details were being formed into infantry companies. As I passed one of these platoons of dismounted horsemen, the commanding officer, a young lieutenant, looked after me as if I were a ghost, for indeed I had been taken for dead. I found Hoeme's black horse tethered near MacSwain's command tent and tried to think of wise things to say when I faced the coward but could not.

The command tent was filled to the walls with staff officers and orderlies mapping an operation that the Second Cavalry could not undertake, for there were no horses to ride out on, whether we attacked or retreated from the Comanches. Still, officers and scouts reported to the command tent in a stream and were dispatched to perform their futile preparations, so that I was not allowed into the rear parts of the tent for some time. There I found MacSwain crouched, half-standing, on a camp chair, Major Clous, his second-in-command, and Hoeme flanking him. Only by the shifting look on the German's face did I know that the sticking mantle of cowardice was to be laid over me. I reported and told of the deaths of the Dutch trooper and of Lieutenant Bass and nothing else. MacSwain studied me with contempt, then spoke: "Can you explain these deaths, each of them, Captain Chapman?"

"The trooper died fleeing the Indians, Colonel. Lieutenant Bass stood and fought."

"Did he? Was your detachment then divided, Captain?"

"It was, sir."

"And how did this division come about?"

"Major Hoeme decided it was wise to ride for safety and Lieutenant Bass and I thought it was not."

"Lieutenant Bass thought these things?"

"He concurred with my opinion."

"Your *opinion?*"

"There was a matter of life and death, sir. There was little cool logic among us."

"Indeed, sir," said MacSwain. "You chose to preserve life by standing and fighting, rather than riding with Major Hoeme, is that correct?"

"It is, sir."

"Yet Lieutenant Bass died by your reasoning, Captain."

"As the trooper died by the Major's. But if the four of us had stood—"

MacSwain slapped the table before him with his stick. "By

God damn, sir! What if the four of you had ridden for your lives under the command of your senior officer!"

"The weaker of us would have succumbed and, perhaps, the stronger survived, as it is in Major Hoeme's reasoning, Colonel."

MacSwain made a sour smile. "Chapman, are you pleased that we are going into Comanche territory?"

"I believe it is our duty to go after the Comanches."

"Duty only? You would not like to avenge the death of Lieutenant Bass? And what of your friend Jones! How can you speak of duty when there is vengeance to be done!"

"Surely vengeance will not be ours, Colonel."

"Oh, it will be mine! That I assure you, sir."

When I did not reply, MacSwain smiled. "I think I understand this fear of yours, Philip, better than you know. You are afraid of the Comanches, are you not?"

"I would not want to ride with any officer or man who was not."

MacSwain reared, but briefly. "Yes. Of course. You do not hate the Indian, do you?"

"I do not."

"Nor do I, nor do I," said MacSwain, having turned his back to study the map. "Do you think they are savages, Philip?"

"I think they can be—as can any man."

"Is there no distinction between civilization and barbarism?"

"None in this war," I said, still angry enough to speak my mind, "but for one's point of view."

Hoeme barked a laugh. "Now I agree. The strong is civilized. The weak must join or be crushed."

Major Clous seemed about to speak but, with a look from MacSwain, held silent. MacSwain addressed me. "You do not like war, do you, Philip?"

"I loathe it, as did General Grant."

"An alcoholic who turned his back on the uniform!"

"In this company I will not honor that with a reply."

"God damn, man, do you no longer address ranking officers with respect? Stand to attention! By God damn, you have no place in an army, Chapman. You belong with the women, the priests and the Indian-lovers from whence you came." He turned sharply. "If you speak once again, sir, I will have you put in irons!" Then his anger drained away, as his energy fled and his pain returned. "I will not disgrace you by placing you under guard, Chapman. But I will ask you to confine yourself to your tent till I have time to reflect—whether it is not indeed time for you to part from our regiment."

At this moment Clous turned to MacSwain and spoke ingenuously, it seemed. "Perhaps there is another way of handling this, Colonel. I have no doubt that Captain Chapman erred in not following Major Hoeme's example of retreating before a superior force. But might not there be some courage, even heroism, seen in Chapman's obstinacy? Two men stood and fought, and fought well, against the Indians, Colonel. I would be loath to imagine the amusement that some officers in Washington might find in our court-martialing Captain Chapman for such an act of bravery."

"Yes, yes. Perhaps you are right," said MacSwain with little attention to any of us. "Please, go away, all of you. You are dismissed."

I went to my tent and waited there. Shortly, Major Clous came. The lines of his face had softened. That became an ironic smile. "It is all taken care of, Phil—"

"All but the court-martial of Major Hoeme."

"Ah! The German doesn't matter. Those boys are dead. Revenge against Hoeme won't bring them back."

"If the German were a private, then his cowardice might not kill again."

"That may be true, but you can't bring a successful court-martial against the German—you must be disciplined in this matter, Phil. There are larger concerns before us." Clous continued after a moment, "Now, when the report goes in to Leavenworth, I will make this an heroic action, do you understand? Now, tell me what happened and then bite your tongue later when you read what I will write."

I recounted our ride up onto the plains, as ordered.

In lieu of the honor denied me by my commanding officer, Major Clous made me commander of the detachment that would retrieve and bury the bodies of the trooper and Lieutenant Bass. For our safety we mounted as many men as the camp could spare, but we found no danger from the Comanches, who had taken what they wanted—their ponies and squaws and our horses—and disappeared onto the plains. It was early afternoon when we set out, and the light had flattened and washed the colors that had been bright at dawn; the earth and sky took on a pallid hue that burdened our spirits as heavily as did our task. We rode up onto the plains, over the white peak which our cartographer would call Mount Blanco, and found the bodies of the Dutchman and Bass where they had fallen. Their remains were a sorry sight, their bodies little more than lumps of flesh bristling with arrows. I had the men break the arrow shafts and roll the bodies in blankets, and we took them down off the plains and buried Bass and the trooper at the foot of Mount Blanco, in rocky soil that would soon yield their flesh to scavengers. Still that seemed a better fate than leaving them on the *llano*. We provided no headstones but piles of rocks and made no eulogy for our fallen comrades but to fire three rounds in the air, which served, as well, as warning to those who had killed them.

There were officers among the command, many of the younger men who had been close to Fred Bass, who demanded that we ride out in hot pursuit of the Comanches, but MacSwain was finally convinced by the senior members of his staff that it would be mad to go onto the plains and pursue the Comanches till we regrouped. The horses we had were sore-footed and raw from the saddle and many wind-broken, and the men were close to exhaustion. Far wiser to turn from battle and rest ourselves and secure fresh mounts from the surrounding ranches and pursue the Comanches in late summer or early fall, when the grass on the plains would be brown and the playa lakes that had gathered the spring and early summer rain dry. Then the Indians would find no place on the *llano* to hide and no forage or water for their ponies and would be forced to surrender or to turn and fight. And too, by fall MacSwain could ride out after the Comanches with written orders in his pocket.

In the days following, scouts were sent out and returned with guides to the country that lay east of the *llano estacado*. These men suggested we make summer camp near the Caballo, a large ranch three days' march to the northeast. I was to be detached from the main command to return and fetch our reserves, L Troop and the infantry companies and the supply train we had left behind, and guide them to the summer camp. Maps of that position were drawn up, and a cowboy from one of the ranches would be our guide.

The following morning the main column rode out northeast toward Caballo Ranch, while my detachment of twelve men and the cowboy guide rode south. We united with the troops we had left in reserve the following day and the day following that were joined by Lawton and the supply train from the Red River. Lawton had brought a hundred horses, and we spent the third day mounting most of the infantry, most of whom would have preferred to walk, and on the fourth day turned northeast to follow the main body of the Second Cavalry. As we rode, going overland, following no trail that I could discern, the cowboy spoke of the rugged country east of the *llano estacado:*

"In the old days, when I first come here," the cowboy said, "there was more white folks in these parts than now, and more Indians, but there was less trouble between the two races, it

72

seemed. The ranches and the cattle herds was not much, the buffalo was still plentiful off the caprock, and the Indians was satisfied with them. True, that beast can be a nuisance to a cattleman, and there was some bad Indians, but somehow we more or less left one another in peace." The cowboy gazed about the countryside we rode through. The earth was brick-red, the scrub oak and cedar a blackish green set against it. The terrain spread upward in a series of low rises, and the footing was firm. Our column of untried riders and forty wagons passed easily through it, though we knew our passage would not have been so effortless without the cowboy's memory and keen eye. "It was not the Indians or the buffalo but the beef prices that did us in, as they have done in all the small ranches in these parts." He took off his hat and pressed his shirt sleeve against his brow. "All along the border of the caprock little outfits combined to make big ones and they combined to make bigger ones, till now there's hardly a head of cattle that don't carry the brand of the Star or the 2222's or the Caballo," he said, and as he spoke each ranch's name he held his hat southeast, north, then northeast in the direction in which each lay. "The Caballo threatens to become one of the largest spreads in the world, or those are the plans for it. The Caballo is where your commander will be making his summer camp."

We rode till midafternoon through blasting heat, then showers swept up behind our column, from the southwest, and we went through the cooling rain hatless. The men gathered the rain in their hats and splashed it on one another, the mood of everyone, even the dour Lawton, gay and cheerful, as it should have been, for we were riding toward a true oasis in this barren land and a summertime to be spent away from war. We made an easy camp that night and rode the next day into the meridian heat that was broken in the afternoon by showers, as the day before. We made the first line camps of the Caballo the following morning and came up on the ranch headquarters late that afternoon, rain-laden wind pushing at our backs, low gray

73

clouds shooting overhead. There lay beneath us a long and narrow valley. Strung along below the valley's far slope was a wood of pecan and willows and elm and cottonwood, the stand so thick we did not at first see the Caballo headquarters among the trees. Though the wood swept down the valley in a meandering line, no river or creek passed through it. The Second Cavalry had pitched its tents in the north end of the valley; the outbuildings and corrals of the Caballo lay to the south. The full display of the regiment and the ranch could not be seen, both regimental tents and ranch buildings disappearing around the bends in the narrow serpentine valley. As we drew nearer, we could see men and animals moving among the trees, engaged in labor there. Some of the men were soldiers stripped of their tunics. Deep within the trees, I glimpsed a tall structure of white stone but could make little of it but that it was the attention of the men's labor.

The cowboy left us, and we turned our column and went to the Second Cavalry's encampment. There the infantrymen were gladly dismounted. According to the Officer of the Day, the main body of the regiment was engaged in drill some distance away. Our men were well fed, and we crept early into our tents, with orders that we need not stand reveille formation. The next morning a headquarters orderly told me that MacSwain could be found at the Caballo ranch house and that I was to report to him there. After a midmorning breakfast I strolled down to the ranch. The sound of hammers and saws and men calling out at work reached me through the trees. The morning was fresh and bright, the lines of the distant bluffs standing as clear as one's own face in a mirror. The stone house would have been considered of fair size in the East, no more, but in this wilderness it rose like a castle. The limestone walls stood completed, two stories tall, with deep eaves and high narrow windows and similar doorways made in the walls. The proportions of the house were likewise tall and narrow, and as the rustling cottonwoods moved from a breeze and the dappled shade and light shifted

74

over the limestone, I thought I had never seen such a graceful structure. The men were laboring to build a long wooden porch along the house front, and another gang was beginning to shingle a plank roof that itself was just being completed. There was no glass in the windows, and a crew could be seen inside the house laying a floor. An architect worked on a plan nearby. He directed me toward a live-oak grove that stood behind the house.

The thick gnarled live oaks grew about in a long oval that had a clearing at its center in which several wall tents had been erected. The grove abutted a stone cliff perhaps two hundred yards from the grove entrance, where I stood as an observer. About a dozen men were gathered before the largest of the three tents, seated in camp chairs arranged about a camp table. I noted several blue uniforms among the men: MacSwain I recognized by his bent posture, Hoeme by his size. Horses were tethered in the trees, visible only by their movement. Beyond the grove I spied two well-finished spring carriages and several smaller coaches and buggies. As I moved forward I saw a woman with the men and then heard women's voices and their laughter nearby. Two young women in pale dresses moved through the trees, passing within twenty yards of where I stood, but taking no notice of me.

I went down through the grove toward the tents and reported to MacSwain. Of the military men there were MacSwain and Hoeme, Lieutenant Quinn, MacSwain's aide-de-camp, and Captain Rister, who was the regiment's Engineering Officer when Lawton was not with the command. The civilians: four were men of late middle age, well whiskered and whiskeyed, ruddy and in good condition, or so they seemed by stance and movement. These men were outfitted in suits, boots, and hats of country gentlemen, as if the West were a shoot. Three of the four were Scotsmen and could scarcely be understood when they spoke. The others were minions of various sorts—servants, drivers, one was dressed out like a gamekeeper—but for one man who might now have been in a position of subordination but would never serve, I thought, not even if he had been born to chattel slavery. This was Ben Cady, the son of the old rancher who was selling the Caballo to the ruddy gentlemen gathered around. Ben Cady was about my age, solid and squarely built, sunburnt as any raw recruit, as he had a reddish coloring that would not allow him to tan. Cady watched me quizzically, as if we were captains of opposing sporting teams.

MacSwain swung his arm about with the flourish of a political orator. "Gentlemen, ladies, please, come out of the tent—it is my great honor to introduce the Second's own Captain Philip Chapman, the hero of Mount Blanco!" This was said with a sarcasm evident to my ears, though it did not seem so to the others. All applauded, all but Hoeme, whose honest dislike deserved some tribute, and the next minute or so was given over to MacSwain's fulsome recreation of what was now called the tragedy of Mount Blanco.

As MacSwain went into his speech, two ladies emerged from the tent behind the men. The first was the woman I had seen from a distance—older, stern, probably a companion to the young woman who followed her from the tent. The latter was a girl of eighteen or so, small as a child; she wore riding skirts and boots, and her hair was done up under a wide-brimmed Spanish hat. Her small head and face were so nearly round that her looks might have been amusing had not she herself seemed amused by her looks. The girl's eyes were wide and so dark as to make her pupils seem quite enlarged. Her skin was tanned, her hair thick: a chocolate curl had fallen from under her hat, and she batted at it distractedly as MacSwain went on. At one point, the girl gazed at me and crossed her eyes, briefly but definitely. My reaction to this might have been taken as the pleasure of a man receiving such high praise as any commanding officer had ever bestowed on a subordinate.

At MacSwain's conclusion there was a flurry of compliments and kind inquiries, after which the young woman in the riding skirt, who was introduced as the niece of one of the Scottish gentlemen, took my arm and abruptly led me away from the others. As we passed through the grove walking toward the stone house, we came upon the two young women I had seen before. My companion—Miss McCorquodale—stopped them and spoke casually of my adventures on the plains. The two young women were a cousin and friend of my companion, and shortly, when she had decided their flattery and flirting had been well done, they were dismissed as if they were servant girls. The cousin and friend teased us as they strolled away. In doing so they called out the girl's nickname, which was Mackie.

"It is how I am commonly called by girls and others in whom I have unfortunately placed trust," she said, piqued. "And by my father and every male in our family and some outside it." She smiled. "But you may not call me that, Captain Chapman, for I am no longer a girl who wants to be a boy."

"I didn't intend to address you so intimately, at least not today, and I would never, at any time, have taken you for a girl who wants to be a boy."

She scuffed at the ground with her boot. "Oh, I have many names, call me what you like. And you, shall you be called Captain Chapman? Yes, you must," she went on quickly, which was her manner, to decide that what she had asked could be best answered by herself, "at least for today. But then tomorrow, we shall see. What do you prefer to be called—by your friends and your family?"

"Philip, if you like."

"Philip is quite nice," she said blandly, "for tomorrow." She had spoken with so little interest that I assumed she was bidding me farewell as she had her cousin and friend. But our stroll had taken us to near the stone house, and her interest had been transferred to it. "Would you live here?" she said, looking at the house in a curious way. "I might one day, you know, come and live here on this ranch that my uncle and his friends are buying."

We passed around the house, Miss McCorquodale peering

through the windows and being greeted by the workmen inside. "Do you know the surrounding country well?" she asked as we drew away from the house, idly wandering among the cottonwoods, though by following their course we made toward the regimental camp. "Tell me, what is this plain like, this *llano estacado,* where you were so brave?"

"It is an immense plain, featureless and perfectly flat but for hundreds of playa lakes, and they are all the same. It is a forbidding place—at least to me—because there is nothing there."

"Oh, it is just a plain," she said. "I have seen plains. They are flat. There is nothing more to them than that. I think you all are afraid of this place because of the Indians there."

"No. We are afraid of becoming lost."

We had stopped and she looked at me squarely. "Will you take me there someday?"

"I think I shall probably go there with you."

"Will you? The hero of Mount Blanco?" She smiled wickedly, and we walked on till we came to a place where we could view the regimental encampment. She stopped and would not go farther. "No. I am forbidden to go into your camp." The main body of the Second Cavalry had ridden in; from the confusion of men and horses moving about, the regiment had just been dismissed from formation. "Tell me something, would you? An honest answer. What is it like to mount a horse and ride forth and make war? Is it splendid?"

"No. Not always."

"I did not think it would be *always,*" she said with a toss of her head and walked quickly back through the trees toward the stone house.

MacSwain vacated the command of the Second Cavalry for the summer and went east, that his old wounds might rest and to press for his schemes for war among the politicians in Washington. Frank Clous was given temporary command of the regi-

78

ment. For a few weeks, this most disciplined of soldiers let military duty relax so that we did nothing but mend equipment and fatten our animals. The scouts we made were but hunting parties, and those on guard more often than not returned to camp with strings of fat fish. That we had become little more than a private army for the Caballo Ranch took the edge off my zeal, and for a time I hunted and fished with the others, worked with our cartographer, and renewed my studies of the Spanish language that one day I might read the journals of Coronado's expedition across the staked plains. Most of the other officers displayed their youth or exerted themselves if their youth had passed. Daily I would see groups of them clustered around Miss McCorquodale and her cousin and friend and other young ladies, riding out to explore the range lands east of the Caballo that were considered safe from Indians. When I tired of hunting and reading and preparing for the fall campaign, I took to volunteering to ride at the head of every scout sent out and was often chosen to lead the longer scouts, when we would not return to regimental camp for days. I became quite popular with the other officers, who desired to stay near the festivities that swirled around the Caballo stone house as it was built and became ever more civilized. Our scouts took us to the west of the ranch, and I came to know that part of the country below the brow of the caprock well. On occasion, when we found a bridge over the escarpment or some rupture in its wall, we rode up onto the plain, but we never went far out onto it, for even in this mild summer air, with the grass green and gently shifting under the wind, the sky as open and clear blue as if we stood in space, even then the plain's vast reach warned us that we were small and would be lost there, and we rode back to where the earth had memorable features to it.

The weeks of riding out and preparing our defenses passed swiftly for me. Summer went into August, and though the days were hot as ever, a breeze from the west cooled us at night and promised fall. There had been little rain since June, and the

grass and earth and air turned dry. On most nights I went to
the bluff overlooking the live-oak grove and the ranch headquarters and there watched the late-summer storms as they
crossed from horizon to horizon. All wind and flash lightning,
these summer storms were dry. When I did not care to follow
the storms or the stars, I observed the movements of camp and
ranch, as a naturalist studies the social migration of another
species of animal. The evening regimen of the camp I knew, or
thought I knew. By the time I had climbed the bluff, the evening meal and duties and games were over, and the men had
gathered around the platoon campfires that went on up the valley, like the tracks of a molten giant. Most of the men remained
in these circles, having been trained for one another's company,
but there were those few who broke off from the rest. As their
dark forms went away from the fires, becoming black clumps indistinguishable from bush or rock unless they moved or smoked,
I wondered if there might not be a poet or scholar or man of
vision among our ranks, someone whose talent or thought would
someday break upon the world in verse or discovery, whose
understanding might in time include my life as a fading memory. At times several men, up to half a dozen, went away from
the fire and stood clustered in the dark, passing matches from
pipe to pipe, talking, debating, it would seem from their gestures. I imagined these men as revolutionaries from Europe, for
there were many Germans and Irishmen among our ranks who
had fled their princes and parliaments for their lives, imagined
that they whispered among themselves of returning to their
homelands, taking freedom there or their vision of it. There
would be one young fellow, I thought, who would suggest they
might bring their political upheavals here, to this country, and
the others would fall silent and look about at the vastness and
desolation of this country and they would return to the fire
thinking that the rebellions that had smashed themselves on the
rocks of European reaction would be lost here, floating aim-
lessly, without contest, on this shoreless sea.

By this time, in August, the stone house had been completed but for glass in its windows and some finishing to the interior. The house had become the focus of life at the ranch, recently having been inhabited by a young Scotsman named Jonathan Weir, who would be the ranch's superintendent, replacing Ben Cady, who would act as his foreman. The friends and associates of Weir were young men like the new master of Caballo, gentlemen of title and wealth who had a love for a certain amount of adventure. For the last week or so I had watched their arrival, in carriages and ambulances and coaches drawn by fine horses. I had seen them riding out with their hounds and guns, though they went east, where the game was not good, as Mac-Swain had forbidden any civilians to approach the plains.

On the August evening of which I write, as on any other evening, men gathered around their campfires, taps was sounded, and the regiment retired. The Second's officers, now freed from duty, made their way through the arcade of cottonwoods to the ranch headquarters, the stone house and the array of tents set in the live-oak grove. There were campfires there, around the tents, and lanterns hung among the trees; light was thrown brightly from the windows of the stone house, for, as one of the young officers had told me, a great chandelier had come from New Orleans and been fastened to the main beam and two dozen oil lamps had been hung from it. On this evening two figures, a man and woman, walked beyond these lights, coming through the grove to stand at the foot of the bluff below me. The couple stopped beneath a tree, and I could not see them. Though I could hear their voices, their words could not be understood. There followed a silence and then the sound of feet scuffing the ground, and then came a sharp report that sounded very much like a face being slapped. The man cursed, which came to me distinctly, and he strode back through the trees.

I called down to the woman who had made herself seen among the trees, and my greeting was returned:

81

"Oh, you," came the bored voice of the Scottish girl, "the stargazer. Do you ever come down off that cliff?"

"I think tonight that it might not be safe."

"Oh, stay where you are. I shall come up to you."

The figure went to the base of the wall, and I came near to tumbling down it trying to dissuade the girl from climbing up. There was nothing to mark her progress but an angry cry shortly after she had begun, and then very near the top, when I could almost reach her, her foot kicked loose a rock and she slipped backwards. "Yoops," she said and came into view and took my hand, and I pulled her over the ledge. The girl was flushed and her voice unsteady, but she had made a remarkable, and dangerous, climb in the dark. "Oh, that was nothing," the girl said shortly. "I have mountaineered in the Alps. And I have climbed this wall before."

"Have you?"

"Yes. And I have received little else but abuse for it. What I might do at home or in Paris is forbidden here. Here, it seems, I am to be a lady. It is ridiculous that I am to be scolded for wearing a riding skirt in this place that is full of britches, but that, according to my uncle, seems to be the case."

"Perhaps it is that in a place such as this with so few women, men especially want them to be womanly."

"Is that it? Then I shall return to Paris, where a woman may be manly and a man womanly, if they choose, since there are near equal numbers of both there. Ah, but then I am imprisoned here for weeks and weeks more! Even so, I will not wear a gown, nor will I sit that female saddle. They are insults—and the latter quite dangerous. This *sidesaddle*," she said with an inflection that a great-aunt might reserve for *blackguard*. "I would like your opinion on this sidesaddle, Captain, as an equestrian—what is the purpose of it?"

"It is so that ladies—"

"Good. Then if one is not a lady—as you and I are not— then one should not be expected—in fact, it would even be thought foolish to sit such a saddle. Correct?"

"The designation of lady is often bestowed on a young woman by others than herself."

"I have heard a few reasons," said Miss McCorquodale, stalking the brow of the bluff. "They say the contraption saves a girl's maidenhead for her husband."

"Miss McCorquodale," I said.

"Good. Then only virgins should be expected to ride these things. Full women should not."

"Miss McCorquodale—I think the matter may be symbolic."

"Which? The maidenhead or the idiotic saddle?"

"No, perhaps I am mistaken. These saddles, they are more than symbolic. They serve a purpose."

"And what may this purpose be, pray?"

"Well—for health."

"Health! Are you afraid that if I ride astride a horse I shall split like a peach?"

I threw up my hands.

The girl tucked her skirts under her and sat on the ground. "It may be symbolic after all," she said. Her skirts gathered, it was revealed that she wore riding britches beneath them. "I think men are sexually jealous of the horse, when a woman has her legs wrapped around the animal's back."

"Miss McCorquodale, have pity on me."

She cocked an eyebrow, all that she would show of her amusement. "Are you making love to me, Captain Chapman?"

"I think it is you who are making love—or something—to me."

The girl lay back, stretched out full on the ground. "Yes, it's true. God, I'm so bored I will do anything for excitement. Perhaps I shall cause a row. Yes—a maiden lured to this cliff by a married officer. I shall beat the grounds with my palms and cry out in that way that men imagine women sound when they make love."

"Ah, now I have heard it all."

The girl sat up, her elbows propped on spraddled knees, chin propped on her fists. Her face came so close to being that of a doll—so nearly perfectly round with a daub of scarlet on her cheeks, her mouth drawn into a pout—that I felt a child's mixed amusement and tenderness and care toward her. "Oh, I miss Paris so," she said, "where women are allowed to say what they do and wear britches when they ride a horse." She leapt to her feet and started away from the cliff. "But then you aren't bored here, are you, Captain, where women and horses are kept in their corrals?"

We walked away from the cliff, without any direction but that. "Yes, well, I would not be bored here either if I could go about killing savages for amusement." The girl softened her tone: "I'm sorry. That was a thoughtless thing to say. I think you are not like the others. I think you take no pleasure in what you do." She continued briskly, "I understand that you are a man of culture, and a scholar, or have some pretensions to be. They say your father is famous, though I have not heard of him."

"I don't think he is yet famous in Paris." The girl remained silent and I said: "Have you studied in Paris?"

"Yes. And I have lived there too. And I have a lover there. That was the reason for their dragging me on this tedious journey. To separate us and break our love."

"And has it?"

"Oh no. Our love, or mine for him, was quite finished before. I only agreed to come here as a way of becoming free of him. He is an artist and quite old—or somewhat older than I—a friend of my father, who is quite famous in Paris. I sat to him regularly; that is how he came to fall in love with me. It is not fair to art or wisdom, I know, but I grew so that I could not endure him, not even his marvelous paintings. He is so talented and wise about everything other than that."

"That I can understand. You are like no young woman I have ever met."

"Oh, I am not! Of course, I go about breaking my neck, or nearly doing so," her laughter murmured, "attempting to seem so, but that is only because beneath these skirts and britches I am just another girl."

"I shall not believe that for a while, if I may."

I could not see the girl's features in the dark—we had walked away from the light that had been reflected up from the camp-fires and lanterns below—but her voice altered as she spoke: "Had you been above us long," she said, "before you spoke? Of course I knew you had," she said quickly. "I knew you were there all along. That is why I took Jonathan there and allowed him to kiss me."

"And to give him a good swat?"

"Yes. That was planned too. Are you displeased that I made such an artifice to meet you again?"

"No, I am pleased. But I imagine that Jonathan wouldn't be, if he knew."

"He is just a boy. He had no business kissing me, even if I did ask him. A man, like yourself, would have refused."

"Would I?"

There was a brief pause, then the girl walked on, speaking lucidly: "Oh, you are right. I am thoughtless. I never think of others, that I may hurt them, but only of myself. I wish I were like you."

"And how am I?"

"You never think of yourself. You think only of others." I could not agree and the girl retorted sharply: "It is true. I have watched you. You are not like those officers who look at a woman as if she were a mirror to their own beauty. If I am not to be seen, I had rather not be seen at all." She turned and pressed a finger against my chest. "I have watched you as you walk, as you ride—it is perhaps most pronounced then—you do not give a hang for your own person. Your thoughts are sub-merged in other things."

"If you mean by thinking of others that I take interest in them, that is correct. But if by thinking of others you mean that I am considerate of them—you are wrong. I am as self-centered as any peacock among our young lieutenants."

"And I shall not believe that for a while, if I may," said the girl, and our laughter joined. She said then: "Philip, there is a ball this Saturday, at the stone house. Will you please put aside your duties and come? You must not remain distant from us forever. And I shall grow desperate and mad if you go on ignoring me. And I shall wear a dress without britches underneath, if that interests you, and have my hair done down in curls. There—is there anything else that can sweeten the invitation?" And she stood on her toes and reached up and brusquely took my collar and pulled my mouth to hers. When we parted she winced, as if the separation caused her pain. Then I saw the dark ragged line of blood on the back of her thumb, where she had injured herself climbing.

We went to a spring and I bathed and cleaned her hand and wrapped it in a handkerchief. As I tended her broken flesh I felt something had torn inside me and that her nearness poured over the wound, cooling as water.

After a week during which I rode out on three scouts and engaged myself in camp duty when not in the saddle, I handed over the red sash of Officer of the Day to a disappointed Captain Ramsey, bathed, shaved, changed boots and tunic, and made myself fit for the ball. I knew of the stone house's interior only from the word of the junior officers, who often came to my tent after their bacchanals, filled with tales of its splendor. The house proved something less than their vinous reports. Its appointments, furnishings, and scale had been judged by frontier standards. Among the walled tents, dugouts, and sod huts that passed for residences, the stone house may have seemed to us palatial, but it was, in fact, small, raw, and unfinished. It seemed a pity that the stone walls and wood plank floors had been hung with faded tapestries and laid with drab rugs, for the ragged white stone and yellow-waxed wood underneath had a natural beauty, in texture and color, that artifice could not match. The furniture too had been covered, and that was equally regrettable: for the log chairs and tables beneath had been fashioned with a rustic artistry. And the grand chandelier from New Orleans was a hoop of steel not larger than a wagon-wheel rim hung by chains from the ceiling sitting a half-dozen or so smoking kerosene lamps. The single object that boasted of Eastern civilization was a spiral mahogany staircase, elegant and elaborately polished and carved, awkward in this place, an embarrassment.

This much of the stone house I viewed from a window near the punch bowl. For a while I chose to remain outside and walked through the trees about the house that had been hung with lanterns and festooned with ribbons and garlands twined from native shrubs. A plank dance floor had been laid at the rear of the house, and a band of fiddlers played waltzes and jigs and promenades, and the younger men bounded about with high energy and some style, for there were ladies here who knew every dance. After a time of dancing and strolling about the grounds, I entered the stone house. The main room had been cleared by the dance—calls and music came to us from the rear—and there remained indoors only the old, the serious, and the weary. I noted Major Clous and various members of regimental staff; the elderly Scotsmen, a half-dozen of them; Jonathan Weir, the youthful heir to Caballo; a collection of Weir's gentlemen friends; and several Texans, among them Ben Cady. Seated before our circle was an old man, his lap covered with a rug, a gnarled cane held across that. This was Ben Cady's father, who had founded the original ranch, now called the Little Caballo. In addition there were several ladies arranged on the spiral stairs and the landing above. The old man turned as I came into the room. His fierce, faded eyes held on me. He took up his cane and shook it:

"And so this is the man who has fought Tehana Storm!" he cried out in the powerful, rattling voice of a street orator calling down doom on the figures gathered around him.

"It is he—Captain Chapman," said Clous in a voice that was timid by comparison.

"Draw near me, sir," commanded the old man, and when I

did he touched my arm with his cane. "There, on the plains, among the Comanche, tell me what you saw. Not of your own movements, but of them."

I recounted what I remembered of the Indians, their tactics or lack of them, of their system of command, the medicine men with their scalp poles and mirrors, and the subchiefs who rode between them, and of the Indian who seemed to be their chief, though he had no means of commanding them that I could see.

The old man put down his cane and touched me with his hand, his fingers as bent and twisted as the cane. "Ah, there you are, sir. It is him. Tell me what you saw of him. Did he ride a white horse?"

I said that among the whirlwind of horses dashing about there had been a horse and a rider unlike the others, that the war paint on all the other light-colored horses had showed vividly, the bands of red and yellow and brown across their chests and flanks, that among them this white horse alone had been unmarked.

"Yes. Yes," said the old man. "And the rider, tell me what you saw of him."

"At first I thought he was unpainted too—the other braves had bright splotches of red across their chests and their arms were painted many colors, red, yellow, blue, green—but then I saw that he was not unpainted, but that he was painted black, his face and chest and arms were black."

"There! Black! Did I tell you! You have crossed the Wanderers' band of Tehana Storm! You are indeed fortunate, sir, to have survived his attack. His loathing of white men would wipe us all from the face of the earth! That is why he paints his skin black and suffers a white animal to bear him!"

The old man tried to stand, but he could not, moving only enough that the rug fell from his wasted legs. Ben Cady reached down and placed a hand on his father's shoulder, not so much to restrain him as that he might rest.

Now I noticed Miss McCorquodale among the ladies on the

landing above, as she rose from them and descended the stairs. She had worn a gown and done her hair down in curls, as she had promised, though by now the curls had been fastened behind her head. She was as tanned as any of the men, and her hands, made large by riding, were thrust out awkwardly from the delicate cuffs of the dress sleeves, and she moved her head against the lace collar, tugging at it as if it might stretch. She spoke to the old rancher:

"Certainly I have missed something," she said. "Why would an Indian paint himself black if he is part white?"

"Why would he paint himself black, Missy? Because he hates white men so and he himself is white and so he hates himself and paints himself black for it."

"How did he come to be," said Miss McCorquodale, "this half-breed, as you might say?"

"This way, Missy. His mother was white. It was in 1836, just after the battle of San Jacinto, after the winning of Texas, that the Comanches raided Storm's Fort there on the Brazos, in Limestone County, and took her away. Ben Storm, the fool, he opened the gate to the devils to make a treaty, and all the men of Storm's Fort was massacred by the savages and some of the women and children. Little Lianna Storm was aged six, and she had a brother aged nine, they was among those captured. Nothing was ever heard of the boy again, and it was accepted he perished. The Comanches took the girl and raised her as one of their own. Nothing was heard of this girl till the year 1860 and she was thought to be dead. This was when a force of Rangers jumped the Comanches on a camp on the Pease River and all but some of the squaws and their papooses was run down and killed. One taken captive was a white squaw, the white girl Lianna Storm, now thirty years of age and as savage in her manners as any redskin. Now the white squaw remembered nothing of her capture by the redskins there twenty-odd years ago, but she was identified as the Storm girl and was taken to Fort Richardson, along with a girl papoose who died not long afterwards. Lianna Storm herself was buried not long after that. Before her death she confessed she had borne two other children, both sons, to the chieftain Lacona. She passed on believing they both had perished in the battle with the Rangers. But Tehana survived, and, some say, the other boy lived as well. The twist to the tale, that which might interest the young lady or any man who takes one," said the old man, "is that Lianna Storm never took to the civilization of her girlhood. No, Missy, she was kept till her death as little more than a prisoner by the people of her birth. She had become a savage and never stopped trying to escape and make her way back to that life. Now, Missy, that I have told you of how Tehana Storm come to be half-white, do you think you can tell me of the frame of mind of a white woman that becomes a savage and cares not to be civilized?"

The Scottish girl spoke briskly, but she was uncertain. "You say she was captured at age six? Why then she had spent five-sixths of her life in another manner, what you call barbarism. I would imagine that time alone would account for her loyalties."

The old man's eyes sparked. "Would you think so? At age six, then, is a girl uncivilized? Can she be said to be blank as paper to take what the rest of her life may make of her? At what age, then, does civilizing take set? At ten or twelve, or is it later yet? At what age do we stay what we was born into? Take yourself, Missy, a fair eighteen, if you was captured at your age, would you take to the barbarian life and love it so that you would never return to your fine gowns and these balls and these young gallants?"

The girl reddened, and Ben Cady spoke to his father, a gentle reprimand that his comments were a trespass, but the girl flashed: "Far from being an insult to me, sir, your father's words have more thought in them than any I have heard since coming to this place where there is talk of nothing but hunting—of beasts and birds, of promotion and women, and of this race of people who do not wish to become Europe's slaves!" She spoke to the father: "As for your point, Mr. Cady, it is well taken. If I were to be captured at this moment by this Tehana Storm, I might very well come to prefer his barbarism to the civilized prisonment of this society and its bondage by gender!" With a quick piercing look at those men around her, the girl turned and strode through the door, out the front of the house.

"Ah, there are some fillies that might take the bridle but are forever spitting out that bit," said the old man, and his laughter rattled at the girl's spirit.

At this point, there came a series of screams from all around outside the house, and before any could move every window of the room was filled with Indians in war paint, all brandishing tomahawks and leering fiendishly and continuing their execrable yowling. The civilians, who did not recognize the Indian attackers as our Tonk scouts, almost to a man dived for cover, and our officers, who had stationed themselves by the windows to protect Poor Man and his boys from their enraged self-defense, stood about with little to do except revive the ladies and one or two of the gents who had swooned. The exception to this were the Texans, who cast looks toward the rollicking young officers in blue that made plain that the end of the war between North and South had not stanched their hatred of us. Relief and amusement soon swept the room, and the Texans' enmity was lost in it.

The entertainment continued outdoors. With recovered dignity the gentlemen and ladies gathered themselves in pairs and strolled out under the stars, making their way down to the Tonk village, where they were to view a scalp dance. I went outside with the party but did not follow them to the Tonkaway camp. I was soon joined in forgoing the entertainment by Jonathan Weir, who was to manage the Caballo Ranch in a few weeks' time. Weir had approached me with a purpose, which he readily admitted as a means of introduction. Candor was characteristic of the young Scotsman—who, like Miss McCorquodale, spoke with an English accent—but it was not an openness to be trusted.

Nor were his innocence, his naive curiosity, and his admiration of me authentic. At heart the young man was cynical and ruthless, so long as his will could be carried out by others. Still, he probed so quickly and with such amusement into his own character and its weaknesses that it passed for charm. Instead of the blandishments that the hero of Mount Blanco had come to anticipate, the young man began sharply, by recognizing a mental equal in a social inferior:

"Some say you are not the hero others claim you are."

"I am not the hero some say or others claim I am."

"Some say you are more of a hero than that. They say you could have ridden to safety, like the Prussian major, that you had the superior horse, but that you did not, hoping to save your comrades on lesser steeds."

"You seem intent on establishing and deflating heroics that do not exist, at least not in me, Mr. Weir."

"I do not believe in them, that is true, in you or in anyone," the young man said, then shifted: "There will be a hunt soon, for my friends, perhaps tomorrow. We want to go up on the plains and kill buffalo. Will you come with us?"

"No."

"Not if you are ordered to do so? We shall have to have a military escort, you see. It has all been arranged."

"I can imagine it has."

"Then you will come, won't you, Captain?" said Jonathan Weir with a faint smile. "You do not like me much, I fear."

"Nor do I trust you."

The smile remained as it had been when the young man conceived it: it did not spread or fade. "You love her too, like the cowboy," he said, then broke away with a frown. "But then everyone does. What," he went on in his gliding manner, "did you think of the old man's tale, that of the half-white Indian?"

"It seemed reasonably accurate from what I have heard."

"Yes, I suppose something like that would be near legend, that all Texans, and those who serve here, would know it by heart. Still, it was an extraordinary tale to the newcomer. And the philosophical questions that are raised by the mother's behavior are profound. That men and women are less the blood of those who give them birth than the creation of those who raise them, that we are not born to what we are but trained to it—it is an uneasy truth, especially to those of us who are socially privileged. But then it may be even more disturbing to those whom life has treated less kindly, mayn't it, Captain?"

"I would imagine that enough rich sons sink and enough poor sons rise that blood may still be considered a factor in either."

Jonathan Weir's cheeks may have reddened, but his voice remained placid: "There was another aspect of the old man's story that intrigued me, perhaps more so that it was passed over by all."

"And what was that?"

"The brother of Tehana Storm, he who escaped the Rangers' attack with him."

"It is assumed he perished."

"Yes. But what if he did not? Let us say that, like Tehana, he lived. There would be two possibilities. The first would be that, like Tehana, he returned to the Indians and remained one of them, indistinguishable from the rest. But let us say he did not. Let us say that he came to live with his mother's people—whites. By all accounts, this Tehana has no white look to him, but for his size, perhaps, and light-colored eyes. But what if the brother physically resembled his mother, what if his skin was light and his hair was fair and his eyes were blue and there was nothing Indian in his looks but his broad face? What if this lad were taken in by a white family, and the knowledge of his origin kept from all? What sort of man would he become?"

"By our previous reasoning, he would become as white as the man and the woman who took him in. He would forget his Indian ways, and, if this knowledge were kept from him and the world, his red blood would be washed white by custom and study."

"And later, if he came to know of his mixed blood, would he hate the Indians as Tehana Storm is said to hate the whites?"

"I think he very well might."

The course of our walk had brought us to the base of the limestone cliff. Weir looked up. "I fear for us if it is true, that all men are made by circumstance." He shivered, for he had come without a jacket. With the breeze came the call of an owl. Weir cupped his hands to his mouth and attempted to mock the bird's cry, then turned to me. "It is late. I should be to bed. For tomorrow will be a big day. I suppose I shall be expected to shoot a buffalo. I will see you tomorrow, won't I?" The young man wrapped his arms about himself and ran back through the trees.

The following morning I rose and made ready to accompany the buffalo hunting party. From Lieutenant Quinn, an admirer of Custer and his rustic dress, I borrowed a deerskin jacket with fringe. Another man lent me a light-colored broad-brimmed hat. I chose from the *caballado* a thoroughbred known for its speed and handsome gait. While the horse was being saddled, I cleaned and oiled and loaded a carbine and a pistol. These weapons and ammunition for them were all the baggage I carried, for I did not expect the hunt would last beyond nightfall, and when I learned it would, saw that provisions for camping—tents, blankets, a camp kitchen, food if the hunt went badly—had been loaded on wagons that would follow us. The number of the party was so great—seventy-five, counting the Second's escort—that it was decided we should divide into four smaller groups. The first was characterized by the very serious hunters and those who desired to be and their hounds and dogs. Another consisted primarily of ladies and their guardians and servants. The third and largest was composed of the older men, those unaccustomed to the saddle, and those who would not hunt. The last and smallest group might have been said to be

Miss McCorquodale and her admirers. In addition to myself and two other officers in mufti, there were Ben Cady and several of his men, several friends of Jonathan Weir, and the young Scotsman himself, who as lord of this range had been made master of the hunt, though we looked more like a Wild West parody of the riding to hounds than the spectacle Weir and his companions knew. That the young Scotsman was stranger to the killing of the American bison made the title ceremonial in any case: the leader of our hunt was the Texan Ben Cady.

The first and fourth parties—ours and the stern hunters—rode off ahead of the second and third, arranging to meet at a spring off the brow of the caprock in the late afternoon. It was our plan to stay off the *llano* the first day of the hunt, going there only if buffalo could not be found in the broken country below the plains. By noon we had seen no buffalo off the plain, and the hunters persuaded the guides that we would find nothing but rabbit in the breaks. "The plains," promised one of the hunters who had read an article on the subject in *Harper's,* "will be black with buffalo!" After a brief repast we rode along under the caprock till we found a trail up, and at about one o'clock we came out on the staked plains.

It was not a good day to first know the *llano estacado,* a day without grace. At midmorning, clouds had begun to drift over us from the southwest, sluggish gray masses that heaved across the sky like doomed regiments marching to battle. By noon the heavens had turned to a solid wall of gray that had no outline or form or motion to it, as if the viewer had been deprived of the perception of color and perspective. The land had lost hue and texture and shape as well. It stretched before us to the horizon like a single slate, smooth, flat, unending, offering no reason for its existence and questioning that of our own.

Jonathan Weir had ridden close to me. He gazed out toward the western horizon. "It is like something amputated," he said. "It is as if what had been here before—mountains, valleys, rivers, cities, forests—it is as if they had become diseased and a surgeon had come and cut away the infected part. It is as if a scalpel, unimaginably large and keen, had in one stroke sliced everything away."

"This plain would then be called a stump," said another young man, a companion of Weir, but his jest was felled by the inhumanity of the plain and brought shudders to those in earshot, rather than mirth.

Such was the effect of the tractless plains on a day without sun that we rode throughout the afternoon not daring to lose sight of the broken land to our left. An hour before dark we saw lights winking in the scrub oak and mesquite below. This was the encampment of the others. Though more encumbered than we, they had made progress ahead of us by riding directly under the plain's margin. Our party had been slowed by the numerous arroyos and gullies and canyons that cut into the plains and that had to be headed, for it was impossible to descend and ascend at every one. After a brief search we found a natural road that could be ridden off the caprock and made our way to the encampment, not long before an early nightfall that looked like winter, though it was not cold. Still we built blazing bonfires and gathered around them, pretending to seek their heat, so intense was our solitude in nature. The game our hunters had taken was supplemented by whistling quail and curlew and green-winged teal shot by the others in the rugged, well-watered breakland. A feast was prepared that rivaled the civilized tables of London and Paris, or such was the opinion of the weary, famished young men who could draw such comparisons. Afterwards the fire was stoked and men mopped sweat and grease away and lit pipes and reclined on their saddles and began the telling of tales that lasted till the fire died to embers and we were returned to night.

The camp rose early and in high spirits. A distant bank of clouds stretched over the east, curtaining the sun, but to the west the sky was clear and high, pastel blue washed over gray, without threat. The air was thin and fresh and carried the fragrances of smoldering mesquite and boiling coffee, of horse leather and frying bacon. The hunters ate and saddled their mounts and polished their rifles with vigor and ambition. Our massed party ascended the road we had found the previous afternoon and by midmorning had, to the last sculled wagon, crossed the caprock. Derision and laughter and challenge were thrown on the *llano,* for what was it, as the girl had said, but a flat place? Where was its threat but in our minds? That which had brought us dread before—that there was nothing to the plain but horizon and these relentless playa lakes—today seemed tame and familiar. Still, some caution was exercised and a camp was established within view of the plain's margin. From this place the women and elder gents could ride out and, with some civilization in view, still experience the adventure of the wild. There was enough small game nearby to satisfy the older men's blood lust, while the smooth terrain proved ideal for ambulance races and the leisurely cantering preferred by the ladies. A polo match was organized by the younger men who did not hunt. A three-man scout had been sent out at dawn, and as the plains camp was being finished, the riders returned with word that a herd of buffalo had been observed five miles to the west. The party of serious hunters galloped away like boys, whooping and waving their hats, some firing their weapons till they were silenced. The smaller party gathered around Jonathan Weir followed at a slower gait. Since we rode gently enough to converse, our column formed naturally into pairs. Miss McCorquodale had been accompanied by Ben Cady since our departure from Caballo, and they led the column. Jonathan Weir and I brought up the rear. The young Scotsman seemed uncomfortable or displeased with some aspect of the hunt. I asked about his horse, which was raw-gaited, or if the California saddle did not fit, but it was Weir's position among men that troubled him.

"It is my place to be here, I think," he said, failing miserably to achieve a lofty air. "Rather than riding ahead. I even considered remaining behind—with the camp—but I think here is my proper place." There began a silence that might have continued without embarrassment to either of us, but he blurted: "Will you kill a buffalo?"

"I don't know. I doubt it."

"Really?" We rode. "Really?" he repeated, and we rode another distance. "Have you killed that many—is that it? Or is it that you have never killed any?"

"I have killed one."

"Only one?" he said, with the uncertain hope of a novice who has just learned how frail but absolute is the barrier to experience.

"Just one. I rode out hunting for meat. But I killed the animal to have done it." The young Scotsman worried his lip with his thumb and forefinger. "It is depressingly simple to kill one," I said.

"Is it? I hear they combine the ferocity of a tiger and the strength of a lion. They say they are as swift as a horse and massive as a rhino."

"They are fierce and strong and swift and huge and stupidly kind to men."

"So I've heard. How did you kill yours? From a distance? I've heard one way to hunt them is with a long rifle. That they may be killed one after another, ten, twenty, a hundred at a time, by shooting them from a distance. That if they do not see or scent one, even if they do hear the report of the rifle, they do not understand the deaths of the others and will mill about the carcasses, drawn there by the smell of blood. They do not run, if one hunts them from a distance. They are sitting ducks."

"Still-hunting is one way to kill them. But we will ride after them."

"Of course. That is the sporting thing. The only way game should be taken. I have hunted every beast in Europe and many in Asia and shot very many birds. Still, I think it should be my position as head of Caballo that after today these beasts must not be hunted, certainly not to extinction. When we extend our range up onto the plains, I think I shall designate a certain acreage as a preserve, that a proper number of the species shall be protected. This, then, may very well be the last of the buffalo hunts."

We observed Miss McCorquodale, who was riding at the head of the column with Ben Cady, turn her horse away from the rancher and gallop back to us. She reined in her horse and slid it between Weir and me. At every moment she seemed about to tumble from her mount, for though she was riding in the lady-like fashion that had been ordered, she did so on an ordinary saddle, with only her left foot in the stirrup, her right leg cocked over the pommel. She had pulled back her shirt like a cape, to reveal riding britches beneath.

"Jonathan, will you do me the kindness of riding awhile with Mr. Cady? I cannot imagine how he has grown so witless in so short a time. His conversation—what there is of it—has become unbearably tedious. Please be a good friend and ride ahead—please, Jonnie, I am so bored with him!"

Weir looked as if he might attempt to assert himself as master of Caballo, but the girl's imperative was modified sufficiently by her boredom with another man that he was able to obey in a lordly fashion.

"Very well. I have been wanting to question Cady on the technique of buffalo hunting anyway. It seems that Captain Chapman here knows very little about it, having shot only one, and that for meat."

Weir spurred his horse and galloped forward. Ben Cady turned in his saddle at the sound of hoofbeats, his shoulders sagging at the sight of his new companion.

The girl and I rode behind the others, chatting idly for a while. Then we felt some disturbance move through the column, from head to tail, as a writhe passes through a snake, and though we could not see or hear what had caused the lead riders to rein in their horses, their concern reached us as clearly as if

99

we had been beside them. Then came the sound of gunfire, distant drifting explosions that only our dread made threatening. All riders broke out of the double column and horses were reined back and forth, turning, wheeling, as the gunfire became more distinct. "By God, the hunt is on!" called out one man, and several others shouted, but they did not turn their horses toward the gunfire, for there was in every one of us the fear that our comrades had found Indians, not buffalo. Then we spied a black dot on the horizon and as we watched it grow our column collapsed into a milling circle of horses, many riders turning their mounts to the rear, galloping back a ways, to rein them in and turn them to rejoin the group, the horses sidestepping and struggling against the bit and tossing their heads. Then at either side of the first black dot there appeared two smaller dots wavering about the larger, growing at the same relentless rate as the first. Then I heard Ben Cady expel the word "buffalo," and we too could see the form of the animal, that of an inverted teardrop, and that the smaller figures possessed a different shape—they were horses ridden by men. All of our collapsed column cheered and waved their hats or rode their mounts around in wide, celebratory circles. Now the hunted animal had come near enough that we could see its massive head and horns and hear the hunters' shouts above the gunfire and the pounding hoofbeats. The buffalo had been making directly for our group, perhaps seeing in our clumped forms allies of its kind that might rise up and smash its pursuers, but now it recognized us as waiting enemies and veered away. Riders broke from our group and fanned out across its path, so that the buffalo wheeled and came back toward us in its pitifully lurching gait. It passed across our front not fifty yards away, its eyes distended, red as wounds, its tongue dangling from its foam-caked mouth like an intestine torn from a belly. The men around us shot into the buffalo's profile as it staggered by, the animal as unconcerned with their fire as if it had been a target in an arcade shooting gallery. A short distance away the buffalo turned to face its pursuers as they circled to fire into its vulnerable flank. Our group drew near this spectacle. The cheering became taunts as the two hunters could not kill the beast, an old bull—its mane torn, its haunches withered—that had been driven from the herd by younger bulls. One of the fellows brazenly leapt from his horse and, less brazenly, went toward the animal on foot. The old bull tore at the ground as the hunter approached, the man's insolence forming as he grew near and saw that the animal could not charge. The man walked to the animal's side and fired into its heart at a place just behind the shoulder, at a distance of no more than ten feet. With what rage I cannot imagine, the bull turned on its killer and with its last breath lunged at the man, so that as it dropped to its knees and sank its great head to the ground and died, the man who had killed it fell in panic on his backside and crawled away on his hands and buttocks in an abased and frantic fear.

At that moment I observed the three riders drawn up in line beside me—Jonathan Weir, Miss McCorquodale, and Ben Cady. By their expressions it would not have seemed possible they were observing the same event. Nearest me, the girl was pale, motionless, her eyes closed—she had seen the animal hunted and killed, as she had wanted, but it had not been as she had imagined. The young Scotsman's face was torn open with a gloating bully's pleasure—he had seen there would be no danger in hunting and killing the beast, and he gloried that the dissipation of his fear might be courage. The rancher's visage had been set by hatred of the hunt, of the crudity of the hunters, and of the stupidity of the beast that could not destroy them.

We left the two hunters and a number of their friends to mutilate the buffalo for trophies and made at a quick pace toward the center of the hunt. The gunfire slackened as we drew near it. Buffalo could be seen scattering over the plain, a few being pursued by riders. Several men left our column to chase a small herd of cows and calves. We were less than half our original number when we reached the playa lake where the buffalo had been attacked. The hunters had stampeded the herd immediately, and few carcasses were to be seen here. Shooting had ceased in the center. Gunfire came from all around us, from beyond our sight, as most of the hunters had ridden in all directions after the scattered herd. Several men were occupied with butchering the few buffalo that had fallen here, taking the animals' tongues and cutting steaks from the humps. The remainder of the party was gathered in a circle around a buffalo that by its immobility seemed to have been roped and tied. The hunters were cheering and popping their hats on their legs. A thick wall of dust and horses prevented us from viewing the spectacle till we rode in close with the gathered hunters. There we saw a huge bull being attacked by the pack of dogs that ran with the hunters. Most of these dogs were mongrels, with little courage, and spent themselves howling and nipping at the besieged buffalo's heels, whimpering and limping about when one of the buffalo's blind charges struck them. Among this pack of curs, however, was a dog equal to the buffalo, a white English bulldog, huge for its breed, weighing well over fifty pounds. The bulldog had clamped its jaws on the buffalo's nose and would not release its grip. The buffalo would fall to its knees and roll about in a rage, slamming the dog against the ground, but the dog would not let go. The buffalo would rise and whirl about and kick and fling its head, snapping and swinging the dog like a whip cord, but the dog would not let go. What began as comedy became a mirthless drama. One could easily imagine the dog locking into a man's throat or a child's leg and the horror of realizing that its sole purpose in life was to hold its jaws closed till the clamped limb was severed or the person or animal attacked was dead. The buffalo went to its knees more often now, attempting to gore or crush the dog. Blood and foam spread from the buffalo's mouth, covering itself and the dog with pink-splattered slime, this then being caked with dust so that the dog and the head of the buffalo became a single thing, something grotesque, unrecognizable. At last the buffalo could not rise. It bellowed, less in rage than in helpless terror, at the thing that could not kill it but would not let it live. "My God, shoot the beast," said a man nearby. "End its suffering." Two men went forward to the huge animal, the height of a horse on its knees, and as the buffalo rocked and swayed in some pitiful animal misery, they placed their carbines behind its shoulder and fired point-blank into its heart. The beast gave a final shudder, a cascade of spasms that ran through its body with such force that the ground trembled beneath it. Then it pitched forward and rolled onto its side dead. The bulldog did not release its grip for a time, till it was sure of death. Then it lay like a companion with the buffalo, so exhausted it could not raise its head.

As we rode away, the hunters had taken the tongue and cut into the hump, and one enterprising young man had sawn off the buffalo's woolly head mop for a mattress he was filling for his mother. Miss McCorquodale, Weir, and I rode with Ben Cady due west, into the wind. We went at a bare canter to save the horses and in a quarter of an hour spied a black clot of buffalo on the horizon, thirty or so of the stampeded animals that had begun to reform their herd. Ben Cady pulled up and spoke to Weir, whose horse halted without the rein.

"Will you be hunting a buffalo today, sir?"

Weir gazed out toward the horizon. "Perhaps I will take a cow."

"You will take a bull," said the rancher.

"Yes. Yes. Perhaps a young one would be easier—for a novice."

"It might be easier to kill, but impossible to catch. You should take the best bull we can find."

"Yes. Perhaps I should. As the master of the hunt. Will you help me?"

"The Captain and I will ride with you. The young lady will ride behind."

The girl unfastened her skirt, and it slid from her waist,

across the horse's rump to the ground. She swung her right leg over the saddle pommel and fitted her boot in the stirrup. Weir scarcely noticed the transformation, while I had expected it, but Ben Cady could not have been more amazed had she disrobed completely. "I shall ride with my cousin, Mr. Cady," she said.

The rancher grimly attempted to keep the matter among men. "Do you think this would be a good idea, sir?"

Weir turned distractedly. "Oh well, whatever she wants. She's a far better rider and pistol shot than I am," he said wistfully.

Cady seemed about to continue his protest when he realized, I thought, that it was not the girl's safety that should concern him. "Then stay to the back of us," he instructed the girl, "if you can hold your horse in." He leapt off his own horse and took the reins of Weir's mount in his hands. "Take Buster," he said of his own mount. "He's a good buffalo horse. He'll do the work for you. And how are you mounted, Captain?" said the rancher, his universal contempt falling freely on government horseflesh. "The young lady has been given a good buffalo horse, if you can prise her away from it."

I thought that hunting buffalo on foot might be easier than that and retained the thoroughbred I had drawn from the *caballado*. The three of us dismounted and examined girth, bridle, and stirrups. As we worked, Jonathan Weir's voice came from the other side of his mount:

"I think they're coming closer."

"Then we won't have as far to go, will we?" said the rancher, pulling his cinch so tight that his horse looked around to see what might be going on.

The herd was moving in our direction but without much pace, grazing as if last hour's stampede had never occurred. Miss Mc-Corquodale raised herself into the saddle, and I followed. Then came Weir. Ben Cady remained on the ground. "What guns will we use?" said Weir when he saw that Cady was loading a rifle.

Cady worked on without speaking, though something in his manner said that we might need every gun we had. "I have both pistol and carbine," called out the young Scotsman. "The pistol's a Smith and Wesson, a .44, I think," Weir said, "and quite good for buffalo, or so it's said. And the carbine's a breechloader specially designed for buffalo—or so the salesman presented it. It has a rather natty twelve-shot magazine—I say, they *are* coming closer, Mr. Cady."

Cady swung up into his saddle, wheeling the horse in a full circle up beside Weir. "Strap your carbine over your back—*no,* the strap over your head—there," said the rancher, assisting the young Scotsman with little *politesse.* "Now take my pistol—no, holster one and carry one in your right—you are right-handed, aren't you, sir? Now, the Captain and I will ride behind you and will hand you reloaded weapons as you ride so that you won't lose the chase—is that clear?"

"You will ride behind me and hand me weapons," said Weir. "Will this be at a full gallop?"

Ben Cady gazed at the Scotsman with monumental puzzlement. "At whatever gait is necessary to stay alongside the buffalo," he answered. "You will use the pistols first and then when the beast is stopped or run out, you will kill it with the rifle, if that is necessary."

"Yes. Yes, that makes sense. Pistols first, then carbines. Then if it's still not dead, we'll attack it with knives and our bare hands," said Weir, his joke so bled of wit by worry that the rancher, by his look, now classified him as daft.

"Now this matter is most important, sir," Cady continued, arranging his horse in relation to me as if he were hunter and I the buffalo. "You must ride to the left of the animal and slightly to the rear. Buster will do this for you if you give him his head. You must fire at a point just behind the buffalo's shoulder here," said Cady, pointing to the spot on his own back. "The shot must be fired quartering *forward,* into the heart. If you override the buffalo and fire directly in, it will do no harm. And if you allow the horse to fall behind the animal," said Ben Cady, turning his mount and speaking low to me, "you will very likely shoot your own horse in the head."

Our attention turned to the hunt. The small herd had come within five hundred yards. We could see the individual buffalo, that there were few bulls among twenty or so cows and calves. Two sentinel bulls stood separate from the herd, but they had not scented us, grazing as unconcernedly as the rest. "We will go at a walk in single file in a beeline for them," said the rancher. "I will be in the lead. If this is done softly, the herd will not stampede, but will move away at a walk or a trot. We will follow them at their own speed, until they break and run. I will spot the bull we want, and then at my sign, Mr. Weir, you will give Buster his head and the run is on. Have you tied your reins? All right," said Ben Cady, reaching across and patting Buster's neck. "Hold him tight, Mr. Weir. He loves the running."

Ben Cady turned and walked his horse toward the herd. Jonathan Weir followed, then I came, and last was Miss Mc-Corquodale. Blocked from view by Weir and Cady, I did not see the bull Cady had chosen for the new master of Caballo till we went after it. We came to within a hundred yards of the herd before the sentinels took note of us, raising their heads, sniffing the air for our scent, switching their tails, pawing at the ground. Another ten yards and the sentinels turned and began to trot away. We spurred our horses to a quick trot and gained on the herd, sitting fifty yards behind the straggling cows with calves. As our pace quickened, we drifted out of line and the animal Ben Cady had set sight on came into view, a trophy bull that seemed half again as large as the male next in size. My horse, which was swifter than the others and uneasy at a trot, went to a canter and moved up on Weir and Cady. Buster, the buffalo horse under Weir, took that for insult and bolted into a dead run, Weir clutching dearly to the pommel. Though my horse had no taste for buffalo, it misunderstood Buster's dash as a challenge to race and sprang into a full gallop. I was set back in the saddle as the thoroughbred took its head and flew after Weir and his mount. Ben Cady and Miss McCorquodale were left behind.

There seemed no doubt in Buster's mind that anyone man enough to ride him would hunt the largest buffalo that could be found. He went after the trophy bull, and we followed. The buffalo grew larger and larger as we drew near till it seemed the size of a locomotive. And still we had only seen the animal from the rear, a prospect that does not do the foreheavy buffalo justice. This, the buffalo seemed to have decided, had to be remedied. My horse had drawn even with Buster, the two of us being more or less twenty yards behind the bull, when, in some piece of time that I did not see, the bull rearranged itself at about-face. My horse got by the bull by leaping so far we flew. When we landed the horse had determined to go on to the side of the earth opposite the bull. It was several bounds later that I was able to seat the bit and turn the horse's head. I saw that the bull had taken flight in another direction, that Buster was on his heels, Ben Cady not far behind, and that Miss McCorquodale had just brought her mount around to follow. My horse's memory was short or its fear of the bull was less than its pique at being left behind, and we were after them at a dead run.

I had passed the girl and moved up beside Ben Cady when the bull turned and made another charge, scattering his pursuers. Buster executed a pantherish leap at full gallop around the bull's horns and was tight on the bull the moment it turned and ran. The charge had allowed Ben Cady and me to close on the bull, Cady on Buster's flank, my horse allowing itself to be rated just behind the buffalo horse. Miss McCorquodale's horse ran to the flank of mine, two lengths or so behind Ben Cady. It was only now that Weir fired the first shots at the buffalo, emptying his pistol into the ground and the air all around the beast. Without command or rein, Buster fell back to Ben Cady's horse and the rancher yanked the empty pistol from Weir's hand and shoved a loaded pistol into it. Buster then pulled up on the bull and Weir fired off six more rounds. Three bullets struck the bull, though with as little effect as had they not. The bull galloped on. Twice more the bull turned on us and charged, but the running had slowed him and our horses were no longer surprised. After the fourth charge the bull turned from us and ran and would not turn again till he was ready to die.

As the pace slowed, Weir's shooting grew more accurate, and though he could not kill the bull with pistol fire, some of the shots were telling, cracking into the bull's hide like the snap of a whip. One bullet had struck a lung, and blood foamed from the wound, while another shot had shattered the buffalo's jaw, so that its tongue jutted from its broken mouth at an imbecilic angle. Weir had just emptied another pistol, with Ben Cady shouting for him to unstrap his carbine, when the ground beneath my horse grew heavy. Cady had begun a cry—of warning, though none knew it—when there came a crack from his horse like a tree limb snapping and the horse went down, throwing Cady out toward the earth like a swimmer diving to start a race. As Cady hit the ground there came two other sounds—the terrible, inhuman screams and the splitting impact of Miss Mc-Corquodale's horse colliding with Cady's damaged, suffering animal. I had turned my head to the rear and was pulling left on the reins to go back to them when I was torn from the saddle and sent flying and was struck on the shoulder and arm with such force that the earth whirled overhead and the sky stood at my feet. I saw it all passing, as if I rode a carousel tumbling through space: my horse running free, weaving, thrusting its head left and right; Ben Cady sitting on the ground rather calmly, arms locked around his knees as if he were resting a spell before hiking on; behind him the two entangled horses, the leg of one broken clean off, pulsing blood like a fountain;

Miss McCorquodale on her hands and knees as if she were crawling after Cady, whose back was to her. So near me it seemed to be another planet; looming overhead stood the buffalo bull, blood falling from its ruined mouth. At the end of this swirling tapestry Jonathan Weir sat astride Buster—he raised his rifle stock to his cheek, and there was an explosion and the world tilted on edge and the buffalo threw itself against the ground, as if it were afraid it might slip off. The animal was dead.

So the new master of Caballo felled his trophy bull, the largest animal taken that day, and became a hero as well, saving my life, it was said, though I think I was in greater danger of being crushed beneath the falling buffalo than perishing from any wounds the weakened beast might have inflicted with its horns and hooves. We had run the buffalo in a great circle, and the kill was made not far from the original stand. Our gunfire had drawn the hunters from their post-kill pleasures, and Weir had dropped the bull to an appreciative audience. The hunters cheered and stood Weir atop the buffalo and toasted and doused the scion with champagne. I took some time coming around, the plains still tilted to one side, but soon was pulled to my feet and dragged about till it was noted that I had suffered only a scraped face and bruises. As soon as I could walk I left the celebration, he whose life has been saved being something of a fool on such occasions. Cady had shot the damaged horse and was tending Miss McCorquodale's mount, which seemed to have survived uninjured. The girl had walked away and stood with her back to everything. Cady's hands had been stripped of skin, and now that he had done with the horses he bathed them in water from a canteen and wrapped them in bandannas. I splashed tepid water against my skinned face.

"Prairie-dog town," Cady said, and I observed at a distance from us the rodents' heads peeking from their holes, which our horses had run upon. "Where is your horse?"

"Gone," I said, but then saw the thoroughbred standing

nearby. He looked sound, but I did not have the strength to go after him. "I must have been thrown. How is she?"

Cady looked toward the girl, who was approaching my horse, speaking quietly and offering her hand. "She is all right, I think. She's asked that you escort her back to the camp. It must be arranged with Mr. Weir," the rancher said unhappily. "You can take Buster. I'll ride in the ambulance." Ben Cady gave a long whistle that dropped the prairie dogs to safety, turned the hunters from their bottles to their guns, if only briefly, and brought Buster ambling toward us, his head dropping low and swinging from side to side as he came. Miss McCorquodale had now taken hold of my horse's reins and led him to us. Ben Cady seemed about to speak to her but did not. The girl asked the rancher to shorten the stirrups, and that done, he boosted her into my saddle.

"Do you mind if I take your horse, Captain?" she said, looking down from the thoroughbred. "Mine may not be fit."

"Are you sure you don't want to ride back in the ambulance, ma'am?" said Cady.

"I am quite sure. Will you tell my cousin that we are going back? Are you coming, Captain, or will I be riding alone?"

I mounted Buster. Ben Cady held the horse by the bridle. "Don't you think you should speak to him yourself, Miss?"

Miss McCorquodale cast her gaze toward the hunters. They were cheering Jonathan Weir as he went to his hands and knees and groped inside the bull's mouth, hacking out the tongue. The girl looked back. "I think it is very likely, Mr. Cady, that I shall never speak to him again." She turned the horse and gave it the rein, as I let Buster pick his way out of the prairie-dog town.

We rode off southeast, the direction we had come, passing around the original stand. The buffalo carcasses there were already being picked over by vultures. We observed a movement near one of the fallen buffalo; one of the dogs that had been injured and left behind was being stalked by a vulture. The bird walked after the dog, its wings spread menacingly. I shot the carrion bird and one other before they flew, and Miss McCorquodale dismounted and took up the dog. One of its hind legs had been broken. "We shall save it," she said and remounted with the dog in her lap. The mongrel was so small she could hold it easily, nestling it under her jacket so that it could hardly be seen. The dog ceased its whimpering after a short time. We rode a mile, at least, in silence, then the girl spoke, looking sharply across the plain. "I have been searching for some reason that gentlemen would take part in such butchery as this hunt, and I have come to the conclusion that you kill these buffalo because they look like Negro slaves."

"Miss McCorquodale, you have some strange notions concerning men, and women, and their relations with animals."

"Thank you. I do believe that men, and women, commit deeds on, with, and to animals that they secretly desire to do to one another."

"Then would you like to have men small and legless so that you might carry them in your lap?"

She whipped the horse and it galloped ahead. The buffalo horse shook its head and blew contemptuously at such behavior. We went after the thoroughbred and its high-strung mistress at a canter. The horse kept at a steady gait, for there was no hope of catching the blooded horse if Miss McCorquodale did not tire of the chase. The girl soon pulled up the thoroughbred. She pointed her crop in the direction we had been riding. A number of rounded white growths had appeared on the distant horizon—the tents of the hunt encampment that had been pitched that morning. Miss McCorquodale said:

"Why are we riding there?"

"I was told it was where you wanted to go."

"I do not. Did Mr. Cady tell you this? I am sick of Mr. Cady's interfering with my life. I want to go home—to the ranch. Which direction is that?"

"There," I said, and she looked toward the northeast and struck her horse and went off across the plains, away from the encampment. I rode after her. She did not pull up till the white domes of the camp tents had dropped beneath the horizon. Her horse was nearly winded, and we walked easily for a while. Miss McCorquodale soon left off her sullen silence and assumed a gay quiet humming, smiling at the jackrabbits that bounded away from us, laughing at the pudgy white clouds that drifted overhead, bearing an exact compass setting for our destination.

We soon came to the caprock and found a way down. I did not recognize the country, which was what the Texans called a shinnery, a large thicket of shin or scrub oak. The land was broken, marked by ragged draws and sinks and low, sharp-crested hills. The soil was leached by erosion, a rotten white alkali. The dust our horses raised tasted sharp and sour, and soon we came upon outcroppings of gypsum rock among marled extrusions of limestone. The plains, even at midafternoon, had been cooled by a west breeze, but here the air was dead and hot and dusty. Water now became a concern. The girl had emptied her canteen, and mine held a cup, if that, of tepid water. We attempted to ride along below the caprock, to search for a spring there, but the draws and arroyos that sluiced down from the plains made our progress tortuous, and soon we were forced to turn east, to follow these ragged ditches away from the plain to flatter terrain. But the landscape did not become easier, and, if anything, the shinnery thickened, the scrub oaks making a maze so that we could not see more than twenty yards in any direction. We were not in danger but near its border, not lost but not so comfortable that we could pretend to be. The shinnery could be ridden out of, and neither we nor the horses would suffer much from a dry camp, and the Caballo could be reached before nightfall tomorrow, but only if our ride went free of trouble. Injury to a horse, wild animals, Indians, a mishap as minor as a scorpion sting might mean death. But the girl's inexperience blinkered her, and in her quest for adventure she scoffed that my caution might be fear.

"Here, hold these a moment," she said, looping her reins over her mount's head and giving them and the dog to me. Thus freed, she stood on her saddle, balancing there like a circus rider. The thoroughbred laid back its ears but, with Buster offering quiet encouragement, held steady, even when Miss Mc-Corquodale cried out: "Look! Look here! There's a woman! Hallo! Hallo!" She began waving her arms, which lost her her balance, and she fell acrobatically back in the saddle. "Oh no, I think I may have frightened her away!" She took the reins and ran her horse through the brush.

The ground began to rise and clear, and soon we had ridden above the shinnery, to the crest of the low hill where the woman had been seen. We dismounted and found the woman's footprints and a walking stick—but we did not see the woman or where she could have gone. There was nothing around us but a sea of scrub oak and an archipelago of low, sharp-crested hills such as we stood on. To the distant north could be seen a projected battlement of the *llano estacado,* but in every other direction there was scrub oak and broken terrain to the horizon. We followed the footprints and, just when it seemed we had lost them on the hill's rocky spine, came on a footpath that led down through the brush. We mounted and followed the path and after a quarter mile came into a man-made clearing. We saw at the back of the clearing a dugout, a low earth mound with a metal chimney protruding from it. Wisps of smoke came from the chimney. We dismounted and went toward the dugout. Now a corral and animals could be seen in the brush behind the dugout. Tools and implements hung from the trees or were set among them, the metal dull and rusted, the wood weathered and unpainted, so that they were by ill-care camouflaged. We stood at the top of the dugout stairs, pieces of slats fitted across steps that had been spaded through the topsoil and hewn into the rock below that. Miss McCorquodale called out, and a skirt hem appeared in the frame doorway and then a woman's hand reached around and then the woman replied:

"Oh, I am so shamed to have run that I can scarce face the light. I didn't think you was Injuns, Miss, I don't know what I was thinking, I had never seen a girl standing on a horse. Can you and Mister come on down, Miss? Oh, it is so good to see visitors here and I act like such a little fool."

The skirt and pale arm withdrew, and Miss McCorquodale and I descended the steps. We came into the gloom of the dugout and for a few moments could see nothing but the sharp traces of objects set near the stairs that were the room's only source of light. The air in the dugout was cool and pleasantly moist and the odor of the earth was cool and moist as well, both rich and clean. There came an iron slap from the stove and a red finger of ember crossed the dark room to a kerosene lamp, which then flamed with waxy light. The woman brought the lamp to a table in the center of the room, near us. By the low light of the lamp we could see how young the woman should have been, not how old she would look when we would ascend to daylight. We were seated and our eyes adjusted to the gloom, and we came to imagine the full objects that the lamplight only traced. The dugout was a single room, without corners, it seemed, though the circle of light may have given it this oval form. The walls were faced with graying plank and the ceiling formed by thick latticework of saplings held aloft by crossbeams thirty feet long that required two standing beams each for support. The floor was earthen and had the spring of thick pile carpet. The table and chairs we occupied were handmade, ingeniously carved and pieced together from the scrub oak and china trees of the shinnery. As the young woman made busy about us, Miss McCorquodale and I sat easy in the dugout's silence, content with the strange aura of this place, that what might have seemed in concept so near a grave was in fact peaceful and satisfying. The young woman moved around the dugout in mysterious operations, as plates and cups and dishes of candy and bowls of dried and pickled fruit and jugs of cider and cooled tea collected on the table before us.

The young woman began to speak in a low, rustling voice that took on, as if mimicking, the similar whispers of her skirt that came and went with her walking.

The young woman's name was Eddie Bird, we learned from Miss McCorquodale's questioning. She was nineteen and had been married for four years, the last two or so having been spent on this range. Mr. Bird had been with the Texas Rángers when they had married but had shortly resigned, and they had left the settlements around Fort Worth and come to western Texas. Mr. Bird had first tried ranching and when that had failed had taken up buffalo hunting with a partner named Bob Johns. They had made this dugout during that time. But the buffalo were soon hunted out in the breaks, and Bob Johns, who was unmarried, left for the hunt on the plains, Mr. Bird choosing not to follow. One day a rider appeared and said that Mr. Bird could earn twenty dollars a month by riding line for the Caballo Ranch, then being formed along the east rim of the caprock, on the grounds of the old Comanche war trail to Mexico. Mr. Bird, the man said, could as well hunt all the buffalo and wild game he could find on the line. So Mr. Bird had taken up riding line and hunting where his duties led him. This explained Mr. Bird's absence, Eddie Bird told us. The nearest line camp was thirty miles, and that circuit and the layover took a week. Mr. Bird had been gone now ten days—she showed us the stick she notched for each day—and she thought he must have come on buffalo and made a stand, for being so overdue. She had been making her daily pilgrimage to the top of the hill to look for Mr. Bird, she said, when Miss McCorquodale had spied her.

"Oh, the loneliness is sometimes awful," Eddie Bird said, "and I do worry and worry when Mr. Bird is overdue, Miss and Mister, but oh how worse it was when Mr. Bird and Mr. Johns was buffalo hunting. Then they would be forced to pack up all the robes and hides they had taken in the fall and cart them in a wagon to the settlements. They would be gone for weeks and weeks. Every evening I would take long strolls out to the hills and through the shinnery in the direction they had gone, thinking I might meet them. But every night I would come home disappointed, so sad and uneasy. Every day I was on giving up in despair but would go out one more time in hopes of meeting them. Then one evening I had walked near three miles from home and I was looking out over the shinnery and I saw a wagon jogging along. Oh, I knew it was them. Mr. Bird saw me standing on the hill and he gave a call and got out of the wagon and started toward me, both of us running. We went down into the scrub and missed each other and had to hunt around in the brush some time before we met. Oh, Miss and Mister, I was laughing and he was crying. I had never seen him that way before. Oh, it was such a joy for us to see one another agin."

Miss McCorquodale had brought in the injured dog, and now that the animal smelled food its trembling head appeared from between the buttons of Miss McCorquodale's jacket, an appearance that caused Eddie Bird to laugh as she may have laughed when she met her husband. The two women spent some time tending to the dog's injured leg, making a pallet for it on the floor and giving it food and water. I went out and unsaddled the horses and took them to the corral and watered and fed them as well. When I returned, Mrs. Bird was speaking of how she fought her loneliness. "Oh yes, Miss, I have tried to keep pets, and a pup like him would be best, but by the nature of how we live we cannot have animals indoors and every pup or thing I would catch would be taken off by the coyotes or the birds or some old loafer wolf." The young woman laughed and bright tears came to her eyes. Miss McCorquodale gently tried to move the young woman to other matters, but her consideration was unnecessary. Eddie Bird's sadness came and went like trailing skirts in the dark. "Oh, I was never so lonely in the daytime. Mr. Bird had given me his Winchester rifle to protect myself when he went away. My, I have learned to love this gun, Miss. I have practiced with it every day, and Mr. Bird gave me training with targets. I hardly ever miss a shot, I swear—would you like to come and see some shooting? Oh, please do, Miss and Mister, I love to show off my shooting! We can have a match! Come, please, I love a match, but Mr. Bird is prouder than I and don't banter on my skill."

Eddie Bird strapped a rifle over her shoulder and I took up a box of ammunition, and Miss McCorquodale and I followed the young woman through the brush to a dry creekbed that pierced the thicket and opened it a few yards beyond its steep banks. We went down the sandy bed a ways, then Mrs. Bird halted us, pointing farther on to a row of targets set like gapped teeth across the bed. The targets looked like fence posts dug into the sand, but shorter and squat, and when Eddie Bird began to fire at them, they could be seen by the dust and their disintegration to be some sort of stone. Miss McCorquodale and I took no part in the shooting, but we would have pronounced Mrs. Bird champion in any case. She did not miss a shot. We left the guns and went down the creekbed to the targets, which were gypsum rock, as I had imagined. In lifting one I saw that it had been carved and the carving was that of a man's head and face, or the half of the head and face that had not been shot away.

"Oh, there is nothing I love like the carving of gyp rock, Mister, it has given me so much pleasure. I work on it every day that Mr. Bird is gone, though I don't do it so much when he is home. These here," she said of the sculpted targets, "I have carved with the faces of Injuns and badmen, but of the other things, most often I follow the shape of the rock and carve out things I see there. I am shamed sometimes when Mr. Bird chides me that they don't look like anything a tall, but toys and baubles and child's things. Would you care to see some, Miss and Mister?"

"We would like to see them very much," said Miss McCorquodale.

We followed Mrs. Bird back up through the brush, going

from one point to the next, without purpose it would have seemed, for the scrub oak was woven dense as a mat, but the young woman had placed her carvings among the brush and knew the exact location of each piece. As she had said, they were things that were like no forms on earth—faces, animals, familiar objects that were in one way or another changed to follow the rock. Mrs. Bird had set them out in the brush, hidden from everyone but herself, to ward off Indians and badmen and evil spirits.

The sun had reached midafternoon by now. I left the women and went back to the corral and saddled the horses and returned with them to the clearing. In a few moments the women came up from the dugout, each carrying a rolled buffalo rug, which we tied onto the saddles. Eddie Bird went back to the dugout and emerged with a cloth saddlebag of meat and dried fruit and a poor bread made of flour ground from peas. She filled our canteens with water and offered us other gifts that we refused. In return for the victuals and the robes, she accepted the injured dog from Miss McCorquodale. It was a six-hour ride to Caballo, the woman thought, more likely ten, and she told us of a roaring spring just under the shoulder of the plains, the formation we had observed from the hill, a place where she and her husband had often made camp during buffalo hunts.

We rode as the young woman had directed us, making north along the creekbed where we had shot targets. After less than an hour we heard the roaring springs and shortly came out of the creekbed. Before us spread a natural park. Cloistered by the dense shinnery and the cut of the creekbed, we had ridden to the base of the *llano estacado* without warning. Our vantage was the foot of a box canyon: the walls of the plains stood around us, forming a deep amphitheater that stretched to the west. The canyon floor was covered with an expanse of river sand, the sand many-colored: a spectrum from the faded lemon yellows of the dry banks to the dull ocher brick of the stream cut. The sand had been terraced and sculpted as the river had fallen from its May crest to the curling silver ribbon now fed from the spring. Each intervening storm had left its cursive mark beveled in the sand, and each terrace of sand was a different color: we turned our horses and rode into the canyon, like vandals scarring some exquisite design in marbled bas-relief. As we drew near the spring we came upon luxuriant stands of cottonwood, wild china, and willows, and, clutched to an island in the streambed, a solitary locust tree, black as char against the fair sands. Cattails and salt grass and wild grape and wild balsam lined the riverbed. In the arroyos grew hackberry and cedar shrubs and wild currants and broom weed and Scotch thistle and wild morning glory and wild larkspur and wild verbena and more shrubs and grasses and weeds and vines than I knew names for. Here we found a wild disorder in the profusion of flora, as if nature, perhaps in atonement for the forbidding constancy of the shinnery, had chosen to set aside this corner in chaos and broken pattern. We dismounted and fell to the sand and sank our faces in the cool clear stream water. Our spirits were washed as well by the grace and the sanctuary of the canyon.

The spring roared at us from up the canyon. As we drew near it, the ground hummed under our feet, the air tingled, the cottonwood leaves shivered like gray moth wings. We came upon a thick bank of willow and cottonwood and live oak and found a bed of Bermuda grass nearby and unsaddled and tethered our horses there. We started out to climb the plain wall to locate the spring and the source of its power, but instead, just beyond the shelter of the trees, found a pool filled by the water cascading through the cliff rocks. We removed our dusty clothes, and Miss McCorquodale unfurled her dark hair, and we bathed in the icy water. When our limbs were numb from the cold we lay on the sun-warmed sands and the flat satiny rocks around the pool that had brushed hollows worn in them that fit the contours of our bodies. We bathed again and lay naked on the rocks and sunned till our skin warmed and pinkened. Time should have been spent, perhaps, concerned with our safety, for we were unclothed, unarmed under the frowning caprock, the *llano* rising over us like an enemy's wall, but we bathed and sunned without any such concern. When the shadow of the caprock drew over us we returned to our clothes and addressed our hunger. We unpacked the saddlebags, then the girl went to gather wood, while I took my carbine and walked up the canyon, into the breeze. I found no game but came on a hole that had catfish. I made a spear by tying a knife to a cedar stick and took two of these fish and skinned them, saving the flat, wide-snouted heads with their drooping, fleshy whiskers for the girl's amusement and mine. When I returned to the pool I found the girl strapping saddlebags, buffalo robes, and a bundle of wood to her back.

"I've found a place for us," she said. "Up there."

We divided the cargo and climbed up through the rocks to the base of the caprock. A shelf had been formed at the junction of the caprock and the sloped canyon wall, and we went easily along it to the cave the girl had found. The cave was no more than ten feet deep—I could stand erect only at its entrance—but we would be sheltered from wind or rain here and could look out over the canyon and not be seen ourselves. I returned to the canyon floor and moved the horses to the base of the wall, so that they might not be discovered, and tethered and hobbled them for the night. I stashed the saddles and bridles away from the horses and went back up to the cave. The girl had started a fire, which soon burned down to coals, and we roasted the oily red flesh of the catfish till it was white and tender.

We ate these steaks with the crumbling bread made from the poor flour and boiled coffee and afterwards looked out toward the arroyos and the berry vines we had passed. But neither of us could manage to leave the cave, and we spoke of the juicy berries for breakfast. We spread the buffalo robes on the cave floor and lay on them gazing out over the canyon. The girl fed the fire dry twigs, but as the air darkened she let the fire die. The moon had risen in the afternoon, but we only saw it as the fire went dark. Bats and nightbirds came with the dying light, crisscrossing the moon in their jerked hunt for insects rising in the dark. The roar of the springs had not diminished with night-fall, but we had grown accustomed to it and imagined we could hear the whirr and rasp of crickets and cicadas down the canyon wall. The girl turned to lie on her back and noticed weather marks and discolorations and patterns on the cave wall. She took up a half-burned stick from the fire and began to draw on the rock with its charred point. She fashioned the marks on the stone into animals and designs that might have been the drawings of Indians.

"Would you think," she said when the moon had risen and cast the wall and her drawings into shadow, "if you came upon this cave and these drawings, that they were the work of primitives?"

"No."

"Oh why not?"

"Because if I rubbed them they would disappear."

The girl smiled and tucked her chin over her hands and studied the canyon.

The moon was well risen now and had lost its yellow plumpness; it had diminished and become flat and bright and cold. The canyon was lit in this white light, the surrounding hills glazed like china; all the trees and rocks and shrubs on the hills were first observed by their shadows, eerie hieroglyphs that, as the moon went across the sky, shifted like pools of ink spreading across a parchment page. The river sand blazed in this light, and the stream lay under it, a snake of glittering ice. The girl turned her head, and her face was caught in shadows.

"Do you think there are any Indians near here now, this very night?"

"I hope not."

"Would they kill us?"

"We might wish they would."

"Indeed. Mrs. Bird told me—while you were saddling the horses—how once Indians tried to kill her. It was a year or so ago, I think, when Mr. Bird was still buffalo hunting and they had camped in some canyon, not this one, some place more distant. They had been on the hunt for weeks, moving around and around till Mrs. Bird was not certain where she was. It was late one afternoon and cloudy and misty and dark and dismal, and Mrs. Bird was alone at the camp. She heard a slight noise not far away, and she went up on a hill nearby and looked up the streambed and through the fog she saw dozens of Indians creeping down toward her. She went back down the hill to the camp, as if she had seen nothing, but once there took up her rifle and ran down the stream away from the Indians as fast as she could. After a mile she came to a large grass-filled basin several hundred yards across. She went to the distant side of this basin and found a hiding place in the tall grass and waited. Soon the form of a man appeared on the edge of this basin coming toward her, from the direction of the camp. She knew it was an Indian searching for her. She could see he was large and had a savage face. She drew a bead on the man. As he drew quite near she squeezed the trigger. But the gun did not fire. Perhaps she had not put bullets in it as she had thought. In any event, the Indian turned and went away without finding her. The next morning Mrs. Bird rose and crept back to camp. There she found her husband sitting over the campfire, distraught and sleepless. At the sight of her he leapt up and cried and held her with joy. Mrs. Bird told him of the Indians, but Mr. Bird had not seen any. They went to the streambed where Mrs. Bird had first seen the Indians—there were no tracks there. Mrs. Bird told her husband of the savage-looking Indian who had come to the basin looking for her and how she had tried to shoot him but her rifle had not fired. She showed Mr. Bird where the Indian had walked, but they found no tracks but those Mr. Bird had made looking for her. This puzzled her husband, she told me, and he grew thoughtful and stroked her hair that morning in a gentle way. Later that day they broke camp and returned home. That is the story of how the Indians came to kill Mrs. Bird, as she told it to me. What do you make of it?"

"That her solitude had maddened her."

"Mad?" said the girl. "Perhaps." The girl lowered her head. Her voice had grown heavy. "I think the old rancher—Mr. Cady—was right about me."

"In what way?"

"I do not think I want to be a captive Indian squaw, nor the wife of a cowboy. I think I would like to marry someone civilized, like you, Philip Chapman. Pity you already are." She yawned. "I am not really sleepy. You once said you would follow me onto the plain. Will you? Oh, let's do something we shouldn't do, Philip! We'll be leaving here soon, you know, and then we must be so respectable."

We rose and went down the canyon wall. We bridled the horses only, to ride bareback. The girl had chosen the slower, steadier buffalo horse, though she did not seem to know the difference between the two, for she cried out that we must race and ran her horse out of the grove. I gave her some head start, then let the thoroughbred go. We flew out of the grove, leaping five yards down to the riverbed. I was thrown from the horse but landed easily on the sand and held the reins, so that I was remounted before the horse recovered itself. The girl and the buffalo horse had disappeared into the stark white-and-black landscape, but the thoroughbred turned up the canyon, and we quickly came upon their tracks. I gave the blooded horse its head and hugged its mane. The horse went smoothly over the sand. We came to the end of the canyon and saw several hundred yards ahead the girl and the buffalo horse going into a heavily thicketed draw that ascended through the caprock to the plains. The thoroughbred went for the draw recklessly and dived into the thicket. I lay on the horse's neck and in a matter of seconds, we shot out of the draw onto the plains, landing there with amazement, for the *llano* lay before us like a sea of ice. Moonlight had spread a shining tent over the sky. The buffalo horse and the girl went like a ghostly ship across the plains, sailing at an incredible speed. The thoroughbred was frantic at the unworldly sheen spread over the plains, but its head was turned and though at first it shied and bucked against the black hole its shadow cut in the moonlit earth, we were soon after the distant horse and rider. We gained on the girl and buffalo horse quickly, for the buffalo horse had grown tired and would not be ridden out. The thoroughbred drew up behind and then alongside the buffalo horse. I reached out and grasped the girl around the waist and lifted her away from her mount. The girl threw her legs behind me, but one or both of us lost our balance and we began to slip from the horse's barrel. We tried to leap running to the ground but with little success. We struck the ground hard for the second time that day, and I, for one, lay for a while gazing at stars I had never seen before. When I sat up I saw the girl lying nearby, laughing, as if she had caused our fall for the laugh. The buffalo horse stood a few yards away. The thoroughbred had run on, whinnying to the other horse that they could be free now—*come along!* But the buffalo horse stamped and would not leave its riders, no matter how mad they might be. After a time, we caught the horses and rode back to the cave, the girl astride the thoroughbred, as if she had known which horse was which all along.

We saw the rider at dawn. He had not come up the canyon as we but had ridden from the south across the *llano*. He stood mounted on the rim of the caprock looking across the canyon at us. He wore a flat-brimmed hat—that was all I could see of him. He turned his horse and rode back from the precipice to a place to descend into the canyon. During the time he was not in sight, the girl and I dressed and rolled the buffalo robes and put her out of sight behind them. I left the carbine with her and took the pistol and went down the canyon wall. The rider had emerged from an arroyo across the way. I waited for him at the head of the willow grove. He rode across the riverbed, studying our hoofmarks in the sand. He pulled up at a point down the riverbank, directly below me. The man was small as a youth, with the shrunken face and body of an old man, his hat and clothes outsized. Whatever his age, life had wasted him. His eyes were scars of gray, his mouth had turned inward, the flesh of nose and the horns of his ears worn away.

I held the pistol slack in my hand that the man could see it, but it did not interest him. By his accent he was from Tennessee or Kentucky:

"They took you for dead. There has been a corn train attacked over yonder by Salt Creek. Comanches, they have tole me. I will saddle the horses while you fetch the Miss. We can ride to Caballo after that."

I returned to the cave, and the girl and I packed the saddlebags and tied them up with the robes. By the time we had descended to the riverbed, the man stood waiting, our horses saddled. We rode out of the canyon due east for several miles and then turned north. By noon I began to recognize landmarks from the Caballo range, and by midafternoon we had come across the first Army outposts that had been set around the ranch headquarters. During this time little conversation was made, though Miss McCorquodale did establish the rider's identity. She had asked by what authority we were riding with the man, and he responded as if delivering a lesson by rote:

"There has been a corn train attacked over yonder by Salt Creek, Miss. Comanches have been said to have done it. They have killed the teamsters. They figgered you all for dead as well."

"What I meant was—are you an employee of the ranch?"

"I was tole to come for you."

"I see," said the girl and pondered her saddle pommel. "And how did you know where to find us?"

"My missus said where you would be."

"Then you are Mr. Bird?"

"I am Emmett Bird," the man said.

We came onto the ranch headquarters from the south, an open approach, and saw that there was great activity surrounding the stone house. As we drew near I recognized the wagons and horses and men from the hunting party and took this to be their return from the *llano*. Instead, they had been warned of the Indian attack yesterday and had ridden throughout the night, arriving at the headquarters early this morning. The turmoil surrounding wagons and horses and gear was not their unpacking but their readying to quit Texas, the West, and any other Indian country while their scalps were attached. After a farewell, Miss McCorquodale parted from us and rode into the hubbub about the stone house. She was noticed by a young man who was stuffing buffalo mops into a bright-yellow valise. There were too many mops for the case, and the balls of wool kept springing out when the young man tried to close the lid. He wiped his brow and looked up from his labors:

"Oh, hello there, Mackie. I say, we thought you were dead or something. Perhaps you should tell someone you're not."

Emmett Bird pulled his horse back as the girl rode into the arms of the thirty or so men and women around the stone house. Their celebration at her safe return might have been the milling and lowing of cattle for his interest in it. He turned his horse and rode away.

I went to the regimental camp, or where it had once stood. Every tent had been dropped, lying in place like discarded napkins crumpled on a banquet table. A detail of men was coming along folding and packing the tents and loading them into wagons. There were fewer than two dozen men performing this detail. The others, I was told, were in line around the ranch headquarters. During our absence MacSwain had returned from Washington, with fresh orders to make war on the Indians. The timing of the attack on the corn train had been exact; MacSwain had taken personal command of investigating the crime, placing a large detachment of men and officers at the site of the massacre. His war now was certain.

I took one of the men from the detail and he secured fresh mounts from the *caballado* and we rode in an easterly direction, where the country was thought to be free of Indians. The massacre site, on a dry tributary of the Pease River called Salt Creek, lay twenty miles away, and we made half that distance before we camped without fire and slept and stood guard in turn. We broke camp at three and were into our men at dawn. We arrived at MacSwain's command tent as a large scout was returning from tracking the Indians. Amidst the confusion of the party dismounting, I chose not to report to MacSwain immediately but had one of the pickets lead me to the site of the attack. This was in an area, fifty by twenty yards; it had been roped off and guards positioned around it. Within the cordon I saw several Texans, men from the ranch. Squatting beyond these men, alone, was Ben Cady, studying some object he held in his hand. I did not see the corpses clearly till I had gone past the rope into the area. The bodies had not been covered or tended to in any fashion. They lay as they had fallen. There were ten or so men, ten or so lumps of flesh: the teamsters had been so hacked and disfigured they were scarcely recognizable as human beings. The bodies were nude. From twenty to fifty arrows had been shot into each body—their torsos bristled with arrows like pins in a cushion. Every man had been scalped and his skull crushed. There had been two Indian guides and a Negro drover; their scalps had been cut away but left at their sides. Except for the Indians, who were the least mutilated of the party, every man had been emasculated, their noses and ears hacked off, their eyes gouged out. The Negro's genitals had been stuffed in his mouth. The men's bellies had been slashed open and their entrails removed. Muscles and tendons had been slashed from their arms and legs. Two men lay on beds of ashes. Their bodies were contorted, unlike those of the others, who had been mutilated after death. The bodies of two other men were tied together; the ground around them was littered with hundreds of cartridge shells. Stretching beyond the cordon was the corn train—six wagons—grain and fodder spilling from split sacks and destroyed beds. In another direction, also beyond the cordon, was a detail of soldiers digging a burial trench. They were near completed, only their heads and shoulders showing aboveground. The soldiers talked in muffled tones as they worked. Steam or ground fog rose from the earth they piled from the trench. Inside the cordoned area two men were going from body to body. One was an artist, who carried a large pad and was sketching the corpses; the other man took notes on a smaller pad. I could see beyond that Mac-Swain and his staff had emerged from the command tent. Mac-Swain stretched his arms as if he had just waked. One of his staff yawned. The burial detail climbed from the trench and began to move the bodies into it. A pair of the men lifted the bodies by grasping the arrows, using them as handles to carry the corpses. The flesh pulled away from the hickory shafts, further mutilating the bodies. MacSwain spoke to his aide, who sharply reprimanded the men. The gravediggers then slid their arms under the dead men, cradling them, as if they were carrying sleeping children.

FOUR

THE morning gun fired on the first note of reveille. Somewhere in the dark a voice sang out with our first call. Outside the tent the ground shook under the men's boots, the sergeant crying out, "Fall in, boys, do fall in!" Then came the litany of names and answering cries, each man's voice of different timbre and each cry coming from a different rank, some far, some near, to left and right, and beneath our troop's rollcall came those of the other companies of the regiment down the line, distant, left and right, the muffled name, the sharper reply, so that we were like a vast choir singing out some primitive chant. Then came the call to mess, and the early-morning dark crackled with campfires, and pots and pans and field trays clashed, and cooks swore at orderlies and orderlies cursed servants and servants pled their woes to their masters. Beyond, the horses and mules could be heard, stamping and nickering, for they knew the calls as well as any man. As the men and animals clamored to be fed, the officers stirred, their tents lighted by tallow field can-

129

dles, glowing in the dark like jack-o'-lanterns. Then the bugle—the voice that told us when to eat, sleep, march, worship, assemble, pack, mount, fight, retreat, fear and hate those of our own kind—blew the general call, and orders were cried out along the line, "Pack up! Pack it up, boys!" and chaos reigned around the fires, everything that was up came down, what was flat was rolled, what was strung out was coiled, the jointed folded, the small fitted into something larger and that fitted into something larger yet. Then boots and saddles was blown, and the horses were brought to their tack and along the line blanket and leather slapped their withers and bit and buckle and halter ring struck their heads. To horse was sounded, and the men in the company formed their horses in ranks before their commanding officer, each trooper standing at attention to the left of the head of his mount. And from up and down the line, from the six companies assembled over a quarter of a mile, came the cries from the commanding officers, "Prepare to mount!" and each trooper turned to his mount's near side and placed his left boot in the stirrup and with the call to mount swung himself into the saddle, woe unto any trooper who was not in time, for he forwent the service of his horse for a half-day's march, and only that if he was lucky. Two sharp punctuated calls were sounded, a rest beat, and came a single trailing echo of the first staccato notes, and the companies came about into a slow walk, moving out in a column of fours, at forward march.

We went out of the Caballo as we had come in, winding through the cottonwood arcade of the false river, crossing the narrow valley and climbing the low shale barrier that formed its western boundary. Colonel James John MacSwain rode at the head of our column, turning in his saddle at the crest of the ridge to look back on his massed regiment, then plunging on. The four buglers who rode next pulled out of line and stood in review. As we passed they sounded the plaintive refrain of "The Girl I Left Behind Me." Then came the mounted troops, the crack F Company commanded by Major Hoeme, then the blue-and-yellow guidons of A, D, E, and B Troops. As each troop passed the buglers, their commanding officers pulled out to exchange salutes with their men. The men returned the salutes and called out to their officers, the heads of the passing horses tossing like waves as they fought against the slow march. From up and down the line came the music of hooves settling into the shale, of horses blowing, the rhythmic creak of saddle leather, the slap of carbine scabbard against saddle, the clank of mess kits against flank and shoulder, the clash and jingle of saber and stirrup and spur. And from the men, hard and brown in their faded blue tunics, their slouch hat brims turned up against the morning breeze, came laughter and low talk and bits of singing to the bugler's call. Then came the scouts, Devereaux, their captain, in his floppy white sombrero, the Tonkaways, squat sullen men, their long black hair flowing beneath bandeaux of calico and buckskin, and the Negro-featured Seminoles who answered to the names of Woman Heart and Eagle Flying and Jerry Half Man. Then came the drums and their beat of our cadence and behind them the infantry chanting to their sergeant's ribald calls. Next the mincing, narrow-hoofed mules, their packs already beginning to slip, their drovers cursing each by name, followed by the wagon train—baggage wagons, ambulances, cavalry forges, Gatling carts, by their names Doughenties, Wilsons, Ruckers. And at last, the rear guard, Company I, rode past, the horses' legs and chests already grayed by the column's dust; tomorrow they would be shifted to advance and some other troop would take their place, last in line. Then the last rider, the commander of the rear guard, came to the crest of the low western wall of the valley. He turned his horse to look back toward the Caballo stone house and the ranch corrals and the meandering grove of trees that some legend gatherer had said followed the course of an underground river. A single smudged blur of light came from one of the windows of the stone house; by the corrals the officer could see the dark shapes of cowboys moving among their horses.

There was nothing else to show that they or any men had ever been here before.

The Second Cavalry rode in a southwesterly line that would have taken us to Fort Pulgas had we pursued it. MacSwain had ordered that the pace be made easy, to save the men and animals and wagons for the rigors ahead. The march was further eased by our knowledge of the terrain of the southeastern escarpment of the *llano estacado*. We knew when to ride in the breaks below the caprock and when better time would be made on the plains. And we knew the natural roadways that would take us up and down. We rode free of the fear of Indians as well, for, despite the attack on the wagon train at Salt Creek, we were in such vigorous condition, in morale and training and equipment and supply, that we knew of no tribe that would be a threat to us. Throughout the summer the horses and mules had been grazed and fleshed out, shod and groomed and rested. All saddles and bridles and accouterments, all wagons and horse furniture had been overhauled. Ammunition and rations and forage and bright fresh canvas had been shipped in from supply depots to the east. The men had been drilled and submitted to rigid camp discipline. Target ranges had been laid out and carbine practice held every day. Company, platoon, and squad movements, both in column and in line, mounted and dismounted, had been practiced. The officers had been briefed and map-trained and had spent countless hours in paper exercises. The enemy and the terrain—the Comanches and the *llano estacado*—had been studied, every conceivable detail of land and foe set to memory. Plans for victory had been drawn up, and as we rode effortlessly across the plains, we could see no flaws in them.

After four days' march we came upon Blanco Canyon, from the northeast, gazing down into it from the *llano* rim, a prospect new to us. This being an hour before sundown, the color and slant of the evening light made the valley seem like a strange place, though the landmarks were undeniable—three miles down the canyon, to our left, could be seen the cottonwood grove, the winding creek, above them the red bluffs, where we had camped and where the Comanches had stampeded our horses the previous spring. Before us sat the table butte, the creek arcing around its far side; and upcanyon, to the right, stood Mount Blanco, where our quartet had ridden onto the plains and the Comanche ambush. Nor were the surfeit of our encampment, the sloth at guard, the ensuing attack, panic, tragedy, and our anger to be forgotten. We rode down into the valley and made our way to the foot of Mount Blanco, where we found the graves of Fred Bass and the trooper Vining, or what remained of them. I led a small detail and we collected the bones that had been scattered and piled other rocks on them. The regiment was then brought up in ranks near the graves and a ceremony performed over the scavenged remains of our comrades. Words were spoken by MacSwain, so low that few could hear, then the regiment fired a volley in unison, near four hundred guns sounding as one. With that we rode up Rio Blanco a ways and camped there and the following day rode deeper into the canyon where it narrowed to less than a mile across. At midday we came to a fork in the river and sent scouts up both branches. The party sent left soon returned, reporting a dead end, a box canyon with a spring of fresh water, good grass, and plentiful wood. We sent riders out after the first scout, firing signals for their return, while the main column went into the box canyon. There we pitched our tents and began unloading wagons and otherwise preparing the area to be our permanent supply camp. Our second campaign on the *llano estacado* had begun.

Early the following afternoon, the forty-odd officers of the Second and another dozen or so of auxiliary status—surgeons, scouts, and sutlers—gathered around the command tent. During the summer MacSwain had purchased a conical Sibley tent, round and high-crowned like an Indian lodge. The front flaps of the tent had been turned back so that its effect was that of a stage, with MacSwain holding forth front and center. In supporting roles were marshaled his staff, maps, charts of the regiment's order of battle, and the veterans of last year's campaign. MacSwain moved among these tools and minions as Hamlet flitted from Polonius to Laertes to Ophelia, no one of them existing but to complete his fractured personality. And it was so, in his role as commander, that MacSwain seemed to be a whole man. Without his power over other men, he was partial, fragmented, without cement for his being. The summer away from the saddle had retrieved his health or the appearance of it. He had not fleshed out but had ordered new uniforms cut, their close fit speaking of his wasting frame but not mocking it, as had his sagging tunic and britches. There was color in his cheeks that was not all rouge, his hair had been darkened at the temples but not so much that those new to the command would notice, and he had regained such energy that he could stand for hours and not display the pain that sitting caused him. Beneath this mask of health, his eyes snapped with intelligence. He spoke with wit and presented his thoughts clearly as he unveiled his winter strategy.

"In the Shenandoah Campaign, we subdued the Rebs by burning their crops and driving off their cattle and chopping down their trees and beshitting their springs and razing their barns and corrals and breaking their machines to bits. Without food or water or shelter, the enemy was defeated and fell. We will pursue this policy in Texas, to bring the Indian to his knees. But here, in Texas, nature had done much of our pillage for us—nature and the buffalo hunter. God has made us a place that boasts fewer of His blessings than did the charred Shenandoah after Phil Sheridan had ridden Rienzi through it!" These remarks were met variously with laughter, applause, cheers, and ribald comments. "Our wasteland is the *llano estacado*. It is here that the Comanches of Bad Hand and Tehana Storm are trapped. On this plain there is not food or water or grain or shelter to sustain them. By the onset of winter the buffalo will be gone, the grass will be gone, the water will be gone, and the plain will become a sheet of ice. The Indians will feed and drink on a winter-long blast of ice and by spring will creep onto the reservation. But we must not rely on nature alone to do our work. If the Indians do not submit to our will, then we must go up onto the plain and punish them." MacSwain pointed out positions on the map with the full fingers of his left hand. "Previously our forces have merely ringed the Comanches in defensive positions. Forts Cobb and Sill in the east. Dodge and Lyon in the north. Union and Pascal in the west. And the Second Cavalry in Pulgas in the south. This strategy has had all the success of storing water in an overturned cup. But now the days of waiting are done. Now, with Miles and DuBois guarding the north and west, with Buell and Davidson hovering here in the east, we, the Second, shall strike upward from the south, closing like talons around the *llano,* plucking the savages from their sanctuary!" And MacSwain moved the stubbed, twisted fingers of his right hand up into the palm of his left, and the officers cheered.

After the excitement had fallen, there were questions. One young officer asked, "If there is no water, grass, wood, grain, game, or shelter on this plain—how shall we survive?"

The mood was such that we laughed. MacSwain held out his arms, and quiet was restored. "There is danger, we must recognize that, but it can be done. The command will be divided into two squadrons. These squadrons will probe out onto the plains from its borders, on the west along the New Mexican line here and on the east along the caprock, from whence we have just come. New Mexico shall sustain our left flank, the Texas ranches the right. Grass, water, and wood can be found in these border regions. In this manner the two forces will move northward, meeting on the Canadian River. The Comanches will be trapped on the *llano estacado.* Then the two forces, united, will descend against the Indian on the open plain and will find and destroy him there. A third force will perform a rearguard action in this area of the plain, where we are now camped, preventing the Comanche from escaping south to Mexico. The Second will be divided in this manner," and MacSwain scrawled the troop numbers of the left and right squadrons on a board and assigned commanders. MacSwain would command the left column, Major Clous would lead the right. I was assigned command of the rearguard. "Gentlemen, I will propose a toast, if we can pillage the surgeon's chest." These arrangements were made, and we raised our glasses. MacSwain's bright eyes went from man to man, till he had gazed at everyone in the tent. Then he cried out his toast to Mars: "Gentlemen, we are at last and truly at war!"

Later that day assignments were detailed by MacSwain's staff. I was informed that I would be relieved of the command of I Troop, which would march with Major Clous. I was to remain at our present camp with a company of infantry, to await the arrival of a new troop of cavalry that had been formed at Fort Richardson and was on the march here. When this troop arrived I was to train them and to scout the area from Yellow House Canyon to a point east of our present position. I was then to follow MacSwain along the New Mexico border or Clous as he made his way up the jagged eastern border of the *llano estacado,* as exigencies dictated.

The divided Second marched out the day following. I mounted a scout and rode with the regiment up on the plains and remained with them till noon, when they split into squadrons, MacSwain marching to the west, Clous to the east. Our scout remained in place till the rearguard of each column had been swallowed by the horizon, then we turned back to our camp. The next days were spent scouting the ravines and canyons

Lords of the Plain

within a day's ride of our position, but we found no Indians nor
any signs of them. Meanwhile, the foot soldiers were set con-
structing a rudimentary supply base. After that we hunted,
read, and drilled, waiting for the approaching troop, which was
to be designated K Company.

Not more than a week after the regiment's departure, one of
the mounted pickets on the caprock above our camp came dashing his horse down the canyon wall. When we returned to the
guard position, we saw what had sent the soldier flying: a column of mounted men that did not look like any troop of U.S.
Cavalry I had ever seen. The uniforms were various, the column line wavering, the horses beasts of wisdom, if age be wise,
and the men in their equestrian attitudes relaxed. Somewhere
among this mob of gypsies I found an officer, though by his
bearing, position in line, and fearful visage, I might have thought
him the tenderest recruit. I detached Lieutenant Fulks from the
column, which he seemed ready to be separated from, and had
my infantry First Sergeant herd K Troop down into the canyon
and set them in some sort of formation for review. The lip of
Lieutenant Fulks trembled as he watched his command coil its
way down the canyon wall, the men cursing their horses, their
commander, and one another like drovers. "Forty Thieves, they
are called," said Fulks, and a tear glistened in the eye of the
young officer, who, I would learn, much preferred the study of
science to the making of war.

The men in the Army during those years after the Civil War
reflected the best and the worst of our nation that was being
moved west. Veterans of the Union and Confederate armies,
professional soldiers who knew how to endure the discipline
and detail of garrison as well as the danger and honor of the
battlefield, marched side by side with adventurers, gamblers,
penniless immigrants, every stripe of criminal who by hook or
crook had secured his release from every prison, jail, and
county farm in the land, and a multitude of those drifting
souls who simply could not manage the responsibilities of civil-

ian life. K Troop boasted a minimum of the former and every variety of the latter. "Most are not bad men, sir, but weaklings," Fulks said. "Cowards, malingerers, and bounty jumpers. But they are *shaped* by a small clique of thugs and thieves and Ship Island sailors, who turn them to their will. There is Chaney, whom I'm sure you noticed at review, a prizefighter and reckless bully who enforces the clique's will by brute strength. And there's Swing, the mutineer, and Parr—I think he is a murderer, he's served a term in the Navy and is not fond of land or horses or officers—and Lister, the pickpocket and thief—oh well, they're all great thieves if it comes to that. I don't have a nickel to my name, though a good deal of that, I must admit, was taken at poker, a game I have not quite got the hang of yet. But the leader among these ruffians is Sergeant Rife, who was educated for the priesthood, which I think may have been the greatest misjudgment of a boy's character since Caligula was not throttled in his crib. From what I can gather, Rife has practiced every profession, legal and illegal, in the West. He's been hanged, scalped, and filled with arrows. The man is indestructible."

It seemed wise to give K Troop one chance to be good, but that, as Lieutenant Fulks foretold, was a mistake. I allowed them free time the rest of the day and watched with amazement as the troop set out their dog tents like Arabs, here and there, wherever they chose, though generally arranging them around a large wall tent that was occupied by Sergeant Rife and his cabinet. At that evening's tattoo the infantry company could scarcely be brought into line, as they strained their necks and peered down toward the K Troop encampment, where the Forty Thieves rollicked about in various stages of undress, drinking, brawling, gambling, and generally occupying themselves with destroying that bounty of nature near at hand. This went on throughout the night, so that not one man in the company answered reveille. This ended K Troop's period of grace. They slept soundly as, during the morning, an infantry detail went through their tent city taking their weapons, horses, and tack. Then two foot soldiers, who may have had some shade in their own histories, crept into Rife's tent and emerged with a collection of knives, daggers, stilettos, and small pistols. The cooks were then instructed to brew a great pot of coffee and calomel. This was served by orderlies to the reclining troopers as they groped through their hangovers. The purgative took quickly, and while the troopers were in the woods beshitting themselves, the infantrymen went through the encampment and struck every tent and collected the few uniform articles of clothing within them. All weapons and noncombustible items were taken away, while anything that would ignite, which included all nonuniform apparel, was cast in a great pile atop Sergeant Rife's wall tent. These things were doused with the whiskey and tequila found in the search and set afire. The members of K Troop wandered up from the creekbed and out of the brush and circled forlornly around the fire. They were themselves encircled by armed members of the infantry and marched at gunpoint into formation. There they shed their remaining clothes. These were collected on sticks and tossed into the fire. The naked troopers were then ordered on their bellies. Armed infantrymen patrolled behind their backs. Lieutenant Fulks, the infantry First Sergeant, and I went along the prostrate company separating the weak, lazy, and infirm from Sergeant Rife's clique, which numbered, when the former were led away, only ten or so. These ten incorrigibles were allowed to simmer awhile in the sun and, in a punishment I had not contrived, to be made feast of by thousands upon thousands of Texas chiggers. Meanwhile the others were clothed in fatigues and introduced by the infantry to soap, scissors, and dismounted drill. After a time Rife and his men were dressed and given spades and set to digging a deep pit, which they finished in time to pass the last three or four hours of night therein. So ended the second day of K Troop among us.

The following morning I asked Lieutenant Fulks to breakfast in my tent. I was ready to go about organizing our march, but Fulks remained skeptical. His doubt proved justified. We had scarcely tasted our coffee when an infantry corporal came in with word there was trouble at reveille. In the dim light of dawn I thought K Troop had again failed to report for morning call. Then I noted fifty or so gray forms spread on the grass, as neatly lined and squared as stars on a flag. Making standing men lie proved far easier than making lying men stand, and after a bit of hauling the Thieves to their feet to have them crumple to the ground, I ordered the sergeants to put a guard around the prone formation and let them have their rest. By midmorning the chiggers had accomplished what rifle butts could not. To a man, yesterday's weak, lazy, and infirm had fled the hard red fleas and resumed their duties, leaving Rife and his companions spread-eagled, suffering torments that I would have thought no man could endure. During the night half their number leapt to their feet screaming and clawing at their flesh and were led away to the medicine tent. Those who remained were Rife's hard core, the aforementioned boxer Chaney, the murderer Parr, the mutineer Swing, the thief Lister, and Rife. These men made but two small surrenders to my will. At dawn I observed Chaney licking dew from the grass, and later Lister gave in to a fit of scratching. But with a word from Rife both brought themselves in line and returned to their positions, as still as the dead. At midday I admitted defeat and had Rife and friends dragged off and tossed in the pit. I called Lieutenant Fulks to my tent. As a gentleman Fulks did not say he had told me so, but he did not find my predicament without its amusements.

"Ah, the character of Rife," he explained in answer to my queries on it. "He's a son of Eire and priest-ridden, or was. By God knows what channels he came to America and set out on a life of adventure. He's a seditionist, by character if not principle. He always seems to be getting into scrapes with those of his own kind. He was a scalp hunter in Chihuahua for a time, and had his scalp taken by members of his own gang. He joined the Kickapoo Indians for a period and after some disagreement over cow or squaw was fitted out with arrows by his fellow braves. He then became a sheriff in some Texas town and was hanged by his own citizenry. A man at war with the world."

"What options do you think we have in handling Sergeant Rife?"

"Shoot him. Allow him to desert. Or," said Fulks with a pale sigh, "give in to his command."

We kept the Thieves in the pit that day but suffered greater indignities from that punishment than they. Rife and his men would fashion balls of earth and their excrement, wads of bread and urine, and fling these up at their guards, the orderlies who brought them food, and any officer who came to question them. The guards knew the worst abuse, for they could not remove themselves from the pit, for Rife and his men would scramble on one another's backs and like acrobats spring themselves out of the pit and be gone up a ravine in a moment. I ordered Rife and his fellows taken out of the pit and, as a last measure, given over to Sergeant Callaghan of the infantry. Callaghan was a veteran of one of the great conscript camps during the Civil War, and while I was off on a scout he had the prisoners carrying the log, spread-eagled on a caisson wheel, tied up by the thumbs, bound in sweat boxes, fitted out with barrels strapped to their shoulders, and marched up and down from dawn to night, from night to dawn, and at length nearly drowned in tubs of vinegar and water. The sole result of these punishments being that we ran low on vinegar.

I returned from my hunt and determined to turn Rife to my will or ship him off to Leavenworth. I asked Lieutenant Fulks to bring the ringleader to my tent that evening. Rife reported with a salute and stood at attention till told to rest. He removed his forage cap, which K Troop had been issued rather than the wide-brimmed hat, and sat when a chair was offered him. The sergeant was a large, red-freckled man, built thick and solid,

141

shaped wide and round at the girth and hips and legs. His head was small for his bulk, extending from sloping shoulders without the usual definition of neck. His powerful arms ended in sharply stubbed hands that looked something like the points of swords. Rife wore a white cotton skullcap over the scar of his scalping, a bandanna wrapped around the scar of his hanging, his tunic over the scars of his arrow wounds. I had during the time of his punishment observed the deep, puckered holes in his chest and back, the flesh about his neck twisted blue and brittle, and the glistening red orb of his skull upon which bits of scar tissue lapped like waves on a choppy sea, and had concluded that Sergeant Rife was exactly the sort of man that I needed on my journey across the *llano estacado*. But this was not to be, it seemed. In so many words I offered Rife second-in-command of our troop, but he refused, showing neither remorse for his insubordination nor promise that it would cease. I explained that court-martial and jail would be the alternative. Rife said he had known both and our interview was done, the sergeant having comported himself like a perfect gentleman.

After the sergeant had gone, I went outside and walked down through the bivouac. The night was heavy and warm, the sky overcast, draped low over the canyon. It was past taps, and a guard challenged me. He commented that it would rain, and I went on my way, through the infantry camp to the K Troop bivouac. The tents there were all dark, thirty ghostly white pyramids curving along the creekbank, all but for one tent near the end in line. That tent's white was warmer than the others, lighted by a candle within. Not far off I heard a low whistle and turned to see a man fading into the dark. When I looked back, the exceptional tent was the same chalk white as the others.

As I stood in the dark pondering by what means I could coerce or beseech Rife and his men to submit to my will, a raindrop struck my neck. I walked back toward my own quarters, not imagining that nature would enlist as my ally. A low rush and crackling came from down the line, past the officer's and command tents, from opposite the way I had been. This was wind coursing through the dry tree branches, but another noise came from beneath it, from the west, where the Tonk scouts had made their encampment. I made my way in that direction and was met by a picket muttering as he came up from the creek. "The Injuns, sir, they figure it's going to rain and so they're moving their tents kit and caboodle to high ground. A ten-foot rise it would take to get a moccasin damp—I will be damned!"

I found my own tent and retired. I woke once, to the first slap of rain against canvas, but went back to sleep, the wind rattling through the parched leaves. Next I woke to the hard din of wind and rain lashing the canvas walls, and beyond a roar like surf pounding a shore. I rose and found the tent floor flooded. I pulled on boots and slicker and went out and saw the tent sitting in the shallows of a lake that reached into the dark, spreading beyond my vision. Most officers and their orderlies were roused by now, and we went about collecting the gear from those tents on lower ground already in danger of being swept away by the flood. That done, we turned to securing the tents above the water that were being ripped apart by the wind. Extra pins were driven into all corner loops and thin cabled picket ropes lashed over the ends of all ridgepoles and fastened with three-foot picket pins driven into the ground. The wall tents secured, we set to double-staking and -tying the large hospital tent, taking care that its three standing poles were buttressed with crates and furniture. By now we had been joined by the Tonks, whose precaution did not seem so foolish, and some of the infantry, whose encampment we had placed on higher ground. Then came a cry of alarm from the K Troop encampment, and I recalled how gracefully their tents had been lined out, only a few yards above the creekbed. We took up our storm lanterns and ran along the silent, rising water toward them.

By now the storm had come on us and the air and sky were

rent and lit as if we had been thrown into a massive artillery war raging on the cliffs above. In the lightning's glare, we could see that the charming, meandering creek was gone, sunk beneath a ragged, boiling lake that stretched seventy yards across. The tops of the elm trees that had lined the stream just showed above the water, the current grasping their branches, tearing and flinging them away. The water had risen ten feet above the creekbed and was rising still. I had Fulks and two men set up gauges at the water's edge to monitor the flood's course, while the rest of us went down to the cavalry encampment where we had heard the cries for help.

The tail of K Troop's tent line had been pitched in a bend in the stream, and the current had torn across it, first isolating that part of the encampment from us, now sweeping it away. We made to save those who might still be alive, dragging tents and the men trapped in them from the water's grasp. Then we went deeper into the water and hauled two bodies from the tangle of canvas and rope but could not revive them. There was such chaos among the men that we could not tell how many were missing—it seemed that a quarter of the cavalry company was not present. I could not find Sergeant Rife among them and, there being no other leader to K Troop, had the infantry sergeant take the drenched and near-drowned horse soldiers away. I took a small group of men who did not fear the water and with ropes and lanterns we went toward the section of the encampment that had been swept away.

Sounds came to us that we would not forget: these were the cries of drowning men. With the next flash of lightning, we saw a dozen men, at least, clinging to tree branches that at nightfall had stood twenty feet above the creekbed. With each flash of lightning the men cried out and beckoned to us, and we saw the heaving water and torn tree limbs and the masses of debris sweeping down on them. With the next bright glare we could see another of the men gone. We hurled and projected ropes to them by every means we could devise and saved three of these

men and another who could not be revived. We worked franti-
cally till all were saved or gone but for one man whose body
was caught in the limbs of a large tree: the man looked lifeless,
his arms lax, his head and face half submerged beneath the
roiled water. One of the infantrymen lashed a rope about his
chest and tied another length of rope to that and then looped
the end of that line around the stoutest man among us. So secured, he ran up the flooded creek as far as the spliced rope
would allow and dived into the water there and with powerful strokes swam out into the current, floating, disappearing,
bobbing to the surface, fighting farther out into the current as
he was swept in an arc downstream toward the drowning man.
We marked his progress in stages, as the lightning lit the sky
every few seconds, till at last he had reached the drowning
man. We saw him lashing the rope around the trapped man.
Then he placed the rope around himself. Then he signaled and
we began to heave on the rope and pull the two men to safety.

As soon as the lifesaver and the drowning man were free of
the tree, they were sucked beneath the surface. We pulled the
rope with all our strength and saw it slicing through the water,
swinging left, the current driving the men toward the shallows.
The two forward men in our line left off pulling and went along
the rope till they came to the two men lashed together and
lifted them from the water. The rest of us then went forward
and dragged the men ashore. They came out a single ball of
mud which split apart as soon as the rope about them was
cut. The lifesaver was revived and carried away. We flopped
the drowned man on his stomach and began pumping water
from his lungs. Great spurts of water and blood came from his
mouth and nose, but he was not yet breathing. A barrel was
brought and he was rolled on that and water poured from the
man but without bringing sound or movement with it. We
turned the man on his back—his face a blue mask of death, his
eyes near coming loose from their sockets—and I pounded on
his chest till every muscle in his body began to kick and his

head snapped forward and then a great amount of foul matter spewed from his mouth. We turned him on his stomach and he began retching, bucking like a horse, bellowing, and, at length, breathing. I left off and gave the man's resuscitation to others, who brought coffee to him and wrapped him in blankets and after a while gave the man whiskey. I went to the water and washed and returned. I saw then that the revived man was Sergeant Rife. He sat hunched, teeth chattering, eyes wild, his skin blue and slick as a snake's. I shared some of the drowned man's whiskey, and Rife raised his red eyes to me. They carried not an expression of worship but something stronger: a sort of hatred: he owed me his life, he thought, and would bend to my will till the debt was paid.

Three days passed before the engorged creek subsided so that we could cross to the main canyon. Till then we recovered from the flood's havoc. We retrieved and buried the seven corpses we could find. We mended and repaired and dried equipment. What could not be recovered or righted, we requisitioned from the infantry company that would be staying behind to garrison the supply camp. The weather turned mild, and the camp became a vast laundry: tents, bedding, clothes, blankets strung from every rope and tree. On the second day the creek had fallen enough that one of the drowned troopers could be seen embedded on the far creekbank. The man's body and face were hideously discolored and swollen, his trunk and limbs bursting his uniform. One of the dead man's arms was lifted, reaching out toward us, like a priest offering his blessing to the damned. Sergeant Rife brooded on the man. He detailed troopers to stand across the bank and shoot the carrion birds and rodents that came to feed on the rotted flesh. He would stand for hours looking across at the blue bloated figure, at times raising his fist and cursing this reminder of his unnatural fealty to me.

It was during this time that I made plans to disobey the orders of my commanding officer. Instead of scouting the caprock east and west and then following either MacSwain or Clous up the border of the plain, I would march north and west from our supply camp, across the heart of the *llano estacado*. Why I undertook this foolhardy insubordination was not clear to me then; perhaps it is still not. There were my military ambitions: to track down the free Comanches and return them to the reservation without war or bloodshed, a goal that would be at least partially realized. Perhaps I thought in some way to emulate the great march of Coronado made in 1541. I could search for the remains of Jeremy Jones and his lost scout. Closer to the truth, I think, was that I had never before been so close to the unknown, in myself and in nature. I would conquer this plain or become ally with it or perish on it.

I called Lieutenant Fulks and Sergeant Rife to my tent and presented them with my plans and the empty map of the *llano*. I enumerated some of the dangers we might face, but found no objection in either man. Sergeant Rife feared nothing on the plain or anywhere else in the world, while Mr. Fulks feared only Sergeant Rife.

On October 5, 1875, we rode out southwest along the caprock to Yellow House Canyon, near the southern border of the plain. There we turned northwest, riding up Yellow House Canyon till it narrowed and rose and fed up onto the plains, beginning our trek across the *llano estacado*. The morning was chill and gray, the sky flat, placed over us like a steel lid, only a red knife of sunrise slicing into the overcast. For a brief time the sunrise gave us light, then gloom descended and we rode over the plains without a sense of direction or of the separation of heaven and earth or of being in any place at all. Men from other places cannot imagine the staked plains. They think of the gentle prairies of Kansas or the tree-strewn *champs* of France or the rising steppes of Russia. Here there were no bounds, no rupture, no undulation, no rise or fall, no break or ornament or movement or change of any sort to relieve the line of the horizon. There was not a tree or bush or shrub or weed that grew above the ground. No formation of any sort, no work of man or nature, was to be seen anywhere. There was the wind, and that might be seen playing across the short stiff grass, and there was what the sky might offer, and there were the playa lakes. But when the day was calm and the sky overcast, when one had left sight of the last lake and there were none to be seen ahead, then there was nothing.

It is difficult to predict how men new to the *llano* will react to it, for during any given day the range of human emotions—from the most abased fear to sublime ecstasy—can be found in a single breast. The plain's monotony and desolation and unboundedness are those of eternity, and, as philosophers have warned us, a thing without end can be either heaven or hell in the mind of man. The plain has a still, arrogant grandeur, but it does not challenge or charm man, as does a mountain or a great river, objects of beauty to be worshiped or obstacles to be scaled or crossed. The plain cannot be conquered. Its beauty needs no man to define it. It has a strange power of deception. Mirages build cities that do not exist. One's mind can become hopelessly lost in the castles of clouds that rear till they seem to scrape the sun. A sound may carry for miles, then nearby a man may speak and his mouth move without sound. The shadows cast by running clouds rise with the malevolence of leviathans surging up from the deep. After a few days the animals and birds of the plains can become as threatening as primeval monsters. A hawk becomes a black angel bearing death, a slithering snake can cause a man terrible doubt and jealousy, an insect circling one's head can seem to embody the devil himself—such were from my own collection of frights.

The open landscape presented military problems, though in planning our campaign we had not seen them. Normally a troop such as ours would have formed in a tight column of twos, with small squads riding flank three or four hundred yards left and right. Another squad would have been sent ahead of the column, and far beyond them three or four troopers would be assigned to gallop to every ridge line, search out every hollow and ravine, peer forward from every divide so that the main column might not be ambushed or flanked. This forward scout was dangerous duty, wearing on the horses, and greatly slowed the march of the column; still many men volunteered for this scout to relieve the boredom of the plodding walk of the main column. Now all offered to ride forward, as the *llano*'s featureless topography would present no danger, no surprises. But then, as the caprock dropped behind, the realization came that a man who could see to the horizon without obstruction could also be seen, and we were forced to mount flanks and forward and rear scouts, sending these parties to the limit of our vision, and then individual riders were sent beyond these scouts, to the limit of their vision, so that danger might be observed far beyond the scope of the main column's field glasses. The men who rode these distant points did not volunteer for this duty a second time and were heard to say they preferred the threat of our enemies lurking in a ravine or woods or just beyond the rise to such relentless security.

We devised a system of gunfire and flags as warning, a certain number of shots determining whether the main column would ride forward to the scout, assume a defensive position in place, or, if something grim lay beyond the horizon, turn and run. In the afternoon of the second day of our ride a single shot was heard, and the forward scout lazily waved the white flag with the centered red circle. We closed the main column and rode ahead at an easy gallop. We joined the forward scout and made toward the lone outrider at an increased pace. The man sat transfixed in his saddle, looking forward through his glasses at something we could not see even when we had ridden up to him.

"I will say, Captain, this place is spooked. It is a ghost train if it is anything at all," said the man, handing me his glasses. "I will be damned I do not like this place."

I moved the glasses till they focused on the phantom seen by the scout: what looked like a great train stretched across the plains, ten feet high, a quarter of a mile long and, as the scout had said, every car a ghostly shimmering white.

"Mirage. Mirage," said Lieutenant Fulks, peering through the glasses, but as we approached, the train did not disappear or become transformed into a natural phenomenon. We saw that the specter was a line of ricks of buffalo bones and then observed that the grass around us still carried the skeletal imprint where the bones had lain before being collected. Hundreds of animals had been killed in the stand, we thought. One of the ricks, standing like an eerie locomotive at the head of the train, was formed entirely of skulls, stacked neatly, with gaping snouts placed forward, so that from a distance the rick had the stare of a wall of eyes. We rode around the ricks and did not pass from their sight and the clawed scars that the animals' bones had left on the plains for over an hour, and even then men turned in their saddles as if we might be pursued by this pale, silent train.

The following morning warning shots were fired again, and we rode forward, as we would throughout our expedition, to consolidate scouts and the main column. Today the outrider's eyes were cast on the ground, toward an object lying before his stamping horse. As we approached we saw that the object on the ground was the body of a man and, as we came up, that the man was an Indian. The column was halted, and Lieutenant Fulks, Sergeant Rife, and I went forward and dismounted. We joined the scout, who was kneeling by the corpse. The Indian was naked and had been scalped; he had not been long dead.

"Comanche," the scout said. "From the looks of it, I'd say his locks were lifted by one of his kind."

We looked about the plain. There was nothing in sight as far as we could see. We could not think of where this lone man had come from or who had killed him or why.

The day following I handed command of the main column over to Lieutenant Fulks and with Sergeant Rife and two other men rode ahead of the troop as the forward guard. The Tonkaway Poor Man went a mile and a half ahead of us as lookout. At one p.m. Poor Man halted his horse and without firing or signaling stood waiting for us. We went forward at a rapid trot and joined the scout, who was looking toward a playa lake several hundred yards away.

"Comanche," said Poor Man, and I found the lake in my glasses and saw forms in the ring of weeds about the lake but could tell nothing of them. "Four braves," said the Tonk. "They have just eaten one horse. Only two left."

"Have they seen us?"

Poor Man did not move his eyes from the lake. "Yes. Maybe want ambush. Maybe want us go round and not see them."

"Are they a scouting party or a hunting party from a larger band?"

The Tonk shook his head. "Outcasts. Cast out from tribe for bad ways. You kill them and it please Comanche gods."

As I turned to send Sergeant Rife back to the main column to bring them forward, my horse bucked, coughed, and went down under me. As I fell I saw white balls of smoke drifting from the weeded lake and heard gunfire. I called out to Rife and the scout and the third man as they spurred their horses forward toward the Indians, but they did not heed me. I fired four warning shots for the troop to come up, but as Rife and Poor Man were also firing as they ran, Lieutenant Fulks did as massed gunfire dictated and halted the main column, dismounted the men, and set them out in defensive positions. I crouched behind my dying horse and watched the miniature battle through my glasses.

Rife and the soldier and the Tonk rode straight for the Indians, firing at the smoke blossoming from the Indians' muzzleloaders, killing two Indians before they could leave their ambuscade. In turn, the soldier's mount was shot from under him, but Rife and Poor Man ran on directly at the Indians, their Spencer carbines rattling fire that the Indians could not match. As Rife and Poor Man ran up on the position, two Indians leapt from the weed cover, one bounding on a pony, the other futilely pulling at his mount's rope, for the horse had been wounded in the attack and could not rise from its knees. Poor Man went after the mounted Comanche. They rode out of my field of vision, as I kept the glasses trained on Rife and the dismounted brave. The Indian had thrown down his gun and was shooting arrows at Rife that either missed or could not bring him down. Rife had dismounted, but he would not release his mount's reins, the horse jerking and plunging and leaping back each time Rife fired, so that he could not hit the Indian fatally. Then Rife's horse was felled, freeing Rife to fire accurately, but now he had run out of ammunition. The Indian had also exhausted his supply of arrows, and he and Rife threw down bow and rifle and closed on one another. They went down, out of my sight, behind the low weed wall around the lake.

I swept the horizon with the glasses and saw that Poor Man had shot the Comanche's horse from under him and was riding after the unseated brave, not firing at the Comanche, content to run him to death, as the Comanche was content to run till he died. I turned the glasses back on the lake and saw nothing. I fired four quick shots and waited, fired four more and saw that Fulks had set about reforming and mounting the column. I put down the glasses and took my carbine and, reloading its magazine as I went, ran toward the playa lake.

As I neared the lake, Rife stumbled out of the weeds, blood squirting from his hand, his face and arms smeared with blood. "It was a fuckin' white man," he said and crawled onto the grass and curled on his side, holding his wrist to stop the bleeding.

I went down into the lake and saw that the Indian was a tall youth, not more than seventeen, with brown eyes and long curling brown hair and fair skin. I counted nine bullet wounds in his body. Rife had also cut his throat.

I went back to Rife. He had not been able to stanch his bleeding wound. One of his fingers had been severed but for a piece of flesh. He asked for help, that I remove the finger and set a tourniquet around his arm. Fulks and the main column thundered in, throwing themselves from their saddles, hitting the ground running. I gave Rife's medical treatment over to Fulks, who had an interest in such things, and went back and shot my horse. When I returned to the milling troop, Rife's finger had been amputated. Fulks and the cook had set about to cauterize the wound with gunpowder. While these preparations were being made, I held Rife's wrist tight. He grinned against the pain, calling out to Fulks and the cook, who were mixing a salve of urine and axle grease, "Hurry it along, laddies, and make it a double dose. I got an arrow busted off in me leg as well!"

Rife's wounds were sprinkled with gunpowder and ignited, and the Sergeant gave out an operatic cry, for it was his belief that a good song helped kill the pain.

We chose to give the white Indian a Christian burial and decided that he was not to be scalped. The men dug a hole and therein laid the youth, who had, we supposed, been captured by the Comanches as a boy. A few words in a language the youth had probably forgotten if he had ever learned it were said, and dirt was thrown over him. The Tonks were allowed to scalp the others and dispose of their bodies as they chose, probably consuming the flesh of the Comanches, as the Tonkaways were a tribe given to cannibalism.

The following morning the cook came to my tent, stamping his feet and muttering curses at Lieutenant Fulks, my second-in-command. I followed the cook to the mess wagon and there found a large pot of soup boiling. The cook ladled into the broth and lifted out the head of one of the scalped Comanches.

I went and found Fulks and spoke to him about his ethnological experiments, that they might be curtailed. I pacified the cook by allowing him to dump from his extra mess tins and jars Fulks's pickled collection of every insect, spider, and small mammal that had ever crossed the plains. May Science forgive me.

Toward noon the day following, the wind shifted to the north and a stench came over us, so foul that many men tied bandannas over their mouths and noses to mask it. It was the rotted smell of death, and soon we came upon the first skinned carcasses, those of buffalo, glistening pink wounds scattered across the plain. To skin these animals of their hide seemed a humiliation to them, robbing them of the dignity that some men and beasts retain even in death. We could not look at the great black heads attached to the naked and shrunken appendages without embarrassment and disgust. We counted ninety carcasses, all shot with a large-caliber rifle. The tongues of the animals had been taken cleanly, the hump and loin meat skillfully butchered—the work of professional hunters. From the state of decomposition we thought the animals had been killed two days before. The men shot a number of the buzzards that circled the carcasses till they saw the pointlessness of that. We rode quickly to the windward of the killing ground and pressed on farther than we might have done, not camping till we had ridden twenty-five miles that day.

The next day we heard the boom of a buffalo rifle in the distance and closed up the column and rode toward the stand. Soon a thick line appeared on the horizon, like that of the bone ricks, but this train was black and proved to be a gargantuan pile of buffalo hides. As we drew near the hunters' encampment we came upon a series of long smokehouses constructed of planks and wattled branches; within them hundreds of tongues were being smoked over buffalo-chip fires. Nearby racks strung from forked poles were hung with hump and loin steaks, curing in the sun. There were also pendant vats fashioned from dried and hardened buffalo hides; these contained chunks of meat being salted in brine. Beyond the smokehouses and curing racks stood the hunters' lean-to tents. In an area away from the camp we saw scores of gleaming white patches dotting the ground—buffalo hides staked hair-down to dry. There were a number of wagons set about the camp. Hobbled horses and mules grazed farther on. Near the racks we found a dozen rifles of various makes and calibers— one a Sharps .50 that weighed sixteen pounds. The wagons were loaded with crates of lead slugs, kegs of powder and primers and paper patches, boxes of used shell casings, cleaning rods and rest sticks and a reloading press and other accessories to the hunt. Littered about the camp were bedrolls, tarpaulins, cooking equipment, and a good number of empty whiskey bottles. Everything necessary for the buffalo hunt but the hunters.

We were set to ride a ways from the buffalo camp and pitch our own tents when one of the outriders cried out and fired his rifle. A distant boom came in return, and we saw on the horizon three black dots that grew till we thought three rogue buffalo were grimly bearing down on us. As the figures grew nearer we saw they were in fact the missing buffalo hunters, all clad in great buffalo rug coats that made them into some hybrid beast with the legs of a horse, the hump and coat of a bison, and the tiny white faces of men.

The buffalo hunters drew into camp, and one, the smallest of the three, dismounted and approached, speaking the King's English as he came:

"Hello there, Captain! I'm Rollie Collins, lord of this hairy manor. Won't you dismount, Captain, and have a steak. Have thousands of them. I think I shall never eat animal flesh again so long as I live. I say, you wouldn't have any wheat flour, would you? I'd give a hundred humps for a buttered scone. And for a beer—a thousand tongues!"

The buffalo hunter—or runner, as Collins preferred to be called—pointed us to a lake a mile on with fresh water, and we rode there. The troop was dismounted, and the men unsaddled and unbridled their mounts and watered them and led them out on the plain. There they drove picket pins into the earth and tethered the horses so that they might graze. Then the men quickly pitched their dog tents, and as the fragrance of buffalo roast came to us across the plain, we marched in loose formation back to the hunters' camp, the cook's helper carrying a fifty-pound sack of flour on his shoulder. We feasted that night on buffalo loin and hump, while the hunters gorged on bread and tallow. After the men were sent back to camp, Lieutenant Fulks and I lingered around the campfire in conversation with our host.

Talk turned to the four Indians we had killed two days before. Collins said that they had been attacked by the same group. "Hardly a major battle. Yes. Four of the poor buggers. Outcasts of some sort. I think we might have dropped one of their horses. Our guns frightened them away. Good luck for us! My boys were so pissed they would have thought scalping a haircut. Sobered them up, though, and we've made a good stand because of it." When told that one of the Indians was a white youth who probably had been captured by the Comanche as a boy, Collins explained, "Ah, pity! May have had something to do with his getting booted out of the tribe. Perhaps he was nightcrawling with the chief's youngest wife. Who knows, or ever will?" He drew on his pipe. "So your business on the plains is the Comanche, is it, Captain?"

"Yes. Comanches. We must convince them they must go onto the reservation."

"Of course. Previously I would have thought you might come up empty-handed. Generally the Comanches come onto the plains only to hunt—but this year they have changed their habits. You will find Indians where you would not have before. The Comanches are wandering the *llano estacado* like the lost tribes of Israel. Not hunting, either—well, they take enough game to subsist, but that is not their reason for being here. There are strange things happening amongst the Comanches. I know only what I hear from the *comancheros*. Rumors of strife amongst the tribes, rumors that an evil medicine man has taken power over one of the tribes—the Wanderers—and that he has forbidden them to hunt or make war. He has decreed that they shall wander the plains till the buffalo return, till their noble enemies return, which, as you and I well know, will never happen. There has evolved some sort of messianic cult amongst them, a death cult. This medicine man has convinced them they will never die. Bullets will not kill them, white men are but wraiths and they must not struggle against them. That sort of thing."

"This is Tehana Storm's Wanderers?"

"Yes. The other great plains tribe, Bad Hand's Meat Eaters, have broken away from the Wanderers. The Meat Eaters seem intent on making peace. Going onto the reservation in New Mexico, I would say. We came across their tracks a few days ago, north of here. Heading west with a great herd of cattle. You may be able to catch them, if you hurry, and have your battle. If that's what interests you."

"It doesn't," said Lieutenant Fulks, having made himself my protégé. "We are peacekeepers."

"Indeed!" The Englishman leaned back his head and stared up into the stars. "I say, would you both care to see something magical, truly magical?"

"I would," said Fulks.

"Splendid!" said the tiny Englishman and leapt to his feet. "Come along then! Come with me!"

Fulks and I rose and followed the tiny figure into the dark. We soon quitted the campfire glow, but our guide urged us on. "Come! Come! It's not here. Not yet." We walked nearly a mile that in the dark seemed like ten, till the campfire shrank to a pinpoint of lighted haze. We kept walking till even that

157

light was gone. There was nothing about us but stars. The earth was black as a pit. "Ah, this is it," said Collins. "This will do. Lie down now." Fulks, game for anything, was already on his back. Collins joined him a short distance away, spread-eagled on his back. "Won't you join us, Captain? It is really the most extraordinary sensation."

I lay down, and when I looked up it was as if I had been shot out into the stars. I was floating in space, the heavens were all about me, there was no earth. Soon I had no body and not much of a mind, for I did not think of anything, floating in the stars. I sat up, before I had gone so far I could not return. Shortly the others rose and we followed the stars back to the camp.

I chose to lay over the troop at the buffalo camp the following day. The horses were weak from the meager grain rations allotted them, and though the men were fit, Sergeant Rife had begun to suffer from his wounds and needed rest. Too, I wanted to gather and dry as much buffalo meat as Collins would allow us to take, which was all we could carry. Collins had come to the end of his days as a buffalo hunter, having grown weary of the slaughter and the waste. He accepted promissory notes for the meat that he had no intention of redeeming.

The next morning, as Collins and I sat before the campfire drinking coffee, talk returned to the previous day's discussion of the Comanches that were going onto the reservation. I asked how we might find the tribe who were remaining free, Tehana Storm's Wanderers, if they had abandoned the canyons and ravines of the borders of the plains and had taken to wandering the *llano estacado*. There were fifty thousand square miles of tableland, and with water-filled playa lakes in every section they might be anywhere.

"That is true," said Collins, "and tracking them is most difficult here, unless they're driving cattle as were the Meat Eaters.

After a day or so the buffalo grass carries as much trace of a horse passing over it as does rock." He pressed the short, wiry grass down. When he released his hand the grass sprang back as it had been. "Still, the *llano* is not limitless. It is grand and austere, but it has boundaries and it has features. The man who will can master it. I have, to a certain extent. And so have others."

"I know its boundaries, but what features?"

"Oh, plenty! Well—some. Let me fetch my map." Collins went off and returned with a rolled sheet of oilcloth. He spread the map on the ground and fastened its corners with rocks. There were S marks here and there on the map, some humped lines in one area, and X's and O's with dates scribbled near them. Four-digit figures were written all over the map. The X's were buffalo stands, Collins said. "The larger stands—some mine, some made by other hunters—they might act for a year or two as landmarks. Though now with the bonepickers coming onto the plains one must keep them up to date. Still, they are a reasonably accurate way of telling one's positions. The lakes don't help, obviously—too many of them. Do you have a cartographer?"

"I have drawn my own map."

"Splendid! You must make up a copy of mine before you go off. Now, here we are at this position." He indicated an X with a current date by it. He then pointed to a mark below that. "These are the bone ricks you passed, and the distance is here." He peered close to read the figure, for it was so small as to be nearly illegible. "The distance between the ricks and our stand is three thousand four hundred and fifty walking horse steps. That is, the number of times a horse's right hoof strikes ground at a walk from this point to this point. It is a necessity that these distances be accurately measured, Captain, as necessary to one's sense of whereabouts as a compass. I know my system may seem strange to you, but believe me, I have never felt safer than when coming on a pile of bleached bones in precisely the

number of paces I had calculated. There is nothing more won-
derful to man, I think, than to know where one is. Now here,"
he continued, pointing at three or four S's about the map, "these
are spring-fed lakes, and this one is a playa lake so large that it
might as well be spring-fed. It contains water but for the driest
times. I, of course, am not suggesting a route of march, but it
might be wise to make next for that lake—which is called, po-
etically, Big Lake." He pressed his nose to the map. "Nine
thousand one hundred and something horse paces from our position at a compass reading of about three forty-five. Perhaps
things have changed, but the Comanches used to favor Big Lake
as a campground during the fall hunt. More reliable even than
the spring lakes, which have the distressing habit of running dry
and being alkaloid. Then a day's march beyond Big Lake, you
will find the trail of the Comanches going to New Mexico. If
that interests you."

I questioned our current position on Collins's map. "It seems
farther east than I had hoped to be, by almost a day's ride."

"Oh yes, that happens to everyone. A horse will always veer
east a bit. The plain slopes, you see—well, you can't really see
it—but it does slope northwest to southeast at a little less than
ten feet a mile. Flat as a pancake, but with just enough tilt to
throw a horse a bit off course. One must make compensations
occasionally and keep a sharp eye on the needle. Two days'
march, a degree off each day, and one is lost."

I asked about the humped marks near the western border of
the map.

"Sand dunes," Collins replied. "Wretched country. Like the
Sahara. A true desert, with no grass. Won't find any Indians
there. Rather unlike some members of my own race, the Indians have a thorough contempt for sand. *Malpais,* the Mexicans
call it. Bad country all around."

"And what is this?" I indicated a circle on the northern part
of the map, with a date by it.

Collins pressed down his thin fair mustache. "A settlement

of sorts. An attempt at one. A collection of dugouts and patches of tilled soil. I came upon the place last year. Deserted. Dugouts filled with sand. Not a trace of the settlers. Don't know where they could be. Dead, I suppose, or moved on to California. They'd even laid out streets, as if they were trying to make a town."

I expressed skepticism that anyone would attempt to settle the plain. Collins replied, "Oh, it's possible, I think. I've been considering settling here myself. Come, let me show you something."

Collins took a deep plate and a canteen, and we walked away from the camp. At a distance he knelt to the earth, took a knife from his belt, and lifted up a clump of native grass. He dug out the soil beneath the grass and scooped it into the plate. He then placed the grass roots in the soil and poured water in the plate from the canteen: the soil was transformed from a grayish brown to a deep reddish chocolate. Collins continued to probe with his knife, digging down a foot or more, till the soil became moist and rich like that in the plate. "The topsoil here goes deep. Three, four, six feet, perhaps deeper. There's no richer in the world when water's applied to it judiciously. Only it never is. It floods or it parches. But there is water here." He tapped the earth. "A great underground river flows beneath these plains. A vast lake, an ocean of water caught in the porous rock that lies underneath the caprock. You've seen the springs that flow from under the caprock? They all speak of this aquifer. But then there's digging a well deep enough to reach it. There were several wells at the deserted settlement. All dry. I like to think the settlers have moved on to another place, looking for this underground river. If they find it, this plain will one day be a garden."

A breeze came across the plain toward us, flattening the grass beneath it, the light skidding across the wind-bent grass silver, like the flash of swords. Collins took the grass from the plate and dumped the earth back in the hole. He put the clump of grass where it had been, tamping the earth around it, replanting it.

I assigned every available man to work with the skinners, to butcher as much meat as we could salt and carry. I remained at camp during that morning, copying Collins's map onto my own. I tacked my work on the wall of the lean-to and studied it. With every step the place I had thought empty was becoming filled.

By midafternoon, the horses and wagons were loaded with meat and the camp was struck. We took our leave of Rollie Collins, again attempting to pay him for the provisions, but he would only accept our thanks. From the buffalo camp, we made for Big Lake, as Rollins had advised. We were by now well into October, and there was no sign of fall but chill in the early morning air. The plains had been swept by showers almost daily, and the native grass stood lush and green. Dotted with sparkling lakes, the plains blazed under the morning sun like an emerald velvet table laid with silver plate. The distant heavens were crowded with cumulus clouds. A profusion of wildflowers grew about the lakes, as if summer might extend forever. At times we would see a lone, branchless tree rising twenty, thirty feet above the horizon, but as we came to it we would find a dried yucca stalk and would wonder at this plant, that it could exist here as a solitary, so far from any member of its own kind. In the sandy depressions we rode into with greater frequency, we found fields of cactus, some flowering in the mild weather; the men savored their tart red fruit out of season. In one of these depressions we came upon a herd of buffalo; the animals considered us, then went off in their humped lope. It was almost daily that a herd of some plains species would approach our column, often with frank curiosity. The red-backed antelope made their distaste for us most plain. They would come bounding nonchalantly to within a hundred yards or less, stop with exaggerated surprise, legs spraddled, neck forward, peering nearsightedly at our column. They would sniff the air, give us another long gaze, then one clown among them would leap high in the air and the herd would bound off as if we were to pursue them in a game of tag. One day I was riding point alone, as this duty was passed among all of us, and saw a cloud of dust on the horizon. Dread struck me, but I held off giving the alarm and soon saw through the glasses that the horses I had feared did not run as if mounted by men. They were a drove of wild mustangs, their long manes and tails flowing like tangled robes as they ran in celebration of their speed. The hunters of the sky became our companions, feeding on our movement. When our column flushed a snake or a long-eared jackrabbit that stillness had camouflaged, these birds of prey folded their wings and plummeted to earth, striking the rabbit with such force that the animal's back was broken, taking the snake so suddenly it had no chance to coil to strike back. These demonstrations made us wonder if man had ever known, even before the invention of his cynical weapons, such cruel and elegant hunting. More prosaically and perhaps more in the manner of man, larks and sparrows and ground birds flocked behind our column, darting into our horses' droppings to pick out undigested kernels of corn. Once when riding at the rear of the troop, I saw some movement in the lead riders, a brief circle out of line that was repeated by each pair of riders, a wave passing through our column. When we last two came up we saw the men had been riding around a meadowlark's nest with eggs. Even my companion in the column, Sergeant Rife, who did not care much for any form of animal life, rode out of line not to disturb the nest, such was our desire to leave nature be.

We came upon Big Lake at the end of the second day's march from the buffalo camp, less than a hundred paces off the distance calculated by Collins. That we had made this ride across the *llano* to a known destination had, as the buffalo hunter said, lifted our morale. Too, the Big Lake contained good water and there was heavy grass around its border, and we passed that night watering and grazing the animals. The following day our column made due north at a fast walk, and at the end of the second day the vanguard signaled we had found the Indian trail that the buffalo hunter had drawn on my map. Word of the Indians had sharpened the troop's interest, for the placidity of the plains had dulled them, but the width of the trail cast a pall over our eagerness. We had come upon a swath of ground beaten bare twenty feet across; it stretched from horizon to horizon. Hundreds of travois marks etched the ground, and droppings from horses and cattle littered the road like paving stones. We found numerous pieces of equipment and artifacts that had fallen from the moving tribe, which concerned our scouts, for the Comanches were known as careful travelers. "Many many warriors and women and children and ponies and cows," said Poor Man. "They ride fast. Leave bad trail."

"Are they riding to battle?" I said, concerned that the Comanches might be striking at MacSwain's flank.

Poor Man conferred with the other Tonks and returned. "No. Comanches do not make war. They do not care who knows the way they go."

"Are they fleeing anyone?"

"Yes. They flee the end of hunting buffalo. They flee the end of the warrior taking coup. They flee the coming of the Woman-Hearted Man."

Despite the Tonks' assurance that we faced little danger riding after the Comanches, we marched with double scouts forward, flank, and rear, and posted extra guard at night. The trail led due west toward New Mexico, a change of march we might have made in any case, for the horses were weakening daily from their low rations of grain, and the water in the playa lakes had begun to drop so that many of the smaller lakes were fields of mud that took digging to reach their moisture. Our maps showed Fort Pascal one hundred miles to the west of us.

164

Marking this journey with water were a spring-fed lake at thirty miles and an old *comanchero* trading post at Las Lenguas, just beyond the New Mexican border. Between the spring lake and Las Lenguas lay the *malpais,* the badlands, twenty-five miles of sand hills without water, grass, or wood. We rode toward this desolation, on the trail of a great body of Comanches, with foreboding. We could now turn and retrace our steps to Big Lake, fill our water casks again, and with good luck find our way to the springs of Blanco Canyon. Each mile we rode north or west might be that distance that our horses and we succumbed to thirst short of known water. The weather taunted us. Gone were the afternoon rain squalls that crossed the plain, the showers that, if they did not fill the lakes, dampened the ground so that the earth might not dry and fissure and suck in any standing water. We had known no rain for four days and had seen no clouds but those trails of vapor that stretched over the crown of the sky, at such heights they were visible only at dawn and dusk. The autumn light that would have pleased a painter with its clarity, with the depth it gave to the turquoise sky, the precision with which it outlined the blanched earth, only exacerbated our alarm. We saw in the finely grained distances the end of rain.

Thinking to cross this desert as quickly as possible, that if we were to come to battle with the Indians we might fight with greater strength sooner than later, I ordered a quick gait that had near exhausted the horses by nightfall. Even at that pace we had come only twenty-five miles, five miles short of the spring lake. I ordered a dry camp for the night, that if we were to jump the Indians at the lake, and they spoiled for a fight, we would come upon them fresh and out of the rising sun. We passed an uneasy night, at half rations of water and less meat, for the salt drove the men to thirst. We rose at three and had covered the distance to the lake by dawn. Shortly afterwards the forward scout signaled us, the slow movement of the flag showing no alarm. We rode forward to the scout. He sat hunched in his saddle at the crest of a low ridge, looking dispiritedly down into the lake. The Indians had gone on, and they had taken the lake with them. We stood on the low ridge and saw beneath us a mile-wide circle of mud: the great tribe and their hundreds of animals had drunk the hole dry. The troop made camp by the lake, and we passed the day digging in the mud but could not find the spring and did not collect sufficient water for the day we spent resting the horses and digging. Our scouts returned at dusk with word that the sand hills would be entered on tomorrow's march and that the Comanche trail had been lost in the drifting sand. The guard was relaxed that night. As we no longer feared Comanche attack, sleep was the only provision I could freely offer my men.

I calculated that Fort Pascal in New Mexico was now closer than Big Lake on the *llano estacado,* and we pressed on. We were but days shy of November, and still the afternoon air quivered along the distant horizon. We had seen mirages daily since coming onto the plains and, after having ridden after some, were used to their flat shimmering lakes. But the phantasms that now played before us were of another sort. A range of mountains grew in the distance. By our maps and our reason we knew these to be the sand hills of the *malpais,* but they reared to heights of hundreds of feet. Moments later the mountains' shape would change—they became sharply serrated and a great blue valley appeared in their wall. This valley, in the next few minutes, filled with water. Then it filled with sand. Then the mountains surrounding this deep tan V fell away and the sand drifted out on the plain like an hourglass whose bell has cracked. Shortly the mountains would appear again and become transformed, to disappear in a different manner.

As we rode west we came upon sand in the native grass, and the grass thinned and at length gave way to rock and sand. But there was life, both flora and fauna, in this desert. We would find bunchgrass and dwarf mesquite and yucca in the sand, and clinging to the rocks, obtaining what sustenance there I could not imagine, would be the stinking creosote bush. And everywhere were cacti, of more types and forms than I knew to exist. Here there were no birds but hawks, no land creatures but reptiles, snakes who fed off lizards and lizards who fed off snakes. All these living things, plant and animal, were fashioned with armor, thorn, or fang. Only the creosote bush was not armed with shield or saber, but by its odor was it made perfectly safe from predator. By nightfall we had come to the sand hills. We knew that in them we would not find even these relentless forms of life.

We pitched camp and rationed water for man and beast. I then had Rife move the remaining barrels to the ambulance, that they might be guarded till we reached water. For the second night no guard was mounted, though sleeping pickets were placed around the horses. I had the bugler sound taps, so that some semblance of military duty might be retained, but so plaintive was the call echoing through the wasteland that its effect was to mock all discipline and regimen as futile. After lights out I drew Sergeant Rife and Lieutenant Fulks, my seconds-in-command in fact and fiction, into the dunes beyond the camp to plan our march through the *malpais* and warn them of its dangers.

"How far did you say it was across, sir?" said Rife, lighting matches over the map laid on the sand.

"The sand hills are twenty-five miles across east to west, seventy-five miles north to south."

"Twenty-five miles?" said Fulks. "That's just a good day's march, sir."

"On the plain. But our horses are weak, and the sand will slow them. You saw how difficult it was to walk only as far as we have come. It will take two days if the horses live. God knows how long if they begin to die."

"And there's no way of skirting this Sahara, then?" said Rife.

"We could, but there's no promise of water if we do go

around. If there's a benefit to crossing the sand, it's that we know that Las Lenguas and Fort Pascal are on the other side. The *comanchero* camp is here and Fort Pascal is thirty miles beyond. We won't know our exact position when we come out of the sand hills, but we shouldn't be more than a day's ride from water."

"Two days across, a third to water," said Rife. "I don't see the problem, Captain."

"The problem is that we only have one day's water left."

"Hell, stretch it."

"It is stretched. One day."

Rife gave Fulks a rather insubordinate thump on the back. "Well then, we'll drink our own piss. Brew it in coffee if you're finicky. I did three days on my own water in Mexico once. Kept it going right on around. Finally dried out and had to kill my horse and drink his blood."

"Really?" said Fulks. "How does it taste?"

"Sweet as syrup. Drank it down like a good hearty soup. Steaming right out of the vein."

"Sergeant Rife, Mister Fulks, we will address what to drink in the stead of water when it comes to that. Now, Sergeant, are the men fit?"

"As fiddles."

"And their morale?"

"Their morale is just fine, Captain. So long as I'm happy, they're happy." And Rife lit a match that I might see his toad's face and the lethal lidded eyes of a snake. A wind came up and blew out the match.

Sergeant Rife rose and went back through the dunes to the camp. After the sergeant was well beyond earshot, Fulks said, "Perhaps I shouldn't be telling you this, sir, as it might be the end of me, but Sergeant Rife has been sending Lister, the thief, into your tent."

"There's nothing there that's worth taking, Mr. Fulks."

"No sir. But the thief has come on some papers of yours

that have caused some confusion in the mind of Sergeant Rife. The things you have been writing about Coronado, well, Rife and his bunch think that these diaries are yours, sir, and it's you, rather than the *conquistador,* crossing the plains searching for the lost city of gold."

"Perhaps it is me, Mr. Fulks."

"Sir?"

"There are many treasures on these plains, I think. There's one in particular—one pointed out to me by the buffalo hunter—that would suit Sergeant Rife to a tee. What does Sergeant Rife remind you of, by look?"

"The meanest man on the face of the earth."

"By profession, I mean."

"I can't think of anything else."

"A farmer. I think I'll encourage Sergeant Rife, the next time he deserts, to come back and settle the plain."

"Farming the plain," said Fulks with a melancholy sigh. "I wouldn't have thought of that, sir."

We rolled our maps and went back to the camp. The wind that had blown out Rife's pipe had become a steady force, drifting a fine carpet of sand over the dunes. When we rose the following morning there were about the camp scores of sandy loaves that shook and trembled and gave birth to men when first call was sounded. We marched directly into the wind that day, our eyes, mouths, noses, ears, every orifice in our bodies, it seemed, clogging with grit and sand. We were wrapped like Arabs in bandannas, scarves, and ponchos, but still our boots and tunics and trousers filled with sand. We could not protect our horses, and by late afternoon they were suffering, so that we were forced to make a camp. During the night the wind dropped and we woke to an eerie calm, the eye of the storm, perhaps, the sky a dark orange, the air so choked with dust that any lantern or match we lit showed only the dullest illumination. Sand had seeped into the water barrels through fissures I thought nothing could penetrate. I issued our last rations that morning, preferring to empty the barrels than watch them fill with mud.

Our horses moved across the sand hills at a pace so slow we seemed to have made no progress by late afternoon, when the sky began to darken and collapse on us. We crested one dune to greet another, seemingly as stationary as a boat turned to windward to ride out a storm at sea. Before true dark we began to move onto stretches of rock between the dunes, and shortly we found bunchgrass and mesquite buried in the sand. At the crest of one dune I looked toward the next and through the gloom saw a dark head resting on the horizon. As we approached the head disappeared, to reappear on the rise of the next dune. On the third dune we galloped the horses forward and saw a child scurrying over the crest of the dune beyond. When we galloped to that height, the child stood before us, in a roadway, two parallel tracks running through the sand, that we thought were the cleverest creations ever made by man. I halted the column and dismounted and went toward the Mexican boy alone. When I drew near he raised his hand to his brow in a military salute. He wore a forage cap of the Second Cavalry and, as if he were indeed a guide from our regiment, turned and at a brisk march led our column toward the village of Las Lenguas.

We came upon an irrigation ditch, a water-filled cut through the rocks and sand. We fell into disarray at the ditch and took a while dragging the animals away from the water, even after they had drunk their bellies bloated. When we had reformed the column and mounted the men, the Mexican boy had disappeared, but the road lay clear before us. Our way was shown through the night by the glow of the parched sand.

We soon came to Las Lenguas, a jumble of dark blocks scattered along the road, tucked among the dunes, many of the low adobe shacks drifted over so that they were but caves bored into the shifting sands. There were no lights in any of the buildings. A search party reported the village deserted, though each shelter was fit to be inhabited, with furniture, provisions, and fuel. A fire was found smoldering in the stove in the *comanchero* trading post. Coffee, sugar, blankets, whiskey, beefsteaks, beads and ornaments for trading, even arms and ammunition were cached in the trading post. Everything but *comancheros.*

"No blood, not a whiff of gunpowder, not a saucer broke, Captain," said Sergeant Rife after we had bedded the troops among the huts, posted guards, and taken the trading post as our headquarters. "Something spooked them off. They're probably hiding in the hills."

"Maybe the Indians we were tracking came through and frightened them away."

"I don't think so, Captain. *Comancheros* do business with Indians. More'n likely they're afraid of us."

By the forage cap the Mexican child had worn and other items found about the village, we knew that MacSwain's squadron had been through Las Lenguas before us. If MacSwain had taken some punitive action against the *comancheros,* I thought we should mount extra guard, as the Indian traders might seek retribution against a smaller command.

Fulks came in from posting guard to report they had found a stable with a dozen or so lame or sick horses, most carrying the U.S. Army brand. "And beyond the stable there's an immense stone corral with several hundred head of cattle, all with Texas brands."

"More than a hundred cattle and no guards?"

"None that I could see," said Fulks, sitting himself before the first table we had seen in weeks.

Rife pondered Fulks's neat cutting and forking on a steak that demanded ruder treatment. He said to me, "You know, Captain, I think we're among 'em."

"The Indians we were trailing?"

Rife nodded. "I wouldn't be surprised if there was a redskin at the window right now."

The windows were empty, as were the streets, but Rife's concern was heeded. I sent him off to double the pickets and appointed Lieutenant Fulks Officer of the Guard. By the time Rife had returned and crawled under a buffalo robe, Fulks was snoring lightly. I let them both doze, posting the first change of guard at midnight, hoping, as the hunter Collins had said, that the Comanches had tired of war.

I woke at dawn and built a fire in the stove and boiled coffee. Shortly one of the sentries came with an intruder, the Mexican boy from the previous night. A white eagle feather had been fastened to his forage cap.

"Buenos dias, joven. ¿Dónde están sus padres?"

"Traficando con los indios."

"¿Están los indios cerca de aquí?"

"Sí. Están por todos lados."

"¿Hay muchos?"

"Cientos y cientos."

"¿Quieren hacer guerra con nosotros?"

"No. Los indios quieren hablar con usted, señor. Usted es el jefe del ejército, ¿no?"

"Sí. Soy el capitán del ejército."

"Bueno. Los indios quieren quitarse. Están cansados de la guerra."

The Indians would come to us and surrender, but first they wanted to talk. The morning was so occupied, making ourselves ready for the council. Runners went back and forth between the camps, till it was arranged that the council would be held that afternoon in the trading post where we had made our headquarters. On our side of the table would be sat myself, Lieutenant Fulks, and Sergeant Rife. Representing the Indians would be Bad Hand, chief of the Meat Eaters band of the Comanches; Hair Grows Short, an elder of the tribe; Nine Pipes, the band's most respected medicine man; and a young chieftain named Kills Few Men. Between us would be Poor Man and two other

Tonks, who would serve as translators. Unauthorized personnel who attended the council were six troopers with cocked carbines that we hid behind curtains in an adjoining room and, from the opposition camp, an unruly claque of squaws, elders, minor medicine men, a representative of the *comancheros* of Las Lenguas, the Mexican slave of Bad Hand, and many dogs and children of the Comanches. The Comanches arrived for the council an hour late. At half past four, then, our negotiations with the Meat Eater band of Comanches, that they might go onto the reservation, commenced.

The Comanches were a graceful people horseback but awkward afoot. Simian in appearance, with long legs and arms and squat trunks, they could sit a horse as no other race of people on earth but scarcely seemed able to walk. The Comanche visage was blunt and powerful: round, flat, coppery faces set with bloodshot eyes. The finely sculpted features and tall, erect carriage of Bad Hand and Tehana Storm were exceptions to this rule. As characteristic to the Comanche as horsemanship was his personality. Shrewd, witty, cynical, the Comanche faced facts and disdained those races, whether white or Indian, that made too much or too little of life. They showed particular contempt for those who despaired in defeat and gloated in victory. Such was the philosophy with which we white soldiers were approached by Bad Hand and his weary, starving band of Meat Eater Comanches.

The elder of the tribe, Hair Grows Short, spoke first. Hair Grows Short was a kind old man, his face soft and wrinkled, his hair white and short as a squaw's. He wore a faded Mexican shirt and deerskin trousers, without breechclout or fringe.

"My heart is filled with joy when I see you here," he commenced. "We all admit it was not always so. But now I feel glad as a pony in spring, for as the young horse must frolic and feed on new grass, an old man must lie down and a vanquished people accept defeat. Though we did not always think so, we now understand that you white soldiers have come to our peo-

173

ple to show us that our ways are as old as the man who speaks these feeble words. Our people must now take up new ways or lie down like an old man and sleep. Old men see these things more clearly than the young. For the young it is bitter medicine we old men make. To be a young brave in an old tribe is like seeing a young bride taken by an old man. It is like an old man who is dying saying to a young man that he must die too. I know that is how my words must sound to those who are not old. They feel the white man has cheated them of their youth. But I see no other way through this pass. The buffalo is gone. The Texan has come. They will destroy our people if we continue to fight them. They have told us this. I think it is a crime against the gods for a man to take his own life. So it is with a people. I do not believe in the bad medicine of Tehana Storm, that the Comanches must die as a people. We Meat Eaters must take the White Man's Road and go onto the reservation. But in such matters as surrender, old men and cowards are often wrong."

The young chief, Kills Few Men, spoke next. He was dressed in faded deerskin with little ornamentation. His own skin was similarly soft and pale, for he did not go out into the sun without an umbrella made of buffalo hide. Though he did at times speak eloquently of the Comanches' passing life on the plains, one felt he claimed experiences he had not had and emotions others had felt. He concluded his address by saying he would follow the medicine of Tehana Storm and the Wanderers band. Kills Few Men and the band of young, unmarried braves would leave the Meat Eaters before they went onto the reservation.

Next came Bad Hand, the Meat Eaters' chieftain. He was a tall, muscular, catlike man among the other thick braves, his looks more Spanish than Indian. He smiled more than any Indian I had ever seen, but those smiles meant nothing: cutting a man's throat would have amused him. The other Comanches were dressed indifferently—breechclouts, vests, leggings, buckskin trousers without any ornamentation—but Bad Hand wore a trim buckskin suit with long fringe, elegantly detailed in blue beads and decorated by blue stitching and blue hourglass designs. His braids reached his waist, for he had tied squaw's hair into his own to lengthen them. He did not pull his facial hair and grew a thin mustache and a few chin whiskers, which he preened as he spoke. He made a display of his wealth and had adopted many traits of his Mexican slave's culture. He rode a fine Arabian horse and mounted it with Spanish equipment. He satirized Kills Few Men's feats and losses by reiterating the young brave's speech, as if he had known no adventures or grief of his own. He concluded:

"The white man struck the first blow. Our women wept, his laughed. We struck the second blow. The white women wept, the Comanche women danced. Now there is a third blow by the white man. Shall we strike a fourth, so that all women will weep that their men are dead? The white man has killed the buffalo. Shall we kill his cattle? He has taken our plains. Shall we take the White Father's City? The white man has sent the Texan to scourge us. Shall we send dog soldiers against him? The Comanches are a wiser people than that. The white man has been wrong to treat us as he has. He has been wrong to make war against us, wrong to kill the buffalo, wrong to take the plain, and wrong to have sent out these Texans. Someday the white man will flood this land in tears for these wrongs, when the buffalo are gone, when the plain is gone, when the Comanches are gone—and there are Texans everywhere. There will be a great wailing in the White Father's City then. But will the Comanche be wrong because the white man is wrong? Tehana Storm and the Wanderers think so. That is their road. Let them wander it. The Meat Eaters will be wise. We will go onto the reservation and take up the little white buffalo—what is the name of the white man's little white buffalo?"

"Sheep," said Hair Grows Short, and the Indians in the room laughed.

"Sheep." Bad Hand smiled. "The Comanches are a wise people. If the white man wants us to take up crooked sticks and chase this little white buffalo, we will do it. I have nothing more to say than that."

The medicine man Nine Pipes spoke last. He was, of the four, most typically Comanche in looks and dress—a short, stout man of fifty with black leathery skin and eyes set close and slightly crossed. He wore a buffalo robe and was round. He seemed angry and bored by all the talk. His speaking style was abrupt, his message to the point:

"I have always said that the time for the Comanche to go onto the reservation is when life on the reservation is better than life outside the reservation. That time has come. Only a fool would stay out on the plain, freezing, starving, and hunting animals that are all dead and gone. We will want goods and presents when we go onto the reservation. What kind of things will we receive on the reservation?"

"You will receive goods and presents when you go onto the reservation," I said. "I don't know exactly what you will receive—meat, corn, seeds, blankets, houses, if you want them. You will also be given instructions in how to farm, and, I think, you will be free to hunt on the plains when accompanied by a guard of white soldiers."

Nine Pipes said to Bad Hand: "Isn't the white soldier good to us? They will give us houses, teach us to plant, and guard us while we hunt. I am tired of this talk. It is time to smoke."

We smoked, then I made a speech extolling the wisdom of the Meat Eaters' going onto the reservation and the virtue of their peaceful ways. Then I asked about Tehana Storm and the Wanderers band: "Do you know where they are camped? Are they on the warpath? We would like to find them, so that we may talk and avoid war."

By now the old chieftain, Hair Grows Short, had dozed off, and Kills Few Men had risen to go with his unmarried braves so that they might prepare to leave the Meat Eaters. Remaining were Bad Hand and the medicine man Nine Pipes. Our conversation grew informal, Bad Hand teasing his Mexican slave with a rawhide string. Nine Pipes produced another pipe, which the three of us shared.

Pressed on the matter of the Wanderers, Nine Pipes tapped me on the wrist. "Their true name is Those Who Cannot Find Their Way, Those Who Are Lost. They are people who drift about without a destination, a people who are forever starting out for some place and then when they are halfway there, they change their minds, they squabble among themselves, or lose interest or decide the place they have just left is where they really want to be. I must give Tehana his due. He has made the Wanderers into a serious band—nothing like the Meat Eaters or the Antelopes—but better than the Wasps or the Worms, who are such cowards and low-lifes I cannot speak of them. But the Wanderers are a lost tribe, no matter the courage of their chieftain."

I said I had heard from a buffalo hunter that Tehana no longer led the Wanderers, that an evil medicine man had taken control of Tehana and his tribe of Comanches.

Nine Pipes turned his sharp black eyes on me. "That is true. The medicine man's name is Coyote Droppings. He is an evil, worthless man—much more like a white man in his thinking and his ways than Tehana, whose mother was white. Coyote Droppings was never a warrior before he became a medicine man. In the old days a medicine man had to prove himself on the battlefield before he took up the ways of a shaman. Nowadays every squaw man in the tribe calls himself a medicine man and does not have to fight. That was how it was with Coyote Droppings, or so I have heard. I have also heard that Coyote Droppings is not a true Comanche, that his mother did some nightcrawling among the Kiowas or the man-eating Tonkaways. Or if Coyote Droppings is a Comanche, then it is said he came from the Worms, whose full name is Worms in the Penis, or

177

from a really disgusting band, They Fuck Themselves, a cross-eyed, addled people who are so slovenly with their habits they allow brother and sister to sleep in the same tipi.

"Coyote Droppings' medicine is bad. Very bad. He says he is like steel against bullets. He says he can raise the dead. He says he can ascend into the clouds and speak with the Great Spirit. I do not know any Comanche who believes such nonsense. It sounds like some tall tale the Cheyenne would think up—they are the sorts who converse with gods. But there is one medicine made by Coyote Droppings that has been very strong. Last summer he said there would be a great star with a tail of fire crossing the sky and that this lost star was angry with the Comanches that they had not made good war against the white buffalo hunters and that the lost star would take the water from the skies till the Comanches stopped their womanly ways and made war against those who made war against the buffalo. All of this happened. The lost star came, the skies remained blue and the earth grew brown, and our people suffered. There was magic in Coyote Droppings' knowing this. But his other medicine was so bad he nearly destroyed the Wanderers.

"Last fall, when there was no water or grass or buffalo anywhere, the Wanderers mounted their war ponies and put on paint and rode up to the great white hunters' camp at Adobe Walls. There were many hundred Comanche warriors, some Kiowas, some Cheyenne even, in the party. Of the white hunters there were only twenty or so. Coyote Droppings had performed magic on all the warriors. They would be like steel to the white man's bullets. If they weren't so much like steel, then Coyote Droppings would return them to life. At dawn the next day the Wanderers made their charge and the buffalo hunters fired their great guns and three of the finest Comanche braves were dead. The Wanderers made a second charge and two more braves lay dead. A third charge and more were dead. The Wanderers rode back a ways to speak with Coyote Droppings and still another of their warriors fell, so that they began to fear that these great guns would fire bullets that would pursue them over the earth and strike them no matter where they hid. So the Wanderers quit the field beaten, humiliated, for there was a Ute among the buffalo hunters and he took the scalps of their fallen braves.

"But the sad part of that tale is that Tehana learned nothing from this disaster. He did not mourn the lost braves at Adobe Walls, he did not cast off Coyote Droppings and his bad medicine. He said that those Comanches who died before the white man's guns were better off than those who would live under the white man's yoke. He said that a brave death is better than a coward's life. This is good Comanche teaching, but only up to a point. It is true that a Comanche brave will always die before he is dishonored, but is this true for an entire people? Should the Comanches fling themselves before the white guns and cease to exist as a people? That was the question raised by Tehana Storm.

"On such matters the people must decide. The people of our tribe provided us with their wisdom. They said that if we chiefs and medicine men wanted to fling ourselves before the white man's guns without thinking, then we were free to do so. The people, however, preferred to live and look for other medicine that might defeat the white man or, that failing, to find some way to live with the white man and retain some of our old ways. When we listened to our people's wisdom we understood that this was the Comanche way of thinking."

"Then what are the Wanderers doing? Are they on the war-path?"

"We do not know. We only know that they remain on the plains and that Tehana has devised a Prophet Dance or Ghost Dance in which the wall that separates the living and the dead is breached and the one passes to the world of the other, back and forth, so that neither life nor death has any meaning. A bad medicine."

The door to the trading post was flung back, and Kills Few Men and a handful of unmarried braves entered. They approached Bad Hand, who did not rise to greet them. They said they had made ready to leave the tribe and asked Bad Hand's permission to ride out. Bad Hand dismissed the braves without much of a blessing. Soon Nine Pipes and the others went out. Bad Hand told his Mexican slave to prepare one of his wives. When the slave was gone, Bad Hand flicked Hair Grows Short with his leather thong. The old man slept sitting, his head slumped on his chest. At length the old man woke, raising his head as if his eyes had been closed but a moment.

A smile came to the old man's face, wrinkles bursting about his eyes like sunrise. "I dreamt, Bad Hand, that we lived in a white man's house and there was a barrel of sugar in the center of it and we were like children again, without cares."

"It was a dream, old man."

"I know, I know," said the old man, with his smile.

So the largest band of Comanche Indians had laid down their arms, the rear of the Second Cavalry was secured from attack, and half of my military mission was accomplished, all without firing a shot. Thinking to present my ideas as deed, that we might take our enemies with talk rather than at war, I set out to join MacSwain before he clashed with Tehana Storm and the Wanderers, now the last free Indians on the plains.

The remainder of the day was occupied with disarming the Meat Eaters while they were still in the mood to surrender. During the afternoon I ordered myself and ten men detached from the troop. We would ride ahead to Fort Pascal, thirty miles northeast of Las Lenguas, hoping to overtake MacSwain's squadron before it rode on. Lieutenant Fulks and Sergeant Rife were instructed to march after us with the main column of surrendered Comanches the second day following. This arranged, our small squad rode out of Las Lenguas, guided by starlight. We dozed in the saddle at an easy gait till three in the morning, when we whipped our mounts and rode hard, the horses making a great effort as if they knew at the end of this ride they would have seen the last of us.

We left the *llano estacado* during the night. At dawn the land burned under the fire of the November sunrise, broken country, cut by washes, dry creeks, and rock-strewn cedar brakes. Along the western horizon stood a great mesa, while about us were scattered smaller tablelands and buttes. The morning air was chilled, but there was no frost. Chaparral and scrub cedar and yucca stood stiff, sharp, and brilliant in the cold, their shadows slashing blue trenches across our path that worried our horses with their icy depth. The ridges and promontories were capped with worn, seared rock, but in the washes and flats gramma grass and wild shrubs and marigold weed grew in abundance. Shortly we saw figures clothed in a dark, familiar blue riding the mesa's rim. We signaled these compatriots, and they rode down an impossibly steep wall to us. Greetings and gossip and tales of our trek were exchanged. We learned we had missed MacSwain. His squadron had passed through Fort Pascal a week ago, MacSwain imagining he was close on the trail of Tehana Storm.

We rode with our escort and soon came upon a valley and a river where water had recently run, its standing pools so fresh our horses had to be spurred out of them. Fort Pascal sat at the head of this valley, backing on the mesa that walled the western horizon. This nestled site, the Pascal officer said, lost most of its charm because of its defensive vulnerability and the long hours they were forced to ride scout on the tableland, that the picturesque camp might not suffer surprise attack from above. Still, military considerations paled as we approached Pascal on that clear fall morning, the fort an eccentric stair of tan blocks thrown along the sloping mesa wall. We rode up a gentle incline, through pin and scrub oak, juniper, piñon and cholla, losing sight of all but those buildings that sat farthest up the slope. These stunted growths soon gave way to *pinos altos,* and we made the final approach to Pascal through their cool shade and silent needle carpet. The ground rose sharply to the bench on which Fort Pascal rested; we came up onto it suddenly. The guiding officer observed that Pascal had been constructed on the ruins of an Indian pueblo; though none of the original mud huts had survived, many of the newer adobe buildings had been raised on the ancient foundations, which, the officer said, explained the cluttered, unmilitary maze of the fort. We passed the last quarter mile to the fort along a drive of crushed red rock lined with whitewashed stone. A tidy parade dusted with the same brick-red gravel fronted the administrative building. About the parade and that building was laid an expanse of grass so trim and bright-green that one dared not touch it, lest like fresh paint its moist color might stain one's hands. There were signs advising one not to step on it. Before the main building stood three flagpoles, which displayed the national, territorial, and regimental banners, these cloths limp in the still air, like gaudy birds just shot and hung to be bled and admired. On the far side of the parade was a small pond whose surface might have been polished metal but for the ducks that moved with all the animation of towed decoys across it, breasting precisely ruled ripples. To the near side was a rose garden, severely pruned and dormant. To my appreciation of so civilized a post, the Pascal officer countered that I might view its charms more closely if I were responsible for hauling water to it, the nearest spring being two miles away.

We from K Troop dismounted in brief formation with the scout and were assigned quarters, and we bathed, ate, and slept. I was roused at dusk by an orderly, who said that Major DuBois, the Commandant of Pascal, had returned from where his duties had taken him that day, one of the neighboring ranches, and asked if I would be his guest at a small gathering in his quarters that evening. The Major and his wife and the officers and ladies of the post and many of the neighboring ladies and gentlemen were eagerly awaiting a more detailed telling of K Troop's odyssey across the plain.

When I emerged from my quarters the sun had gone behind the mesa, and though the hills and buttes to the east were still bronzed, our winter shadow was dark as night. A carriage had been arranged for my transport. We went up a good ways farther than I had anticipated, passing through a street of adobe houses, none much larger than two rooms; these were the enlisted men's barracks. We left this lower section of the fort, which was all we had seen from the valley below, and made along a winding road toward the officers' complex. Shortly we entered a black tunnel of trees that the driver said were mahogany and came out of that into the officers' village, a rambling string of adobe houses that were larger than those below, some reaching two stories, with low rooms and patios attached. Music from many guitars came through the night, the serenades of the *tertulia* toward which we went mingling with the solitary strumming of those servants who had retired to their quarters.

The servants' dark children ran alongside the carriage, laughing and crying out in Spanish. We came to an adobe wall, the only fortification I was to see at Pascal, and were waved through to a courtyard. The carriage passed around a mechanical fountain—more work for the drawers of water—and came to rest before the arched entrance to a Spanish *hacienda*. White-clad servants escorted me through a hall into an interior courtyard that had been abandoned to the night air by all but a Mexican band, four guitarists, one of whom sang a song of lost love whose plaint may have rather been the longing for hearth and fire. We came to another archway, through which I observed a spacious low-ceilinged room filled with officers, gentlemen, and ladies. From the wild reel being danced, the fête seemed to have started without me. Major DuBois came forward and led me through the guests, the Major tossing out informal introductions as we went.

"Good many of them drunk as lords," said DuBois of the established merriment of the guests. "You see, Chapman, there are such great distances between *haciendas* here in New Mexico that these functions tend to go on for days." We came upon a woman of thirty, perhaps, with small, almost stunted arms and shoulders and bust, but whose hips grew immense beneath her close-fitted satin dress. "Bertha dear, have you seen Rebecca? Rebecca is my wife, Chapman. Chapman, this is Bertha. Miss Wylie. Bertha is one of my wife's innumerable sisters. Bertha, this is Captain Chapman, from Texas."

Bertha sported a good mustache for a woman, and a crazed crooked grin, and was given to forward flirtation in a heavy Southern accent that the author will not attempt to render. "Why, Captain Chapman, I do so admire you saddle-hardened, sun-bronzed Texans—"

"Oh, Bertha, do go and find Rebecca!" Bertha went off rather quickly, it seemed. "What a tiresome thing rutting is among women. We simply must make a match," said DuBois, wiping his brow with his hands and then studying them as if he could not imagine where his handkerchief had gone. "Well, so you see, Chapman, though we did not pour the first goblet till sundown, officially, the party has been going on for a week at Don de Silva's *rancho* and will go from here to Richardson's place on Mesa Lica. It won't stop till someone gets shot. Is Texas as dreary as they say? Nothing but those grim Presbyterian Irish?"

"It is not like this."

"I suppose not. New Mexico is a rather remarkable place. It is so *old*. Did you know that Santa Fe is older than Boston? It was founded before those outcasts landed at Plymouth Rock. These people came as *conquerors,* Chapman. What is truly remarkable is that one would find such a civilization bordering on Texas. It's the beauty of one and the desolation of the other. The Spaniards were no fools. I've never been to Texas, except down toward our bit of the *llano estacado*—the people here call that Little Texas. Tell me, is it really like Hades?"

We made more of this talk, of the holes and gardens where we had seen duty, posts that had been heaven or hell, of the

184

commanders who had been mad or bad or sad, and of the women, honest or free, we had known or hadn't known, talk that bore me more pleasure than I might have admitted, for Major DuBois, in having no interest in Texas, Indians, horses, or war, passed as a cultured, witty man.

Unlike those of us who after the Civil War had followed adventure and advancement from one post to the next, DuBois had remained fixed, for the last ten years, in the New Mexico and Arizona territories. He readily admitted that if he were transferred to some other place, he would resign his commission. "At the mention of Texas, Chapman, I shall fall on my sword." These and similar revelations were offered as we moved through the Major's guests, the most intimate speculation, such as where his wife might be passing the evening and with whom, spoken in a voice that could easily be overheard by nearby revelers but evidently was not, for we drew no attention from them. DuBois told me of the problems he would face when his guests learned of the capture of so many Comanches. "You see, Chapman, we in New Mexico do business with the Comanches. The *rancho* of every man in this room, my own modest place included, is stocked and stocked heavily with cattle bearing Texas brands. Of course, the glory of accepting the surrender of Bad Hand tempts me—you understand, Chapman, that as ranking officer in this military district this role is forced on me. I must weigh fame against fortune," said DuBois, casting a forlorn eye across the gala. "Whether to resign the commission or sell the *rancho,* that is the question. Oh, Chapman, I've heard this scandal that you're married—are you? Yes, I feared so." DuBois sighed and bowed toward his sister-in-law, who stood across the room gazing at us with twisted grin and crooked eyes. "I simply must find her a mate soon. The wife in good health? The only real bachelor we have here is my adjutant, Leverman, and well, Leverman is, I'm afraid, one of those young men who wouldn't be interested even if not being interested weren't perfectly sane." At this point DuBois blanched and grasped my arm as if it were the crank to some machine he could not make run. "Oh my God, Chapman, I had forgot about Don Alvaro! You see, I'm afraid word of your trek across the staked plains has got around. Making you famous. Why couldn't you have skirted the damned thing like Marcy or MacSwain? Now you must pass the entire evening with Don Alvaro, enduring his endlessly tedious scholarship. I mean, who could possibly care whether Coronado camped on the awful *llano* or off it—or whether this wretched lost city of gold was on the Canadian or the Arkansas? Chapman, who shall dance with Bertha!"

The day following, an alarm was blown and we went up onto the mesa and there observed a great column of dust rising to the southeast. This was K Troop in escort of the tribe of Meat Eaters and their herd of ponies. DuBois sent a troop out to meet them. It was arranged that the Comanches would set out their village in a canyon below Fort Pascal, which was rimmed by cliffs, so that we might guard the Indians against outbreak or attack by whites. It was further arranged by DuBois to honor K Troop and Bad Hand with a parade in review. This was done that same afternoon. Stands were constructed, bunting hung, the parade swept and made ready for the review. The officers, ladies, and notables of Fort Pascal gathered at three o'clock, and shortly a column of riders—Bad Hand and his foremost braves and K Company led by Lieutenant Fulks—came up through the pines toward the fort. I had chosen to stand inspection of my command rather than ride with them and so, as they approached, saw them through the eyes of a garrison soldier. Previously I had been sharp that my men be fitted in proper uniform and with regulation equipment and still so maintained myself, but on this campaign I had allowed Rife and the Thieves to return to their old ways, to improvise such gear and uniforms as suited the plains. As K Troop passed in review I did not observe a single regulation uniform. The men wore light-colored slouch hats and pile caps made from buffalo wool and buckskin trousers and moccasins and irregular boots. I might have taken pride that there was an occasional blue flannel shirt among the column and that one or two men had retained their forage caps and that some had rolled their greatcoats and strapped them across the saddle pommel and one young trooper had slung his carbine over his left shoulder; but there was not a black campaign hat, not a pair of blue woolen trousers or any high-topped boots, not a sash, plume, or saber among them.

It was thus that the entire company passed in review. After the parade was done, Major DuBois, who had not said much during the affair, turned and cast a high glance over me.

"Bit difficult at times to tell the Indians, Philip."

There passed a few days of intense cold that allowed the men to recoup their energies and their military bearing. All went well with the surrender of Bad Hand. It was arranged that the Meat Eaters would winter on an Apache reserve nearby, to march to Sill in Indian Territory the following spring. I lost the services of Lieutenant Fulks during these few days. Major DuBois, it seemed, had found a mate for his wife's sister in my second-in-command, and I did not see how I could refuse happiness to all three. I signed orders that Mr. Fulks would stay on at Fort Pascal on temporary duty.

At this point in our campaign my will to pursue the remaining free Comanches had weakened. Though I pored over my maps well into the early morning, I had all but decided to follow MacSwain's path north, skirt the plains, and rejoin the regimental encampment on the Canadian River, thereby effectively ending our winter campaign. The march across the plains and the surrender of Bad Hand seemed achievements enough. But though I passed hours rationalizing that I could now quit the field with honor, I knew further that the success of the march was that we had avoided disaster simply because of clement weather and that the coming onto the reservation of the Meat Eaters was their wisdom rather than our prowess. To a reasonable man, accomplishment should be reward enough, but I strove to mark the world with my will. So it was on that morning the Mexican youth came to my quarters that I chose to strike out again, to earn by my own labors what fortune had already given me.

I was dozing over my work when I heard the Mexican boy arguing with my servant. I ordered the boy admitted. The youth burst into tears and thanked me for saving him from the Texas devil.

"¿Un diablo tejano, joven?"

"¡O sí, señor! ¡Hay un diablo tejano en la cantina, señor, que quiere hablar con usted, señor! ¡O pobre señor!"

I went down to the village cantina to see the *diablo tejano* who wanted to talk to me. The Texas Ranger sat at the end of the bar studying a sheet of paper laid out before him. There was no one else in the cantina save for the bartender, a yellowish Mexican. The Ranger was of medium height, stocky, dark, his face burnt deep red, his brows and mustache black hoods over mouth and eyes. His manner was easy, his speech quiet; he smiled without trouble, for he seemed generally amused by the human condition. The paper he had spread on the bar was a Spanish journal from Santa Fe. To the left of the newspaper sat a glass of tequila, to the right a Colt .45, cocked. The Ranger apologized for his rudeness as I joined him, but, he said, he did not believe in shaking hands in the presence of a Mexican. The Texas Ranger's name was Hartsell, a major by rank. His business was to ride out on the plain in search of a fugitive from justice. Before he was hanged, this fugitive, the Ranger promised, would tell me of the whereabouts of the lost tribe of the Comanches. Little time was taken in arranging that the Ranger and his partner would guide us back onto the *llano estacado*.

*　　*　　*

The empty map I had inherited from Marcy's cartographer had filled beyond expectations these last weeks. To the knowledge gathered from the *comancheros,* the Indians, the hunter Collins, Don Alvaro's studies, and my own location of natural features was now added the Texas Ranger's intelligence. Hartsell pointed out the abandoned settlement drawn in by Collins and added three other such sites to the map. These were not several separate attempts to settle the plains, he observed, but the traces of one man's effort to make a town. "These spots are where Holland Law and his people have once been," said Hartsell, " 'seventy-two, 'seventy-three, here in 'seventy-four—all failures. They keep moving on, looking for a place with a bit of water and some luck." The Ranger tapped the map. "This was their position last year. They were gone by a year then. Not a trace of them but their dugouts. By the time we had come on this last settlement, we were in trouble. We had run dry of water and we had to turn back. Now we have come again and we will see where the trail leads to, whether Holland Law has died or gone to California or is waiting for us on the plain."

"The man who founded these settlements is the man you are riding after?"

"He is."

"His name is Holland Law?"

"It is."

"And you know him?"

"I do," said the Ranger. "Once we rode together. One day we parted, or it could be Holland Law riding out with a noose for me."

The Ranger was accompanied by a partner called Terry, a youth whose eyes were gray and merciless, the smooth pink button of his face unmarked by any concern for life. Despite his youth, Terry was a full member of the Texas Rangers and, though outranked by Hartsell, thought himself no man's inferior. He was given to reading the Bible during odd moments of the day, and though he showed no signs of religious belief, his speech was colored by that book's angry prose, as was his morality steeped in its vengeance.

One bright, frigid morning when Hartsell had ridden forward with the scout, the youthful Ranger approached me. Preamble had no role in Terry's manner of speaking. "What has the Major told you of Holland Law?"

"Very little. That he has founded a village on the plains that you cannot find."

"Escondido is its name," said the youth, who did not pronounce the Spanish correctly. "You have some learning in the greaser tongue, I hear. Does that word mean 'lost'?"

"It is Spanish for 'hidden.' "

The youth cackled. "Lost or hidden, we will find it." Terry drew a paper from his jacket. "Have you seen our warrant? Holland Law is wanted by the State of Texas for the crimes of murder, treason, espionage, rustling, and false immigration."

If there was any amusement in the equal weight the Ranger attached to these infractions of the law, I did not indulge in it.

"He is also a seditionist, a Quaker, and a member of the Socialist sect."

"That is quite a lot."

The youth agreed, then went on darkly: "No one knows where this Escondido is but them who live in it, and maybe they don't even know where they are. We have found the remains of it, the empty dugouts shed like the skin of a snake. Have you ever heard the likes of it, Cap'n, a farm village that crawls about like a serpent, that creeps from place to place, leaving hut and field behind, to crawl on to the next? Now do you think this is likely the town and fields of a peaceful farmer or do you think it is more likely that these are the camps of outlaws?"

"I would think they might be farmers. If they were wandering outlaws, why would they plant and dig huts at all? They could live in tents and feed by hunting, like the Indians, and leave no trace at all. On the other hand, there are many reasons, all children of failure, that farmers might move from field to field, leaving their previous town a ruin, till they found the water, soil, and climate that would make them prosper."

"I would think flight more likely if the threat were lynching."

Terry made a noise that tore in his throat. "I can see that you are taking this matter lightly, Cap'n, but I will tell you, you will change your tune when you meet Holland Law face to face. Maybe the Major has told you some romance that fits your Eastern ways of seeing us, but I will tell you this Holland Law is no peaceful farmer searching for his Eden on this plain. He is a criminal. He is a cruel and clever man. If I was you, I would drop to a knee and pray that when you do come on him he is cowering alone in some hole he has dug in the earth, for if you come upon him astride a horse, a gun in his hand, you will be dead. And as for what you think of me, that I am crazed or a rogue or just a Texan, I will tell you that I am a friend of the law and none of this Law!"

With this the youthful Ranger whipped his horse away.

Toward evening we came upon the last settlement abandoned by Holland Law. We saw from a distance the scout standing their horses amidst a number of low mounds. Had it not been for the great size of the mounds our men might have been mourners in a graveyard. We rode to them and dismounted and made camp. The two Rangers stood away, studying their maps. The Major bade me join them and indicated our position on the map. "From what we know, this is the last settlement of Holland Law. The others gave signs of being much older, the dugouts filled with sand and the bones they left behind bright as new. Wouldn't you say that is so, Terry?"

"I would say so," replied the youth.

"Now we must decide, Captain, where Holland Law has gone to now—if he and his families have not perished or gone to California."

"Have you looked in the dugouts? There might be some sign of their intentions there."

Hartsell looked at the youth. "The Captain and I will search the dugouts, Terry, if you will make us a torch."

"That will be fine with me," said Terry and went off to find oil and rags.

"The boy does not like snakes and crawling things," said the Ranger with a smile. "I trust they don't bother you, Captain."

Carrying torches, the Major and I went to the largest dugout and slid down the sand-filled steps to a doorway covered by a woolly white mass of cobwebs. Hartsell burned a hole through the webs and we entered the dugout, crouching low, for the ceiling and walls were wrapped thick in the gauzy webs. "I'm not sure if what we might find here will be worth the effort, Captain," said Hartsell. "Tarantulas." He touched his torch to one of the woolen walls. The webs sizzled, and behind them, clinging to the webs, the walls, to each other, was a glistening black mass that writhed under the flame. We went quickly back up to the surface, brushing at our clothes and bedrolls throughout the night at the thought of what might be creeping over us.

Around noon the following day we came upon the feature that the Ranger said would guide us to Escondido. It appeared on the horizon as a human figure in white and soon came to be seen for a scarecrow built with bones, shaped like a man, its head the horned skull of a buffalo. "It marks his road," said the Ranger, "so that Holland may find his way about the plains and that we may find him. Here, Captain, lend me your good glasses." I gave him the glasses, and he scanned the horizon. He stopped when he came to look toward the northeast. "Another marker there," he said and leapt to the ground and tore several bones from the pile and laid them out as an arrow in that direction so that the troop might follow us.

We rode the rest of that day, following the bone markers that were placed at a distance that they could be seen only through glasses. All these markers were of a different shape, as if he who had made them had grown bored with simply stacking bones to mark his road and had attempted to fashion forms that might please or frighten the traveler. We camped that night in a state of expectation unknown to us since the first day of the campaign. The road grew clear the next day, as wagon ruts were observed in the grass. Three hours into our march we saw the low mounds of another settlement rising from the earth like great fish breasting a calm sea. We came upon fields of broken earth, all fallow and sere in the wintry light, some having returned to grass, some bearing the stalks and stems of their summer growth. Plows and other implements had been left to stand and blanch in the fields. We saw no animals anywhere. The dugouts here were placed farther apart than at the previous settlement, as if the village had begun to lose its center and was spinning apart as its masters crossed the plains. Though the morning was bright and clear there was no movement of man or beast about the dugouts. The settlement might have been deserted but for thin smoke playing from two of the chimneys. Riding in the van with me were the two Rangers and Corporal Chaney. When the smoke was sighted, the Ranger Hartsell halted us.

"Captain, I think it would be best if you and I rode in alone and if Terry and the Corporal went back to the column and stopped them off a distance." He watched as the youth took his pistol from his holster. "There will be no danger to the Captain and me if we do not create any."

"I figure we should circle them," said Terry, "so that the hound won't run."

"Holland Law will not run from us," said Hartsell. "You will keep the soldiers off a ways, Terry, while we talk."

"I would like to know what you will be talking of," said the youth.

"We will be talking of Holland Law's crimes and deciding his fate," said Hartsell.

"That fate has done been decided," said Terry and holstered his pistol and turned his horse and went with the Corporal back to the main column. Hartsell waited till the riders were small in the distance, then we turned and walked our horses toward the nearest dugout.

"Has the man's fate been decided already?"

"It has been sealed by the State of Texas," said the Ranger. "I only want a word with Holland before we hang him."

We came to the first dugout and dismounted. Hartsell went onto the dugout roof and tapped his pistol on the metal chimney. He then went to the head of the dugout stairs and squatted so that he might better see the door below and be less readily seen. He called out,

"We have come for Holland Law. Is he here?"

There was no movement or sound for a time, and the Ranger repeated his challenge. With no answer then, he went down the dugout steps with his pistol drawn but with no intention of using it, it seemed. He pushed open the door and stood just inside the dugout, peering into the gloom. He stepped back to the sunlight and looked up to me. "There is someone here," he said. "Come on in."

I went after the Ranger down the dugout steps. I paused just inside the door. The Ranger had gone into the dark cavern. I could hear him speaking to someone there. Their voices were low; I could make out no words, only that the person conversing with the Ranger was a woman. A match flared, but it lighted only the Ranger's face and immediately went out, the air being so foul it could not support its combustion. Another match was struck and the Ranger lit a lantern, whose flame was little brighter than the match. I moved toward the dim flame and saw in outline the Ranger Hartsell kneeling on the floor by a low bed. A woman lay in the bed, her head propped by a pillow. I could tell nothing of the woman but that she was young and that she held a bundle in her arms that I took to be a doll. The woman spoke in a light, rushing voice, eager, expectant, to the man at her side. So great was her loneliness that her outpouring knew neither stranger nor secret.

"He has knowed you was coming for years. Wherever we went he was ever thinking on the wrong he had done and was ever looking over his shoulder. He tried to be a good man to make up, but the Lord cain't accept goodness in token for bad. Goodness ain't heaven, Mister, the Lord don't care about it."

"Where are the others?" said the Ranger. "Are they in the other dugouts? Where is your man? Is Holland Law here?"

"Oh, the others are dead and gone! We have lost so many this year. My man Mickey he is dead and gone. He could not fit to our ways, old Mickey. Him and Holland was always flaring up, and now he is gone."

"Did Holland kill him?"

The woman turned her face away. "All of us have been afflicted for his sins. We come to bear it, Mister, but there was them like Mickey who said the Lord don't punish the righteous and we have all sinned to have suffered so. One day he walked off from here and left me and the younguns alone."

"Is Holland Law here now?"

"Me and Holland are the only souls here now."

"Is Holland in another dugout?"

"Yessir. Since I cain't walk he has been coming to me ever day, but he did not come yesterday and I fear he is dead. He was blinded in the fire and he can't see no more than I can walk. He would come ever day to tend to me, but he did not come today or yesterday and I fear the Lord has called old Holland home. Oh may the Lord call him home!"

"I think we should look for Holland, ma'am. Will you be all right here alone?"

"I do not much care to be left alone."

"We must see Holland, then we will come back. What can we bring you?"

"A sip of water. I have lost the taste for food."

"Which dugout will Holland be in, ma'am?"

"There in the next one over. That is his."

195

The Ranger poured a bit of water in a cup and fed it to the woman. The drinking exhausted her, and he laid her head back on the pillow. Her skin was so pale and her face so thin she seemed made of glass. She wore a cap, for most of her hair was gone. Her body stank of the illness that was killing her.

"I will leave the light on for company," said the Ranger.

"God bless you, Mister," said the woman. "God bless you for coming at last."

I went up the dugout steps, and the Ranger followed. A tendril of smoke, near invisible but for the heat it poured into the air, came from the next dugout chimney. We tethered our horses and walked to the dugout. This was a larger affair than the others and less submerged, so that there were slits high along the interior walls that admitted air and light and provided prospects to the north and to the south. We found no one in the dugout, but the Ranger bade me stay. He had stopped before the stove and had absently placed his gloved hand on the belly door.

"He is here," he said. "I can feel him about."

We searched the cabinets and walls and floors of the dugout and found nothing: everything was solid earth. Then the Ranger looked at the earthen ceiling, a lattice of thatched saplings supported by crossbeams. The Ranger went outside and returned with a pitchfork. Beginning at one corner, the Ranger went along probing the ceiling, pushing the pitchfork between the saplings into the earth cover. At one point he found some resistance and withdrew the pitchfork. One of its blades was running with blood.

"Would you die, Holland, rather than speak?" said the Ranger, his face uplifted.

There came a strangled, muffled laugh from above. "I had dozed asleep and you have waked me."

Dirt began to drift from the ceiling, and we saw a section of it move and saw that section of the ceiling was a board painted black and smeared with coffee grounds and dirt and crossed with saplings in the same pattern as the rest. We took chairs and stood on them and lifted the cover and the man lying on it and brought them down. The man was coated with dirt from his burrow. He coughed and choked, bringing up the dirt he had breathed and swallowed while hiding. The Ranger brought the man water, and when he had cleared his mouth, he drank. There was not much to be seen of the man for the filth but that he was old and his eyes were wrapped in bandages.

"Were you hiding from me, Holland?" said the Ranger when the man had drunk and came to breathe freely.

"Aye, I was at first, but I come near to burying myself there later."

"Where did I get you with the fork, Holland?"

"In the lungs, I'm feared," said the man, and we saw that blood was mixed among the dirt he had brought up.

"Why didn't you cry out, Holland?"

"I didn't have the air, sir," the man called out and was taken with laughter and coughing that tore away at his injured lungs till it seemed that every fiber in his chest would come up. When the convulsions ceased, he took more water, moving his tongue over his teeth to clean them. "I hear an old sound in your voice, sir," he said, his covered head moving from me to the Ranger, as if he were a sighted man. "Do I know you?"

"I am known to you, Holland," said the Ranger. "It is Flukey Hartsell."

"Flukey? It is Flukey," he said, turning as if he were speaking to another person in the room. "Flukey, why have you come for me, boy?"

"I have come to see you hanged, Holland."

A smile yanked at the old man's mouth, his lips jerked. He rubbed his hand around his neck. "Oh, don't hang me, Flukey, boy, it ain't no way to die."

"It is the law, Holland."

"But I *am* the law, Flukey! Don't you remember, boy? I *am* the law!"

197

"I remember, Holland," said the Ranger and waited till the old man's coughing fit had passed. "You were the law."

The old man sat, his hands placed on his knees. He breathed hard, sweat coming from under the bandages wrapped around his face. "When is it going to be, Flukey? When am I going to die?"

"There is some business first, Holland," said the Ranger. He took a folded paper from his jacket and opened it before the man. "Will you confess, Holland, to what you have done?"

The Ranger placed the dry, crackling paper in the man's hand, but the paper slid from his shaking fingers. "What crime will I be signing to, Flukey, boy?"

"To most that you have done." The Ranger brought a low stool and placed it between the man's knees and placed the paper on the stool. He fitted a pencil in the old man's hand and put the pencil to the paper.

"This is it, then, Flukey, boy?" said Holland Law and scrawled out something on the paper. The Ranger took up the paper and looked at what the man had written. He then folded the paper and returned it to his jacket.

"The soldiers are here with us, Holland."

"Soldiers? Yes, yes. I could smell the wool."

"They are looking for Comanches, Holland."

"They will never find them, boy. The Comanches have gone from this country."

"Do you know where they have gone?"

The old man threw back his head. Blood had begun to dribble from his nose. He smiled and more blood—pink as flesh—could be seen in his mouth. "They have gone beyond the Canadian River. You will find them there."

"Are they on the warpath?"

"No. They have had their run at it and are done."

"I want to find them, that they may go onto the reservation."

The old man moved his head from side to side. "Go north of here to the ends of the plain and you will find them there." Holland Law raised his head and spoke out with the false hysteria of a preacher. "Flukey, boy, my eyes hurt bad! Is there some salve or lard to put on them? Look there in the cupboard. Maybe I can open them and see before I die, Flukey!"

The Ranger went to the cupboard and returned with a jar of salve. He unwrapped the bandages from the old man's face. Two patches of cloth had been placed over the old man's eyes. The cloths may once have been saturated with salve, but they had dried now and when the Ranger tugged them off bits of flesh came away with the cloth so that the man's blinded eyes could be seen through the torn blistered lids. The Ranger cut fresh pieces of cloth from a bandanna and soaked them in the medicine and pressed the cloth against the man's eyes. He found a sheet and tore strips from that and wrapped these fresh bandages around the man's head so that they were the only thing about him that was white and clean.

"How did you get burned, Holland?" said the Ranger. "What has happened to you here?"

Holland Law laughed softly. There was no more fear in him. "The Lord has struck me down for my sacrileges, Flukey. He put some bomb in one of the stoves. The children heard it frying in there like the devil's talk and I opened the door and He plucked out mine eyes. And He took the children to Him as well. He gave them shirts of fire! I could hear them running around me, *burning,* but I could not catch them, Flukey, before they had burnt up. I dug holes for them in the walls. They lie buried there if you want to find them."

"And where is your wife, Holland?"

"Oh, I have many wives, Flukey, since I became a free lover."

"Who is the woman in the other dugout, Holland?"

"Oh, that is May. She is my beloved, beloved wife, Flukey, of all the others."

"What happened to her man, Mickey, Holland? Did you kill him?"

"Yes, I killed him. He walked off from me and I followed

199

him and when we was off a distance I killed him and buried
him. You will find him buried east of here a ways."

"You killed him for his woman?"

The old man nodded. "She has poison in her, Flukey. It has
poisoned her milk, but there was nothing else to feed the poor
little feller, and he was crying so. I would give the little feller
sugar and water, but at night she would feed him from her breast
and he took to convulsions and he died."

"What happened to the others, Holland?"

"They walked off from us."

"Did you kill them, Holland?"

"Oh no. I did not kill any of them but Mickey, that was
May's man."

The bare earth floor began to shake and then the sound of
our horses came to us and the old man bowed his head and
gasped for air, for the fear of death had returned and taken
hold of him just as he had thought it was gone. The Ranger
rose and came to me.

"Will you stay with him, Phil, till I get a guard on him?"

The Ranger went up the dugout steps. I could hear him calling out to the others and the others calling out in return. The
floor and the walls of the dugout trembled from the horses galloping above us, and dirt seeped from the ceiling. The old man
raised his head and turned toward me. The medicine that Hartsell had placed on his eyes was running from under the bandages, flowing down his face like tears.

"My philosophy was simple, sir, but none of them came to
it. Man is one and that is it. There is no pleasure nor pain that
is all mine or all yours. Can you feel it, sir, can you feel the
rope on your neck?" And the old man reached out and his
hand came closer to grasping me than I would have thought
possible. "I must flee, I must flee," he said and turned his band-
aged eyes toward the bugle calls, the galloping horses, the cries
of men and the clash of equipment as the troop came up in
formation to dismount. Men could be heard running about

above us. Dirt spilled in thick falls from the ceiling. Men came down the stairs and took Holland Law under his arms and carried him up into the sunlight. There a wagon had been pushed before the troop, its tongue fixed to stand upright, a noose tied to the standing tongue. Holland Law was walked to the rope, and there I ordered my troopers to stand away. Without their support the old man fell.

"Will you not help us hang this dawg, Cap'n?" said Terry, the youthful Ranger.

"I do not think I will allow it."

"And how will you stop us?" said the youth.

"There are enough of us to do it," I said, and the troop moved around us, so that the wagon, the condemned man, the two Rangers, and I made the center of their circle.

The Ranger Hartsell spoke. "What is it that you object to, Captain? How can we put your mind at ease?"

"This is not a legal execution—it must be done in a place made for hanging," I said, and the old man on hands and knees cried out—

"Aye! Aye!"

Terry came toward me. "We can take him off somewhere and hang him there, if you won't countenance it, Cap'n!"

Hartsell pushed the youth back. "This is Texas, Captain. We are the law now. The War is done. The boy has showed you the warrant. Holland Law has been tried and convicted and has signed his confession. There is only justice left to perform. We have come to hang him and we will do it. You tell the soldier, Holland," said the Ranger. "Have you committed these crimes and been tried for them and sentenced to die?"

The old man bayed his answer. "No! No! These liars! I have done no harm to anyone! By God, I swear! I swear to the Mother of Christ!"

"You are the liar!" cried the youth.

Hartsell knelt by the old man. He spoke evenly. "Do you know that voice, Holland?"

The old man turned his head. "Is there someone else there, Flukey?"

"Do you recall Zeph Terry, Holland?"

"Zeph? No. No, I don't ever recall him."

"It is his son, Holland. You shot Zeph Terry down and let him die. He is here to see you hung."

"I am here to see you hung!" cried the youth.

"Now is the time to come up to it, Holland. Don't go out squawling like a child."

Holland Law raised his hand, and Hartsell took it. "Oh, Flukey, it is so awful to die without seeing the light! Strip these rags off and let me try and see."

"You are blind, Holland. Leave the bandage be."

The old man was lifted to his feet by the two troopers who had helped him previously. They tied his hands behind his back and fitted the noose over his head. When they were done, the old man threw back his head and turned his bound eyes to the sky. "Oh, I can see you all now, Flukey, all you angels come round. Oh, the grass is green, ain't it, boy, oh and the heavens is blue!" His legs gave way beneath him, and he would have fallen to the ground but for the rope about his neck. The troopers moved to hold him firm. His voice came thin now from his fear, his words squealed out. "The woman, is she here, Flukey?'"

"She is too sick to move, Holland."

"It was that love of her that scattered and tore us, Flukey. There was nothing ever to parallel it!"

Hartsell pulled the noose tight around the man's neck so he gasped to breathe. "There is no proper gallows or a tree here, Holland, so that your neck likely won't break. We will try it a couple of times, but we may have to let you hang and choke."

Laughter hissed from the old man's constricted throat. "Build me a gallows, Flukey, ride me down to a tree!"

"I can shoot you, Holland, if the suffering grows too bad."

The old man cried out in wild mimickry, "Flukey! Flukey, boy, shoot me if the suffering grows too bad!"

Hartsell turned to me. There was nothing changed in him but that his eyes had dimmed and his voice beat at his words, not hard but hard enough, like a man striking a friend who would not quit the fight. "We are ready to commence, Captain. The death sentence will be read, and Terry and I will drop him as best we can. Will you witness the execution or will you stand away?"

"I do not think this should be done here and now."

The Ranger looked off. "Will you be a witness to it, Captain, or will you stand away?"

I turned and had Sergeant Rife form the men in ranks and had the company drum beat a roll so that the man's last words and his strangulation could not be heard. I walked off and went to the dugout where the woman lay. She was nearer death than life, it seemed, lying rigid, her huge glistening eyes fastened on something above. Her breathing came hard, her words escaping in terror at the drumroll that came down through the earth to us.

"Did you find Holland Law?" she said.

"We found him. He was in the dugout as you said."

"Oh Lord, oh Lord, they have found him. Was he alive?"

"He was alive. His eyes are badly burned. We will be taking you both to the settlements, so that you can be cured."

"Can I see him now?"

"Not yet."

"Is he resting now?"

"He is."

The woman turned her face to me. I did not think she saw me any more clearly than had Holland Law. "We will be together by and by. What—*what!*" The woman sat upright in bed, a harsh movement that she had not the strength to hold. Her limbs and face quivered from her effort and from her fear. The drumroll had stopped. "Oh Lord, oh what was that?"

"Those were our horses. They were running and now they have stopped."

"Oh, and they was running round and around!" she said and

went back to her pillow and after some time of silence closed her eyes.

Holland Law was left to hang till his heart was cold and then was cut down and buried that afternoon. The Rangers made camp with us and rode out the next morning. They rose and left in the dark, and I did not see them go. I sat with the woman till late and posted Corporal Withers, who had some medical training, to stay with her. She died so easily during the night that the corporal did not come to me till after dawn. We wrapped the woman in sheets as white as we could make them and uncovered the fresh soil over Holland Law and placed her body there with the man in a common grave.

We turned our column, then, due north and made for the Canadian River, knowing that we would come upon MacSwain's encampment there if not the Indians'. Late the second day the earth began to move against the horizon, swells and troughs formed under us, and we left the *llano estacado*. During the second night it began to snow, and we woke to these rolling prairies blanketed in white, the air smothered with drifting flakes. We marched that day through the deepening fall but felt no threat from it, as there was no wind or ice or bitter cold in the storm. As the weather throughout the fall had been a mild ally to our campaign, with rain when we thirsted and dry when we cared to march, now winter laid down a pure white carpet of snow so that we would come upon the tracks of the scout that would lead us to MacSwain's encampment and the tracks of the lone brave that would lead us to the hidden Co-manches. I stood over the tracks made by the single Indian pony and marked the direction they led by my compass, know-ing that our campaign was nearly over. We continued north and soon crossed the broad, clawed swath made by a column of heavy, shod horses. We followed this trail till near nightfall, when the prairie gave way before us. Below we saw the curving string of lights that was the regiment's campfires burning under a veil of snow. Dark figures moved across the dimming white. As the bugler sounded our call, more of these black forms crawled from their snowy mounds. These then became larger, stranger figures as the men mounted their horses and came toward us. We nudged our horses and rode down to them, calling out our greetings.

We had not thought of such things for months, that it was Christmastime and that men would be playing like boys in the snow. Some were pulling sleds up the riverbank to ride them down, some skated on the icebound river, some flung snowballs as we passed, someone among them had built a snowman with the stripes and scowl of our Sergeant Major. The camp had been made at an abandoned stage depot. When our horses had been taken from us, we were led to an adobe building and entered a banquet hall. There a long table had been laid with turkey and antelope roast and venison steak. Before us were placed bowls of oranges and bread baked from white flour and mugs of wine and coffee. A tree stood in the center of the room; it was hung with strings of berries and bits of bright cloth, and candy canes and candles had been set among its branches. Mail had come from the East, and letters were scattered under the Christmas tree like gifts. As we ate, men sang Christmas carols. Afterwards we went out and saw our tents had been pitched for us and our horses and equipment cared for, and our troopers retired for the night relieved of their duties. The regimental smithy had removed the wheels of a buggy and fashioned runners for it; a pacer was harnessed to the makeshift sleigh, which was strung with bells, and more officers and buffalo rugs and bottles of whiskey than were thought possible were piled into the sleigh. We rode through the trees alongside the river till the runners came undone and we tumbled into a snowdrift and lay drinking and singing as if the day when the buggy would be returned its wheels, when the tree and its trimmings would be taken down and cast away, when the bottles would be emptied and the husks and bones of our feast would be thrown to the dogs, when the carols would become cadences and the winter games would be played by men at war—that night we did not think the morrow would ever come.

Now the Second Cavalry was reunited. The fall campaign had been called a success, and the winter campaign promised to be the end of our Indian wars. MacSwain was at the height of his powers. He glowed, he preened, he flexed his ambition that his military plans had been so faithfully executed, that now we stood ready to capture or destroy the last of the free Comanches on the plains. MacSwain's squadron had marched up the western border of the *llano estacado,* passing through Las Lenguas and Fort Pascal, as we knew, scouting that part of the plain that lay between the *malpais* and the Pecos River. That MacSwain had found no Indians in this region had amounted to the pacification of Comanche New Mexico, or so it had been written in the reports to Leavenworth and Washington. Nor had Major Clous, in command of the second squadron, found any Indians along the eastern border of the *llano.* Clous's march, however, had not been made with the ease of Mac-Swain's. While the latter had ridden more or less directly north, never more than a half day's march from water and wood, Clous's squadron had been forced to search and head the twenty or so canyons that formed the ragged eastern border of the staked plains. But even Clous's campaign fit neatly into MacSwain's pattern for success. The difficulties of that right wing flattered the easy march of the left, while MacSwain's stroll up the New Mexican border paid homage to the struggles of Clous in the east. But the stitching that bound up the brilliance of the Second's fall campaign was K Troop's anabasis through the heart of the *llano estacado,* the brave scout of my command. That K Troop had made peace and not war with the

Indian was forgotten. For now I and my Forty Thieves were martial heroes of only slightly less stature than Crook and Custer.

It would have been a sensible decision to have K Troop made rearguard again, for the men and the horses were jaded from our effort, but MacSwain would not hear of it. We would share in his glory if we had to crawl to do so. It snowed another two days, and the men were given that rest, and the honor they received further bolstered their morale. As well, the news that we would soon be fighting the Indians brought them vigor and ambition, for in the last months they had fashioned themselves into a fighting unit.

It was during the dark morning hours of our third day at the Canadian camp that MacSwain's orderly waked me with the word that the snow had stopped and we would be marching out. As I dressed I heard the trumpets call reveille and went out and saw that the snow had thinned: individual flakes danced like ivory moths over the men as they struggled from their snowbound tents and plowed through knee-high drifts to make formation, their attenuated forms causing them to look like boys shivering in the cold. As the men broke formation for breakfast, the officers gathered in MacSwain's tent for final orders. The Second would be divided again into two wings, for there were conflicting reports issuing from the scouts and many tracks had been found in the snow, and we could not agree among us on a single line of march. Clous's weary squadron was assigned to rearguard and was to follow with the pack train, itself split between the two unequal squadrons. Of these MacSwain was to command the larger left wing, which would march to the Palo Duro Canyon, the largest of the canyons on the eastern plains, where most thought the Comanches would be found. The smaller right wing under the command of Major Sully would head the Palo Duro and march south to the lesser canyons, the Tule and the Quitaque. It was to Sully's diminished squadron that K Troop was to be attached. If we found nothing in Tule or Quitaque canyons, then we were to turn north and proceed to the southern rim of the Palo Duro and make contact with MacSwain. Huge flags had been fashioned for signaling across the canyon in the event MacSwain had not crossed from the northern rim. If all went well, the Indians would be sighted in the canyon below, and the two squadrons would descend the walls from north and south, trapping the enemy between them. If the larger squadron came upon the Indians first, it would attack alone; if our smaller unit found the Comanche encampment, we were to wait till the main column could be sent for and then the united Second would engage the enemy. All unnecessary baggage, clothing, and equipment were left behind. Each man carried five days' rations for himself, a like amount of forage for his mount, and three hundred rounds of ammunition. It was hoped we would feed off the Indians we would destroy. There was no talk of peace with the Comanches now, not from this writer or anyone. We were at war and would strike the Indians till they surrendered. When we emerged from this briefing, the snow had stopped and a livid uneasy dawn was spread across the clearing eastern sky.

Though the march of Sully's squadron was to be longer than MacSwain's, it was the easier of the two. We would mount the plains where the snow had drifted little and the footing was firm and the visibility unlimited, while the larger squadron would follow the Canadian River, to scout its drifted banks and quicksand tributaries, before turning south to the Palo Duro. During the first two days of our march there was no sun and the air remained still and cold, so that we did not suffer from the ice and mud of a daily thaw and nightly freeze. We rode to Tule Canyon in those two days but found no Indians en route nor signs of them. The men and horses were in good condition, but if we dared march another day south, away from the Canadian encampment, we would be forced to halve rations and forage for fear we would be caught out short of our return. There were few among us who felt there were Indians in the canyons to the south. We argued with Sully that we should discard our orders to proceed to Quitaque Canyon and instead turn north to the Palo Duro. Many of the younger officers charged that we had been sent south on a chase and speculated wildly that a fight might be raging in the Palo Duro as we palavered. Sully deliberated. His fear, though he did not express it directly, was that if he turned our column north now and marched to the Palo Duro and we found no Indians there, then MacSwain would imagine the enemy had escaped through our net to the southern plains. Most of the older officers, myself included, found Sully's concern reasonable: MacSwain could hunt out scapegoats where no fault but his own existed. Sully was at the point of adopting some half measure which would have likely lost him both glory and rank when chance delivered us to battle. One of the troopers had dropped his carbine in the snow during the day's march, and as punishment the man was to be walked back to retrieve it. On retracing our tracks, the punishment detail had come upon tracks in the snow, laid at a tangent to ours, but fresher. Word of these tracks was delivered to us too late to make a scout that evening, but at first light Sully, his aide, myself, Captain Billings, the commander of the squadron's second company, and several Tonk scouts retraced our march. We stood off a ways while the Tonks studied the tracks.

"Comanche spies," the chief Tonk told us on our approach. "They come on our tracks maybe half day after we pass. Look 'em over and hightail back north."

"Were they following us?" said Sully.

The Tonk shook his head. "They come from off yonder. No follow. Come on tracks and see many soldiers pass. They turn and run."

"Off yonder?" said Sully, looking north. "To the Palo Duro?"

"Many many Comanche camp in Palo Duro."

"And we have a trail leading right to them," said Sully as he gathered Billings and me away to confer. "What a piece of good luck. We'll have them all to ourselves, gents."

"It might even be luckier than that," said Billings. "This

scout may have mistaken us for the entire Second. It's possible. Not only will they not be expecting us to turn and come up from the south, they won't even begin to imagine that Mac-Swain is to their north. We will catch them entirely unawares."

Sully set back his head and crowed: "My lads, not even Custer has such luck!"

His ambition now fired, Sully rode the command north along the Indians' trail at a killing pace, and still we did not reach the Palo Duro by nightfall. The weather warmed during the day and chilled little that night so that the snow had greatly melted by dawn. We were slowed in tracking the Comanche scout as the snow wasted throughout the morning and had lost their trail entirely by noon, when we came upon the rocky escarpment of the Palo Duro Canyon. The squadron was halted a ways back from the canyon, and those in command crept forward, crawling the last few yards to the precipice on hands and knees. Lying flat on our bellies, we studied the canyon through our glasses. The immense scale of the Palo Duro chilled us. At the point we had come upon it, the chasm stretched eight miles across, and the canyon floor lay a thousand or more feet below. The canyon opened gracefully to our right but closed sharply to the left, to the west: at the first bend upstream we could see the precipitous walls standing less than two miles apart. This narrowing produced little rise in the canyon floor, and the thousand-foot declivity carved out a gorge whose bottom could not be seen. The December sun stood high and white above us, casting a pallor over the landscape, fading the multicolored striations of the canyon walls, bleeding the sky of its blue, so that we did not believe that the haze the Tonks observed up the canyon was more than the ashen light of winter. We returned to the column and rode hard for the next upstream bend. Again we dismounted away from the precipice and approached the canyon with caution. The haze was thicker now, a dark band of smoke lying over the canyon at a level just below the caprock, trapped there by the warmed atmosphere of the plains. The smell of wood burning was strong in the air. The canyon continued to narrow and twist upstream, but the haze grew so dense there that we would not have seen more than two miles had the view been unobstructed. We returned to the command with the word we had come upon the ̇Comanches and gave orders to make ready for battle.

It was decided among the officers to ride the squadron along the plain upstream, making our way a mile or so away from the canyon rim, sending outriders to scout along our exposed flank. When the Comanche village was sighted we would then draw up our column and either attack or attempt to make contact with MacSwain, depending on the size of the Indian village. Many agreed with the Tonks in thinking that from the great pall of smoke the village would be too large for our force of a hundred to stand alone. Sully detached a small scout of two Tonks and two troopers under the command of Second Lieutenant Beaumont to cross the canyon at our present position to search out MacSwain on the northern rim, to apprise the larger squadron of the Comanches' presence and try to coordinate our attacks. We stood on the precipice edge and watched these men leading their mounts down the sheer canyon wall and saw the danger that would face us on our descent. A surprise attack would be nearly impossible. The descent to the canyon floor would take a half hour at least, during which time we would be visible to the Indian sentinels and vulnerable to their rifle fire. A danger greater than that was that once on the canyon floor we would be there to fight to the finish, for there would be no retreat up the walls. We considered descending to the canyon floor here, to ride upstream through the gorge. But to relinquish the heights of the canyon walls meant risking the greater dangers of ambush by the Indians and losing all contact with MacSwain for the lesser advantage of a surprise attack on a village whose unknown size and location might turn the surprise on us. We would keep the high ground and hope, as Captain Billings thought, that the Comanches might be so little expecting us that we would catch them sleeping. To secure this advantage, Sully ordered that we would attack the village at dawn, even if that meant waiting out an uneasy night. When we saw that Beaumont's scout had made the descent to the canyon floor and had begun the laborious climb of the north wall, we returned to the squadron and rode west by northwest along the canyon border, sending out flanking scouts to the escarpment.

By midafternoon a dark wall of clouds had heaved up along the northern horizon. In a half hour the wall had reached around us, to the west and the east, and had grown black and thick. The air about us became dense and still. The sun weakened, then disappeared, dying as meek as an empty lamp. We were struck by a mass of frigid air and passed through the portal of the norther with no hope of escape from it. We saw our flanking scouts signaling, and Sully and Billings and I detached ourselves from the column and rode toward the canyon into a whistling wind. Sleet lashed our faces as we stood on the precipice looking down at the glittering string of lights scattered like a trail of broken glass along the canyon floor. Then the falls of the storm spilled over the canyon and the Indian fires winked out and the canyon began to fill with dark. We turned our horses away from the precipice and rode back toward our squadron. We crawled under what canvas we could stake to the ground and passed a freezing, sleepless night, our only solace knowing that the Indians, unaware of our presence, would suffer our storm on the morrow.

We sat on our horses waiting for light. It came gray, a blur that we could not wipe from our eyes, a streak that opened along the eastern horizon, a colorless slash in the dark. Gradually I began to see the troopers about me, their faces pallid, so pinched from the cold that I was startled not to recognize men I had ridden with for months. The men hunched over their saddle pommels, exhausted, wet to the skin, their reins clamped under their arms or tied off and left to hang free. The horses' heads drooped near the earth, their unsteady legs stood wide, their bellies raw under the girths, for we had not unsaddled them during the night, the mouths of many bleeding, as we had gone to harsher bits that they might obey our commands this final day. The column sat like a lifeless thing, still but for a mount that might wearily shift its burden, silent but for a sick trooper coughing down the line. Then the sound of hoofbeats came from the north, from the canyon. The men straightened in their saddles, the horses jerked up their heads. The men pressed spurs into the mounts' flanks and held them under the tight rein, walking their horses about, that they might leap into a run when set free. Sully, Billings, and I rode forward to meet the scouts, who came into view just as the sun broke through the overcast, flinging wild colors across the earth and the approaching riders. The scouts reined in around us, their eyes flashing, their horses circling under them.

"Major, we have come on a good one!" cried out the chief of the scout. "The Comanche village goes on up the canyon as far as we can see!" He wheeled his horse among ours, who had become infected by the excitement and were dancing against the bit. "And better than that!" said the scout. "We have seen riders on the far canyon wall—our boys have hooked up with MacSwain!"

"And what are they signaling?"

"They have signaled attack!"

"Have you found us a way down the wall?"

"Yes! We have found a good trail down!"

"Have the Indians seen us?"

"Major, there is no smoke from a single lodge! The Indians are sleeping!"

Sully swept off his hat and brought it across his horse's rump. We wheeled with him and rode back to the column that had begun to shift and heave, men and horses straining to run. Sully turned at the head of the column. "Boys, there's a fight ahead! Close up, close up now! Chapman! Billings! We'll run them to the canyon to pump them up. Now close up!" With the drovers cursing and cracking their whips, the saddle train was brought up as tight to the column as we would see it that day. That done, Sully cried out, "Let's gallop, boys!" And the column sprang forward into a sweeping run. The wind pressed against our faces and we gasped open-mouthed for air, tears streamed down our burning cheeks, the blood in every man pumping for the fight.

The scouts led us to the trail they had found east of the Indian camp so that we might descend the canyon wall unseen. When we came to the precipice we found the canyon still sunk in night, with only the upper far wall in sunlight. But on that wall we saw a zigzag blue line of troopers hand-leading their horses down into the gloom, and on the plain above two hundred more soldiers dismounting, preparing their mounts and equipment, waiting their turn to enter the trailhead. We unfurled a flag and signaled across the chasm but received no answer in return. MacSwain had ordered the attack with no thought of us, and we quickly dismounted to make our way into the canyon to join his command. We could only hope that our smaller squadron reached the canyon floor before Mac-Swain had regrouped and mounted his larger body and left us in his dust. With a mad grin Billings held out a coin in his hand and tossed it in the air. As I caught the coin my opposite number called the side that came face down. Billings flung the coin out over the abyss, and I ordered Sergeant Rife to dismount the men. K Troop would lead our squadron to battle.

The scouts had found a fissure in the caprock palisade which, but for the shale at the very bottom of the canyon wall, proved the most difficult section of the descent. I rode at the head of the column and, though my mount negotiated the steep grade with ease, I feared at times, laboring under a storm of dirt and rocks, that one horse or man above might slip and that we all would go scattering down the canyon wall. The bright morning air was filled with the curses of the men and horses neighing in fright and the clash of saddle equipment. Once we had passed through the caprock, the trail became a linked series of traverses whose only difficulty lay in the constricted switchbacks which the horses had to be guided through a step at a time. One long traverse led to a sharp bulge in the canyon wall that shielded us from view from the Indian village. As the others were straggling above me, I hobbled my horse and climbed to the crest of this ridge and looked upcanyon. The Indian encampment stretched as far as I could see. There was no smoke or any movement about the huge camp. The sun had not risen to strike the canyon floor: the Indians slept in night. I lifted my glasses across the canyon. The upper reaches of the north wall were flooded with sunlight. The trail on the far side was steeper than our own and our comrades' descent slow and difficult. We would reach the canyon floor in good time to be among the van of the attack.

We came down the final thirty yards to the canyon floor in a rushing slide of shale, horses, men, and equipment. In ten minutes K Troop had completed the descent, gathered up our equipment, and grouped in a formation of fours. On the canyon wall above we could see Sully signaling us to move out, and our company went at a quick trot upstream toward the boiling cloud of shale dust where MacSwain's troops were debouching onto the canyon floor. There we found great confusion—horses and men tangling as they plunged down off the wall. We went on through this chaos toward a bend a quarter mile upstream where we could see a formation of troopers swirling about, as if making ready to charge. We rode at a high gallop toward the troop running ahead of us up the canyon. We came to their assembly point and saw MacSwain and several of his staff there, all pumping their arms, signaling a charge. The Second was attacking the Indians in detail, with no order of battle but that provided as each company came off the canyon wall, with no coordination between companies but that we knew there were units riding ahead of us and units coming up behind. We whipped our horses and ran them all out but did not gain on the troop ahead, as they too dashed to catch the riders before them.

We were into the fight quickly, running headlong into it. Everywhere about us was dust and men on horses cutting and striking at things we could not see, the cries of the Indians and the cries of our men calling to one another through the blinding pall, the crushing, thunderous beat of hooves and gunfire, the earth and air trembling from our attack. I dismounted our men as I could and we fought in fours, moving in among the lodges on foot. The troop ahead of us had remained mounted and had now ridden on through this village to attack the next. With their parting the dust cleared and the strange pyramids of the tipis rose through the haze, beyond them the grotesque ballet of our holders, each man straining against the four horses he held as they reared and fought against their restriction. Our men went through lodge after lodge and found no braves there, only women and crying children. Nor did we find any bodies of Indians about the village; we began to wonder what enemy we had been fighting. The troop riding behind us now came up, and I signaled for them to run on through us, up the canyon toward the gunfire. These men galloped past, led by an officer whose eyes were bright as medals. I ordered K Troop to regroup, to sling arms, and we went through the village to see if we could save any of the dying.

As we turned to aid the wounded, cries were heard from a ravine above the village. I detached two men and we scrambled up through the dense mesquite brush to a place where four of our troopers were crouched behind rocks, peering farther up the ravine.

"Indians up there, Captain!" said one of the men, and as we looked up into the thick undergrowth we saw a lone brave walking down toward us. The Indian was six feet in height, with broad shoulders and a high head. There was little of the savage about the brave. His eyes seemed to carry some understanding that was not rightly his: he laughed at us as he came down, casually throwing back his head to keep his hair from his eyes. He carried a bow and he shot arrows against the rocks that shielded us, though he seemed little concerned whether the arrows struck us or not. One of the men raised up and shot the Indian, the bullet shattering his ribs, but the brave kept laughing and sending arrows down at us without hurry, tossing his hair back from his eyes. Another man shot the Indian and then another man shot him and the first again, which killed him.

I went through the village and saw to the wounded and the gathering up of the captives, all women, children, and old men, forty or fifty in number. Some men had taken to looting the tipis, and that was curtailed. All troops of the Second but the rearguard, I was told by Sergeant Rife, had ridden through us into battle. I detached a squad of men to move the captives and the wounded to the rearguard position and turned with the rest of the company and rode up the canyon toward the sound of gunfire and a rising cloud of dust and smoke. At the next village we found a small detachment from F Troop tending to the wounded and guarding captives as we had done. We rode on through to the third village, where we found the injured without aid and the hale members of the village scattered. Another detail was left off here and the rest of us rode farther up the canyon toward a sharp elbow that had blocked our view of the fighting ahead. When we made this turn the canyon opened before us. On its floor was spread an immense collection of lodges and tipis, not only the great Wanderers tribe of Tehana Storm, we would learn, but many lesser Comanche tribes as well. Blue-coated riders moved through the village lodges, riding back and forth, circling, dashing their horses about. Farther up the valley at a point just beyond the village, where the canyon narrowed and its floor began to rise, skirmish lines had been formed. These weaving blue threads of dismounted soldiers had been moving up the canyon, it seemed from the position of their horse holders, but now had turned left and right to face the walls above them. As we observed them they were just taking cover and beginning to fire upwards. We could not at first see the Indians on the canyon walls above, for their brown skin and hide clothes lent them camouflage on the immense breastwork of rocks, but then by looking at no fixed position one could discern a constant movement on the walls, as if the rocks were protozoa being viewed under a microscope, writhing with life. We knew then that the Comanches had been forewarned by our attack on the lower villages and their braves had fled to the heights with little loss to their number, though they had left behind their women and children and many ponies. Strings of white smoke drifted down from the Indians' muzzle-loading rifles, while below a gray haze hovered over our troopers' modern weapons. We were distant from the battle, and the gunfire came to us like children slapping palms in a game. We did not stand long before the panorama of battle. Columns of riders poured past our position, some riding to attack, others falling back: we must join them. We rode onto the broad canyon floor, where we were immersed in the mad swirl we had observed from afar. The earth rocked from hoofbeats and the air was filled with the animals' neighing and blowing. The screams of the Indian women and children came to us, but we could not see them for the dust. Our men called to one another, officers shouting orders to their troopers, the men crying out in exultation. Over all this came gunfire, a constant beating. The dust rose and became so thick we could see only a few yards around us. We too began to ride about without purpose and fire at the cliffs we could not see and cry out to one another senselessly.

Ramsey's A Troop, the horses all grays, rose out of the pall of dust and came toward us hard. Ramsey pulled up his blooded mount before me, the horse rearing, wild to run and fight. Ramsey cried out,

"My God, Phil, where have you been! We have routed them!"

"What is happening forward?"

"They are gone! They have fled!"

"Are they gone from the cliffs?"

"Yes! We have killed so many of them with our fire that the others have run! Join in, Phil, let your men go!"

"We are collecting prisoners. We will go forward, but we must do that."

"Right! Good thinking, Phil! We are to burn the villages!"

"That is MacSwain's order?"

"Yes! To destroy them all!"

"Where is MacSwain?"

"To the rear, I think! Clear the villages, Phil, so that we can burn them!" Ramsey reared his horse and laughed. "Or we will burn them all!"

The line of gray horses turned behind their leader and went into the dust.

We rode through to the far end of the huge village, to the place we had observed the skirmishers being formed and deployed. There we saw the skirmishers had remounted and ridden up the canyon, the rearguard of their unit just now passing behind a sharp bend in the canyon wall. The cliffs above us had been cleared, as Ramsey had reported, the bodies of scores of warriors littering the rocks. Behind us we could see detachments of dismounted men moving through the Indian lodges, looting robes and food and weapons and other things that might be useful to us. This done, the lodges were brought down, the poles chopped and broken, the tent skins torn and shredded. Then these and all the belongings of the Indians that did not interest us were gathered in great piles, taller than a mounted man could reach. These piles were doused with grease we found in the village and lighted, and the canyon floor blazed with dozens of bonfires, their flames red as sunrise, the smoke leaden, dense, acrid. We turned and went down into the stench and heat of the fire and saved and collected all those captives we could, though many of them did not care for our work. It took two, often three troopers to pull some away from the fires, the women weeping for their lost possessions, the children weeping for their mothers. Only the elders did not lament: they seemed to find deliverance in the destruction of everything they had as if our fires were ceremony. The smoke rose in a mass above the canyon floor to be collected like a ceiling by the plain's atmosphere, black and flat over us. The sun darkened till it hung like a rotted fruit in the sky. The conflagration sucked the oxygen from the canyon floor, and we suffered from breathing the scalded stench that was left. The men draped their tunics over their heads that they might breathe and not be burned, and our column moved down the canyon like mourners in sackcloth. The horses became wild with fright at the flames that cracked like whips. A trooper was thrown, and his mount fell and rolled into one of the fires, becoming so burned that it ran through another fire and went into a frenzy of agony before it could be shot. The captives we herded between our lines fell to the ground, clutching at the earth for coolness and breath. Those who could not be prodded forward were roped and dragged along with the column. We came through the fires, our uniforms scorched and baked with ash, our faces blacked by soot. We sought water, not to drink but to douse ourselves and our animals, but could find none anywhere, for the springs that had fed the Indian encampment were upstream from us and the beds in the lower reaches of the canyon were dry. Our canteens were so hot they could not be touched barehanded, nor was the steaming water in them fit to drink or dampen our clothes. But as we moved down the canyon the air became clean and fresh and we stripped off our uniforms and bathed in it and drank it till we were cooled.

At a point not far from where the cliff trails had debouched us onto the canyon floor, we came upon a large camp of other prisoners and gave our number over to those in charge. Like all captives we were to take that day, these were women, children, and the old—there was not a male over twelve or under fifty among them. There were several hundred in this camp, and we heard of other camps that, though smaller than this, would double the number of captives. We also learned of a great herd of ponies that had been captured, numbering in the thousands. I could find no order in the regiment here below the fires, all troops having been separated from one another and then themselves split into platoons and squads for various duties ancillary to war. Thinking to keep K Troop intact, I marched us away from the prisoner camp before we could be detached or dismembered. A ways down the canyon we found a small spring. There I dismounted the men and sent a rider on to the command to report on the captives and the burning of the villages and asked for further orders. In a short time two riders from MacSwain came up to us in a dead run, urging us to remount and make down to the command as quickly as possible. Imagining that MacSwain was under attack, we galloped our exhausted mounts toward a battle we did not think we had the strength to survive. We came instead upon a command camp no less disorderly than usual, horses fresh and ready, men and officers in uniforms that seemed bright as parade dress to us. As in any battle, excitement ruled those in command, though their attention now was directed toward the rear and the cliffs above us. The rearguard troops were deployed in defensive positions below us. There were other troops on our flanks with their weapons and their eyes raised to the sky. I was taken through the cordon to MacSwain, who was scanning the canyon walls and the caprock rim with his glasses.

"Look here, Phil, we are being surrounded!" said MacSwain. "Do you see them there? There! No, they are gone now." He jerked the glasses from his face. He moved his arm in an arc from west to east. "Don't you see, the Comanches have climbed the walls and gained the heights! They are gathering their forces above us and will attack down these trails if they are not defended. We will send K Troop up here, Phil," said Mac-Swain, marking the steep north trail on the map. "And Johnson, who is less used to this than you, he will climb the south wall. Phil, there are a thousand braves above us. We could be doomed if you do not make this climb. There will be no end to glory if you save us!"

I returned to the men and saw them in their saddles, though they could scarce believe that our fighting was not done. We passed through the fresh troop of the rearguard and ran our horses down to the northern trailhead. Farther on I saw Johnson's B Troop starting the climb of the southern wall, his men leading their horses up the trail's Jacob's ladder. I swept the cliffs and the caprock above us with glasses and saw no Indians nor any smoke or dust or other sign of them. But the sheer canyon walls heaved out like swollen bellies, so that an army might have gathered ten feet back of the caprock rim and not been visible from the canyon floor. We thought there were Indians above us and made preparations to combat them.

We commenced our climb dismounted, leaving our horses and their packs on the canyon floor, a quick ascent more important to us than mobility at the top. Each man carried only his weapon and fifty rounds of ammunition. We went up the trail quickly on foot, making half the height of the wall in twenty minutes. We stopped there to breathe and tend to the minor injuries we had incurred. I had not given much attention to such matters during the climb, but now I saw the light had grown sallow, casting blurred shadows across the rock face. The sky had gone from blue to a metallic shade that had no color. The smoke from the villages burning upcanyon had begun to drift down on us, the atmospheric pressure on the plains above acting as a lid, collecting the smoke in the canyon under the caprock. I could just make out Johnson's column on the far wall. The caprock toward which he climbed was obliterated. Our own trail disappeared into a grimy haze. Our eyes had begun to tear, and the air burned our lungs. We doused our bandannas with water and wrapped them around our faces and started again. Soon we could not see the rocks we put hand to; our eyes burned and we wept. Then our blindness was forgot-

ten: the smoke grew so dense we could not breathe. We drove
our faces into fissures in the rock and sucked at what air we
might find in the earth. All climbing stopped. We clung sight-
less, choking, to a wall that in our minds grew to stand perpendicular. Fear crushed our senses. If we moved one finger we
would tumble into a bottomless, smoking abyss. I came near to
tearing my hands away from the rock—I would fall that I
might breathe! Then some force struck my back. My arms were
pinned to the canyon wall. A monstrous form began to pull me
upward, a voice hissed in my ear that we must climb or we were
dead. I moved one hand and the other and went upward.

The smoke thinned as we rose, and soon I could breathe
deeply and make out the pitted rocks beneath my face. A voice
called out from above. A rope tangled around my hand. I
looped the rope over my head and shoulders and was jerked
free of the canyon wall. I swung back into the wall with numb-
ing force but was then pulled up to the caprock escarpment to
come face to face with the red, sweating gargoyle of Sergeant
Rife. Rife grabbed my tunic and flung me up onto the flat
earth. I lay gulping in its thin pure air. I could hear Rife calling to those below, exhorting them to climb up, to take the rope
he threw them. As the men came up they scattered across the
plain to escape the smoke.

As those who were first brought up revived, we set out to
make a defense of the trailhead, though there was no need for
it. Sergeant Rife and I scanned the horizon and saw nothing.
The Comanche braves, a thousand of them, had vanished. We
thought we were lucky in this, for a single brave with a club
could have taken our entire troop one by one as we clambered
over the caprock. I saw that the men completed their defenses,
then walked along the canyon rim to a promontory from which
I could survey the battlefield. The smoke had thinned. Through
the glassy air I saw the fires had burned out; their black smoldering ashes scarred the valley floor. Farther up the canyon I
noted two troops had dismounted and were climbing the can-

yon walls, thinking as we that there were Comanche warriors ready to attack from the heights. There were no Indians there or anywhere, on the plain or in the canyon. I turned my glasses across the chasm to the plain beyond. There a dark sea moved over the earth: the captured Indian ponies were being herded into corrals. In the canyon directly below lay the camp of the captive Comanche women and children and elders. This great milling body was being herded downstream by soldiers, their blue line so fragile that it seemed the massed captives might break free at any moment. To the left more troops had gathered at MacSwain's command post. Though they were but specks of blue, clotted here, drawn out in long cursive strings there, I knew their celebrations of victory, the toasts, the boasting, the exultant refighting of the battle over the map table. Now I heard a bugle playing recall. The lines of the troopers on the cliffs wavered in their upward surge, then held fast, then, like a tide that has worked itself out, the skirmishers began to return to the valley floor. I looked back to my men and saw that the last of them had come up the wall. These few men stood on the canyon precipice, still suffering from the smoke. Above a faint azure haze was gathering around the sun. Soon the sky would be cleared. A hawk soared over the canyon, gliding down, circling lower, down into the canyon, till it disappeared into a speck against the valley floor.

Our Indian wars were over, but for a final blow.

Soon thereafter we quit our defenses on the plains and joined our comrades in the canyon below. There was still some accounting of the victory being held among the officers—the number of braves killed on the canyon walls, the number of captives taken, the number of ponies captured—but such talk was slackening. By our arrival, haste had overcome the command. The Second Cavalry was in saddle, moving down the canyon toward a place where we could regain the *llano* and flee south, away from the Comanche counterattack MacSwain feared was to come. K Troop joined in this mob of mounted soldiers, captives, pack animals, and scouts, and by late afternoon we had marched out of the canyon. There on the plains we joined the great body of Indian ponies. Four troops formed a hollow square around the ponies and a lesser number of men encircled the captives, and we began to herd these desperate humans and their animals across the plain. The column marched quickly, following the trail K Troop had made from Tule Canyon. We sent scouts in every direction, but they found no trace of the Indians. But the vanishing of our enemy did not pacify us. That the Indians could be gone so suddenly gave us worry that they might so reappear. We rode at a trot till nightfall, pushing our dismounted captives at the same pace, then made a wary camp. Our commander's fear of reprisal had infected us all. Every man in the regiment stood his own guard that night. At midnight Major Clous came for me. He and the staff had been meeting for hours with MacSwain, attempting to assuage our commander's trepidation, but with little result.

"He feels we must make a forced march across the plain, Phil, to the ranches east of here."

"That will be impossible with our train."

"Exactly. He has ordered us to lighten our burden."

"How? Shall we release the ponies?"

"No. We will kill them."

"There are two thousand ponies in this herd, Frank. Will he kill them all?"

"No. The best will be taken by the Tonks. The others will be shot."

"And what number will that be?"

"One thousand five hundred."

"More or less."

"Yes."

"We could release them, Frank."

"The Indians would recapture them."

"That would take weeks if we scattered them."

"Yes, but they would gather them in again in time and remain a fighting force."

"Without their women and children, without their lodges and robes, without the buffalo, the Indians are done for, Frank. We do not have to kill these animals."

There was a silence between us. "There are worse things being thought, Phil," said Clous. "We must destroy the horses or their masters—do you understand?"

"I do not think MacSwain can be considering that."

"Men will consider anything. We are all savages in thought, aren't we, Phil? We will destroy the horses and not their masters and we will be thought barbarians for it. Now I'm sure you understand."

Arrangements were made to kill the horses the following morning. The Tonks cut five hundred of the best ponies from the herd. The remainder were divided into three herds of that number, five hundred each. Each of these herds was corraled in a dry playa lake. This placed the horses at a level below the men who would shoot them, so that our fire would not cross the circle and strike our own kind. The captives were likewise placed in a dry lake bed at a distance and surrounded by a heavy guard, for it was feared they might rise up or attempt to flee when they heard the slaughter of their animals. The Tonks would drive their ponies far away so that they would not be spooked by the gunfire. Precise calculations for the slaughter had been made. Two troops were assigned to each herd, one troop, or that number of men, firing in line, the other placed in reserve behind, in case the animals attempted to break out of their encirclement. Seventy men would form the firing squads, with a slightly larger number placed in reserve. The firing troopers were each given fifty rounds of ammunition: nearly four thousand rounds for each herd of five hundred horses, nearly eight rounds to kill each horse. If that was not sufficient, then the reserves would be brought forward to finish the killing. These men had also been rationed fifty rounds each. If any of the ponies survived this barrage, then it was agreed they would be allowed to run free, though few of the planners thought this would come to pass. After the killing three smaller detachments composed solely of officers of the regiment would move among the horses to finish off those animals left wounded. Then we would march away, leaving the carcasses in piles in the dry lake beds.

The regiment was roused before dawn and stood in formation as each troop commander drew near to his men and told them of that day's duty. No volunteers were called for: every man was to share in the killing. As before battle, no breakfast was offered the men but coffee and tobacco, this being taken in ranks. As we waited in the dark we listened to the Tonks moving their herd of ponies from the others, the ponies neighing to one another, for some separation of mare from foal, stallion from mare, was bound to occur. Then came the sounds of the captives being taken away, their progress marked by the rush of leather over grass, dogs barking, women crying as if they harbored presentiment of what was to be done. Dawn came without color. The earth seemed chiseled from gray stone. The men rose and reformed in dismounted columns, moving out in silence. The three columns—two troops to each—were marched out by voice command, no bugle calls being played. Each column went away from the camp toward its own destination—A and F companies to the north, C and D west of that line slightly, B and K troops making due west, away from the others.

As we went across the plains, dawn opened behind us, casting shadows in our path. We saw in the distance a circle of figures, the horse holders, arranged about the playa lake. Twenty or so in number, they stood in a circle three hundred yards across, looking inward, their attention directed down to the horses they had gathered in the lake. Nothing could be seen of the horses from this distance but the very crowns of their manes as they milled about: this appeared to us as some faint disturbance moving over the surface of the earth. We came upon the lake, and the two troops of the column divided and proceeded in single file, B circling the lake to the south, K Troop moving to the north. The column halted when the two guidons met on the far side of the lake and the circle was completed. Then Lieutenant Johnson and I went along the semicircles of our men, standing back those of even number, bringing forward the odd numbers. As the senior officer I had been given command of the detachment. The lake bed lay in shadow. I walked down a few yards so that the sun would not blind me. I could only see the shape and movement of the ponies, the white animals and those marked with white moving among a dark mass, as the herd restlessly circled the lake. I returned to the line of men and looked north toward the other two columns formed on the horizon like rings of totems. Among all our planning it had been forgotten to arrange the signal that would start the killing. But then someone in one of the distant circles fired the first shot, and a mass of gunfire swept over the plains. The commencement of the killing came to us unlike thunder or stampede or raging water or any sound of nature, or war or any engines made by man. The gunfire and the cries of the horses were a massed sound of savagery and grief that neither we nor God could have made alone. I turned and went to the line of my men. There I raised my saber. As the sword fell, I called out *"Fire!"* and directed the first shot at one of the white patches moving among the shadows.

The killing did not go as we had planned. We had begun firing too soon, with the lake bed in deep shadow, and shot only generally into the herd, killing few animals cleanly or swiftly. Most were wounded or maimed. Those with injuries to their legs writhed on the ground, pathetically attempting to rise and run with the herd. They were trampled instead. Those with belly wounds ran until their bleeding felled them, many with their intestines spilling from their wounds and dragging along the ground. Some of the ponies were shot in the face or jaw and not killed, their heads shattered and disfigured so that they flew about like hideous beasts from the netherworld.

Our shooting did not improve as the sun rose. The sight given us by light was taken away by the cloud of dust beat up by the ponies and the smoke that spewed from our rifles. Too, a great number of the men were not shooting at the horses: they fired their rifles into the ground. I found myself maddened by the screams and the suffering of the horses, from the roar of the gunfire that kept me from being heard. By now most of the front-line troopers had discharged their fifty rounds. As these men finished their ammunition they let their rifles sag to the ground and stood gazing at the slaughter they had done. We had fired three thousand rounds and had killed less than a hundred horses, a like number having been wounded. As the gunfire diminished I understood its narcotic kindness: without its roar the horses' screams came to us clearly. When my voice could be heard, I ordered the reserves in line, and they commenced firing. But many of these men would not fire, not even into the ground. A dozen of their number threw down their weapons and walked away. As the encircling line thinned, some of the ponies made their escape. But by now most had been driven into a frenzy by the firing and the killing and had gathered in a tangled circle in the center of the lake. As those among them were shot and felled, the surviving ponies climbed in terror on their bodies, so that a pile of horses was formed in the center of the lake. The reserves ran through their ammunition quickly or did not fire all of it. Only twenty-five men stood in our line firing at the horses—and still only half the herd were dead or wounded. I went to the men who were still firing, one by one, and spoke to them, telling them to put down their weapons and leave the line. I came to one youth whose mind had been seized by the killing. He had fired his magazine and had taken up another trooper's weapon and was firing it. He had collected several other weapons about him so that he might fire them in time. After a while, only that one trooper and five or six others in line around the lake still fired. These few men killed the ponies with great efficiency, felling as many as a hundred horses among them. Soon they began to see they were alone and, one by one, put down their rifles.

Now that we had stood away from the lake, I thought the surviving ponies would escape onto the plains. A few did, but a great number remained in the lake bed, some running about madly, others standing over a downed horse, a mate or a foal. These would not quit the lake bed till they were driven from it. I did not count the number that escaped, but they could not have been more than fifty. The men were formed into ranks and their injuries cared for: these were mostly burns from the heated rifle barrels. One trooper had been struck in the leg by a stray bullet, but the tear was minor. Several of the younger troopers were weeping; they were taken away from the others and treated as if they had been wounded. I detached two volunteers from the troop and had Sergeant Rife march the other men back to camp. Desultory firing now came from the other circles, and I set my mind to the task that occupied them, going among the horses and finishing the wounded. The two volunteers bore the weapons and the ammunition I needed. The finishing went quickly. We went from horse to horse, the bearers aiding me in searching out those still alive, often killing a badly suffering pony before I arrived. I viewed the dead horses closely. I noted their color, their size, their age and health and gender. I noted their wounds and how they had died, whether they had suffered or had been killed cleanly. At length I failed to see the horses individually but perceived them as variegated colors and shapes, as the pattern in a rug or the markings for islands and hills on a map. We went with no particular system toward the center of the lake, where the greatest number of ponies lay, many piled on one another, stacked four or five high.

It was then, as I looked at these horses piled one on another, that I understood I was doing wrong. I returned my gaze to the ground and did not look up again, and again the finishing came easy.

During the afternoon the Quartermaster's detail went about the lake beds dragging the carcasses into great piles in the center of each lake, covering the piles with lime, making monuments to our slaughter. The captives were brought back to the camp in a state of terror: huddled in a lake like their animals, ringed by guards, they had imagined they too would be killed. The troops were offered a large midday meal, but few ate it. Some men sought sleep but found sleep, too, impossible. Morale was low among the men and discipline tattered, for the other troops had seen many men refuse to shoot the Indian ponies. MacSwain ordered a march to take us away from our shame and bring the men into line. We were in the saddle by four, but winter night came early and we had not gone far enough, it seemed, by dark. We marched another two hours or so, till eight in the evening, when a halt was called. It was thought we would make a dry camp here and then on the morrow ride for Quitaque Canyon, not more than a day east of us. The men were exhausted from battle; many could barely sit upright in the saddle. Their minds, too, needed release from battle and killing, and it was hoped that sleep would bring them peace. But MacSwain called all officers to his map table and told us of a scout that few believed had been made. Killing the Indian ponies had not dispelled his fear; rather it had gained fear's ascendency.

"Indians have been sighted here, here, and here," he said, his hand skittering across the blank page that stood for the *llano estacado*. "We did not get all their horses in the Palo Duro. The warriors drove many of the best away before our attack. You saw today the caliber of the animal we took. The best escaped.

At this very moment the Comanches are riding behind us, on our flanks, waiting for us to sleep to make their attack. Can you imagine their rage when they come upon the ponies? Can you imagine what awaits us if we allow them to overtake? No, we must have a night march, and not here, not to Quitaque or Tule." He swept his hand over these canyons drawn on the map. "These holes teem with Indians. Every gully, ravine, and arroyo is fitted with an ambush. No, we shall not fall into their trap. We shall ride here, directly across the plains, to safety among the Texas ranches, here." And his hand fell to the place where we had made our summer camp.

"That is a hundred miles," said one of the officers. "It could be more."

"It could be more—let's say it is more," said MacSwain. "Is there a man among you who cannot ride a hundred miles or more for his life? And this plain—no king ever built a finer road. And look at this light." He swept his hand from the unbounded horizon to the high pale winter moon. "Who among you wants to sleep when we can ride! Tie the captives to their ponies, make your men ready—we will have a good night!"

"A hundred and thirty miles," said one officer as we dispersed. "We will have two good nights."

"With the captives," said another, "we will have three."

We returned to the men and told them of the night march. This was not received ill, for many shared MacSwain's fear of the vanished warriors, while others who sought to escape the last days' war and slaughter thought that dreams might return them to it more surely than memory. The captives were tied to their horses and the horses were tied one to the other, so that none might escape. We set out under the moon and stars as bright as moons and, as our commander had said, made good time across the plain, riding at a fast walk, covering four miles an hour. Our first night of sleeplessness passed easily. We suffered from nothing but the desire to sleep. We tracked the moon as it moved across our path. We spoke to one another of the stars and what lay in our futures now that our campaigns were over. To the rear a trooper played a mouth organ, another sang—

"I dreamt I dwelt in marble halls . . ."

—the horses blew and nickered among themselves, the murmur of their hooves moving over grass soothing our spirits. The moonlit night, the low talk, the music, the whisper of the horses' walk, all these things spoke of sleep so that during that first night we did not forget it. Many of the men dozed in their saddles and were waked by the sergeants who rode the line. Even the keening of the Indian women told us who we were and what purpose we had, that we were a column of soldiers mounted on horses, riding our captives away from war.

I did not see the fog till we were in it. One moment I was looking at the moon, the next there was nothing about me but my arms and hands and my horse's head. I let my horse fall back to the rider behind. Saying that I had dozed in the saddle, I asked how long we had been in the fog.

The man replied, "For an hour, I think, but it could be less than that. I may have slept as well."

I spurred my horse and went forward toward the head of the column. The horse did not run well, shying as the form of each horse and rider loomed out of the fog. But I kept the animal headed and soon heard hoofbeats rising like echoes from the mists. Our two horses almost collided, the approaching rider and I crying out, the horse before me rearing as did my mount, as if some ghostly self-image had leapt through the gray wall of fog.

"Who is it?" cried the rider.

"Chapman!"

"Phil, it is Billings! Are you still behind us?"

"We are—I think. Where have you come from?"

"From the head of the column. We are fine there. We are

following the needle. We should be out of this soon—or it will lift."

"How long have we been in it? I must have slept in my saddle."

"An hour—maybe more," said Billings. "Phil, we will be all right, but we must not let the men sleep. We must keep the column intact. We must draw the horses up, croup to head, and no one must sleep. A single rider who loses his senses could lead the entire column astray. Ride back along the line, Phil, and close them up. And keep them awake!"

And the rider wheeled his mount and returned to the fog.

I went back along the line, speaking to every man to close up behind the rider ahead, shaking each man, not leaving him till I heard him speak. I made my way to the rear of K Troop, identifying each of my men. There I passed on the instructions to the commander of the troop behind. Then I turned and went forward along the line of my troop, speaking to each soldier as I overtook him, shaking those who did not respond, closing up the column. At the head of the troop I turned and made my way back to the rear, a circuit I would ride till I lost count.

We came out of the fog at midday. Our watches pointed at twelve and the sun stood overhead: having sleep and dawn taken from us, these things meant little. Again we thought we would pitch camp and argued with MacSwain, but not forcefully, for exhaustion had made us tractable. MacSwain would have his forced march across the plains, to crown his victory. The men were not allowed to dismount as pemmican and bread were distributed by the Quartermaster. We set out riding through the winter afternoon, the sky thin and white, the air crisp, as if newly made. In this march K Troop had been assigned rearguard. This placement gave us strength. We felt privileged over those who went at the head of the column, with nothing but a compass reading before them. The sun set and we marched on, keeping to the regiment's trail that was marked clearly in the grass.

Sometime after dark a strange cry came to us from the rear of our troop. We rode back and saw that of one of our men had lost his senses from sleeplessness. The man had dismounted and was running in circles, laughing, barking, howling, jabbering in some tongue known only to himself. We caught the man with ropes and bound him to the saddle of one of our horses.

The settling of this trooper had caused us to lose sight of the column ahead. We put our horses into a lope and soon came on the trail, well marked in the moonlight. By three a.m. the lack of sleep had become torture. Our eyes were so swollen we could not close them. Our heads felt as if they might explode. Flesh hung on our bones like mail; muscles yanked involuntarily: an arm might fly up in an exaggerated salute, a boot kick pointlessly in the stirrup. The moonlight cast each of us in his own hell. Rife saw imaginary animals and birds and would twist and flinch from their attacks. One of the other men had taken it in his head that he was a grand field marshal. He rode over the empty plains as if he were passing in victorious review through a great city, beckoning, gesturing, blowing kisses to the damsels that packed the fantastic balconies above. The trooper who had lost his wits leaned back his head and crowed or barked or sang—now we let him be any animal he liked, while I could only laugh at the others and myself. So we passed the night, each of us wandering in and out of the mad maze that wakefulness had made in our minds.

By dawn all but Rife and I, who dozed and waked fitfully, were fast asleep in their saddles, leaning over the pommels, their arms wrapped about their horses' necks. At length we came to the end of the *llano estacado* and looked out over the broken land beyond. Below we saw the camp made by our regiment. We rode down over the caprock and dismounted and fell against the red, rumpled earth, many of us already dreaming as we struck the ground.

FIVE

THE valley had been stripped by winter. Before, in the summer, we had stood above the valley and seen only the crests of its limestone cliffs and the meadows near us and the thick bodice of trees—cottonwoods and live oaks and willow—that had hidden the ranch buildings from us. But now the trees were a file of skeletons, and we saw through them the cliffs beyond and bits of sky and anything else there was to be seen. The stone house stood as we remembered it, as did the outbuildings and their maze of fences and pens and corrals, but the rest—the visitors riding, hunting, and strolling about the grounds, the cowboys and their horses and the cattle—but for a few animals in a distant pen, all were gone. As we rode down into the valley, figures emerged from the bunkhouse and watched us. As the trees had been shorn of their foliage, so these men were without human curiosity or welcome. Though one man moved, none made offer to approach or greet us. We turned our weary troops and marched them up the valley to where we had made our summer camp. There we were dismounted and the horses set out to graze. Our captives were herded into the empty corrals and guards placed about them. Our tents were erected and fires built. The few animals we had seen in the ranch pens were requisitioned and butchered, while arrangements were made to purchase more cattle from nearby ranches. Some of our summer supplies had remained in storage at the ranch; these stores were broken open and distributed so that our first night's camp at Caballo Ranch was passed in pleasure.

Toward evening a cowboy carrying a sack over his shoulder came up through the stark trees, their late shadows casting spikes and bars of night across him. The sack contained mail that had come from Fort Pulgas in the fall, before our mail had been rerouted to Fort Sill for delivery to us in the field. By this chance we would be reading letters dated before those we had received at the Christmas camp on the Canadian River. As the mail was distributed, the cowboy spoke of the vacancy of the ranch, where once commerce and entertainment had thrived.

"Oh, it has gone back to the way it was before they all come," said the man. "The rock house there stands to their folly, and there is more board fence than this place will ever need. But as for the rest of it, it is much the way Little Caballo was before they come, so far as the herd and them that work it."

Pressed for details on the fall of the Great Caballo, the man continued, "Well, the lords and ladies, they left soon after you fellers. They went off in their traps and carts to Denver, Colorado, I think it was. Seems these whiskers, who talk no tongue that was English for my money, it was learned that they come up short on some corn exchange or t'other. They then went and pulled the rug out on the Caballo, like the rug was pulled out on them. All them little spreads that was bought up by the whiskers, they went unpaid for and was returned to them that had owned them previous. This at a value of a dime on a dollar, the herds being sold and the money squandered. And the price of what beef they did get back not a nickel a pound."

"These small ranchers are ruined?"

"They are ruint and they will be ruint some more. There is the debt the whiskers and young Weir has totaled up. Now every man who says he owns the Y-L or the Jinglebob, he owns a piece of that debt. We will see some bankers ahorseback before long."

"And the Cadys, are they ruined too?"

"Well, young Ben has him a mighty fine house, as you can see, but that will go too, like a rock tied to his neck. As for the old man, he is dead."

"Ben Cady, is he here now?"

"He is. He sets in the house right now. He don't go out much no more. Sets and rocks like an old woman lost in his grief."

The following morning I went down through the bare trees toward the stone house. Dry leaves walked nervously across the ground, clutching at my trousers, cartwheeling joylessly off with the breeze. The sky was clear, cloudless, the air warm as early September, when the Second had marched out of Caballo. As I approached the stone house, I caught a glimpse of a woman in a back window. In a moment the woman, a pretty young Mexican servant, came to the rear door.

"*¿Está en la casa el señor Cady?*"

"*Sí. Sí, señor, el patrón está al dentro. Pase, pase.*" The woman moved from the door and led me into the house. She waved her hand forward. "*En la frente, el patrón está en la frente.*"

Ben Cady sat in the front room, which had been little improved since the summer *baile*. There were pieces of stiff leather-covered furniture put about, and Mexican blankets had been hung on the walls—wild bars and splashes of color. The grand spiral staircase was gone, replaced by a ladder. The chandelier was gone; lamps, their chimneys sooted, and candles had been attached to the walls. But for the fouled lamps the room was clean. The plank floor was still moist from scrubbing; the windows sparkled; had not their glass been imperfect, distorting the landscape beyond, one might have imagined they had been removed with the chandelier and the spiral stairs. Ben Cady sat near one of the windows so that light would fall over the book he held. He wore slippers and a supple deerskin jacket that fitted him like a robe. His eyes were reddened and swollen, his look one of relentless malice toward me. As I came into the room, Ben Cady closed the book on his lap, a children's primer, and commented on it,

"I am learning to read."

"I see. Have you got far?"

He nodded. "I began it with a purpose. But now I find pleasure in it, and some strength. I will begin the Bible soon, or some other history."

"That is a good place to begin."

Ben Cady looked at the book in his hands. The book's cover was worn to a shine; he smoothed it once, like stroking a pet. "Did you get your letters?"

"We did. They were welcome. We thank you for keeping them."

"There is one you did not get. I did not keep it for you."

"I see. Whose letter was it?"

"It was from the young lady, Miss McCorquodale. It went there." He gestured to the fireplace across the room. "It was to you."

"You burnt a letter for me?"

"I did."

"Mr. Cady, you shouldn't have done that."

"And there are things you should not have done, Chapman."

I did not speak.

Ben Cady said, "I read it before I burnt it."

"Ah well, now that is *fine*, Mr. Cady—is that how you are learning to read, opening other people's mail?"

Cady darkened. "I did cipher it well."

"And what did you cipher, if you don't mind telling me?"

Cady twisted the primer in his hands. "That you have done wrong by the young lady and your wife and Mr. Weir."

"And yourself, Mr. Cady?"

His delivery became suddenly lame. "You have made love to an unmarried woman, one who was herself about to be spoken for, and you are married."

We sat for a while without speaking. Our anger went. I said at length, "Would you mind telling me what she wrote, Mr. Cady?"

He spoke slowly: "She wrote that she cared for you, but that you were not free."

"That is all?"

"There was not much to it." He raised the book. "I learned most of the words from here. I studied the writing like a scholar. I can recite it, word for word, if you want, though there was much of it I did not understand."

I waited, then said, "I have not ruined her, Cady. I love her and will marry her."

The man looked away. "But you are married."

"These are modern times. I will divorce my wife and marry her."

"You will ruin all those around you to have her, and when you have had her you will cast her off, as you cast off this wife, to look for someone new."

"That is not true, Cady. I will never cast her away. I love her."

"And the wife you have now, who you have tired of, did you not once love her?"

"No. I never loved her."

The primer slipped from the man's hands and clattered to the floor. His fingers twisted where the book had been. "Tell me, how do you marry a woman you do not love?"

The victory over the Comanches was now complete. A rider from Sill reached us that afternoon, and with him came word that the braves of the Wanderers band led by Tehana Storm had walked onto the reservation at Sill and surrendered themselves. The taking of their women and children, the pillage and burning of their lodges, the killing of their horses had broken their will to be free. Now there was only the matter of transporting the Comanche women and children to the reservation and our duty on the Texas frontier, but for scouting and garrison, was done. Wagons for the captives were secured from Caballo and the surrounding ranches, and this march was made with ease through gentle weather, two hundred miles being covered in a week's time.

From our southwesterly approach the Red River made the border between Texas and Indian Territory. After fording the Red River, a real river, a body of moving water that would not vanish in a week or rise in an afternoon to become a raging car of Juggernaut, we marched over rolling prairies blanketed in thick yellow grass. We soon came upon a stream and made camp there, feasting that night on perch and bass and trout and catfish. The following morning we continued our march over this gently rising plateau, toward evening coming upon the southern outpost of Fort Sill. There we were greeted enthusiastically by the members of the Eleventh Cavalry and remembered we were heroes. We gave over our captives—twenty wagons carrying over two hundred women and children and elders—to the garrison soldiers and were free of duty. Soon a detachment of guards came from the post headquarters, and they escorted the captives to a compound that had been built not far from there. We followed our guides and near dark came to a precipice overlooking a valley backed by the Wichita Mountains, whose summits were etched crimson against the darkening sky. Fort Sill was nestled in the foothills beneath these peaks. The faint call of retreat was heard, and we saw a dense grid of men set in formation in the parade. The dull boom of the sunset gun came across the valley, and a tiny flag was drawn down from its stanchion in the very center of the parade. We stood on the bluff as if taking part in the evening ceremony, not moving out till the soldiers had broken ranks and spread over the post grounds.

By the time we had ridden down the bluff the mountain shadows had reached across the post and valley floor. True night followed quickly, and it was dark as we rode into Fort Sill. The officers of the Eleventh and their wives came onto the porches of their stone houses, calling out as we rode past, lamp-light streaming from the windows and open doors. Our men cried out to them in return, as if these were families of their own, and the night was filled with the sounds of homecoming. We stood a brief formation in the dark, and the men were dismissed and marched off to eat at tables and sleep under roofs for the first time in nearly a year. The officers were billeted that night in the fort hotel, which provided us with such wonders of civilization as the bedbug that would not die. Many men yearned for cold ground and canvas, and this writer passed the night dozing fitfully in a rocking chair.

At first light the tramp and call of men at drill came to me; I went to the window and saw a company of Negro soldiers of the Eleventh wheeling about the parade in formations unknown to us. East, beyond the parade, I could make out the outlines of a row of tipis, smoke curling from the lodge vents. From somewhere in the hotel came the smell of our cooking, and I returned to bed so sleepy and so hungry. When next I turned, the room was flooded in sunlight, my bed surrounded by fellow officers, all grinning and studying their watches.

"Eleven o'clock, Phil," said one. "Not bad, but only third ribbon. Vorster and Beaumont are on for the blue. Beaumont is odds on. There's a twenty here that says the lad'll go past noon."

Nothing was done that day but eating and more sleeping. No formations or duty of any sort were called. After that rest we were given five formations a day, which soon became three.

The men were set light duty and the officers freed from all but Officer of the Day, as the noncommissioned men took charge of the regiment. Otherwise we spent our time hunting and fishing or however we chose.

Sill was an open fort. It had no moat or parapet or battlement set with cannon. There were not even the rude defenses of Fort Pulgas, where the buildings were connected to form a stockade. Large stone stables and a corral on the southeast corner of the post and an ill-tended earthen redoubt to the southwest were the fort's only defensive works. Nothing else was needed, one came to realize. The enemy was all about us, but here they were turned outward. The Indians themselves were our ramparts. An immense grass parade dominated the post: all permanent structures but the stables faced onto it, with perfect military logic, as one might stand at the centered flagpole and be roughly equidistant from the barracks, officers' line, post headquarters, the commander's quarters, mess hall, the chapel, and the Sill Hotel, where we visitors were quartered. Only the stables and Suds Row were to be found beyond this great military village square. The permanent buildings were made of a light-gray limestone, built low and deep, their interiors dark, damp, but with moderate temperature no matter the season. The parade was bounded by gravel paths, a shade lighter in color than the winter grass; it was pacing these walkways, as broad as roads, that I spent my two days of rest.

The morning I decided to seek out amusement I was directed three miles north to the establishment of Nye and Co., the Sill post trader. I took a horse and rode along the way I had been told. Shortly a cloud of dust appeared ahead. Within the swirl I could see horses dashing about and carriages and wagons being circled, with Indians and blue-coated soldiers and cowboys all whooping and crying out. But the horse under me did not seem particularly concerned and went on ambling along the road and I with him.

The Sill trading post was pandemonium. The crowd of a thousand or so could be divided into three masses: Indians of the Pacer band of Apaches, who had traveled here to draw their rations; white civilians, farmers, ranchers, horse traders, and salesmen who had come to trade with the Indians; and the soldiers who had been assigned to regulate the trading but were often involved in the commerce themselves. Indian braves, squaws, children, dogs, ponies, and every imaginable sort of wagon, cart, and sled were gathered in a mob at the commissary door. Within the commissary the chiefs of these families and lodges were exchanging their monthly ration cards for so much coffee, sugar, flour, and meat—bacon, beef, or pork, depending on the supply. As each chief received these goods—some bound in packages or sacks, others, such as the stiff brown sugar, handed out by the fistful—he would call in his squaws, who packed and lashed their bundles onto the backs of animals and children and one another. This laden train then moved in a mind-splitting confusion away from the commissary door, and the next family entered to receive their bounty. What was not handed over to the women was taken by the chiefs and braves to the white civilian traders. These goods, such as pork, which the Indians had no use for, were swapped for fine-spun garments, tall hats, walking canes, cheap jewelry, and other items the government did not see fit to issue. So outfitted, the chiefs and braves attracted the local ranchers and horse traders. In an effort to domesticate the Indians, the government had awarded each family livestock scrip that could be exchanged by the licensed white dealer for cash. The good Indian, endeavoring to become a rancher or farmer as the White Father wished, went to these traders and bought cattle, sheep, and draft horses. The discouraged Indian, having tired of ranching or farming, returned to these traders to resell them this livestock for rifles and ammunition that he might return to the hunt. The bad Indians exchanged the chits for cash, went off a distance from the trading post—for such commerce was illegal—and bought or bartered for whatever liquor these merchants would serve them. Then there commenced among those whose fortunes and spirits were low the selling of their women to the soldiers for the night. This sorry business done, the Indians fell to trading among themselves. Dog swapping gave way to games of running, riding, and marksmanship with bow and arrow. Contesting the skills of bygone days lasted a while, but as the liquor ran free, boxing and wrestling matches began; as night fell these became brawls. It was a rare morning that did not see an Indian family packing a young brave back to its village, to dress and hold ceremony over his wounds, all that remained of the glory of making war with ancient enemies.

A young officer of the Eleventh broke off his amusement with the unmarried squaws and directed me to a building adjacent to the Indian commissary, the white man's or upper trading post, I was told, as no liquor could be sold in the Indian or lower store. Therein I found a spacious, well-stocked emporium served by three obsequious clerks. One of the clerks unhitched his apron and led me down a hall toward the back of the building and the sound of merriment. We entered a room as large as the store, packed to the walls with soldiers, ranchers, a few Indians in Western dress, and a half-dozen chubby prostitutes. The decor was simple: a bar, a piano, a stool for the piano player. The clerk stood me a drink, then, at the sound of a small bell above the door, hurried back to the front. I was hailed by a group of young officers from the Second, Beaumont's crowd, who were mingling with a like number of dandies from the Eleventh. These young men were gathered about a window, all looking out.

"Phil, just in time for the show," said Beaumont, and a place was made for me by the window, offering a view of the rear and side of the nearby Indian commissary. Moments before, I was

245

informed, a family of squaws had been called to the front of the commissary to pack their goods. The squaws had taken their papooses from their backs and had left babies and backboards leaning like black-eyed dominoes against the commissary wall. Now, from the rear of the building, came three members of the Eleventh, all junior lieutenants. One of this trio sauntered to the front of the commissary to act as lookout; the other two went to the line of papooses, who twisted their little brown heads about to see what the large white men could possibly be up to. At a signal from the lookout, the two men went quickly along the line of backboards, turning them upside down, transforming the two round eyes at the top of each board to a single singing mouth at the bottom. The wails of these upended babies soon brought their mothers running, putting our pranksters in retreat. The trio burst through the clubroom door and were treated with cocktails of hospital alcohol and plum juice for their entertainment.

"Beau!" called out one of the Eleventh as their group had surrounded several of the prostitutes and were making toward the door. "Are you coming along? Time to feed the animals!"

"Yes. Yes," said Beaumont. "We're riding up to the Comanche compound, sir, if you haven't been there. I'll promise you a better show than this."

We went out and found our horses and rode north till we came upon two stockades fifteen feet high, logs driven deep in the ground and strung with barbed wire. Near the top of the fence ran a plank walk for the armed sentinels. A rude gunhouse rose above the compound gate: there more armed guards surveyed the captive Indians. One compound was large, fifty by fifty yards, the other less than half that size. The former held the Comanche women and girls and children under six: several tents were set about, fires smoked, an area had been arranged as a playground for the children. The second, smaller stockade, without tent or fire, contained the men and the boys of any age. I had thought that our prisoners—the women and children and elders—had been a sorry sight when we had given them over to the Eleventh, but their condition in these confines had worsened. The women had aged terribly in but a week of imprisonment. Their clothing and hair and skin were filthy; they crawled with lice and vermin. In our custody these women had shown life to them, be it fear, anger, and hatred of us. Behind these wires their eyes had grown dull, without hope or care. Littered inside the fence line were the elders of the tribe, who had rolled in their blankets and ponchos and had taken to the ground. The children played, no matter their misery, but willfully, their games the joyless mimicry of the stalking and killing of war. The officers of the Eleventh ordered the guards to swing open the gates, and several of these young officers and a number of the prostitutes entered the enclosure. The women were instantly surrounded by the squaws, so that we worried for their safety, but the Indian women had gathered to stroke the prostitutes' fair skin, their satin dresses and soft leather gloves. We went to the men's enclosure, though not one among the Eleventh called for these gates to be opened. Perhaps some of the Comanche men had been seated or were lying about at our arrival, but now all stood, facing us, even the smallest boy. One of the Eleventh identified those he knew—Walking Bird, Horseback, Broken String. Tehana Storm was not among them. He and other tribal chieftains of note and some of the younger braves were being kept away from these stockades, in a prison fashioned from abandoned stables.

"There was a terrible row when the savages first came in," said the officer of the Eleventh. "Several guards were attacked with knives. Wounded too. They had to separate the troublemakers."

Another said, "And there's the matter of the trials as well. They were put away for hanging, I think."

"We plan to try these men?"

"Not the Army. The Texans want them. Dickering's going on now."

247

"What crimes will they be charged with?"

"Murder, I suppose. You were there, weren't you, Chapman? The corn-train massacre at Salt Creek—it's their work."

A cheering came from the officers and the prostitutes. We turned toward a wagon lumbering over the brow of the hill. The wagon was drawn by a single horse, driven by a single teamster. Dogs followed along behind the wagon, barking, snarling at one another, flinging themselves against the wagon's board sides. Birds—crows we could see as they came near—flew above the wagon. Too, the teamster took shape and form as the wagon came close: the man was an imbecile, a toadstool of reddish-brown flesh sitting square in the center of the wagon bench. The horse did the imbecile's work for him, drawing up to the fence of the large compound. The imbecile rose and lifted arms that were caked with the brown slime of old blood. The officers of the Eleventh cheered him as he clambered over the bench back into the wagon bed. He stooped and came up with lumps of raw, bloody meat in each hand. He held the meat over his head, like a champion. The officers gave out with savage, sarcastic cheers. The imbecile turned and flung, both hands at once, the raw pieces of meat over the wire fence. In the stockade, the Indian women fought like beasts for the meat, not for themselves but for their children. The screeching and clawing subsided when there was enough meat for all. Then the imbecile took his place on the wagon bench and held the reins slack in his hands and the horse went to the men's stockade. There the spectacle was repeated. The imbecile held the meat aloft and received his ovation from the officers of the Eleventh. He clapped the hunks of meat together over his head, spraying himself with blood, and flung the meat backwards, over his shoulders, without turning to the fence. Some of the blindly thrown meat cleared the upper wires, some did not, falling to the ground outside the compound, to be ripped to pieces by the dogs. The Comanche men and boys did not move as the hunks of meat rained about them. Then one youth could not discipline himself; he fell on one of the pieces of meat. The boy was taken up by two men and stood away in shame. But then another, a man, snatched up a piece of meat and began tearing at it with his teeth till he was stopped. Then another boy snatched a piece of meat and ran to the far side of the compound, and the others could not be controlled. All but a few of the Indian men and boys had taken the raw meat and had gone away from the spectators to eat. Those few stood watching us in defiance, but there was little interest among the officers of the Eleventh and the prostitutes and our men in that. We mounted our horses and rode away, planning that evening's entertainment.

That afternoon I went to post headquarters to arrange that our Comanche captives might be fed cooked meat served in a more civilized fashion. In return I was offered, as an antidote, perhaps, to the barbaric treatment of the Comanches, a tour of one of Sill's civilized villages. A guide, one of the post interpreters, was provided me. We rendezvoused after dinner and went across the plains north of Fort Sill. Mount Scott and the Wichita Range stood to our left, a string of rocky foothills strewn across our path. Clouds swept the moutain summits, icy gray tendrils that seemed to be lighted from within, for they glowed against the dark backing sky and the storm curtain hanging beyond the horizon. For now a jar might have been placed over the valley—air and sound and light stood still. The native grass we rode through burned yellow as lamps. The land was void of all moving game. The birds did not sing or fly but huddled in their grounded nests. We came upon a doe, who started at our appearance, but the animal went to earth immediately when we changed our course away. We went due north and crossed Medicine Creek and made our way up a gradual trail that led between two hills of equal height. Like every promontory in this valley, the crowns of these hills were shattered rock. My companion theorized that once the hills had been gigantic boulders pushed down from the Rockies by glaciers, abandoned here to disintegrate, sundering and eroding to become enormous cairns of stone that over the centuries had collected blown sand and flood silt, to form such natural castles as we rode through.

From the top of the pass between the hills, we looked back into the valley, as we had come. The hewn geometry of Fort Sill—the neat square of small gray blocks about the parade, the long even lines of the stables, the barracks radiating from them—spoke of our civilization and its brooding regularity standing amidst this chaos of stone.

We went down the north slope away from Sill and soon came into a valley. There we found the civilized Cherokee village the interpreter had spoken of, a collection of neatly painted frame houses scattered over several thousand acres of tilled land. Here were roads going about among the fields, strict paths leading from house to house, wherein dwelled dark men and women with close-cropped hair, all dressed in Western clothes and answering to such names as Bill Redd and George Hunt. Plump haystacks dotted the land. The earth was a dark mahogany loam that would in the spring and summer burst forth with corn, oats, alfalfa, and every fruit and vegetable to be found on the finest farms in the country. The pens and corrals were filled with horses and hogs; fat sheep and cattle grazed on winter wheat. Mules plowed in harness, chickens and geese roamed the yards where sturdy dark women scrubbed wash in buckets and hung bleached clothes on lines to dry. Black-eyed children in laced boots and denim pants and woolen jackets and caps lined the road and waved and called out, not always in English, as we passed. We soon came to a building larger than the others, with high eaves and tall narrow windows. This structure, my guide said, served as a church on Sunday, a school during the other days of the week. We dismounted and went in and stood at the rear of the room and observed a class in geography being led by a hardy young woman whose eyes smiled at the presence of the young interpreter. In proud demonstration, the

Indian pupils chanted the names of the thirteen original colonies and had commenced on the Presidents of the Union when we saw fit to leave. As we went to our horses we observed a buggy approaching at a rapid clip. "Reverend Clark," said the interpreter and went to meet the vehicle. In the buggy sat a man and a young woman. The man was a full-blood Cherokee—with the mixed Negro and Indian features of that tribe—and the young woman his daughter by a white woman, the only trace of her patrimony being the broad nose and full mouth of her father's race and flesh that might have been dusted lightly by an evening sun. The minister was dressed in clerical garb—long black frock coat and vest, a white collar and white lawn tie. He spoke excellent English and conversed knowledgeably with the interpreter on topics of agriculture, as the minister was the largest farmer in the village. The daughter possessed a refined air, as befitted a young woman who had just returned from a college for ladies in the East. She regaled me with tales of the officers at Sill that seemed to interest the young interpreter far more than her father's concurrent discussion of farm technique. In time we were invited to the minister's house for tea, but my guide, whose countenance had grown dark as the northern sky, declined, allowing we must return to the post before the rain. We bid the minister and his daughter farewell and rode back through the civilized village, up the trail between the hills as we had come. We halted on the pass, the civilized village behind us, the Sill compound ahead. Lightning rent the sky beyond the Wichita Range. A spike buck bounded through the deep yellow grass as the interpreter spoke:

"I often wonder in my work, Captain, what it means to be civilized and what it means to be free. Can they mingle? Sometimes I feel surrounded by invisible walls of accepted conduct. Tell me, who are the more strictly jailed—those Indians you have just observed, or those behind wire?"

"Neither are free, perhaps, but at least the Indians we have just seen are civilized."

The interpreter studied me briefly. "Then civilization is what we have when freedom dies?"

"There is the wire."

The interpreter made no further comment and we rode back to the post before it rained.

Soon our time of rest was done and we were to be returned to duty. A meeting of the officers and staff of the Second Cavalry was called. We reported to post headquarters as ordered, but found neither Colonel MacSwain nor Major Hoeme nor any other senior officers there. Shortly Major Clous came and spoke to us, making clear the absence of our regimental commander. The Second Cavalry was to remain at Fort Sill to replace the Negro Eleventh, which would be reassigned to Texas and Arizona. After the meeting Clous told a few of us that MacSwain was suffering bitter disappointment. Having won, he thought, the most brilliant Indian battle in the Army's history, he was now assigned the task of feeding, clothing, and policing the savages he had defeated. As for my own K Troop, they were being detached from the Second and sent to Kansas, where they would join Custer's forces which were marching north to Dakota Territory. Gold and silver had been discovered in the Black Hills, on the Sioux reserve, and now white prospectors were encroaching upon Indian territory. Custer was being sent north to keep the peace, or so Frank Clous presented us the boy general's mission. Those in K Troop that I spoke to were honored to be attached to Custer's Seventh, imagining no danger amidst the glory, as we truly thought our defeat of the Comanches in the Palo Duro Canyon was the last of our Indian wars.

I did not review K Troop before they marched out and so did not expect to see Sergeant Rife at Fort Sill days after their departure. This was at Nye's bar: Rife stood drinking among the traders and sutlers and local ranchers who had gathered for trading day. Rife wore civilian dress and had made no effort to hide his identity. If the man could desert with such aplomb, I would be the last to interfere, and I went to the far end of the bar to tend my own business. Rife, however, had caught sight of me and came down the length of the room, his red face swollen, his stubbed hands rolled in fists.

"Captain Chapman," he called out a few paces away, and I thought before turning to face him, what a fitting end to my military career. Having survived floods, droughts, stampedes, Texas chiggers, buffalo hunts, Major DuBois's sister-in-law, ambushes, *ennui,* the *llano estacado,* and a total of seven Indian battles, I would meet my end here, in the backroom of Nye's Trading Company. "Chapman," Rife said and drew nearer, "I think we had an understanding that I owed you my life and when that debt was paid, we would be free to pursue whatever trouble lay between us."

"If we did, it was unspoken," I said and took hold of a bottle.

"Well, I have been thinking about it, Cap," Rife said and pushed one of his hands in my direction, "and I have decided that me pulling you out of the smoke ain't quite up to you pulling me out of the soup." The red hatchet of a hand grasped my own and began pumping it, the diabolical face cracked with a grin. "I owe you one more, Cap." He thumped my back and ordered drinks. "Oh, and you don't have to worry about having me arrested, Chapman, as I have been discharged legally." He proudly showed me his papers. Several drinks later Rife hunched his shoulders under the tight civilian suit. "Funny thing, Captain, now that I am well out of it, I kind of get to missing the wet blue, every now and then. Ain't that something after all these years?"

As with soldiers, talk turned to our old wars, even if they had been fought only yesterday. Then we spoke of our future as civilians. Rife said he would be off for California soon to look for gold.

By now we had had many drinks. "You won't be returning to the *llano estacado* to set up a little farm, Sergeant?"

"Settling that godforsaken place? Don't be daft, sir. I will be going back to New Mexico to do a little business with Mr. Fulks, though." The Sergeant gave me an uneasy look. "To buy my finger back. You remember the three Comanches we jumped that day and the boy I killed before I could explain it to him he was white? Yes, then, you'll recall my finger was done in and it had to be severed. Well, Mr. Fulks bought it from me for five bucks to pickle there, you know, in a jar with his collection of bugs." Sergeant Rife stared morosely at the finger stub, now healed and shiny as a brass doorknob. "I been thinking about me finger sitting in that pickle jar and I decided I got to get it back from that little heathen and give it a Christian burial."

As for my own prospects, I was to return to Fort Pulgas to serve out the rest of my tour of duty. En route, I was to command the escort of the ten Comanches who were being held in the post jail, to ride them to the town of Bobsboro, Texas, where they would be tried for murder. As I was one of those who had come upon the scene of the corn-train massacre that had occurred near the Caballo Ranch, I would also act as witness to what I had seen. The prisoner escort were not men from the Second, but a Negro company from the Eleventh that was to be stationed in Texas. Likewise my second-in-command would be from the brunette regiment, a Negro lieutenant by the name of Julius C. Flipper. Lieutenant Flipper was an overly dignified officer, though some of his starch may have come from being spoken of more often than not as the first member of his race to graduate from West Point. I think beneath his perfect conduct Mr. Flipper would have much preferred to have been the second member of his race to have graduated from West Point.

On my last day at Sill I went to post headquarters to bid farewell to Colonel MacSwain. There I was halted by MacSwain's new Adjutant, a young lieutenant I did not know.

"The Colonel is not in today, sir."

"Then early tomorrow."

"Nor tomorrow, nor the rest of this week. The Colonel is gone out with a hunting party."

"But Colonel MacSwain doesn't hunt."

"He's taken it up," said the Lieutenant with a wisp of a smile.

I stood on the steps of the post headquarters looking out across the parade. There was great activity around the hotel and officers' quarters. A mail detachment had ridden in from Fort Leavenworth, and the officers of the Eleventh and the Second were gathered around the commander of that unit, to receive letters from home and the gossip spreading from our Western headquarters. As I watched, a hunting party of a dozen men and as many pack animals rode onto the far side of the parade quadrangle. A stream of men and officers spilled from their barracks and quarters to assist the hunters in unpacking and laying out the carcasses of dozens of wolves. The officers around the mail train crossed the parade to join in the inspection of the kill. Over the course of the next quarter hour the wolves were examined by all and found to be worthy prizes; then the parade gradually emptied but for a number of Negro servants or soldiers acting as servants who went among the wolves, that dead and disemboweled looked like nothing but dogs, making preparations to skin them. The hunters and the officers had gone off to Artillery Hill, a mile to the south of us. A storm had come near, enclosing the Wichita Range. Thunder cracked through the mountains, and the hunters and the officers wheeled about the three-inch ceremonial cannon to face the storm, cheering wildly as if they might return nature's fire.

On March 10, 1876, I, the lone white man among them, set out in command of the strangest of trains, a group of men who had once been the freest on earth imprisoned by a company of those who but recently had been the least free. Our destination was the Texas frontier town of Bobsboro and neighboring Fort Ichard. This march we made in five days. During the afternoon of the last day we came to the high country north of Bobsboro and looked down on a broad colorless valley. Bisecting the valley we observed a straggling village, beyond which lay Fort Ichard. We rode through the town without incident, perhaps taking the populace by surprise, and then to the fort, where we were received without grace. The guard seemed reluctant to open the gate, suspecting perhaps, Lieutenant Flipper suggested, that he and his men were Seminoles disguised as soldiers, bringing prisoners to Ichard as Greeks had born gifts to Troy. Our welcome did not warm once inside the fort. The Officer of the Day was insolent, the men on duty spat frequently, the Post Adjutant took a pedantic quarter hour studying our orders, and the commander of Fort Ichard, one Captain Vernon Starr, refused to admit Lieutenant Flipper to his office when I went to surrender the prisoners.

I knew Vern Starr well without knowing him at all: aging, alcoholic, long a widower or divorced or a bachelor, given to the company of men and a life of hunting, gambling, and debauchery, too long in his rank, too near retirement to resign and nowhere to go if he did, no family, no friends, no home, nothing but the Army and that, saddest of all, had never been his anyway. Starr was fifty at least, too unwell from drink to be obese, not quite dirty, not quite clean, poorly shaven, his uniform dank, as if it had been washed out by hand the previous night and put on this morning before it had dried, as Starr himself oozed sweat in the airless room, leaving moist traces on everything he touched.

Starr let my order drop to the desk and spoke in a squeaky voice: "Fifty darkies, ten redskins, four thousand Texans, and right in the middle of them a bluebellied Yankee. I'd say that someone somewhere doesn't like you, Chapman." Starr's eyes flicked over me. "Look, Chapman, let's talk. It's not your Afri-

cans that are giving me a bellyache, but your noble savages."
He lifted my orders from the desk and let them drop. "The
Texans want to take them away to a local jail. I've tried to stop
them, but I can't." He lifted another sheaf of papers on his desk
and let them drop. "Washington has made a deal with the State
of Texas. The Army gives over the prisoners to the Texans for
trial. In return the Governor will commute any death sentences
the prisoners will receive, so that they can rot in Huntsville."

I read the documents in question. "What troubles you about
this—other than its being illegal?"

Starr's lips stretched wide without parting. He lifted a third
file of documents from his desk. He read the topmost:

"*Deer*—spelled like the little animal we shoot at instead of
one another—*deer Bluebellies, them redskins won't nivver*—
never, I suppose—*won't nivver reach trail*—trial is meant, I
think. *Signed, the Citizens' Protective League.* There are more."
He dropped these letters on the desk.

"Then our only problem is retaining custody of the prisoners
during the trial. We still have some extraordinary powers in this
state—don't we? One jail is as good as the next—if we can post
the guard."

Starr leaned back in his chair and kicked his boots on the
desk. The leather was remarkably well kept, considering the
rest of him. "Chapman, it's a shame they're closing this dump,
for I'd sorely like to see you in command here. Over the years
my men and I have chased murderers, guarded the courtroom
from their kinsmen once captured, executed the poor devils
who were guilty as hell and illegally convicted and condemned,
collected taxes (far more dangerous than pursuing murderers),
put down race riots, put out prairie fires, put in the fix for the
Mayor's bordello, and put up with just about every form of insult, abuse, and attack known to mankind, if that's what it is
crawling around in this great State of Texas. For this public
service we have been called carpetbaggers, scalawags, and yel-
low-bellied bluebellies—and that's from the pulpit. My men

have been shot at, beat up, robbed, spat upon, and umbrella-whipped by silver-haired grannies. Now, Chapman, I only just now read your orders, and in haste, but I'll swear if it doesn't seem to me that you and your brunettes are in charge of the prisoners, not me, not my white trash. Now if you and your black boys want to go into Bobsboro and guard the redskins so they can be lynched legally, be my guest. But me and my white boys are staying home from this picnic."

I stood. "Thank you, Captain Starr. I had intended to request that duty. You have saved me the effort."

Starr called out to me at the door. "All right, Chapman, come back. Damnit, come back." He drafted an order, signed it, and dropped it on the desk. "Hand this to Lieutenant Day on your way out. We'll split it up—one black bean and one white bean. You take command on the weekdays, I'll see if I can keep their red necks from being stretched Saturday and Sunday."

I took up the draft order. "Then you'd like to meet my second-in-command, Lieutenant Flipper."

Starr scowled. "Dinner in my quarters at seven. Lieutenant Day and the first member of his race to graduate from West Point or anywhere else for that matter will buy the wine. What name did you say he took?"

"Julius Caesar Flipper."

"Julius Caesar Flipper—is that a joke?"

"Is Starr?"

And the man who looked more like a soiled dumpling than any celestial orb spread his lips and excreted genuine amusement.

The following morning, after an evening during which Lieutenant Flipper almost gained a sense of humor and Captain Starr a skull dented by a wine bottle, I left my penitent fellow officers and secured a buggy, not caring to see a saddle for a while, and drove into Bobsboro. There I drank a brandy at an establishment called the Tanglefoot, then crossed the dusty, milling main thoroughfare to a hotel with the name Cross Timbers. I rented a room and sent out for a bath, a laundress, and a tailor, all of whom arrived in the person of a Chinese man named Yi. I handed over my soiled uniform, stepped into the near scalding water, and in a short time was returned a clean, pressed uniform. I ordered breakfast and sent for the local papers, the Bob County *Hesperian* and the Bobsboro *Avalanche-Journal,* both of which more or less called for the lynching of our Indian prisoners.

When I finished reading and breakfast, I dressed and went to the Bob County courthouse, where I found Floyd Lockney, the Sheriff. After receiving my credentials, the Sheriff and I left the courthouse and went to inspect the county jail, which we found on the north side of town, well away from Main Street and the courthouse. The jail was not of stone as I had hoped—Sheriff Lockney said the courthouse was the only stone edifice in the county—but made of great, square-hewn green logs, a massive, windowless blockhouse twenty feet in height, the outside thickly studded with sharpened nails. The sole entrance to the jail was a door cut ten feet above the ground. A deputy lowered a ladder to the ground, and Sheriff Lockney and I climbed into the jail. The top floor of the building was a loft, about twenty by twenty feet, with a trapdoor in the center of the floor. With the deputy and the Sheriff straining hard, they just managed to lift the massive door. The ladder was then lowered to the cell below, and we descended. The Sheriff thumped the green logs, harder and heavier than any stone, and I was convinced that the people of Bob County had constructed a jail impregnable from without, all but a grave from within.

I returned to the fort that afternoon and set Lieutenants Flipper and Day to the task of bathing and dressing the Indians in fresh habits, that they might be presentable for the trial that was to commence the next day. I came to wonder if our cleaning the prisoners served their cause. The ten Comanche prisoners, after weeks of captivity in the stables of Sill and the hard, dusty march to Ichard, were near the state of dogs—filthy, cowed, perhaps, to a pitying mind, they might even have appeared blameless. When they emerged from their baths moderately scrubbed, their black hair plaited and shining with fresh grease, outfitted in what spare clothing we could find in Ichard's stores, I saw that we had transformed cringing animals into men. Not the fierce nomads we had known from the plains, splashed with war paint, naked but for breechclout and moccasins, astride their steaming war ponies, but still men—proud, disdainful of their captors and their fate, not merely looking capable of murder but rather inclined toward it.

Lieutenant Flipper and I walked down the line of cells to the last. We stopped before the grated window in the door. Therein we observed a tall muscular man, standing, with his back to the door. I called out, "Tehana," and the man turned and we saw he was white. I had known that the Comanche chieftain had darkened his skin with a paste made from charcoal, dirt, ashes, and berry juice. His hair had been likewise dyed, and the years of living in the sun and the grime from the stables and the dust from the wagon column had further darkened him and disguised his parentage. But now that was gone. Cleaned, Tehana's skin was light, his hair brown; his size and stature had diminished under his prison garb. But it was in his look and expression that he truly became white. His primitive hatred of us had been replaced by the sneer of a European: an appraisal brimming with conceit and contempt for all races and classes and peoples not his own. It was as reflected in the face of Julius Flipper that I saw most clearly that we had imprisoned a white man.

That night we rode our prisoners in a circle around Bobsboro's main district and deposited them before dawn in the log jail. At the jail I was joined by Sheriff Lockney, and we went together back into town. It seemed that every man, woman, and child in Bob and the adjoining counties had been informed of the impending trial and had made their way to the county seat. The crowds stood so thick on Main Street that the Sheriff and I left our horses at its north end and went to the courthouse on foot. After much effort, we gained entrance to the courthouse and pushed into the courtroom.

The courtroom was a scene from Bedlam. We entered what seemed a cave of people. The walls, floors, benches, chairs, aisles, every space in the courtroom was lined and hung with humanity. Laps were filled, arms entwined necks, chins were propped on shoulders, faces appeared under arms, younger visages occasionally popping from between legs. As one's senses recovered from the shock of so many of one's fellows so compacted and near, there came the successive blows of sound, heat, and stench. All therein ran with sweat and choked for breath. The windows had been filled by those who could not gain admittance to the courtroom; there they perched on anything that would give them a view inside. A path was made in the throng, and the Sheriff and I passed to the front of the courtroom, where men vacated seats for us. Now some order could be seen in the chaos. At a high desk at the head of the room sat the judge, a darkly florid man in black robes. To our left stood two long benches, one behind the other, the back bench flush against the wall and elevated a foot above the other. This was the jury box, though I did not believe it for a while, for the men seated there all wore pistols at their hips and more than one fellow in the back row had taken out a knife and was carving and whittling at the bench before him. To the right, across the room from the jury box, stood the prisoners' dock—empty. Immediately before us, between the crowd and the judge, spread a table nearly twenty feet in length. At one end of this table sat the defense attorney and his assistant, at the other end the District Attorney and his aides. These men wore high stiff collars and town suits and silk vests and polished shoes and gold watch chains and stick tie pins and rings with stones and other accessories that served to set them off from the populace. But this effort of distinction proved futile: the attorneys had the same lean, leathery faces, were the same dried and weathered men as the cowboy in chaps or the farmer in denim. Like the jurors and every other male in the courtroom, the attorneys wore pistols at their waists. Finally, there was a witness stand, placed to the right of the judge's desk, and a large flag of the State of Texas to the left.

As we took our seats our attention was fixed on a man occupying the witness stand, a farmer by the look of his flat shoes and straight-brimmed straw hat. The farmer was a prospective juror being questioned by the judge and the attorneys concerning his prejudices and foreknowledge of the alleged crimes.

"And how long have you lived here in Bob County, Terrill?" asked the judge.

"Three year," said the farmer, a simple man. "Make it four."

"And what do you know about the Salt Creek massacre that happened up near the stake plains, Terrill?"

"All about it," said the farmer, and gazed about wide-eyed when the crowd erupted in laughter.

The judge battered his desk top with a steel hammer, having broken or despaired of a gavel, I supposed. In time he could be heard: "Now, Terrill, let's get this straight. Were you there at the massacre?"

"No."

The judge worked his hammer. "Now by damn, Terrill, then you can't know nothing about it!"

"No."

"Now, Terrill, I want you to think this question over a bit, because I want a straight answer out of you. I want you on this jury, Terrill, because you are a good man. Now, Terrill, this is the answer I want from you—what do you think of our red brothers, the noble Indians?"

"Skunks."

The District Attorney, a man short as his chair, leapt up and made himself heard over the cheering: "I want this man Terrill disqualified, Judge! Pitch him out!"

The farmer Terrill looked crestfallen. The judge eyed the District Attorney. "Now hold on there, Mr. Lanahan, it should be Mr. Tomball, the defense attorney here, who finds exception to this idiot sitting as a juror."

The District Attorney wheeled with his back to the judge and played to the crowd. "No sir, your honor—I don't want empaneled on any jury of mine some sob sister who thinks them red snakes in the grass are mere skunks!"

"Varmints!" cried out the prospective juror, for he was about to lose the best seat in the house, banished to the buzzard roost.

There followed a period of uproar during which I observed the players in this farce—the preening District Attorney, the besieged judge, the hopeful prospective juror—and became aware of a focus of repose in this maelstrom. This was the defense attorney, Wendell Tomball. During the arguments Tomball sat quietly at the attorneys' table, his chin resting on one hand, writing out what looked like a letter with the other. A faint smile creased his face, evincing, I thought, boredom with these legal proceedings. The seriousness with which Tomball would defend the Indians would not become evident till in a few moments he stood to question the prospective juror, the farmer Terrill. Then Attorney Tomball rose to near seven feet, strode across the room at once, spread his arms till they seemed to reach from wall to wall, and gazed down on the prospective juror Terrill. He spoke terribly:

"Terrill, I ask you, who killed those poor teamsters at Salt Creek?"

"Injuns," came the faint reply.

"Say again?"

"Injuns," came the faint reply.

The defense attorney straightened his frame. He clasped his giant hands together and rubbed them in a deliberate circular motion, as if he had trapped a small mammal therein and was

263

slowly grinding it to powder. "Now, Terrill, how do you know that Indians killed these boys?"

"It's what they say."

"Yes," rumbled the voice. "Yes, in-deed. Let me rephrase my question, Terrill. Let us say you were one of the teamsters on that wagon train that was attacked. Picture it. You witnessed this slaughter and you escaped and have come here to tell us exactly what happened. Now tell us, Terrill, how did you know that your attackers were Indians?"

The prospective juror looked about for help, but there was none. The courtroom was still as death. "They whooped."

"They whooped. Is there anything else that told you they were Indians?"

"And hollered. They whooped and they hollered."

"They whooped and hollered—was there anything else of the Indian about these killers, Terrill? Surely there was something more Indian about your attackers than the racket they made."

"They shot arrers. They shot the fellers full of arrers, stuck like pincushions, I been told."

"They whooped and hollered and they shot arrows—what else was of the Indian about them? Were they dark men?"

"Yep. Complected dark."

"And red?"

"Yep. Dark and red."

Attorney Tomball placed his hand on the judge's desk and spread his fingers over it. "Dark and red, like Judge Clark here?"

The prospective juror shook his head. "Nope. Nope. Not like the judge there."

"That's all right, Terrill," the judge commented blandly. "I am a quarter Cherokee. You might not be too far off the mark there."

"Quarter, is it?" said the shaken juror. "Didn't know that, judge."

When there was quiet, the defense attorney continued, "Now,

these men who whooped and hollered and shot arrows and were dark and red in coloration, were they covered with war paint? Were their faces and arms and torsos splashed and striped with red and green and blue and white paint?"

"Yep. Like a picture."

"And they wore feathers and bells and animal skins and bone chest plates and breechclouts and beaded moccasins and horned headdresses and the like?"

"Yep. Dressed out just like Injuns."

"Dressed out just like Injuns," said the defense attorney, his smile cutting open his face, folding flesh in deep, beveled creases about the corners of his mouth and eyes, as a proscenium curtain is drawn back in pleats. "Now is there anything else? Oh yes—did they scalp the dead?"

"There you are. They skint 'em all. 'Cept the nigger, they tole me."

The defense attorney struck a fist into a palm. A bull whip spoke more gently. "Now let me get this straight, Juror Terrill. These attackers were men of dark and red skin which was covered all over with war paint, they whooped and hollered like drunken cowboys, they wore bells and feathers like any New Orleans whore, and they fleeced the dead with the skill of a Milesian sheepherder. Now is this how you knew they were Indians?"

The prospective juror agreed, but without enthusiasm. "As I recollect it."

Tomball seemed about to continue, but he stopped and stood over the prospective juror and smiled so that the man might be seen to tremble. "I like this man Terrill, Judge. I will ask you to empanel and swear him as our twelfth juryman."

The judge looked toward the District Attorney, who was not pleased with the state of mind of this juror, but Lanahan signaled acquiescence and the judge struck his hammer and the farmer Terrill took his seat on the benches to the left of the room.

"Time o' day, Bailiff?" the judge called out.

"Bearing on noon, Judge!" cried out the bailiff, a wise man, it being a quarter past eleven.

Down came the hammer and the court was adjourned till one o'clock. The judge requested that the two attorneys of record retire with him to his chambers, and the Sheriff and I with them. We rose and went out.

The officials of the trial—the judge, the attorneys Lanahan and Tomball—were found in a small room at the end of the hall. Though there was the usual backstage camaraderie amongst these legal adversaries, some disagreement had risen between Tomball and Lanahan. The District Attorney's courtroom cheer had been touched with frost, while the bitter irony of Tomball's official mien had become amicable teasing. The District Attorney was speaking as we entered:

"By damn, then you follow out this line of questioning for me, Wendell, as I do not like where it takes *me* at all."

Tomball pushed his chair back. "I was merely trying to establish in the jury's minds by what skill and method any witnesses you might have would identify their attackers. I sure would feel better about this case of the State's, Dub, if you had some witnesses to this crime."

The District Attorney released his exasperation. "Wendell, I thought we agreed these savages were guilty or would be found so and that we would enact this thing in a manner that would give the court and ourselves some dignity and keep the redskins from decorating the willows along Lost Creek."

The prospect of a lynching caused the judge to look up from his steak, the fare provided the officers of the court. "That is a fact. That was agreed, Wendell."

The giant defense attorney hooked his thumbs under his braces and thrust out his chin. "Well, then, I have changed my tune."

The District Attorney looked darkly at his adversary. "Wendell, tell me, what *in the world* is on your mind?"

The defense attorney sat back, his head propped against the wall. "What concerns me, Dub, is how we go about telling one sort of man from another. The meaning of my questioning of Terrill is that any man can make a wild shout or darken his skin or don a wig or paint his face or fly arrows or take a scalp. Now, you have been in these Cross Timbers as long as I, Dub, you were here in the days of the Brazos reserves, before Major Neighbors moved the Comanches up to Sill, and you know how much cattle rustling and barn burning and simple grudge killing went on by the white race and was laid off with some grease paint and a war bonnet at the feet of the red man."

"Will you be making the defense, Wendell, that the men who did this massacre were *white*?"

"I have made no defense but to set free some doubt, Dub, as is my right as a defender against injustice. There can be no wrong when there is doubt what is right. That is our system." The defense attorney smiled. "You know, there was a white man among them. You yourself have so charged, Dub."

"Now you are falling into trickery, Wendell. If you are speaking of the half-breed Tehana—he is as much a white man as Jim Clark here is red."

The District Attorney queried me:

"Captain Chapman was one of those who came upon the scene early and saw the teamsters before they were buried. Do you think white men could have done what you saw done, Captain?"

"No civilized man could have done it. What was done was done by savages."

The defense attorney gazed at me, then turned away. "Then there only remains the question, gentlemen, which race among us is civilized and which is savage."

The District Attorney cried out, "Damn you, Wendell, this line of defense will take us straight to riot!"

The defense attorney smiled. "I know, Dub. That is why I have abandoned it."

Lanahan studied his opponent without trust. "And what will your line be?"

"I have decided instead," rasped the great voice, "to take up a line of defense that will lead us straight to civil strife and revolt."

The District Attorney struck the table, desperate to establish some accord with his adversary. "Hang you, Tomball, if I do not sometimes think you are a woodshed Republican!"

The defense attorney let go a laugh that was like a cannonade in its report and its purpose.

The afternoon session commenced with a show, the marching of the accused Indians from the jail to the courthouse. We first knew the Indians were approaching by the silence that came before them. The quiet began at the north end of Main Street and swept down to us, spread about the courthouse, and then, like rising water, seeped into the halls and stairways and offices of the building till at last it flooded the courtroom and all about us was silent but for the barking of a dog, a horse's nickering, the playful babble of a child outside the window. First we heard steps across the quiet, then bootfalls, then the rhythmic tramp of marching men and an officer calling out cadence. We saw from the window four columns of soldiers, two columns of twos, each pair marching at the very edge of the street. Between this double cordon walked ten men in motley dress, our prisoners, their heads covered with blankets so nothing could be seen of their faces but shadow. Leading the procession from the flank came the Negro lieutenant, Julius Flipper, smartly marking time for the crisp stepping detachment of black and white soldiers of equal number and checkered arrangement.

Lieutenant Flipper marched his guard and their captives down Main Street, up the steps, and into the courtroom, seated the captives in the prisoners' dock, and threw a heavy picket

line about them all before the Texans could believe their eyes
and do what rioting and lynching they had dreamed all winter
to accomplish.

I was called as the afternoon's first witness, to describe the
scene of the corn-train attack as I had come upon it last year at
Salt Creek. I followed the words written previously herein, giving the true account of what I had witnessed but with a minimum of detail, as would soon be supplied by the District Attorney. Philosophy and experience clashed during my time on the
stand. I did not want to believe that Tehana Storm or any men
under his control or any men of any kind could have committed
such atrocities. But by the mere recollection of the condition of
the dead bodies did I become witness for the prosecution, and
my words, when translated to the Shoshonean tongue, caused
a chittering whistle of derision to rise from the Indians. This did
little to lower my esteem with the prosecution and friends, and
I stepped down from the stand a hero among my own kind.

But for its closing argument, the prosecution rested its case.
Attorney Tomball then rose, his shoulders slumped, as he
reached down to papers scattered over his table. He chose one
of the papers from all the others and declaimed to the judge:

"I call as a witness in his own behalf, Tehana Storm of the
Wanderers band of the Comanche Nation!"

A hush went through the courtroom as Tehana cast off his
blanket and made his way through the soldiers and took his
place on the witness stand. Tehana's appearance has been de-
scribed—he was by his features and his look a white man—but
now we saw by his bearing, dignity, elegance, by his native
arrogance, that he was a lord among us, that he looked out over
us with the mingled contempt and pity with which any regent
surveys his people. In this, Attorney Tomball's purpose was
defeated. These Texans stood now as the Roundheads had before
Charles I, as the *sans culottes* before Louis XVI—they would
fear and respect such men but they would hate and kill them
too. If the attorney had sought to free us of our loathing of

269

those beneath us, he had given us in its place the loathing of those above.

By his speech Tehana further emulated the doomed kings he could have known nothing of. "I will not beg for my life, I will urge you to take it from me. I will not ask for my freedom, but will warn you that you must keep me forever in chains. This I have prayed to your gods. Do not give me my life, for I will take yours from you. Do not think of mercy, for I will wage a merciless war on all your men and women and children. Never free me, for your blood will lie in seas across the land. Never free me, for there will be a fire on the land that will burn forever. Never free me, for I shall know every face in this room and shall visit death on you all. Such were my prayers to your gods.

"Then I turned and spoke to my gods. But they did not answer me. I spoke again and still they were silent. I begged for my gods to speak, but they did not. But then I saw that their silence was words. In their silence they say that I am dead. They say that you, my conquerors, should have no fear of me. They say that you may sleep well, that your lands will never burn, that your women will not weep, that your children will not perish—not by my hand. They say I am a ghost. They say I died with the buffalo. That I died with my ponies. That I died with the coming of the white savages on our plain. And so as I die, I make a gift of these things to you, my conquerors. I give you the buffalo that you may starve. I give you my ponies that you may wander about lost. I give you my country that you may live in an empty place, alone, without man or beast among you but your own kind."

The translator rendered this as a vague *mea culpa,* that Tehana had agreed to accept whatever justice and punishment his white masters meted out.

Now the witnesses were done. There remained only the closing arguments, the jury's deliberation, the verdict, the sentence, and the punishment, the last to be delivered, we hoped, some time distant. The District Attorney, W. R. Lanahan, would present his final argument first. He called out:

"Bailiff! Have you cleared the hall of all women and children and those who cannot stomach the facts and the truth?"

"All be gone that wanter be gone!" cried out the bailiff.

The District Attorney commenced, his voice low and manner calm, as he would comport himself throughout his presentation.

"We shall speak now of burning and pillage and plunder. Of murder and rape and torture." He took a paper from the desk and read from it, as he would read from other sheets to mark each of his charges. "You are a young woman by the name of Annie Abel. You are living twelve miles from the forted town of Post Oak in Shackelford County. Your husband Jim has gone into this forted village for supplies. There has been no unrest among the Indians for three years. Jim feels it is safe to leave you and your little baby girl, Melinda by name, alone. You are working in the yard when you see the Indians. There are four of them and they approach without menace. You give them food and drink. You say your husband is in the fields not far away. The Indians leave. But they return. They are angered. They say you have lied to them. Your husband is not in the fields. They take you and your babe with them. You are mounted on the back of one of the Indian horses. Your baby commences to cry. She will not hush. This angers the Indians. They sign-speak that the baby must be quiet, as they will be found out from her crying. You press your hand over the babe's mouth till it near suffocates. You must let it breathe. You take away your hand. The child cries out. This enrages one of the Indians. He takes the child from you. He grasps the child by one leg. He whirls the child above his head like a whip. As he whirls the crying child above his head he walks to a tree. There he smashes the child's head against the tree till its brains fly from its skull."

The District Attorney held this sheet of paper before the

jury. He released it from his hand. Every juror, everyone in the hushed courtroom, watched as the paper floated to the floor. The District Attorney went to his desk and took up another paper from which he read of another Indian atrocity. For an hour—perhaps it was not so long; it passed like years—the counsel read of murder, rape, enslavement, and torture; of humiliation, brutality, and cruelty so unspeakable that by his mere recitation, in his quiet voice, were we made ill with anger. As each tale of horror was concluded, the attorney would let the paper he had read slip from his fingers and drift to the floor till, at the end, the floor about him was covered with white blots. As the attorney moved among the papers, he took great care not to step on any one, and as he walked among them, we began to see them as did he, as we were meant to see them, as the graves of our people scattered over the Texas plain.

There was but a single sheet left on the attorney's desk. He took it up. "You are a teamster named Willie Marshall on a corn train bound out from the settlement of Bobsboro, Texas, to the hunting camp at Adobe Walls on the Canadian River. You are a man of family. You have a wife and three children in Tennessee. You have arranged for them to come to this small settlement of Bobsboro when you have completed your trek to Adobe Walls and have returned with your corn wagon loaded with buffalo hides. There is little worry among your five fellow teamsters and six guards and two Indian scouts. The Comanches have been chased out on the staked plains. The Army is near, you will pass within a few miles of one of their encampments. One of the scouts is crying a song in his Mexican tongue. You are riding easy on your wagon bench. The mules are good in their harnesses, for you have got the best of them at Bobsboro, by knowing your trade. There is one other experienced muleteer among you. This is Cap Helms. He is older than the others, like you a veteran of the Confederate armies. This day Cap rides ahead of you. You call out to one another, jokes and recollections, when the way is smooth and the wagons are quiet.

Then terror strikes. It is midafternoon. A mild summer day. You have called out to Cap Helms ahead of you. The road is quiet. Cap Helms should have heard you, but he does not answer. You call out again. Then you see Cap slide down on his bench, toppling sideways. You see the long feathered stick protruding from his neck. Then there are two more feathered sticks sprouting from Cap's back and then a fourth arrow shatters Cap's head, and he is flung from his bench and falls beneath the wagon wheels. Now you are struck hard on the thigh—the blow of the arrow comes with the force of a hammer. An arrow strikes the lead mule, another the wagon wheel beneath your bench, another rips through your shirt, another drives into the corn heaped behind—you hear it hiss as it drives through the grain. That is all you have heard, the hissing of the arrows in flight, the various sounds as they strike flesh, bone, wood, earth, the heaped corn. But now there is sound, too much for your ears. The cries of those wounded ahead and behind, the terror of the mules, the war cries of the attackers—and there is your own cry as you fall from the wagon bench, twisting the arrow in your leg till the shaft snaps off, so that you may crawl beneath a wall of chaparral and hide and wait and pray for your life.

"It seems for a time that your prayers will be answered. A gun battle ensues. Two of the teamsters, Henry Dawkins and the colored man Bob, put up a great resistance. Their bodies will be found surrounded by hundreds of cartridges. But their shells are now spent, and there is silence. Dawkins and the colored man Bob are allowed to die quickly, for they were brave in their resistance. Fear spreads over you. You did not go to your comrades' aid. You lay like a coward in the chaparral as they died. If the Indians find you, you will suffer an unspeakable end. All is quiet now. You hear the Indians moving among the train. They speak to one another, as calmly as buyers on market day, as they move among the corn wagons. Then there are shouts of excitement. Soft leather moccasins rush past your sanctuary. There is more shouting among the

273

Indians. Then above that the cries of a white man. He is pleading for mercy in a tongue that these savages do not know. He is pleading for mercy in a tongue that even the Lord cannot understand. Death is the Lord's only mercy, and that will not come for what passes like an eternity. Night falls, and still there are the man's moans. They do not cease. On occasion there is a scream—it comes to you like wild laughter, for the moans of the tormented dying man are terrible. You know that your best chance of survival, maybe your only chance, is to lie where you are, in the chaparral. But you can no longer stand the sound of the man dying—*how is he dying? how are they killing him?*—and you rise to your knees and crawl from your hiding place, away from the fires of the wagons, toward the dark.

"You crawl till your knees are raw and bleeding from the rocks. You come to your feet. The reflection of the fires is distant now. You turn your back to the hideous light and take a step into the dark. And another. You want to shout with ecstasy. You remember how as a child you were afraid of the dark. How can any man ever again be afraid of the dark! You are now walking, not well, because of your wound, but you are moving away. You are going to live! Then you sense some movement in the dark. To your left. You stop, not moving, not breathing. There is another movement, to your right. Then there is movement all around you. Low to the ground. Then sound. An animal snarling. Wolves—you think you are surrounded by wolves and laugh at their pitiful threat. Then there is another sound—one that freezes your blood. A bark. These are not wolves but dogs. One of the dogs begins to bark. You fling yourself at the animal, to crush the sound in its throat. But in the dark the dog leaps away. Now the others are barking—all around you. You have stumbled into an Indian dog den. Everywhere the dogs are barking and leaping at you and snarling and snapping. You can hear cries in the distance. The dogs have roused their masters. You run. Your leg is whole again—fear has healed it. You run and run. But the dogs are there, all about you. Why

can't you outrun the dogs? You see that you are barely walking. The dogs have you encircled. You fall and grasp one of
the dogs and tear at its throat like a wild animal. The other
dogs attack. They will kill you, and you bless them for it. And
then you are dead. You must be. You no longer feel the dogs'
fangs at your throat, their breath in your face. Then a dread
comes over you, a fear blacker than death itself. The dogs are
gone. You are surrounded by men.

"They take you back to the wagon train. The wagons are
aflame, the corn spilled and smoking. You see Henry Dawkins,
you see the colored man Bob. Their bodies have been mutilated. But they were dead when these things were done. They
have been honored for their bravery. The Indians walk you
through the smoldering wreckage of the train. You see all
the others—Cap Helms—dead. Robert Dixon—dead. Johnny
Holmes—dead. Another body—you do not know the man, for
his nose and ears have been cut from his face, his scalp taken,
his eyes gouged from his head. You come to the end of the
train. There is a campfire. The Indians have gathered around
the fire. The fire has been built between two wagons. Strung
between the two wagons is an animal the Indians have been
roasting. The animal has been left too long over the fire—it is
charred black. The Indians turn the animal and you see it is
not a beast, but a man. You are crying now, babbling senselessly. You are saying the names of your loved ones, your wife
and your children. Susan, John, James . . . you cannot remember the name of your baby daughter. Susan, John, James.
. . . The Indians have cut down the black charred hunk of
flesh. They are churning the fire, stirring the coals. Now the
Indians are tying wires around your hands and feet. Susan,
John, James . . . One of the Indians takes the wire that is tied
about your feet and yanks. You strike the ground hard, but the
other wire grasps your wrists and you are borne into the air.
Susan, John, James . . . You are weightless. It is like flying
into the night. Susan, John, James . . . Then there is a pain

you could not have imagined, it comes from your groin and spreads through your body and erupts from your mouth. And now you are lifted toward the sky. You go up, up into the black night. There is something at your back. There is some terrible gnawing into your back, something eating there . . . but you do not care, for you are sailing into the heavens. Dark is coming to you. But then with a cruelty that encompasses the mind of God, you are taken from the dark. You are turned away from the stars and the night. You are turned slowly till you come to look into the flames of Hell. You look and sink into this raging fire till your eyes are burned black in your head, and then, even then, with blessed death so near, they turn you again, and now you face the dark, the starless, eyeless dark. And the color of that dark is the red fire of life that will not go out! O merciful Lord, your last thought is prayer that the fire of life will soon be out!"

The last sheet of paper fell from the attorney's hand. It sailed across the room, sliding to the floor distant from the other white squares. The District Attorney watched it till it settled and then he spoke, as quiet as ever.

"Susan, John, and James . . ."

There came then a sound that we knew to be the united cries of those white men in the room—for the faces of all about me and everywhere I could see were disfigured by their mouths spread open—but it struck in a single blast of rage, like two blows clapped against our ears.

Amid the roar, Attorney Lanahan sat down and the defense attorney, Tomball, stood and went before the crowd. There he waited till we were silent. Then he spoke:

"Shall I tell you of the Indian babes who have been slaughtered by white men? Shall I tell you of the Indian women raped by white men? Shall I tell you of the Indian braves savaged, tortured, murdered, and scalped by the white men? Shall I have the bailiff clear the room of the faint at heart and the weak of stomach and tell you tales that will make the recitations of my honorable adversary seem like child's play? No. No, I will not speak today of the defeated nations of those who are native to this land and have been so ruthlessly, mercilessly, cruelly driven from it. No, today I will speak of the invaders of this land, the conquerors, the Europeans, the white race of mankind. Today I will speak of you and me."

The attorney turned and addressed the men in the jury box: "Farmer Terrill, do you know what tribe you come from? Ben Stack, what tribe is yours? And Bill Walker, Jim Baird, McKnight there, Jackson, McClellan, Scott, Poage, Young, Mac-Bride, Coulter, Houston, Peete, Hays—what tribes do you hail from? Where does Tomball come from? We are Englishmen, some of us, Scotch, Irish, some Welshmen, a good Dutchman now and then, a Schmidt who has made himself a Smith, but by and large, you and you and you and you, we are what they call Scotch-Irish, lowland Scots, Presbyterian Irish, Ulstermen, Orangemen, we are what the good Ben Franklin once referred to as white savages. We are in truth the first real Americans. The Dutch, the Germans, the English, the French, the Spaniards, they have all come to this country and gone back, or have come and clung to the seaboard, near that water that connects them to their homelands. No, it is our race, by whatever name you call us, a race without a true homeland, we are the ones who have come to the heart of this country, to settle and to live and to call it our own. It is we who have taken this land from those native to it, it is we who have cheated, stolen, lied, tricked, burnt, murdered, raped, pillaged, and destroyed and driven from this land those who are native to it."

There was some restive movement among the crowd, some voices were raised in protest, some men moved angrily in their seats, but the attorney looked out at these men and by his anger that was like their own, he calmed them. "And why have we done these crimes—why have we been so *good* to them? It is because we, you and you and you, Terrill, Danley, and Baxter, Johnson, Reilly, and Cummings, it is because we have been cheated, stolen from, lied to, tricked, burnt out, murdered, our women raped, our villages wrecked, our cultures destroyed, ourselves driven from our homelands, driven from land to land till at last we came to this wild place and saw that if we did not make it our own, there would be no place on this earth for us. And what race of people have so despised, tormented, and vilified us? Why, they are of our own kind. Their flesh is white—whiter than our own. They speak our tongue—and do so more gracefully than we. Their garb and get-up is like our own—but more fashionable, sometimes it is even cleaner than our own. Their houses, their horses, their children, their churches, their God, these too are like our own—but finer, finer and fairer than our own. Oh yes, it is men of our own kind—like us but better than we—who have made us into a wandering tribe of nomads little different beneath the skin from these aborigines we call savages. Old Ben Franklin was right about that after all. We are like these Indians here, and like them too we were made to be savage. That is what I have come to say to you—no man is savage by nature. We did not cheat, steal, lie, burn, murder, rape, pillage, and destroy but that we were taught it by those of our own kind, those men who are like us but are better than we."

The attorney walked about, now tracking across the sheets of paper dropped there by the District Attorney, kicking them from his path, with contempt not for the meaning that had been given them by his adversary but for the subterfuge he had employed. "Shall I tell you how the tribes of Tomball and Grady—my mother's people—and the McCrackens and Jameses—the peoples of my father's mother and my mother's mother—came here? We began as lowland Scots, the Tomballs and the McCrackens did, not a Celtic people at all, but some collection of Danes and Angles and Saxons that had been pushed north by the reign of conquerors that fell on the British Isle after the Romans had gone and left this northernmost outpost of their great empire to seed. These people collected there in that neck of rock and sea between England and Scotland. There they made themselves Celts and settled to an existence of crippling poverty, of scratching from the weak soil little more harvest than the seeds they had sown. These people came to act as a buffer between the highland Celts to the north and the English to the south and so suffered the plunder, massacre, and rapine of the near-constant wars that raged between these two so superior races. These lowland Scots were not a people, not a race surely, scarcely more than a collection of bandit tribes that preyed as viciously on one another as on their enemies, till a wandering native son by the name of John Knox returned to them and brought with him a religion, the Protestant religion, that gave these brutal subhumans a sense of themselves as a people and a race; churches that drew together under the same roof clans that had been warring for centuries; pastors that brought learning and enlightenment to what had been a wasteland of mind and soul; and a God that they feared more than any race or kind of man on earth.

"Now after Knox and his followers had forged this race of nomad bandits into a people, they grew to be a thorn in the plump English side. The English were then ruled by a putrid king who sought to unify the British Isle while subjugating the neighboring Irish. This king thought to kill these two angry birds with one stone—to smother two rebellious peoples with one immigration—and he settled scores of thousands of lowland Scots in northern Ireland, to set Scot against Irish like dogs loosed on bulls. The Irish were a hard people—their misery at the hands of the English can be chronicled as well—but they could not stand up to the invaders, the Presbyterian Scots, and the Irish were driven from the northern reaches of their homeland and Ulster, a fortified nation within their nation, was gained. Oh, but what the Ulsterman had won by his own military prowess, the English banker and politician and priest took away. Punitive tariffs and taxes were levied against the Ulsterman; no Presbyterian could hold political office; the ministers of Nonconformity were forbidden to offer public worship and to perform other sacramental rites. By the beginning of the century before this, the Scots in Ireland were in a state worse than they had ever known in Scotland, starvation being a more dreadful weapon than the sword.

"And so we, the Tomballs, and those like us, looked to America. With the Teagues and the Logans and the Campbells and the Rutherfords. No matter where we entered the country—my people went into the Pennsylvanian Appalachians—there is a pattern of sameness to our history here. We were land clearers. We were mountain tamers. We were, first and last, Indian fighters. We were men and women who pushed back the frontier, who made forests into fields, who flattened hills and valley, who drove the Indians ever to the west, so that these refined coastal people might extend their fortunes without so much as grubbing a root. The Tomballs were among these people. After we had settled the wilderness of Pennsylvania, the value of our cleared land tripled and we were moved out by the richer and steadier colonists from Germany and England. From Pennsylvania we went down into the Shenandoah of Virginia and were once again driven out by our successes in clearing land of trees and Indians. From Virginia we scattered south and west. You all know the names of the places of your fathers and your grandfathers. Tennessee, Kentucky, Georgia, Alabama, Mississippi, Arkansas, Missouri—is there a man among you who does not have roots in one of these states? There we met the same fate as before. We knew nothing but the felling of trees and the planting of grain and the killing of Indians, and time and again were we felled ourselves in the dollar wars that we could understand as little as the Indian understood our loathing of trees. We moved again, to new forests, inhabited by other Indians, and began again our war, the only war we knew, against nature and those native to this land. Oh, I have seen the highfalutin writing in the silk-stocking papers and journals and books back East. They say that the West is being settled by greed, land greed, by men who want more land than they have a right to, men who come to the land and savage it and move on to new, virgin land to savage that, to move on again. I have read these opinions and I have thought how true they are. This land has been ravaged by greed—how true—but it is not the greed of the settler, the man and woman and child in a Conestoga wagon. These are not the people who have despoiled this land. No sir. It is the Eastern banker who has pushed them out of Pennsylvania, he is the despoiler. It is the Virginian squire who has deeded them from the Shenandoah, he is the ravager. It is the genteel planter who has made slave of all within his purview—white or black, by wage or chattel—he is the thief. Oh, these gilded despoilers, these titled ravagers, these elegant thieves, they have run these people without a home from Pennsylvania and Tennessee and Kentucky and Georgia and Arkansas till they all have come here to this land we call Texas. It is here that we have declared our home. It is here we will take our last stand, that we shall be pushed and run no farther by dollars and deeds and debts. No Wall Street banker, no Tidewater royalist, no antebellum flesh peddler, not even those native to this place—no one will ever take this homeland from us. That is why, like cornered beasts, we have lied, cheated, stolen, murdered, raped, destroyed, and driven those native to this land from it. *We have no goddamn where else to go!"*

There came a cry from the crowd that dwarfed the response drawn by the District Attorney. As before, Attorney Tomball waited for the shouting to subside, making no effort by gesture or speech to silence the throng. At length quiet came and he delivered his finale.

"I will now speak to you of reason and mercy, of forgiveness and understanding. I will speak to you against violence and hatred, against blind passion and brute strength. I will speak to you of vengeance and its folly. I will speak to you of wrongs begetting wrongs till there will be no end to wrongs. I will speak to you of making ourselves good men, strong and gentle, who will put an end to our war and vengeance and stupid, stupid bloodshed. I will speak to you of the way we are now and of the way we may yet be.

"And so it is that we in this court, if wrongs will not forever beget wrongs, must hand down kindness, understanding, and mercy to those who have wronged us and, in turn, beg such forgiveness from those whom we have wronged, those native to this land that we have taken from them for our home."

With this Attorney Tomball turned and hailed the bailiff in a voice so great that the man flinched at being so addressed: "Bailiff! Clear all those men, women, and children who have lost the power of reason and its great wings of mercy and understanding, clear all those who cannot think and forgive and beg forgiveness from this hall!" The bailiff, a man who found importance in himself and his duties, opened his mouth to cry out, but the attorney had gone to the cordon of soldiers about the prisoners' dock and placed his hands between two soldiers and parted them so that we might see the Indians we would hang. He named the Indians there, calling each by his name in their native tongue, and still speaking in that tongue, he asked their forgiveness, that we did not know what we had done. That such foreign words had been memorized and delivered with many errors little diminished their effect on those who knew the Indian tongue and mattered not at all to those who did not, as translation paled before the attorney's gesture.

The judge rose and ordered the courtroom cleared, and the crowd filed out of the room. Those remaining in the courtroom were the jurors, the officers of the court, the soldiers, and the prisoners. The judge spoke to the jurors, then joined the attorneys Lanahan and Tomball, who had gathered in the back of the courtroom, like gladiators who had dueled to a draw and had been awarded their lives for it. The jurors conversed among themselves briefly, then called the judge to the jury box. A verdict of guilty had been decided and declared in less than five minutes.

Night had begun to descend. The courtroom was lighted by lamps within and from without by the glare of the torches that were being made and ignited and handed out, as children are given candy at a fair, along the length of Main Street. The windows had now been closed, but still we could hear the growing voice of the mob and see men who had placed themselves above the others haranguing their fellows. Though we could not make out the words of these speakers, there was little doubt as to their purpose. I went to the window and saw that Main Street was a river of men and torches, with the speakers set among them like islands, causing the flow of the crowd to collect and swirl about them. For the moment, these many speakers divided and diverted the mob, but one could see that soon one by one these speakers would tire or be pulled down till only one remained. Then, so united, the mob would rise like a flood against us.

As dark collected about the town, the torches cast monstrous shadows across the courtroom, in effect dimming and, as true night came, dousing the lamps within. In such a ghastly lit scene, Judge Clark approached and told me of the guilty verdict handed down. He spoke of whisking the prisoners away to the railhead at Weatherford tonight, before the mob learned of the verdict and that the sentence would be imprisonment, not death. We were wondering how we would transfer the Indians from the courthouse to the wagons and drive the wagons to the Weatherford Road without riot when Vern Starr, a soiled, rumpled angel of deliverance, appeared at the courtroom door. Starr had brought with him ten troopers, the number of Indian prisoners. Each trooper wore a field pack, which, at Starr's order, he slung from his back and opened. Within each trooper carried a blanket, a pair of nondescript trousers, and moccasins or soft shoes. The troopers removed their boots and uniform trousers and donned the faded, worn attire and the Indian foot-wear. They then pulled the blankets over their heads and, but for a glimpse of a white finger that we hoped would not be noted in the torchlight, passed for the ten Indians.

Starr moved his disguised men into line and spoke to me. "If we can make the first fifty yards we should be fine. I'll march the boys to the jail and keep them there a half hour, no more. Then they'll get back into their boots and proper dress and we'll get out of there. I don't want to be around when the Texans decide to smoke us out. With some luck you'll be on the Weather-ford Road and up to the ridge by then. Now, I've had your wagons brought to the livery stable two blocks east of here. When we have drawn the mob away, trot your redskins over there and scat. It might be best to move them now into the hall by the rear door. I want to file my boys past the windows here. Men will believe just about anything they learn by peeping."

We moved the Indians into the short hall directly behind the judge's bench, then watched as Starr put his blanketed men on view past the window and marched them under guard out of the courthouse and into the hellish night. We waited by the side window and thus lost view of Starr and his men as they formed up in front of the courthouse, though we knew of their presence by the reaction of the crowd. A silence moved through the throng; there was no sound but the crackle and hiss of the torches. Now we could hear Captain Starr ordering his regular troopers into formation, cursing with great authenticity those disguised as Indians. As Starr made his guard detachment ready to move through the mob, a man shouted,

"We got 'em in hand, boys! Let's hang 'em now!"

But before the crowd could move, Starr's voice rang out. "By goddamn, we will not hang them now, but later! And as for *you*," he cried, we imagined, at the man who had spoken, "if you do not move from my path I will shoot *you*!" And we heard Starr's pistol cocked and the order to forward march called out. The men jammed in the street parted and allowed Starr and his guard detachment and his false prisoners to pass through them, north along Main Street toward the jail. As the soldiers moved along, the mob turned and followed Starr till the courthouse was left unguarded by the mob's vigilance and Lieutenant Flipper and I, our detachment and our prisoners, were able to effect our escape as planned by Captain Starr.

We made our way to the livery stables and found our wagons within its barn. We mounted and chained our prisoners in the wagon beds and moved southward through the darkened back street of Bobsboro till we reached the outskirts of town. There we joined the Weatherford Road. We followed the stage road south from town at a more leisurely pace than any of us desired, the last thing we could tolerate being one of the wagons to break down. We were soon past Fort Ichard and on the rise toward the ridge that Starr had spoken of. As the head of our column made the ridge, I gave over its lead to Lieutenant Flipper and stood aside as the wagons creaked and lumbered to the ridge crest and there pitched down into the next valley. As I stood waiting to take up the rearguard, I looked back at Bobsboro and knew with an eerie exactitude the mind of the mob. There on the northern border of Bobsboro was gathered a clot of flame: this was the mob surrounding the county jail. During the five minutes it took the wagon train to pass, I observed this ball of fire break into five or six pieces, these forming into as many fiery snakes that began to stream south through the town toward us, moving not only down the marked avenue of Main Street but through the back streets and alleyways, a half-dozen vertical molten lines racing toward us.

As the last wagon went by, I turned my horse and galloped to the head of the column and called out to my second-in-command, "To hell with the axles, Mr. Flipper, put them into a good run and get us out of here!"

The wagons rattled at a good pace across the valley, and we had made the crest of the second ridge as the first torches of the mob began to outline and spill over the ridge we had just left. Again I took the rear position and noted that the river of flame seemed to have halted on the ridge behind, only a ribbon of fire dribbling down the stage road. I did not remain to see if this hesitation was the beginning of an ebb in the mob's fury or the gathering of their forces for a final assault, but went with the column at the same good pace across the valley to the third ridge, where I again stood as rearguard. No torches appeared on the ridge behind us, the second we had crossed, nor did any appear on the third or fourth. When the wagon train had cleared the sixth ridge and I could look back and observe nothing but its black form dimly outlined against the sky, only then did I order our pace slowed to a walk. The old wagons creaked and sighed at the reduced pace, as if sharing our relief.

Tehana Storm met his end the following day. We had intended to march throughout the night, to arrive at the railhead in Weatherford no later than midmorning, but one of our wagons lost a kingbolt, which we spent an hour futilely attempting to repair. We abandoned this vehicle by the road and doubled up the prisoners it had carried and started again. But soon another wagon went down, and we made a dry camp that night while a detachment of troopers went back to retrieve parts from the abandoned wagon. The second wagon repaired, we were off at dawn, moving over a sea of ridges and valleys such as we had known since leaving Bobsboro. The country was grassland, dotted about with clumps of black, gnarled live oak, some of the crippled trees being centuries old. By some means I did not know, the Indians had during the night concluded they were being taken to be hanged, an odious and dishonorable death to them, and no amount of persuasion by me or the interpreter could convince them that their fate was to be imprisonment. As the sun rose, the Comanche prisoners began to prepare for their execution, each man singing his death song. After some time the Indians' screech began to tell on the men's nerves.

286

Lieutenant Flipper, who was not suffering the caterwauling well, rode forward from his rear position to see if there could be an end put to the death songs, but neither I nor the interpreter could imagine how to do it. Flipper unhappily returned to his post. One of the troopers nearby joined in with an old Comanche chief's song, ostensibly mocking its tuneless squawl, but in effect joining the Indian's lament.

Toward midmorning we began to climb a long, gentle hill that our guide said would be the last rise before Weatherford. We would have the Indians at the railhead by noon and be done with them by dinner. At the summit of this final ridge stood a massive live oak tree. The tree's branches twisted among themselves in a maze so coiled and intricate that they formed a cage that one could imagine a child or an animal entering and being unable to find its way out. As we marched toward this disfigured arbor, hoofbeats came up from behind, the interpreter whipping his horse into a run. The interpreter turned his mount into mine:

"Captain, I don't like it at all! Tehana Storm has taken to chanting his death song now. He says he will die before he reaches that tree. You had better come back, quick!"

I looked forward to the ancient tree that had grown to mythological dimensions, a Medusa that we had to battle to pass, when some attention jerked the interpreter and his horse to the rear. I turned and viewed the wagon train stretching down the road behind us. The Indians had risen in the wagon beds and had cast off their blankets and had raised their manacled hands. All were turned toward the last wagon in line, that which carried Tehana Storm. The interpreter had already spurred his horse down the hill, and I went after him. As I rode I saw that Tehana had raised up in his wagon, like the others, but that his hands were free. In one of his hands sparkled the steel of a knife. He moved toward the wagon teamster who was riding the near wheel animal. This man was not aware of any danger from his rear, his attention focused on the Indians in the wagons ahead. Tehana reached for the man, and the two of them went over backwards, beneath the mules' hooves and the wagon wheels. When the wagon passed over them, the teamster could be seen sitting in the roadway with a knife handle protruding from his leg. The Indian had taken the teamster's carbine and was crouched nearby, working its mechanism. He turned the rifle and looked up toward the head of the column. He raised the rifle and aimed it at me or the interpreter. It was then that Lieutenant Flipper, who had been riding alongside, leveled his pistol and shot the Comanche chieftain at close range, bringing him down with the first shot.

The Indian was not yet dead. We took him to the crest of the ridge and laid him out under the live oak tree, as if it were summer, that he might be shaded from the sun. The other Indians set up a lament so strident and mournful we could scarcely make ourselves heard. Lieutenant Flipper knelt off a ways from us, his head held in his hands, for he had never killed a man before. We saw that Tehana had stripped the flesh from his wrists and his hands in freeing himself from his manacles. We wrapped these wounds, but with little purpose, for the Indian had been struck in the lung and was dying. He had secreted the knife in his leggings, but how he had come by the weapon we never learned. As the life fled from the man, his eyes faded till they looked blue as sky. It was reported later that with his dying breath Tehana Storm had asked after his white mother, whom he had not known since he was a boy, but this was not true. Before he died Tehana did try to speak to those of us who had gathered around him, but when he opened his mouth only blood spilled from it.

Upon delivering the Indian prisoners to the railhead at Weatherford, I was ordered to journey to Dallas, to secure two deserters and transport them to Fort Richardson for court-martial. This assignment was readily accepted, as it would postpone my return to Fort Pulgas and my duties there. I was to be accompanied by a Sergeant Chalmers, a good soldier by his record, who was as weary of war and horse as I. We performed our tasks in Dallas, arresting and detaining the deserters in two days' time, and were set for a third of relaxation when on that morning I was approached by a hotel clerk.

"I am sorry for the delay, sir," the clerk said in hushed tones. "The telegram arrived last night, but there was some confusion—we did not immediately think of you. I am very sorry indeed."

I took the cable to a sunlit corner of the lobby and there opened it. The yellow paper lay like pollen on my hands. The message read:

MRS. CHAPMAN VERY ILL   PLEASE COME QUICK

I arranged for Sergeant Chalmers to stay in Dallas till a replacement for me could be sent, refusing his offer to accompany me to Fort Pulgas. The rail line, I learned, went west from Dallas, through Fort Worth, Weatherford, and Mineral Wells, where it ended. I made plans to take the train to Mineral Wells, buy a horse there, and ride to Fort Pulgas, two hundred miles to the southwest, securing by trade or cash fresh horses along the way. I left Dallas at noon and arrived at the westernmost city on the rail line at midnight. I woke a boy at the livery stable and bought a horse and equipment and before dawn, without supplies of any kind, set out toward Fort Pulgas. I went due west along the unfinished rail line, riding the ties between the saber-bright rails till light came and I could see beyond the roadbed. The country therearound was rugged, sharp-crested hills, steep valleys, all spread over with scrub cedar and brush. I kept along the rail line, waiting for the land to flatten and clear, to be freed of gorge and river, before I commenced my trek overland.

As the sun rose I overtook a succession of work crews, laying rail, setting ties, building beds, clearing the land of tree and

289

shrub. At the van of these workers were the surveyors. These men gave me a map of the region and told me of obstacles and difficulties no map would carry. "Two weeks ago there was a great prairie fire, here," the chief surveyor said, "stretching from the *llano estacado* to near Fort Pulgas." He drew these positions on the map. "So far as I know it may still be burning down toward the south. You won't find man nor beast, not any forage and little water, if you cross it. You might skirt it to the east, here, but no telling how far off that will throw you and how many hours that will add to your journey."

I left the advanced railhead and went cross-country into the Texas wild, riding in a southwesterly direction, as the compass pointed me toward Fort Pulgas. I knew no difficulties that could not be overcome or avoided. I came upon many ranches in this wilderness; everyone I encountered gave me fresh mounts and food and water and wished me Godspeed. But to change mounts, I did not leave the saddle on this the second day of my odyssey. On the morning of the third day, sunrise came gray, the east blanched, the low sun tarnished yellow. In my stupor from two nights without sleep, I had ridden senselessly into the fields of ash carried away from the prairie fire. I dismounted and walked a distance. All was covered by a layer of the deadest matter on earth. The air was suffused with particles so fine they could be observed only by the pallor they cast to the light and the sooty ring collected about the sun. I mounted and galloped my horse across this country, as sick at heart as if the entire world had died. I reduced the gait and saw even then that the horse was near gone. Lope gave way to trot and trot to walk as, similarly, my mood fell in stages to despair. I tied my compass to the saddle horn and set the flagging horse on a southwesterly course and followed the needle, whose butt end pointed the way I must go.

Toward noon the horse ceased walking. I quirted the horse but he would not go. It did not much seem to matter, but I chose to strike the horse again and would have, I think, kept striking the beast till he moved or fell, but a voice called out to me from a distance. There I observed a small gray-bearded man gesturing for me to dismount. This was the rancher whose land I had ridden onto. The old man helped me from the saddle and took me into his house and fed me bacon and coffee. While I ate he studied my map but could make little of it. He swept his arms about as he spoke of the lay of the land. "Fort Pulgas—that'll be there." He pointed out a bearing a bit south of my previous course. "And the burnt country will be between them and you. The flames did not creep down to Pulgas but was turned by a sou'wester and went on east of there. You will be ninety-nine miles from Pulgas standing at the barn door, and half of that is burnt. No grass nor water nor any other place left standing. You will be wanting a horse that will carry you all the way." He removed our plates and cups to the wash sink and stood by the window, gazing out. "The zebra dun will do it," he said, as if speaking to himself.

We went to the stables and found the horse the old man had spoken of, a mare—Jessie, he called her. He talked the horse away from the others and led her by her mane outside the fence. The mare was a medium-sized, perfectly proportioned animal, with a gentle temperament and powerful stride. She would be the horse, the rancher said in bidding us farewell, to carry me the twenty-four hours to my wife.

We set out at one in the afternoon on the bearing the rancher had given me, the horse moving well at all gaits. We came to the end of the ash an hour before dark. I had been in the saddle now forty hours and without sleep for sixty. We were riding over tall spring grass when night fell. Not long after, the stench of the burned land reached us. Soon we came to the border of the burn, and I dismounted. I led the horse out onto the vast burnt field, so that she might grow accustomed to its stench and acrid dust and the unstable footing it provided. I remounted and went onto the black field at a diminished gait. In a short while a bank of clouds hove over the sky and we were trapped in a night so dark I could not see the mare's head before me. The black earth came up, the black sky came down, till they were joined around us in a coffin of night.

The mare kept fighting at the trot, and at length I let her go to a lope. She drifted between strides, till I imagined that she flew, gazing about at the earth below for her next safe landing place: there seemed to be no other explaining how she ran in the dark. At length I recovered my sense enough to see the danger of this gait at night and pulled her into a trot. It was at this gait that I first knew the mare was suffering: the quick, hard jog shook her with coughing and chest spasms. When I dismounted, the horse lowered her head and strangled till she passed matter from her lungs. Then she raised her head and blew. I wiped my hand across her nostrils and lit a match: the mucus was streaked with blood. She ran a fever, and the glands under her jaw were tender to the touch. She coughed again and strangled up more foul matter from her illness, a fever of the lung and throat, perhaps brought on by the ashen air. I remounted and struck another match: two o'clock. Four hours till daylight. There might be that much left in her before she weakened and could not be ridden. I raised the quirt but did not strike her. The movement of my arm was sufficient to make the mare run.

We went till the horse fell off the pace. Her lungs had filled again. When we stopped she was taken with coughing and strangling, bringing up a great amount of foul matter. We rode a ways and stopped for the mare to clear her lungs. She was taken with fits of shivering now. Her chest and head were hot with fever, while her ears and legs were cold. She kept turning her head back as if to examine her flank. She stood with forelegs wide apart and head drooping slightly, but came up when I rose into the saddle and went off at a good walk.

By four the horse could not go for ten minutes without being halted by a convulsion of choking. Blood dripped from her nostrils. During her worst times of suffocation the horse would open her mouth as if to take in air by that manner in which she could not breathe. Her heart beat wildly and her fever burned in her barrel and head, while her extremities were like ice. After these halts, the mare found going difficult at first. Her hooves dragged along the ground, one often striking the other, as if she had forgotten the mechanics of walking. I would have to lead her these few minutes, till her legs warmed and she could be ridden again.

It was still dark when the mare first fell. By the time I had risen and regained my senses, the horse was up, walking away from me. I went after the horse and stopped her and saw that she had not injured herself in the fall. Her breathing was shallow, quick as a panting dog's. She still bled from her nose, though no longer did she choke up mucus. I placed my foot in the stirrup and raised into the saddle; the mare winced and her legs buckled under my weight. I struck her with the quirt—for the first time—and she went off, her head dropping low as if she were inspecting the ground over which we passed.

Before dawn some taste or aroma rose in the air that I did not recognize. It was not till the horse had broken down again and I dismounted that I saw we had left the burn. The air was sweet. I knelt and tore up a piece of grass. The grass was filled with juice. The eastern sky carried a pale smudge of dawn. As I watched, the gray haze took on coloration, faint bars of purple and blue. The sunrise would be wild with color and the earth tropical with life. I took up more grass and went to the horse and held it before her muzzle, but she turned her head away. Nor would she take any water or the small bit of forage I cupped in my hand. There might be dawn and spring all about and hope within her rider, but the mare was dying.

It was not long before the mare fell a second time. She rolled to her side and nickered and came up with her legs under her, but when she pulled up her forelegs to rise, she lost balance and rolled to her side. I pulled her to her knees, but once again her raised forelegs were not steady and when her heavier hindquarters came up, her forelegs went from under her and she fell to her side. Again I got her to her knees. Now she tried rising hindquarters first and came up well and stood as if she could be ridden, but when I put foot in stirrup, she fell. I whipped the horse, but she could not come up, crying out against my cruelty and stupidity.

I put down the whip and approached the beast's head. She took my arm between her teeth, but her strength was gone and the bite she delivered was so weak it came as a nuzzle of affection. I removed her bridle and loosened the cinch and laid the saddle off her back. A shudder passed through the mare, every muscle in her back and barrel trembling. I removed the flannel shirt I had bought in Dallas and wiped the horse down. Her legs and feet were swollen and tender, her lips and gums livid; the glands under and between her jaw had begun to swell. I formed a blanket by fastening shirt and jacket together and laid this over her back. I poured what water there was left in my canteen in my hat, but she could not drink. I went a few steps away, and the mare struggled a final time to rise, but she fell back. She whinnied once—a cry I had not heard before, as if to say I must not leave her—and then was quiet.

I walked across a valley spread with morning and spring. The grass was coming green and birds sang, and now and then some animal I could not see, a rabbit or mouse or snake, rustled through the brush. Shortly I came upon a road that ran east and west. I walked along the road west till a wagon lumbering out of the rising sun overtook me. The rancher rode me on to Fort Pulgas. We arrived there in the late afternoon, the day after my wife had died.

SIX

AFTER months there came the time to leave Fort Pulgas. I found great satisfaction in preparing to close the place, as one would gloat at the prostration of an enemy. There was much movement of personnel during this time, and military protocol and discipline were eased so much as to be dismissed. This also pleased me, for I had grown weary of drill, inspection, and formation. As I gradually shed my uniform for civilian dress, I achieved my greatest success as a soldier: receiving promotion to major, being appointed Commanding Officer of Fort Pulgas and the decimated battalion assigned to its closure, and learning that my resignation from the Army had been accepted. I was to be discharged in June.

Our primary work during these final weeks was the accounting for and transfer or sale of supplies and equipment at Fort Pulgas. I assumed direct charge of these accounts and saw that none of us was jailed for the plundered stores, unbalanced books, and missing cash. There was good trade between Hidetown and the post, as we chose to sell at a fair price rather than haul vast amounts of *matériel* across the plains to market it slightly more dearly in San Antonio. I had previously had no love for Hidetown and expected it would pass the way of most frontier scabtowns, to thrive or waste with the fort that supported it, but during my absence the place had been brought about. An industrious element had risen to power and were set to continue and prosper after our departure. Unfortunately fate, in the person of a sleepy smoker, decreed otherwise. One night a fire swept Hidetown (to have been renamed Angela for the wife of the man who would be its first Mayor), and there was little we could do but gather at the banks of the dusty Pulgas River and watch the flames.

For some reason that eluded me, life went on at Pulgas as if there would be no end. The relaxing of military responsibility brought on such a burgeoning of our social life that I considered sending the men out on patrol, though there were no hostile Indians within a thousand miles. The activities that generally aid the begetting of our own kind—teas, dinners, dances, flirtations, trysts, moonlit buggy rides, and strolls hand-in-hand about the parade—increased to a pitch that I found appalling. This nonsense culminated in the inevitable—the announcement of the wedding of the Post Adjutant, Captain Nolan, and Helen Fuller, governess to the children of Captain and Mrs. Morrison, to be celebrated in late May, the last week of our tenancy at Pulgas.

On the morning of the wedding, I was found in the company of the prospective bridegroom and Doc Armand, Post Surgeon, both men, like me, widowers. Our trio walked the perimeter of the fort as if inspecting it. There was during our stroll a great deal of remembrance of our days at Pulgas. All that was spoken of were the good times, as each of us had lost a wife in this stark, desolate quadrangle. At length we completed the square, coming to stand where we had begun, at the main gate looking toward the charred remains of Hidetown. For a man nearing forty who had been through the ordeal at least once, Captain Nolan was anxious to an unreasonable degree and soon went off to shine his boots, trim his mustache, and polish his brass for the dozenth time since sundown yesterday. With the bridegroom's departure, the physician took to the healing of my sorrow. Armand was a tall, corpulent, hard man, with the look of one who has known all the wickedness in the world and all its cares and is bored to death by them. The physician had been friend to me—tormentor and supporter—during the weeks following Ann's death, when I needed goad as often as balm. He spoke, gazing across at the burnt sticks of Hidetown:

"I think we are a people who will leave no ruins. Do you know there are architects who design buildings with that purpose alone—that they may be magnificent in decay?" We had taken to walking again, once more around the fort's perimeter. "Will you be leaving your wife's remains here, Philip?"

"You know I will not."

"Will you bury her at home?"

"I will."

"And will that be an end to it?"

"Perhaps."

"Ah, you will make such a fine ruin, Philip. Isn't that what you've had in mind all along, making a monument to Ann, of sorrow rather than stone?"

"If my mourning has lasted overlong, it is because I did not care for her when she was alive."

"Bah! Did that cause her illness?"

"I wished her gone."

"Did you wish her dead?"

"I wanted to be free of her—by any means."

"Did you wish her dead, sir?"

"What would you advise if I did?"

"That you should take up your revolver and join her." The physician clasped my arm and halted our walk. "Philip, these crimes of the mind must be ignored, near forgotten, before they can be dealt with. For now put your mind in order and call it clean. Soon forgetfulness will come, it will be like night, and in its gloom these guilts will pass into neglect."

"And when morning comes?"

"Then there will be some dust in an obscure corner that you will sweep into the street."

It came time for the wedding, and Doc Armand and I went to the chapel, where the denizens of Fort Pulgas had gathered. From camp follower to Commandant all were turned out in their finest attire, every face but those of bride and groom set with joy. The chapel stood near the postern gate, befitting our early commander's opinion of its functions. On one side of the chapel sat Suds Row, on the other the latrines, backing it the guardhouse. The building had been constructed quickly and cheaply, with green cottonwood lumber purchased in the days before our quartermaster knew the curing properties of that wood. Now every board in the chapel—from spire to knee pew—was warped to some degree. Every winter there had risen a cry from the faithful that some effort more permanent than chinking be made to halt the whistling wind in its progress from porch to presbytery, but nothing was ever contemplated till summertime, when the chapel became the only pleasant, airy edifice on post. So it was today that a breeze drifted through the chapel, cooling the overdressed multitude therein.

The ceremony commenced with the efforts of the post marching band to render some tunes by Wagner, Brahms, and Schubert. During the music guests were seated, like litigants in a courtroom, one set of intimates and kin directed left, the other right. At length the chapel doors were closed. Then Mrs. Grundy, as matchmaker, was escorted by the groomsmen to the first pew, in lieu of the bride's mother. Then the groomsmen marched in pairs down the center aisle, stationing themselves at the sides of the nave of the chapel. The bridesmaids followed, also in pairs, to divide and arrange themselves on the steps to the chancel. The matron of honor, the Widow Badgett, then came, she standing on the left at the foot of the chancel steps, opposite where I, as groom of honor, had been placed. Then came the bride on Doc Armand's arm, sweeping along in a gauzy haze of veil and train, the latter being attended by the groom's children. I had previously considered the bride a plain girl, but on making her approach she seemed a lovely creature, this illusion cast, I thought, by the veil and cool bluish light of the chapel. As the bride approached, I assisted the groom down the chancel steps to meet his beloved. Once united, they returned to the altar. When all were in place and the last strain of the processional hymn had faded, Chaplin Bischopp appeared from the vestry. Looking down on us all, the old charlatan cried out, "Who giveth this woman?" and the marriage vows were exchanged.

The traditional ritual of arched swords concluded the ceremony. By Captain Nolan's request, many of his civilian friends were to stand in the arch. These men had brought a mixed bag of weapons—ancient ceremonial sabers, broadswords from China, a fencing foil in Doc Armand's hand. This gave a great variety to the arch, but the bride and groom ran the gantlet without losing any part of them that could not be replaced by needle and thread. At the cry of *Return sabers!* the wedding was done and the celebration could begin.

The wedding festivities were held at the Commandant's quarters, which I had left vacant upon my ascendancy to that post. There we found that the ladies of Fort Pulgas had set up a banquet that featured chilled oysters, champagne, and scores of cakes of all types. There was such movement among the celebrants as they circled the room, passing around in pairs and trios, that an observer might sample all their opinions by placing himself by a window and turning his back to the affair. There was Mrs. Hightower, Fort Pulgas's first bride, who told and retold the story of her wedding and of the hailstorm that had preceded it and the flood that had followed. There were those who remembered that flood or the next that took the life of Pulgas's second bride, Jenny Waller, as she attempted to cross the swollen Pulgas River to Hidetown to save her husband from a fate worse than death. As these moved away others came.

". . . a pity that the Morrisons weren't at the wedding. Is it Captain Morrison who is on bad terms with Miss Fuller? Or is it Mrs. Morrison who has rather a shine on Captain Nolan . . . ?"

". . . there is at least one more cavalry officer at Pulgas who needs a good marching to the altar. Did you see how he gazed at Georgia Badgett . . . ?"

". . . and Captain Lee—but he has too good a cook to need a wife . . ."

". . . and Lieutenant Hannah—if only he weren't so skilled at billiards . . ."

So the carousel of garrison life passed by. At length I let them go reeling about unheeded, their gossip revolving with the same gaudy regularity as toy wooden horses fixed on a turning wheel. For a time I watched the children playing in the yard outside. They ran and ran in some game of chase and capture. There was my daughter, now five, already with the gangling arms and legs of a girl. She was followed about by a chow puppy I had given her after her mother's death, now as round and red as a Christmas pig. Once Kate stopped in her play and looked toward me, smiled and waved as if I had not intruded. Now I turned from the children and saw that I had been joined by another guest, a figure I did not know, whose features I could not make out in the dimming light. Nor did I recognize his voice, though, had he not been so old, it could have been my own—

How many years has it been since this wedding took place? How many years since this fort has been left a ruin? Surely you can tell us something of what lies in store for these souls. Or will you leave them trapped in time on that May afternoon on the Texas frontier? Only a few minutes of freedom will do— there, as all the guests pause in their circumambulations to raise a toast to bride and groom, you know that in a few minutes the bride will steal from the hall, that her husband's carriage has been made standing ready to take them to a honeymoon in San Antonio. But then you know, too, that a few short years hence, at Fort Apache in Arizona Territory, a few short weeks after the death of his beloved wife Helen, Captain Nolan will send his servant from the room, write a few words of instruction to his attorney, take up his pistol and put a bullet into his brain. Now you have released these two from your frozen grasp, now free the others. Doc Armand, tell us of him. And Captain Lee and Lieutenant Hannah, the second and third most eligible bachelors at Pulgas, such good friends as they toast bride and groom. Ah, comes the redoubtable Widow Badgett, and so many of the others circling the room. . . . But then the clouds do darken as the years pass—is that why you have chosen to leave them here? Not only Charles and Helen Nolan, so many of them are dead and gone now. So many of their lives have come to nothing. I think I understand now. You will leave them all here at this wedding party on the Texas frontier, May 24, 1876. Doc Armand, Captain Lee, Parson Bischopp, the sutler Lowenthal—you will turn your back on them, that, as the children and the dogs run after the Nolan's bright yellow carriage, they might live eternally here on this afternoon, glasses raised, the music stopped, your own eyes closed, pen lifted from the page.

During the final days, train after train left Fort Pulgas, till there was only the closure party remaining. These were my family and our belongings, which included my daughter and her menagerie; Mrs. Grundy, who had fastened herself to us as Kate's governess and was welcome to her; a wagon bearing the silver zinc coffin of my wife; an escort led by Lieutenant Hannah; and a train of perishable surplus goods that we thought to use or sell on our way to San Antonio, our military destination. We rode all before dawn that last day, to bid Fort Pulgas farewell in the dark. Lieutenant Hannah and I stood our horses at the main gate as wagons and troopers passed out. There were no bugles, no flags, no formation. The last wagon rumbled through the gate and we were gone.

"Shall we put a lock on it, Major?" said Lieutenant Hannah.

"Is there anything there that needs keeping pent-up?"

"By God no!" said the Lieutenant and gave the gate a fling that it would fly loose in the wind.

We joined the San Antonio stage road during the morning and made good time, as the rivers had fallen and the soft banks and fords had dried. Our first day we made to near old Fort McKavitt and camped on the San Saba River or a tributary of it. After supper I went on horseback to search out the old fort but could not find it, as darkness returned me to camp. We continued to make good time in a southeasterly direction and on the fourth day out pitched our last tent camp before we reached the German settlement of Fredericksburg. That night we bade true farewell to the Texas frontier, the last evening many of us would ever spend under canvas. Mrs. Grundy had prepared a frontier feast for the occasion, and all officers and men came to our tent and the grounds around it. Someone remembered that one of the wagons had been loaded with the instruments of the post band, and these were taken out and a wild symphony ensued, great musical enthusiasm if little trained talent evident among us. As Kate and Mrs. Grundy were the only females present, they danced whenever they chose. Midnight saw all but Kate going strong, and she, wrapped in robes and rugs in a corner of the tent, kept watch on the dancing boots till weariness drifted her asleep.

We began to leave the Edwards Plateau the next day, and the country changed to steep wooded hills and sharp limestone-buttressed valleys. Near evening our outrider came back with word we had made Fredericksburg, and we went more quickly along that we would find lodgings before night. I remained with our horses as Kate and Mrs. Grundy went to investigate one of the local hotels, a palace by our frontier standards. I smoked as I waited, leaning against the wagon frame, lost in some reverie. Shortly I noted two men walking rapidly along the street, German immigrants by their clothes and manner. As they drew near, they could be heard speaking in their native tongue, arguing, it seemed, about some passage in a book one of the men carried. So intent was their debate the two men did not see me till they had drawn alongside: there they started at my presence. With great elaboration they both lifted their hats and said, "Good even-ning!" Eyeing the zinc coffin in the wagon, one of the Germans began lifting his stiff black hat on and off his head, as a boiling pot jiggles its lid. "Good even-ning. The Society cemetery is a nice place by the river if you are going there. Very very nice place if you are lost."

"Not a friend?" inquired the second German, shaking his head.

"My wife," I said.

"Ah, so sad. So sad. This street turn and down by the river. Good even-ning."

"Good even-ning."

The German cemetery sat on a green prow of land lifted over a bend in the river that those before them had named the Pedernales. The land we gathered on shifted and sloped away at all points; headstones had been placed in angles natural to the land, a pleasant desertion of the geometry fixing so many military cemeteries. Ann was to be buried at one of the lower reaches of the ground that was quite steep; from here it was but two paces to the grated iron boundary fence and then, twenty yards below, the washed limestone cliffs and rubble that made the riverbed. There was mist that morning and cool; the grass was damp from this and the night's dew, and we proceeded with caution down the slope to the pit that, like the headstones, had been dug perpendicular to the slanted ground rather than at a right angle to the true horizon. There was no intention among any of us to make Ann's exequies a military rite, but most there were officers and troopers, and we paid our last respects to this woman as a fallen comrade. In honor the officers had strapped on sabers and donned their bright-plumed dress helmets. A drum and fife had been taken from our store of musical instruments, and the bearers came down the grass slope with the coffin to the beat and shrill call of the Dead March. As the casket was lowered into the pit and all gathered around, an officer spoke a few words of loss for the women who had died on the frontier with us. Then I went to the head of the pit and took my saber and gouged a small hole there. I turned my saber blade upward and placed its grip and guard in the hole and tamped the earth about it. I took a piece of cloth cut from our regimental flag and fastened it to the saber's point. On this cloth had been written that which would later be carved in stone:

Ann Parsons Chapman
Beloved of Philip her husband
and Katherine her daughter. After
life's fitful fever, she sleeps now.

This done, heavy pieces of earth began to slam against the coffin wall, and there came muffled sobs from nearby. The fife played taps and then there rose an angry cheer from the officers and men, for soldiers cannot mourn, and the sergeant cried *"Twos right!"* and the drum broke into a snapping quickstep and the fife picked up the lively, taunting cadence and we all walked at a rapid pace away from the grave.

I was to receive the official documents of my discharge in San Antonio, but arranged with Lieutenant Hannah that my family and I might leave the military train at this point, that these documents be sent on to meet our ship at New Orleans

304

or, that failing, to New York, our final destination. We were but family now, and though we did miss the company of the men in blue, there came a sense that our journey was no longer an ending but a beginning. Kate, Mrs. Grundy, one chow puppy, two cats, a cage of a variety of birds that had been taken in injured by my daughter and nursed to a healthy loathing of one another, a horned toad, whose prehistoric little scowl I had grown quite fond of, and I set our wagon due east, following a good road along the banks of the Pedernales River, toward Austin, sixty miles distant. In Austin we sold our wagon and mules and boarded a train, a *train*, for Galveston, and for the first time in five years were propelled along not by some beast of burden but by the magic of man's mind. At Columbus we found the bridge over the Colorado River down and were delayed there three days while it was repaired.

During the day Kate and I wandered the fields around Columbus. The prairies here billowed under an ocean of wildflowers. As far as the eye could see, flowers grew without number, countless varieties mixed among themselves; then suddenly upon making a rise they would be segregated to their own kind, throwing across the hills immense blankets of yellow, scarlet, orange mixed with crimson, that shading into purples, blues, and whites. Toward one hilltop we might see a stretch of sunflowers, then at the next summit, reaching to the horizon, painted cups, yellow indicus, purple lupines, California poppies, verbenas, sweet peas climbing the long-stemmed grass, marigolds, scarlet phlox, passionflowers, field violets, lilies, their delicate white tendrils shaded as soft as a woman's neck. Among these was Kate's favorite, a sensitive little plant whose leaves folded up at the touch of her hand, however light, and whose round fuzzy balls of crimson petals emitted the most fragrant perfume. Beyond this chromatic storm stood the distant southern sky collecting rising cathedrals of thunderheads that would deliver the afternoon showers whose warmth we bathed in as we ran through the rain and the flowers toward the hotel.

*   *   *

Our vessel of departure, the *Terra Nova,* a captured block-
ade runner with two stories of cabin and staterooms built on
her decks, was scheduled to sail from New Orleans bound for
New York on June 14, 1876. Though modest in size, propor-
tion, and accommodations, the *Terra Nova* loomed over my
landlocked daughter as the most fearsome vessel ever set afloat.
Kate found intrigue and adventure in the ship's name as she
translated the Latin sounds directly to English. She speculated
we were boarding a pirate ship and occupied herself with mari-
time fantasies that the Captain, a good man with a yarn, did
nothing to dispel. I did not consider the cargo of the *Terra
Nova* till I saw the cavalry horses being herded down to the
dock. I had sailed on such transport vessels before and knew
what sufferings these beasts would endure in their cramped, airless holds below. At least these horses were all done in—old,
scarred, weary warriors—and bound for their end. The injuries
and illnesses they would incur during the voyage would be but
prelude to that.

We were underway with the tide and into the Gulf by nightfall. Dawn found us in a calm sea, but the light was sallow and
the air slick, greasy to the touch, and the Captain was not
pleased with it. The Captain and the crew made preparations
to secure the ship, among them setting up the great wooden
roadway that reached into the hold, so that we might drive the
horses below into the sea if necessary. The fodder and coal that
had been stored on deck made the old vessel precariously top-
heavy and in stormy seas would threaten to capsize us if we
did not take measures to store them below. The prospect of
this sacrifice cast dread over us all, but during the afternoon
the barometer began to rise and that night the wind shifted
and we woke to a blazing dawn and the sea a plate as vast and
still as the plain. By evening we had come into easy swells, and
our spirits rose and we dined with the Captain and celebrated our

good fortune. The *Terra Nova* rounded the cape of Florida our third day out; on the morning of the fourth we made the Gulf Stream, which swept our bare-masted craft up the Eastern Seaboard as if we were a yacht racing before the wind. We docked at the port of New York on our seventh day out from New Orleans, a day ahead of schedule, all aboard well and in good spirits.

Max Crawford was born and raised near Mount Blanco, Texas. This community is gone now, but once it could be found in the country between Floydada, Crosbyton, Matador, and Dickens, Texas, on the southern rim of the *llano estacado,* less than a mile from the caprock of Blanco Canyon.